A TEXT BOOK OF

I0681472

COMPUTER ORGANIZATION

WITH MULTIPLE CHOICE QUESTIONS (MCQ'S)

FOR
Semester – II
SECOND YEAR (S. E.) DEGREE COURSE IN COMPUTER ENGINEERING

As per New Revised Syllabus of
University of Pune (Pattern 2012)

Mr. AMOL R. KALUGADE

Assistant Professor, Comp. Engg. Deptt.

AISSMS's Institute of Information technology

Pune.

Mrs. MALAN SALE

Assistant Professor, Comp. Engg. Deptt.

Sinhgad College of Engg.

Vadagaon (Bk) Pune.

Mrs. JYOTI SURVE

Assistant Professor, IT Deptt.

JSPM's Jayawantrao Sawant College of Engg.

Hadapsar, Pune.

Mrs. VEENA KADAM

Assistant Professor, IT Deptt.

JSPM's Jayantrao Sawant College of Engg.

Hadapsar, Pune.

NIRALI PRAKASHAN

N 2875

COMPUTER ORGANIZATION (SE - COMPUTER)

ISBN : 978-93-83971-06-0

First Edition : January 2014

Published By :
NIRALI PRAKASHAN
Abhyudaya Pragati, 1312, Shivaji Nagar,
Off J.M. Road, PUNE – 411005
Tel - (020) 25512336/37/39, Fax - (020) 25511379
Email : niralipune@pragationline.com

DISTRIBUTION CENTRES
PUNE

Nirali Prakashan
119, Budhwar Peth, Jogeshwari Mandir Lane
Pune 411002, Maharashtra
Tel : (020) 2445 2044, 66022708, Fax : (020) 2445 1538
Email : bookorder@pragationline.com

Nirali Prakashan
S. No. 28/25, Dhyari,
Near Pari Company, Pune 411041
Tel : (022) 24690204 Fax : (020) 24690316
Email : dhyari@pragationline.com
bookorder@pragationline.com

MUMBAI
Nirali Prakashan
385, S.V.P. Road, Rasdhara Co-op. Hsg. Society Ltd.,
Girgaum, Mumbai 400004, Maharashtra
Tel : (022) 2385 6339 / 2386 9976, Fax : (022) 2386 9976
Email : niralimumbai@pragationline.com

DISTRIBUTION BRANCHES

NAGPUR
Pratibha Book Distributors
Above Maratha Mandir, Shop No. 3, First Floor,
Rani Jhanshi Square, Sitabuldi, Nagpur 440012,
Maharashtra, Tel : (0712) 254 7129

BENGALURU
Pragati Book House
House No. 1, Sanjeevappa Lane, Avenue Road Cross,
Opp. Rice Church, Bengaluru – 560002.
Tel : (080) 64513344, 64513355,
Mob : 9880582331, 9845021552
Email:bharatsavla@yahoo.com

JALGAON
Nirali Prakashan
34, V. V. Golani Market, Navi Peth, Jalgaon 425001,
Maharashtra, Tel : (0257) 222 0395
Mob : 9423491860

KOLHAPUR
Nirali Prakashan
New Mahadvar Road,
Kedar Plaza, 1st Floor Opp. IDBI Bank
Kolhapur 416 012, Maharashtra. Mob : 9855046155

CHENNAI
Pragati Books
9/1, Montieth Road, Behind Taas Mahal, Egmore,
Chennai 600008 Tamil Nadu, Tel : (044) 6518 3535,
Mob : 94440 01782 / 98450 21552 / 98805 82331, Email : bharatsavla@yahoo.com

RETAIL OUTLETS
PUNE

Pragati Book Centre
157, Budhwar Peth, Opp. Ratan Talkies,
Pune 411002, Maharashtra
Tel : (020) 2445 8887 / 6602 2707, Fax : (020) 2445 8887

Pragati Book Centre
Amber Chamber, 28/A, Budhwar Peth,
Appa Balwant Chowk, Pune : 411002, Maharashtra,
Tel : (020) 20240335 / 66281669
Email : pbcpune@pragationline.com

Pragati Book Centre
676/B, Budhwar Peth, Opp. Jogeshwari Mandir,
Pune 411002, Maharashtra
Tel : (020) 6601 7784 / 6602 0855

PBC Book Sellers & Stationers
152, Budhwar Peth, Pune 411002, Maharashtra
Tel : (020) 2445 2254 / 6609 2463

MUMBAI
Pragati Book Corner
Indira Niwas, 111 - A, Bhavani Shankar Road, Dadar (W), Mumbai 400028, Maharashtra
Tel : (022) 2422 3526 / 6662 5254, Email : pbcmumbai@pragationline.com

www.pragationline.com   info@pragationline.com

Preface ...

It gives us immense pleasure to present this book on **"Computer Organization".** The book is written for Second Year Degree Course in Computer Engineering as per the revised syllabus.

As per the policy of University of Pune, Engineering Syllabus is revised every five years. Last revision was in the year 2009. New revision is coming little earlier, as university has introduced **Online System of Examination** from year 2012.

As per the new system, the **Online Examination** (separate Phase-I and Phase-II) will be conduced based on first, second and third and fourth units respectively. The **Online examinations** will have objective types of questions with multiple choices. End semester examination will be based on all the six units and that will be conducted in traditional way.

This book provides an introduction to the theory on computer organization. The concepts of computer organization are presented with ample numbers of examples and programs. Multiple Choice Questions are also given to test the understanding of the students.

Unit 1   Provides the Concepts of The Evolution of Computers and Number Operations.

Unit 2   Provides the Concepts of Processor Organization.

Unit 3   Provides the Concepts of Data Paths and ALU.

Unit 4   Provides the Concepts of Control Design Organization.

Unit 5   Provides the Concepts of Memory and I/O Organization.

Unit 6   Provides the Concepts of Advanced Computer Organizations.

My sincere hope is that the material presented in the book will be useful to readers.

Our sincere thanks to Shri. Dineshbhai Furia, Shri, Jignesh Furia and Shri. M. P. Munde. The books could be completed in time, due to sincere and hard work of Nirali Prakashan's staff namely Mrs. Deepali Lachake, Mrs. Shilpa Kale, Miss Pallavi Kumari, Mrs. Prajakta Shrimandilkar and Mrs. Sonal Pokhjarkar.

Valuable suggestions from our esteemed readers to improve the text will be most welcome and highly appreciated.

January 2014   **Authors**
Pune.

Syllabus ...

Unit I: The evolution of computers and number operations   (8 Hrs.)

Mechanical Era, Electronic computer, VLSI – Integrated circuits. SOC Processor architecture performance consideration performance measure speedup techniques. System Architectures – Microprocessor, Micro controller and parallel processing. Designing for Performance, Von-Neumann Architecture, Data flow architecture, Computer Components, Interconnection Structures, Bus Interconnection, Scalar Data Types, Fixed and Floating point numbers, IEEE 488 Number representation, Signed numbers, Integer Arithmetic, 2's Complement method for multiplication, Booths Algorithm,

Unit II: Processor Organization   (6 Hrs.)

Processor Basics: CPU organization, CPU Bus Organization: Central BUS, Buses on periphery, Additional features: RISC & CISC types representative commercial microprocessor of RISC & CISC types, Co-processors Data representation –Integer and floating point representation, Instruction set –Addressing modes formats, Machine Instruction characteristics, types of operands, types of operations, Instruction formats, Processor organization, Register Organization in 8086/88, 80386Dx and i7 microprocessors,

Unit III: Data Paths and ALU   (6 Hrs.)

Data Paths: Fixed point and floating point Arithmetic, ALU, Pipeline processing Case study of Intel Nehalem organization, pipelined and non-pipelined machine cycles

Unit IV: Control Design Organization   (5 Hrs.)

Control Design: Basic concepts Hardwired and micro-programmed control, Pipeline control, Example of ADD Instruction macro/micro design,

Unit V: Memory and I/O Organization   (6 Hrs.)

Memory systems, DDR3 Memory Organization, NUMA and UMA, caches memory mapped I/O and I/O mapped I/O, DMA, buses and standard interfaces –serial parallel buses –PCI, SCSI USB. USB bus organization to interface display and Printer, Case Study: Intel Nehalem Memory Organization.

Unit VI: Advance Computer Organization   (6 Hrs.)

Advanced computer Organizations (Block Diagrams only) The AMD Multicore Opteron, The Sun UltraSparc T1, The IBM Cell Broadband Engine (CBE), The Intel IA-64, The IA-64 model: Explicitly Parallel Instruction Computing, Prediction, Speculative Loads. 64-bit architectures i5/ i7 Desktop version and mobile version, NVDIA GPU architecture (Block diagram only).

Contents

THE EVOLUTION OF COMPUTERS AND NUMBER OPERATIONS

1.1 MECHANICAL ERA

In 19th century, attempts were made to design mechanical calculators to perform faster computation.

1.1.1 Babbage's Difference Engine

In 19th century, Charles Babbage designed first automatic multistep computer. This was called as **difference engine.** It is used to print mathematical tables automatically and was able to perform only one mathematical calculation i.e. addition. However, the method of (finite) differences embodied in the difference engine can calculate many complex and useful functions by means of addition alone.

1.1.2 The Analytical Engine

Analytical Engine designed by Babbage was much more powerful than Difference Engine. This is considered as first general purpose programmable computer ever designed.

The overall structure of Analytical Engine is shown in Fig. 1.1. This machine introduced all major components which are using in present machines/computers.

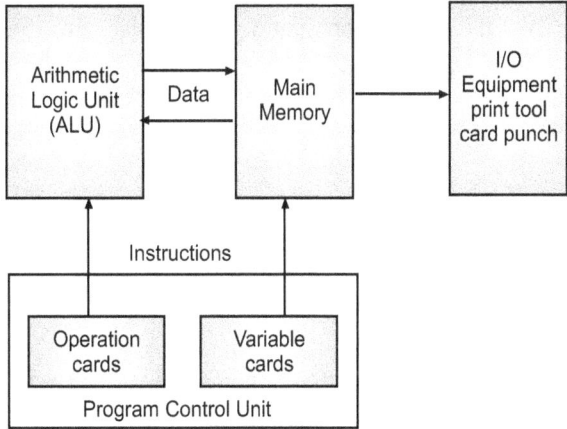

Fig. 1.1 : Babbage's analytical engine

Here, main components are a memory called the store and ALU called the 'mill'. A program for Analytical Engine was composed of two sequences of punched cards.

(i) **Operation Cards :** Used to select operation to be performed by ALU.

(ii) **Variable Cards :** Used to specify the locations in the store from which inputs were to be taken or results to be sent.

For example : An action a × b = c, would specified by an instruction consisting of an operation card denoting multiply and variable Cards Specifying the store locations assigned to a, b, and c. Use of conditional branch (i.e. if-then-else) was first done in Babbage's Analytical Engine.

1.2 ELECTRONIC COMPUTERS

Mechanical computers has the following drawbacks :

First, its computing speed is limited by the inertia of its moving parts, second, transmission of electronic digital information by mechanical means is unreliable.

On the other hand, electronic computers have moving parts as 'electrons' which can be transmitted at speed of light (3×10^8 m/s). Thus, electronic computers were becoming more popular in early 1900's.

1.2.1 First Generation

These machines were using vacuum tubes as electronic components. The first popular computer was Electronic Numerical Integrator and Calculator (ENIAC). Similar to Babbage's Analytical Engine, ENIAC used to generate mathematical tables. It was used in U.S. Army. It was heavy computer of 30 tonnes containing 18,000 vaccum tubes. The ENIAC was programmed by a critical process of plugging and unplugging cables and required manually setting a master programming unit to specify multistep operations. This turned into its drawback.

In 1945, Von-N. Neumann proposed a new computer, Electronic Discrete Variable Computer (EDVAC). EDVAC used to store and process numbers in true binary or base 2 form. Data was processed serially or bit by bit. EDVAC had main memory of 1 k words and secondary memory or 20 k words.

In 1947, Van-Neumann designed a new computer known as IAS computer.

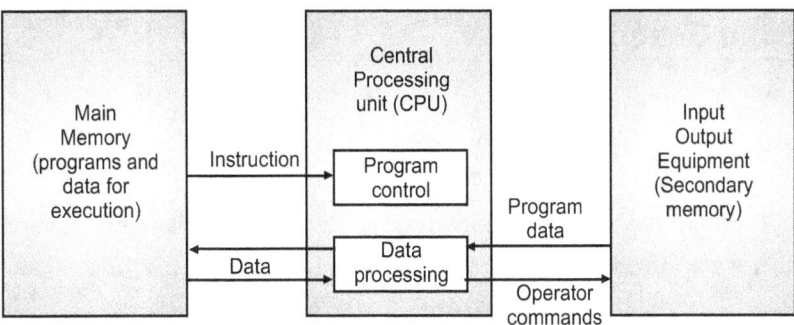

Fig. 1.2 : First generation computer

As shown in Fig. 1.2, this machine has a CPU for executing instruction, main memory for storing action programs, secondary memory for backup storage. These machines had their instructions written in binary code known as **machine language.** e.g. An instruction in machine language meaning add two memory location contents will take the form.

   001110110000000010011001100100000111

Machine language programs are extremely difficult for humans to write and thus, error prone.

Substantial improvement is obtained by allowing operations and operand addresses in an easily understood symbolic format

   $ADD \times 1 \times 2$

This format is known as assembly language. An assembly language requires a special system program (known as assembler) to convert assembly language into machine language.

1.2.2 Instruction Set

IAS machine had near about 30 types of instructions. These instructions were chosen to provide balance between application needs. To represent instructions a notation called Hardware Description Language (HDL) or Register Transfer Language (RTL) is used.

Fig. 1.3 explains notation for a simple three instruction IAS program that adds two numbers.

Instruction	Comment
AC = M(100)	Load contents of memory location 100 to accumulator
AC = AC + M(101)	Add contents of memory location 101 to accumulator
M(102) = AC	Store the contents of accumulator to memory location 102

Fig. 1.3 : IAS program to add two numbers stored in main memory

1.2.3 Second Generation

Vaccum tubes used in first generation were too heavy, delicate and costly. They were replaced by low cost, low space and cheaper 'transistors' made by silicon in second generation.

Similarly, in CPU more registers were added to facilitate data and address manipulation. e.g. Index registers were introduced to store an index variable 'I' of the kind appearing in the statement.

$$(CI) = A(I) + B(I)$$

1.2.3.1 Input-Output Operations

Designers realized that I/O operations, i.e. transfer of information to and from peripheral devices like printers and secondary memory can degrade performance if handled inefficiently

To eliminate this problem computers such as IBM 7094 introduced input-output processors (IOP's) which are special purpose processing units designed exclusively to perform I/O operations.

1.2.3.2 Programming Languages

A High-level language is intended to use on many computers. Thus, a system program (known as compiler) translates the user program from high-level language to low-level language (i.e. assembly language)

Then assembler will convert that low level language program into machine language.

First successful high-level programming language was FORTRAN (Formula Translation). It permits specification of numerical algorithms in a form approximating normal algebraic notation.

For example : vector addition in FORTRAN.

$$\text{DO} \qquad 5 I = 1,1000$$
$$5(CI) = A(I) + B (I)$$

1.2.4 Third Generation

This generation is associated with introduction at integrated circuits (ICs). As in second generation transistors were used here. But, they were integrated in huge number on a small size chip (i.e. IC).

Organisations like IBM, Intel were major manufacturers. IBM developed main frame system based on this technology. Pentium 1 processor of intel was having 95,000 processor mounted on it. This was the revolution in computer field.

1.3   VLSI (VERY LARGE SCALE INTEGRATION)

VLSI allows manufacturers to fabricate the CPU, main memory or even all electronic circuits of a computer on a single IC that can be produced at very low cost.

Table 1.1 : Summary of Computer Generations

Generation	Approximate Dates	Technology	Typical Speed (Operation Per Second)
1	1946–1957	Vacuum tubes	40,000
2	1958–1964	transistor	280,000
3	1965–1971	Small and medium scale integration	1,000,000
4	1972–1977	Large scale integration	10,000.000
5	1978 onwards	Very large scale integration	100,000,000

1.3.1 Integrated Circuits (IC)

IC is an electronic circuit composed of transistors and manufactured in small rectangular 'chip' of semiconductor material. It is covered by plastic or ceramic package, which provides electrical connections called 'pins'. In multichip module ICs are mounted on a single Printed Circuit Board (PCB).

1.3.1.1 IC Density

IC density is number of transistors mounted on chip. As manufacturing techniques are improving, number of transistors mounted on single chip are also increasing.

Earlies ICs contained fewer than 100 transistors, they were called SSI (Small Scale Integration). The terms medium scale, large scale, and very large scale (MSI, LSI and VLSI) are applied on ICs containing hundreds, thousands and millions of transistors.

1.3.1.2 IC Families

Based on transistor and circuit types IC families are employed as bipolar and unipolar. Unipolar is also known as MOS (metal-oxide semiconductor).

Bipolar circuits use both negative and positive carriers while unipolar circuits use only one carrier positive in case of p-type MOS and negative in case of N-type MOS.

1.4   PROCESSOR ARCHITECTURE

According to processor in use, computers are classified as :

- (i)   mainframe computers
- (ii)   minicomputers
- (iii) microcomputers

Mainframe is a large computer having thousands of ICs and costing millions of rupees. Typically, they are used as central computing facility in large organizations such as universities, factories or bank. Minicomputer is smaller and slower version of mainframe used for shoring between multiple users and useful in small business. Microcomputer is even smaller, slower and cheaper version.

1.4.1 Performance Considerations

In 1970's due to advances in VLSI technology computer designers started increasing the use of complex, multistep instructions. This reduces N, the total number of instructions getting executed for a task. i.e. a single instruction can replace several others.

For example a multiply instruction can replace a multi-instruction subroutine that implements multiplication by repeated execution of 'add' instruction.

Reducing N in this way tends to reduce overall execution time T. By using this strategy 'intel' designed a set of complex instructions known as CISC (Complex Instruction Set Computers). But soon later it became clear that complex instructions have some disadvantages. i.e. execution of even small part of such instructions, sometimes reduces overall performance of a computer.

For example suppose a computer executing only fast/complex instructions each requires k units of time to execute. Thus, 100 instructions will get executed in 100 k time.

Now, it 5% of instructions are slow, complex instructions require 2k time units each. To execute an average set of 100 instructions therefore requires (5 × 21 + 95)k = 200 k time units. i.e. 5% of complex instructions can double the overall program execution time.

- Considering these drawbacks, RISC (Reduced Instruction Set Computer) were designed, whose detailed discussion will be there in further chapters.

- Apart from instruction set, some other factors also affect computers performance like time required to move data between CPU and main memory M, time required to move data between memory (M) and I/O devices. CPU requires 5 times more time to read a word from memory (M) than its internal registers.

RISC computers limit access to main memory by doing access of load of store instructions.

1.4.2 Performance Measures

CPUs processing of an instruction involves several steps, each requires at least one clock cycle.

1. Fetch instruction from main memory (M)
2. Decode instructions opcode
3. Load (Read) from M any operands Needed
4. Execute the instruction
5. Store (write) the results in main memory (M)

Consider, execution of a program 'Q' on a given CPU that takes 'T' seconds and involves the execution of total 'N' machine instructions. Here, 'T' can be determined accurately only by measurement of 'Q's runtime. 'T' is depending on some parameters, one of them is 'instructions executed per second' denoted as IPS. Here,

$$T = N/IPS$$

Another measure of CPU performance is average number of cycles per instruction i.e. CPI.

Here, $CPI = \dfrac{(f \times 10^6)}{IPS}$, f – CPU clock frequency in MHz

Hence, program execution time 'T' is given by

$$T = \dfrac{N \times CPI}{f \times 10^6} \text{ second}$$

Note : [CPU performance is measured in MIPS (million instructions per second)

where $MIPS = IPS \times 10^6$

$$MIPS = f/CPI$$

Following are three factors determine that performance.

1. **Software :** The efficiency with which the programs are written and compiled into object code influences N (number of instructions executed). Reducing N will reduce execution time T.

2. **Architecture :** The efficiency with which individual instructions are processed affects the CPI (Cycles Per Instruction). Reducing CPI will reduce execution time. T.

3. **Hardware :** The speed of processor determines f, the clock frequency. Increase in 'f' reduces T.

1.4.3 Speedup Techniques

Table 1.2 explains some important speedup features of modern computers.

Table 1.2

Feature	Objective
1. Cache Memory	To provide CPU with faster access to instruction and data.
2. Superscale processing	To increase performance by allowing several instructions to be processed in parallel (full overlapping).
2. Pipelined processor	To increase performance by allowing the processing of several instructions to be partially overlapped.

A cache is a memory unit between CPU and main memory M. It is silicon built memory having its physical location on CPU. Cache memory is faster than main memory as well as costly than main memory.

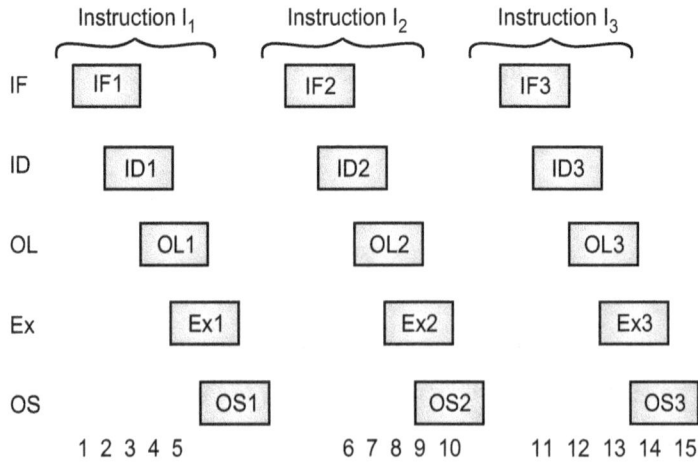

Fig. 1.4 : Non-pipelined

Pipelining allows processing of several instructions to be partially overlapped steps involved are Instruction Fetching (IF), Instruction Decoding (ID), Operation Loading (OL), Execution (Ex), and operand storing (OS).

As shown in Fig. 1.4 in non-pipelined CPU, the instructions are executed strictly in sequence while as in Fig. 1.5, pipelined execution permits partial overlapping.

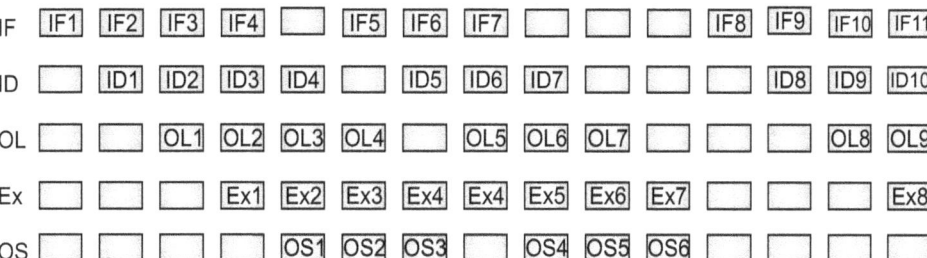

Fig. 1.5 : Pipelined

Here, we can observe, upto 5 instructions can be overlapped, provided the necessary pipeline stages are available.

Note : Sometimes, performance reducing delays occurs. In Fig. 1.5 in case of instruction I_4, which is using Ex stage for two consecutive cycles.

A microprocessors effective MIPS can also be increased by replicating various instruction processing circuits so that several instructions can be in same processing phase at the same time. CPUs with this capability are known as **super scalar**.

1.5 SYSTEM ARCHITECTURE

Overall system architecture is based on basic organization of CPU, main memory, I/O ports, microprocessor, microcontroller and parallel processing unit with network.

1.5.1 Microprocessor

This is key hardware element. It works as computer's CPU and is responsible for fetching, decoding and executing instructions. Data and instructions are typically composed of 32-bit words. CPU is identified by an instruction set which contains instructions to be executed on CPU. These instructions perform data transfer, data processing and program control operations.

1.5.2 Microcontrollers

Microcontroller is embedded in the controlled device and often it is invisible to end user. It is used for performing task that previously employed either special purpose control circuit or had no control logic at all. e.g. controlling washing machine.

The microcontroller has an organization around a system bus which includes CPU, RAM, ROM, I/O port. Fig. 1.6 illustrates typical structure.

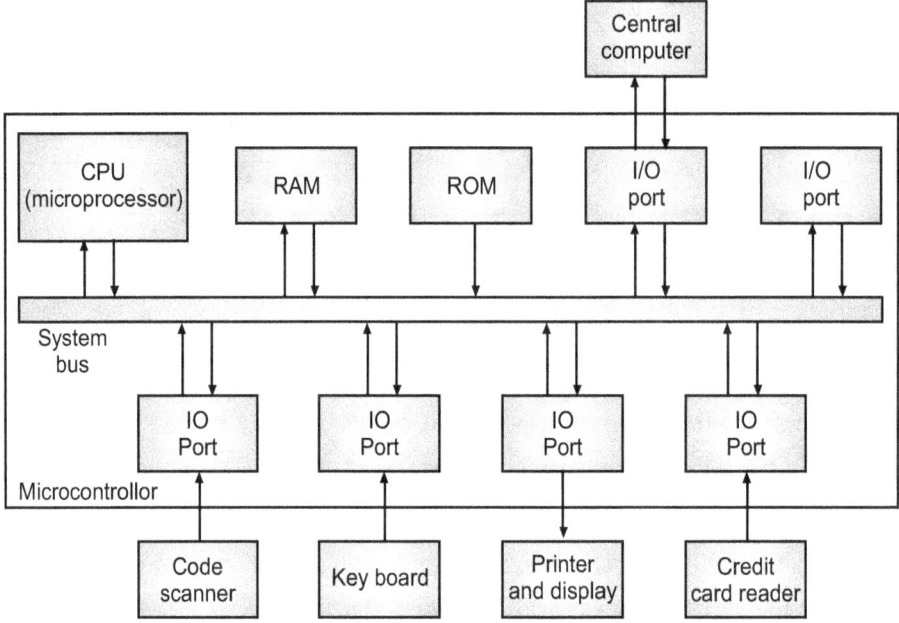

Fig. 1.6 : Microcontroller based of sale terminal

1.5.3 Parallel Processing

An approach of parallel processing involves, several instructions to be in process simultaneously in each pipeline, resulting in a potential increase in performance.

An alternative approach in getting unlimited degree of parallelism is to use multiple independent processors working in union.

For example, network computers can be programmed to work concurrently on different parts of same task. Such systems are known as loosely coupled or distributed systems. To address interprocessor communication problem, computers are built to employ in separate CPUs that are tightly coupled (i.e. can use each others shared memory). Processors in these machines can access each others data are multiprocessors.

Two types of multiprocessors are shared memory and distributed memory machines. In shared memory all processors have access to common main memory, in distributed memory, each processor has only a private or local main memory.

1.6 VON-NEUMANN ARCHITECTURE

[May 08, 11, Dec. 09, 11, 8 Marks]

In the first generation, Originators of ENIAC designed the first stored program computer named EDVAC (Electronic Discrete Variable Computer) and the EDVAC project was further developed by Von–Neumann Machine with his collaborator at the Institute for Advanced Studies (IAS) in Princeton.

General von Neumann machine consists of the following components :

- **A main memory :** Data storage is one of the core functions and fundamental components of main memory, which stores both data and instructions.
- **An Arithmetic and Logic Unit (ALU)** capable of operating on binary data.
- **A control unit,** which interprets the instructions in memory and causes them to be executed.
- **Input and output (I/O)** equipment operated by the control unit.

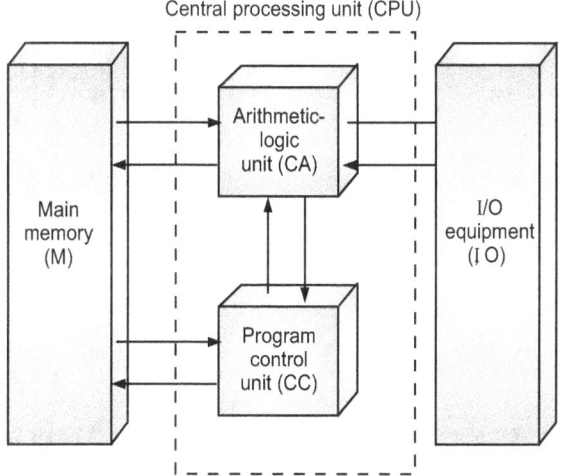

Fig. 1.7 : General Structure of Von–Neumann Machine

Von Neumann memory unit consists of 4096 storage locations ($2^{12}=4096$) of 40–bit each referred to as words. These memory locations are used to store data as well as instructions. Let us see one by one.

Data Format :

The left most bit (bit 0) represents the sign of the number (0 for positive and 1 for negative) while the remaining 39–bit indicates the number size in two's complement form.

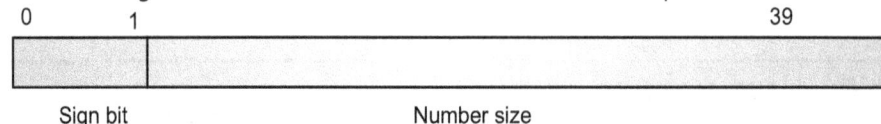

Fig. 1.8 : Data format

The numbers are assumed to have an implicit binary point corresponding to the decimal point in ordinary decimal notation. It may be placed in any fixed position within the number word format hence these are called fixed point. If the implicit binary point is assumed to lie between bits 0 and 1, then all numbers are treated as fractions.

+0.5 = 0100 0000 0000 0000 0000 0000 0000 0000 0000 0000

+0.1 = 0000 1100 1100 1100 1100 1100 1100 1100 1100 1100

Zero = 0000 0000 0000 0000 0000 0000 0000 0000 0000 0000

–0.1 = 1111 1100 1100 1100 1100 1100 1100 1100 1100 1100

With binary fixed point between bits 0 and 1 fractions are restricted to lie between –1 and +1. Out of range calculations adjusted by some suitable scaling factor.

Instruction Format :

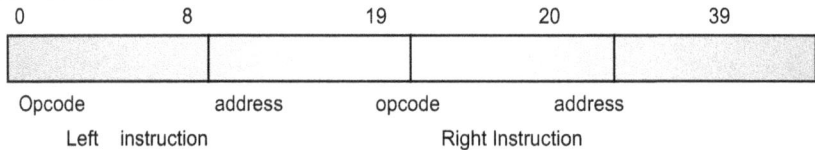

Fig. 1.9 : Instruction format

Each instruction is of 20 bits so that two instructions can be stored in each 40 bits memory location. Instruction consists of two parts: an 8 bit opcode (operation code) and 12–bit address. The opcode defines the operation to be performed (add, subtract etc.) and address part identifies any of the 212 memory locations that may used to store an operand of an instruction.

1.6.1 Detail Structure of IAS/Von–Neumann Architecture

The von Neumann structure describes a design architecture for an electronic digital computer with sub-divisions of a processing unit.

The control unit operates the IAS by fetching instructions from memory and executing them one at a time this figure reveals that both the control unit and the ALU contain storage locations, called registers, defined as follows :

- **Memory buffer register (MBR) :** Contain a word to be stores in a memory or is used to receive word from memory.
- **Memory address register (MAR) :** Specifies the address in the memory of the word to be written from or read into memory.
- **Instruction register (IR) :** Contain, 8 bit opcode instruction being executed
- **Instruction buffer register (IBR) :** Employed to hold temporarily the right hand instruction from a word in a memory.
- **Program Counter (PC) :** Contains the address of the next instruction–pair to be fetched from memory.

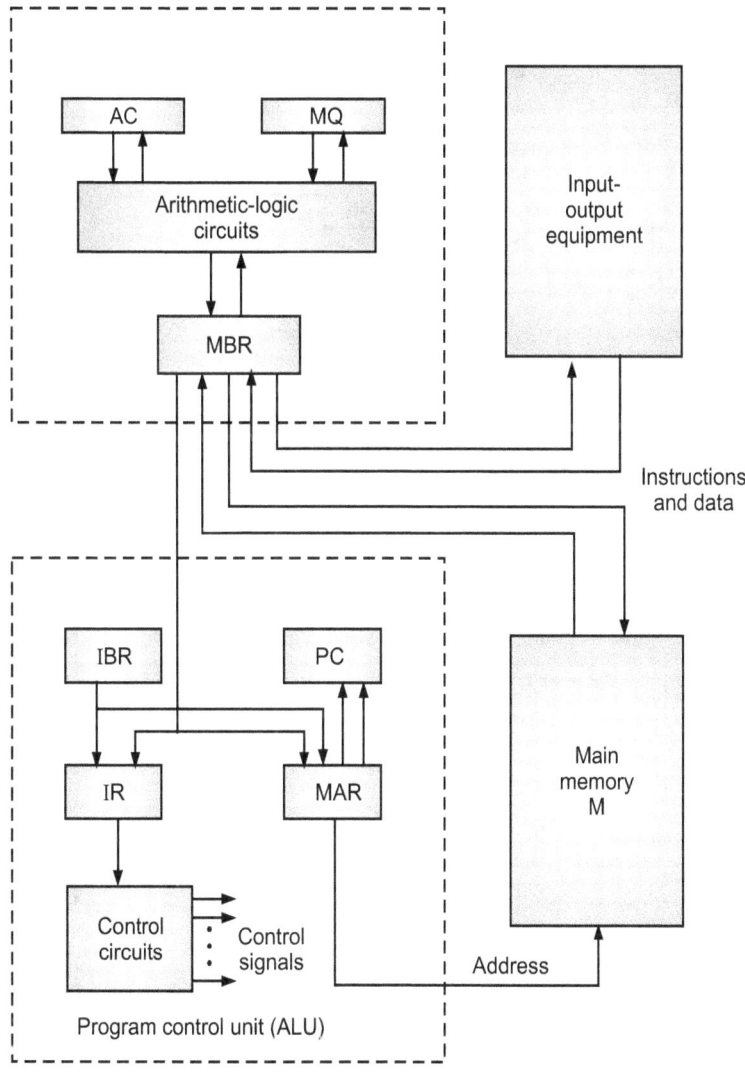

Fig. 1.10 : Detail Structure of IAS computer

Accumulator (AC) and multiplier quotient (Mg) : Employed to hold temporarily operands and results of ALU operations. For example, the result of multiplying two 40–bit numbers is an 80–bit number. The most significant 40 bits are stored in the AC and the least significant in the MQ.

IAS Operations :

The complete instruction cycle involves three operations : Instruction fetching, opcode decoding and instruction execution. The control circuits in the program control unit are responsible for fetching instructions, decoding opcodes, routing information correctly through the system, and providing proper control signals for central processing unit (CPU) actions.

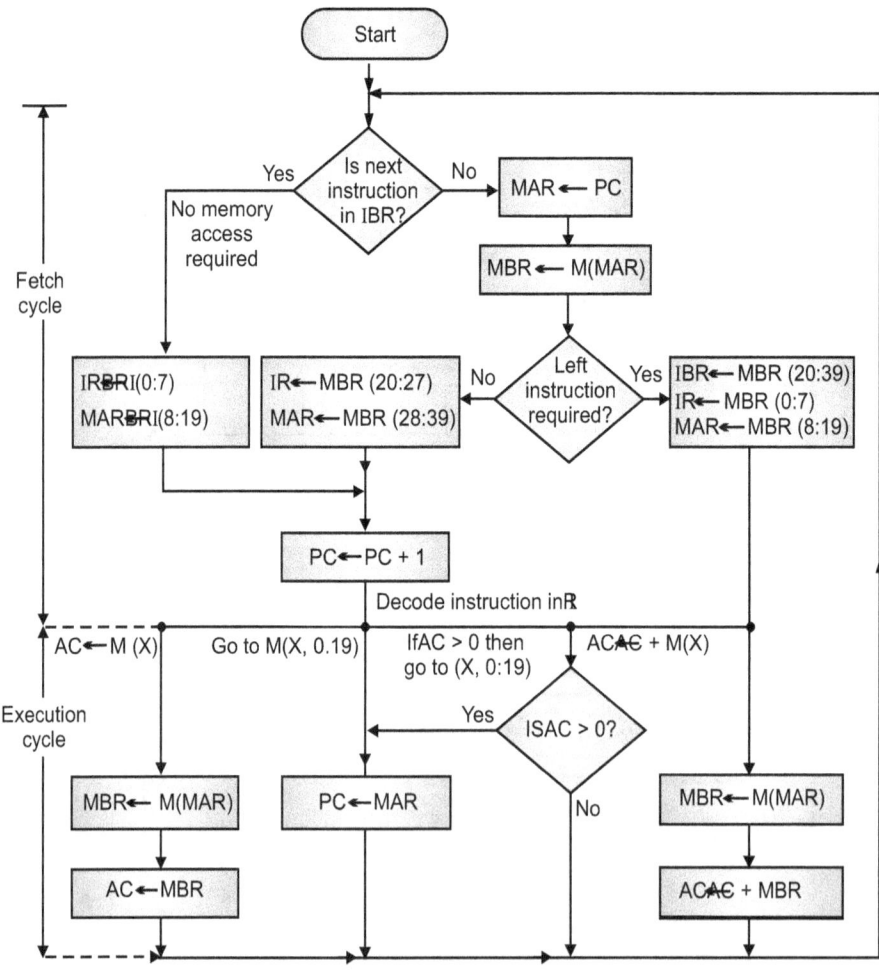

M (X) = Contents of memory location whose address is X

(X : Y) = bits X through Y

Fig. 1.11 : Flowchart of IAS operations

After decoding, the arithmetic logic circuits of the data processing unit perform actions specified by instruction. An electronic clock circuit is used to generate the basic timings signals to synchronize the operation of different parts of system.

The instructions of IAS computer

The instructions of IAS computer are divided in five groups :

- **Data transfer :** Move data between memory and ALU registers or between two ALU register.

- **Unconditional branch :** Normally, the control unit executes instructions in sequence from memory. This sequence can be changed by a branch instruction. This facilitates repetitive operations.

- **Conditional branch :** The branch can be made dependent on a condition. Thus allowing decision points.

- **Arithmetic :** Operations performed by the ALU.

- **Address modify :** Permits addresses to be computed in the ALU and then inserted into instructions stored in mentor. This allows a program considerable addressing flexibility.

After each instruction cycle central processing units checks for any valid interrupt request. If so, CPU fetches the instructions from the interrupt service routine and after completion of interrupt service routine, central processing unit starts the new instruction cycle from where it has been interrupted. The complete cycle involves three operations : instruction fetching, opcode decoding and instruction execution.

Fetch cycle :

o The fetch cycle common to all instructions.

o Program control unit fetches two instructions simultaneously from memory.

o It is the process by which a computer retrieves a program instructions from its memory determines what actions the instruction requires and cames out those actions.

o It check whether the next instruction is available in the IBR or not. If not the previously incremented contents of the program counter are transferred to the address register and a read request is send to memory (M).

o The required data at memory location X(M(x)) is then transferred to the data register DR. The opcode of the required instruction register and address part is sent to the address register while the second instruction may be transferred to the instruction buffer register IBR.

o   If the next instruction is available in the IBR, opcode part is sent to the instruction register and address part is sent to the address register.

Program counter is incremented only when instruction is read from memory i.e. when the next instruction is not available in the IBR.

Decode Cycle :

o   In the decode cycle, the instruction in the instruction register is decoded by the control circuits in the program control unit.

Execution cycle :

o   In the execution cycle micro–operations depending on the instructions are carried out.

o   Four basic instructions are

- M (X) $\leftarrow$ AC.
- Go to M (X, 20:39)
- if AC $>$ = 0 then go to M (x, 20:39)
- AC $\leftarrow$ AC – M (X)

o   Instructions executed by sequence of micro-operations. M(X) $<\!\!-\!\!-$ AC requires two micro-operations.

- First the contents of accumulator are transferred to the data register and then the contents of data register DR are transferred to the memory location specified by the address register AR.

1.7   COMPUTER COMPONENTS

There are four basic components of the computer :

Input/output, CPU and Memory

CPU :

- The CPU exchanges data with memory. For this purpose, it makes use of two internal registers :

    o   **A memory–address register (MAR)** which specifies the address in memory for the next read or write and o **A memory buffer register (MBR)** which contains the data to be written into memory or receives the data read from memory.

o Similarly, an I/O address register (I/O AR) specifies a particular I/O device,

o An **I/O buffer register (I/O BR)** is used for the exchange of data between an I/O Module and the CPU.

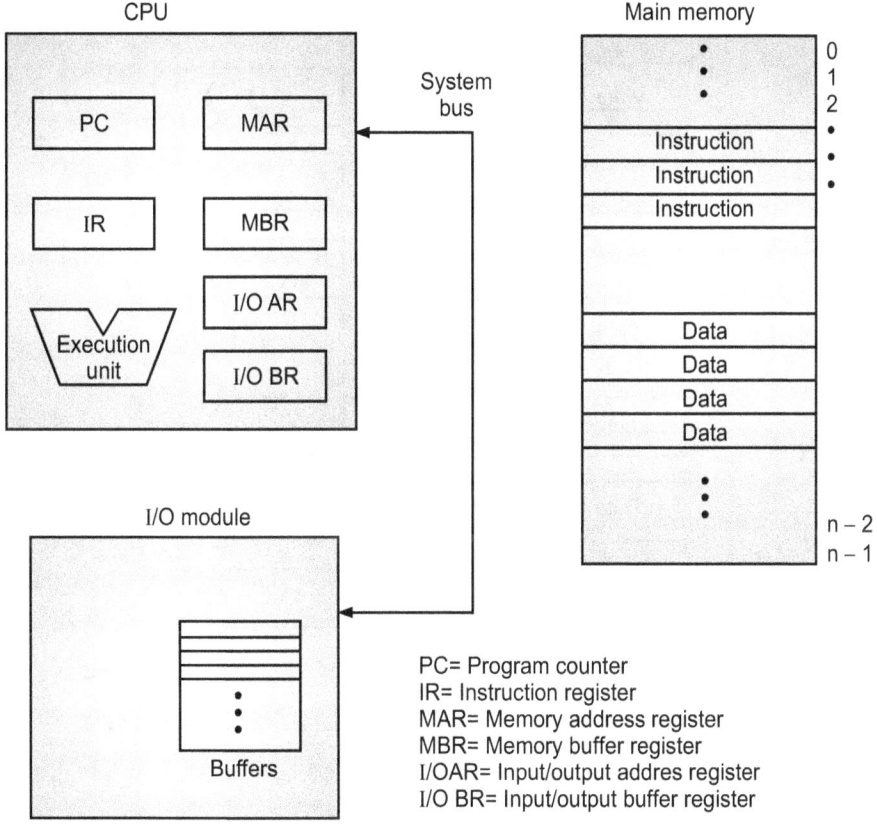

PC= Program counter
IR= Instruction register
MAR= Memory address register
MBR= Memory buffer register
I/OAR= Input/output addres register
I/O BR= Input/output buffer register

Fig. 1.12 : Computer components

1.8 INTERCONNECTION STRUCTURES

A Computer consists a set of components or modules of three basic types processors, memory and I/O. That communicate with each other. In effect, computer is network of basic modules. Thus, there must be paths for connecting these modules. The collections of paths connecting the various modules are called as interconnection structure. The design of this structure will depend on the exchanges that must be made between modules.

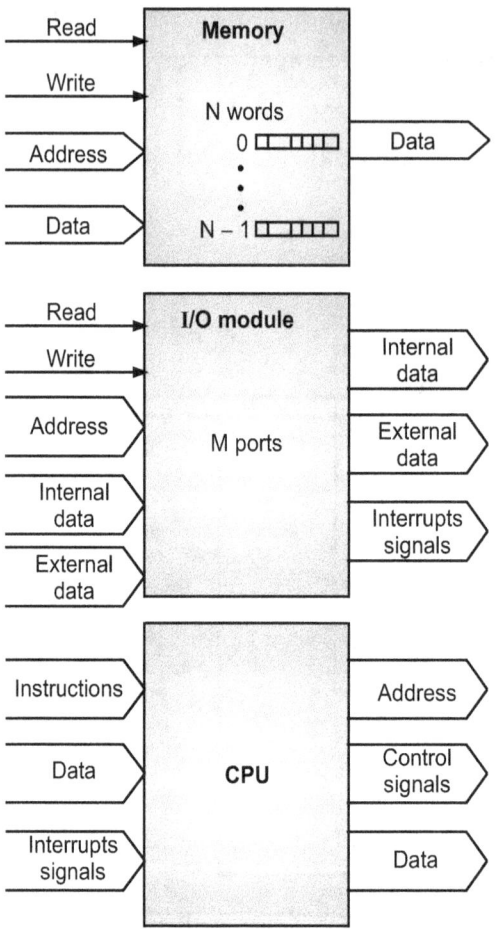

Fig. 1.13 : Interconnection Structures for each Computer Module

Fig. 1.13 suggest the types of exchanges that are needed by indicating the major forms of input and output for each module type.

Memory : memory module consists of N words of equal length, each word is assigned a unique numerical address (0, 1, ... N−1). A word of data can be read from or written into the memory. The nature of the operation is indicated by read and write control signals. The location for the operation is specified by an address.

- **I/O Module :** From the internal point of view I/O is functionally similar to memory. There are two operation, read and write. I/O module may control more than one external device. We can refer to each of the interfaces to an external device as a port and give each a unique address (0... m−1). In addition, There are external data path for input and output of data with an external device. Finally, I/O module may be able to send interrupt signals to the processor.

- **Processor :** The processor reads in instructions and data. Writes out data after processing and uses control signals to control the overall operation of the system. It also receives interrupt signals.

  The preceding list defines the data to be exchanged. The interconnection structure must support the following, types of transfers :

- **Memory to processor :** The processor reads an instruction or a unit of data from memory.

- **Processor to memory :** The processor writes a unit of data to memory.

- **I/O to processor :** The processor reads data from an I/O device via an I/O module.

- **Processor to I/O :** The processor sends data to the I/O device.

- **I/O to or from memory :** For these two cases, an I/O module is allowed to exchange data directly with memory without going through the processor, using direct memory access (DMA).

1.9   BUS INTERCONNECTION

1.9.1 Bus Structure

It consists of typically 50 to 100 separate lines. Each line is assigned a particular line or function. Bus lines are classified into three functional groups.

Data Bus : Consists of 8, 16, 32 or more parallel signal lines. The data bus lines are bidirectional. This means CPU can read data on these lines from memory or from port, as well as send data out on these lines to a memory location or to a port. Data bus is connected in parallel to all peripherals. Communication is activated by output enable pulse to peripheral.

Address Bus : It is a unidirectional bus. The address bus consists of 16, 20, 24 or more parallel signal lines. On these lines the CPU sends out the address of memory location or I/O port that is to be written to or read from.

Control Bus : The control lines regulate the activity on the bus. The CPU sends signals on the control bus to enable the outputs of addressed memory devices or port devices. Typical control bus signals are :

- **Memory Write :** Causes the data on the bus to be written into the addressed location.

- **Memory Read :** Causes data from the addressed location to be placed on the bus.
- **I/O Write :** Causes data on the bus to be output to the addressed I/O port.
- **I/O Read :** Causes data from the addressed I/O port to be placed on the bus.
- **Transfer ACK :** Indicates that data have been accepted from or placed on the bus.
- **Bus Request :** Indicates that a module needs to gain control of the bus.

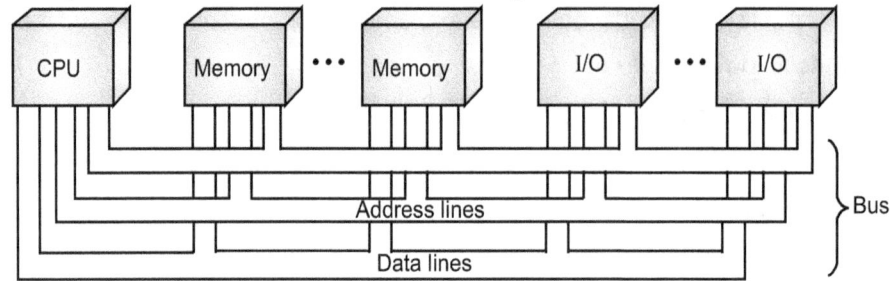

Fig 1.14 : Bus interconnection

- **Bus Grant :** Indicates that a requesting module has been granted control of the bus.
- **Interrupt Request :** Indicates that an interrupt is pending.
- **Interrupt ACK :** Acknowledges that the pending interrupt has been recognized.
- **Clock :** Used to synchronize operations.
- **Reset :** Initializes all modules.

The operation of the bus is as follows. If one module wishes to send data to another. It must do two things :

(1) Obtain the use of the bus, and (2) transfer data via the bus. If one module wishes to request data from another modules. It must (1) Obtain the use of the bus, and (2) transfer a request to the other module over the appropriate control and address lines. It must then wait for that second module to send the data.

1.9.2 Bus Configurations

Fig. 1.15 shows two bus configurations.

The traditional bus connection : Uses three buses: local bus, system bus, and expanded bus.

The high speed bus configuration : Uses high–speed bus along with the three buses used in the traditional bus connection.

Cache controller is connected to high speed bus. This bus supports connection to high speed LANs, such as Fiber Distributed Data Interface (FDDI), video and graphics workstation controllers, as well as interface controllers to local peripheral buses including SCSI and P1394.

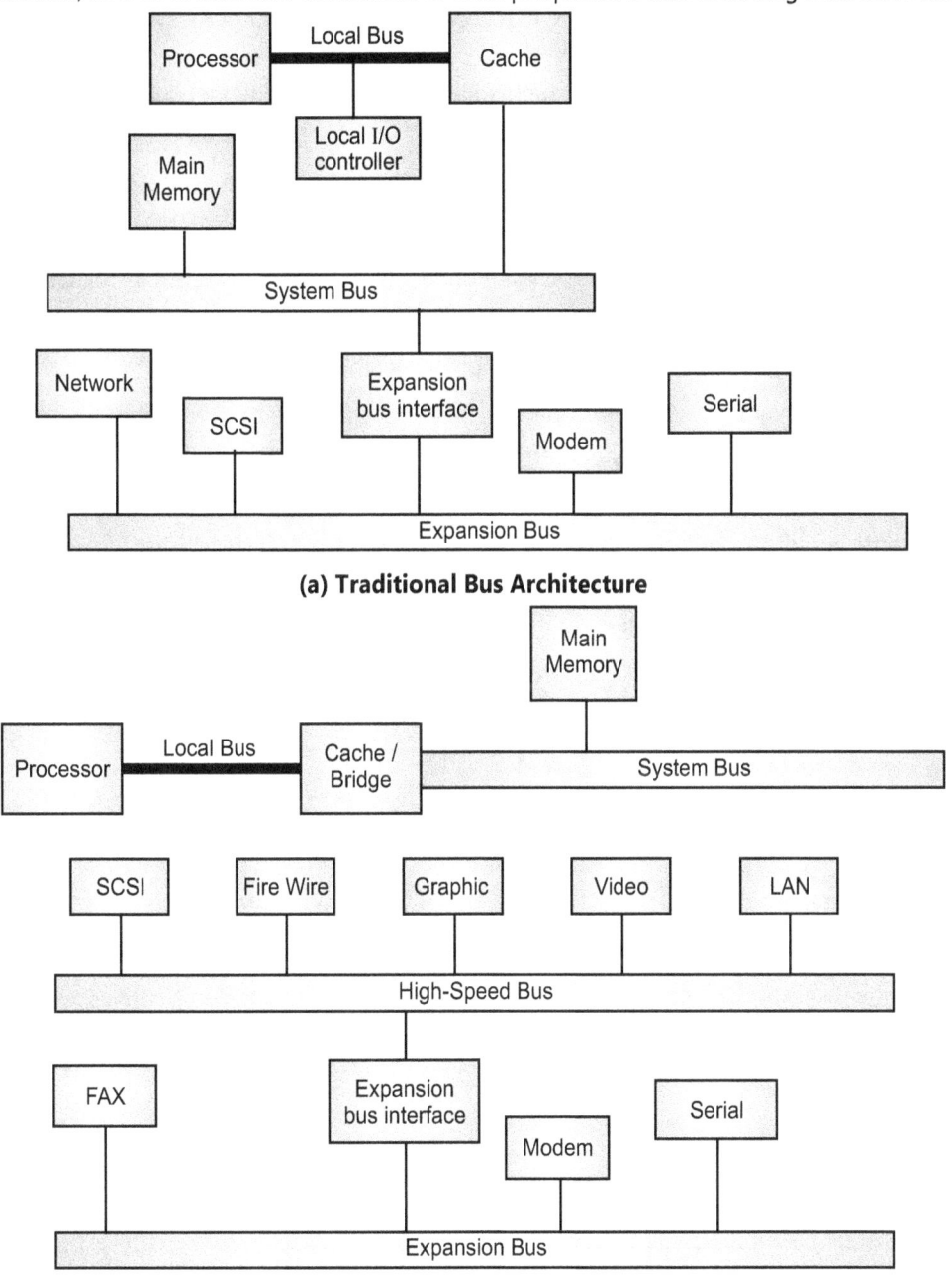

(a) Traditional Bus Architecture

(b) High-performance Architecture

Fig. 1.15 : Bus Configurations

1.9.3 Inter connection Networks [May 07, 3 Marks]

The important characteristic of a processor used in multiprocessor system is its ability to share a set of main memory modules and possibly 1/0 devices. This sharing capacity is provided through a set of two interconnection networks.

Interconnection network are a class or high speed component network usually composed or processing elements on one end of the network.

1. Between processor and memory modules.

2. Between processor and 1/0 subsystem.

Different physical forms available for the interconnection networks these are as follows :

1. **Time shared bus or common bus :** It has common communication path among number of processors. Networks have passive components.

2. **Crossbar switch :** It has separate bus associated with each memory module maximum number of transfers can take place simultaneously.

3. **Multiport memory–control :** In which switching and priority arbitration logic are distributed throughout the crossbar switch matrix which is distributed at the interfaces to the memory modules.

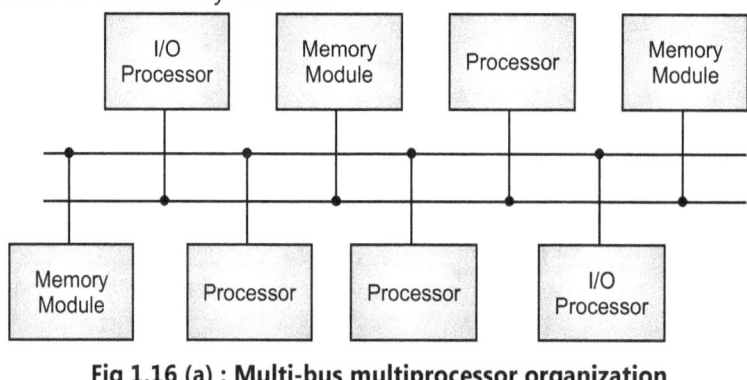

Fig 1.16 (a) : Multi-bus multiprocessor organization

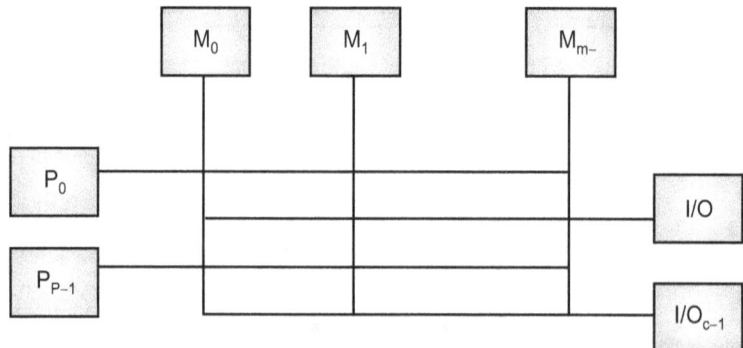

Fig. 1.16 (b) : Crossbar system organization for multiprocessors

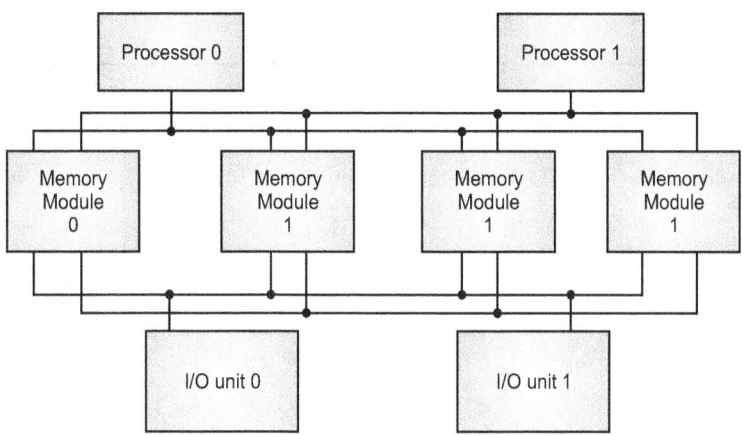

Fig 1.16 (c) : Multiport memory without fixed priority assignment

Important point related to three multiprocessor hardware organizations :

Table 1.3 : Multiprocessor hardware organizations

Sr. No	Time shared bus	Crossbar switch	Multiport memory No.
1.	Lowest overall system cost. For hardware and least complex.	Most complex. Highest. Total transfer rate.	Most expensive since most of control and switching circuitry is in the memory unit.
2.	Easy to modify hardware system configuration.	Functional units are simplest and cheapest.	Functional units permit low cost processor.
3.	Overall system capacity limited by bus transfer rate in rate bus fail then whole system fail.	Usually cost effective for multiprocessors only as basic switching matrix is required to assemble any functional units into a working configuration.	Potential for a very high total transfer rate in overall system.
4.	Expanding may degrade system performance.	System expansion improves Overall performance.	Difficult to modify as the design decision is made quite early.
5.	Lowest efficiency.	Expansion of the system is limited only by size of the switch matrix.	Large number of cables and connector are required.
6.	Organization is suitable for smaller systems only.	Reliability of system can be improved by segmentation or redundancy within switch.	

1.10 SCALAR DATA TYPES

Data processing unit performs all arithmetic and logical operations. Scalar data types are data types of operands used for arithmetic operations in computer. Scalar data types are classified as fixed point numbers and floating point numbers. Representing numbers in such a data types is commonly known as fixed point arithmetic and floating point arithmetic.

1.11 FIXED AND FLOATING POINT NUMBERS

Floating point describes a method of representing real numbers in a way that can support a wide range of values. Both the values are in binary. Depending upon design the hardware can interpret number as an integer or fraction. Radix point is never explicitly specified. It is implicated in design and hardware interprets it. In integer numbers radix point is fixed and assumed to be to the right of the right most digit. As radix point is fixed the number system is known as fixed point number system. With fixed point number system we can represent positive or negative integer numbers. Floating point number system allows the representation of numbers having both integer and fractional part.

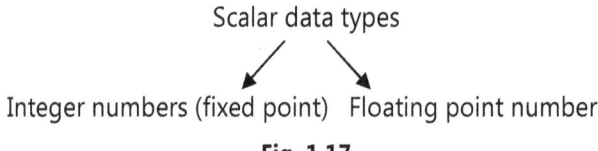

Scalar data types

Integer numbers (fixed point)   Floating point numbers

Fig. 1.17

1.11.1 Fixed Point Numbers

These are represented in two forms. (1). Signed integer (–ve) and (2). Unsigned integer (+ve). Computer doesn't have provision to represent negative sign. So we can represent negative number using the following methods.

(Represents using)

1. Signed magnitude
2. 1's complement
3. 2's complement

1.11.2 Signed Magnitude Representation

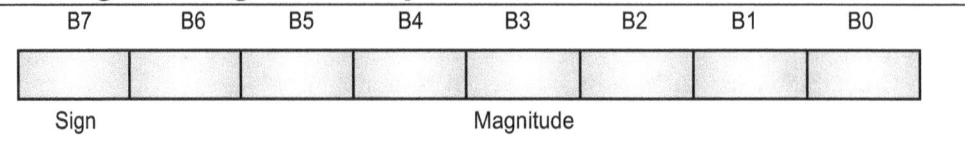

B7	B6	B5	B4	B3	B2	B1	B0

Sign   Magnitude

Fig. 1.18 : 8–bit signed number representations

Signed number represents negative as well as positive numbers.

The most significant bit (leftmost bit-B7) is used to represent the sign of number. If it is 0 the number is positive and if it is 1 the number is negative. For example, +7 represented by 0000 0111 and −14 represented by 1000 1110. Unsigned 8bit binary numbers has range 0 to 255. This is divided into 0 to + 127 for +ve numbers and 0 to −127 for negative numbers.

Some drawbacks are :

- For addition and subtraction it is necessary to consider sign of both the numbers and their relative magnitudes
- The 0 can be represented by two ways :

  + 0 = 0000 0000

  − 0 = 1000 0000

Due to two representations of zero it is difficult to test for zero operation of computer arithmetic.

1.11.3 One's Complement Representation

In this method, negative number are obtained by complementing each bit of corresponding positive number. For −3 representation complement each bit of positive 3(0011) so you will get 1100. This operation is equivalent to subtracting that number from $2^n - 1$ that is from 1111, in case of 4 bit numbers.

Example 1 : 1's complement of $(1001)_2$.

$$1 \quad 0 \quad 0 \quad 1 \quad \text{number}$$
$$0 \quad 1 \quad 1 \quad 0 \quad \text{1's complement}$$

Example 2 : 1's complement of $(1010\ 0011)_2$.

$$1 \quad 0 \quad 1 \quad 0 \quad 0 \quad 0 \quad 1 \quad 1 \quad \text{number}$$
$$0 \quad 1 \quad 0 \quad 1 \quad 1 \quad 1 \quad 0 \quad 0 \quad \text{1's complement}$$

1.11.4 Two's Complement Representation

The two's complement number is obtained by subtracting corresponding positive number from 2^n. The 2's complement number is obtained by adding 1 to the 1's complement number.

Using 2's complement we can distinctly represent +0 and −0. As 2's complement have only +0 representation. In 4–bit numbers −8 is represented by only 2's complement system i.e. 1000. This method is popularly used in computers for addition and subtractions.

Example 1 : 2's complement of (1001)2.

Find 1's complement first

```
        1  0  0  1   number
        0  1  1  0   1's complement
    +            1   add 1 to 1's complement
    ------------------------------------------
        0  1  1  1   2's complement
```

Example 2 : 2's complement of (1010 0011)2.

```
     1  0  1  0  0  0  1  1   number
     0  1  0  1  1  1  0  0   1's complement
  +                    1      add 1 to 1's complement
  --------------------------------------------------
     0  1  0  1  1  1  0  1   2's complement
```

1.12 INTEGER ARCHITECTURE

Computer process only binary number and not decimals or hexadecimals. So in integer arithmetic we process only binary addition, subtraction and division.

1.12.1 Integer Addition

Rules :

A + B	SUM	CARRY
0 + 0	0	0
0 + 1	1	0
1 + 0	1	0
1 + 1	0	1

Example 1 : Add 28 and 15 in binary.

First find the binary equivalent of 28 and 15

```
2 | 28 | 0          2 | 15 | 1
2 | 14 | 0          2 |  7 | 1
2 |  7 | 1          2 |  3 | 1
2 |  3 | 1          2 |  1 | 1
2 |  1 | 1              |  0 |
2 |  0 | 0
```

Binary equivalent of 28 = 11100

Binary equivalent of 15 = 01111.

Addition is

```
        1  1  1  0  0  ...28
    +   0  1  1  1  1  ...15
        1  1              ...carry
    -----------------------------
        1  1  0  1  1  ...43
```

1.12.2 Integer Subtraction

Rules for subtraction

A – B	Difference	Borrow
0 – 0	0	0
0 – 1	1	1
1 – 0	1	0
1 – 1	0	0

Example : Subtract 15 from 28 in binary

Convert 15 and 28 in binary

Binary equivalent of 28 = 11100

Binary equivalent of 15 = 01111.

Subtraction is :

```
        1  1  1  0  0  ...28
    -   0  1  1  1  1  ...15
        1  1  1     1  ...carry
    -----------------------------
        0  1  1  0  1  ...13
```

1.12.3 One's Complement Subtraction

Subtraction performed by using only addition by two numbers.

Subtract smaller number from larger number :

1. Determine the 1's complement of smaller number.
2. Add the 1's complement to the larger number.
3. Remove the carry and add it to the result. This is called end–around carry.

Example 1 : Subtract 0 1 1 1 1 (15) from 1 1 1 0 0 (28) using 1's complement.

```
          1  1  1  0  0      ...28
    +     1  0  0  0  0      ...1's complement of 15
    ----------------------------------------------
    -     1  0  1  1  0  0   carry as 1
    +                    1   add end around carry
    ----------------------------------------------
          0  1  1  0  1   ...13
```

1. Determine the 1's complement of the larger number.
2. Add 1's complement to the smaller number.
3. Answer is in 1's complement form. To get the answer in true form take the 1's complement and assign negative sign to the answer.

Example 2 : Subtract 1 1 1 0 0 from 0 1 1 1 1 using 1's complement.

```
          0  0  0  1  1   ...1's complement of larger number 28
    +     0  1  1  1  1   ...add 1's complement to smaller no.
    ----------------------------------------------
          1  0  0  1  0   ...answer is in 1's complement form
          0  1  1  0  1   ...final answer 13 (take 1's complement)
```

1.12.4 2's Complement Subtraction

Like 1's complement subtraction is achieved by addition.

(1) Subtract smaller number from larger number :

1. Determine the 2's complement of smaller number.
2. Add 2's complement to the larger number.
3. Discard carry.

Example 1 : Subtract 0 1 1 1 1 (15) from 1 1 1 0 0 (28) using 2's complement.

Calculate 2's complement of smaller number

```
          0  1  1  1  1
          1  0  0  0  1      ...2's complement of 15
          then
          1  1  1  0  0
    +     1  0  0  0  1      ...add 2's complement of 15
    ----------------------------------------------
          1  0  1  1  0  1   ...discard carry
          0  1  1  0  1      ...13 final answer
```

(2) Subtract larger number from smaller number :

1. Determine the 2's complement of the larger number.
2. Add the 2's complement to the smaller number.
3. Answer is in 2's complement form. To get the answer in true form take the 2's complement and assign negative sign to the answer.

Example 2 : Subtract 1 1 1 0 0 from 0 1 1 1 1 using 2's complement.

Calculate two's complement of 1 1 1 0 0.

$$0 \quad 0 \quad 0 \quad 1 \quad 1 \quad ...1's \text{ complement of larger number 28}$$

$$+ \qquad\qquad\qquad 1$$
_____

$$0 \quad 0 \quad 1 \quad 0 \quad 0 \quad ...2's \text{ complement of 28}$$

$$+ \quad 0 \quad 1 \quad 1 \quad 1 \quad 1 \quad ...\text{smaller number}$$
_____

$$1 \quad 0 \quad 0 \quad 1 \quad 1 \quad ...\text{answer in 2' complement form}$$

$$0 \quad 1 \quad 1 \quad 0 \quad 1 \quad ...\text{final answer 13}$$

Example 3 : Subtract smaller number from larger number.

(1) 25-10

Subtract 1010 from 11001

    11001   ...25
    01010   ...10

    2's complement of 01010

    10101

+   11
    _____
    00110

      11001   ...25
+   00110   2's complement of 10
    _____
    |1|1111   discard carry

      1111   ...15 final answer

Example 4 : Subtract larger number from smaller number.

10-25

Subtract 11001 from 1010

01010   ...10

11001   ...25

2's complement of 25.

   11001

   00110

+   '1
_____

  00111 ...2's complement of 25

           01010   ...10

       + 00111   ...2's complement to 25
       _____

           10001   ...answer is in 2's complement form

           01110

       +   1
       _____

           01111   ...15 final answer

1.12.5 Hardware Implementation of Addition and Subtraction

The figures suggest data paths and hardware elements needed to accomplished addition and subtraction. The central element is binary adder which is presented two numbers for addition and produces a sum and an overflow indication.

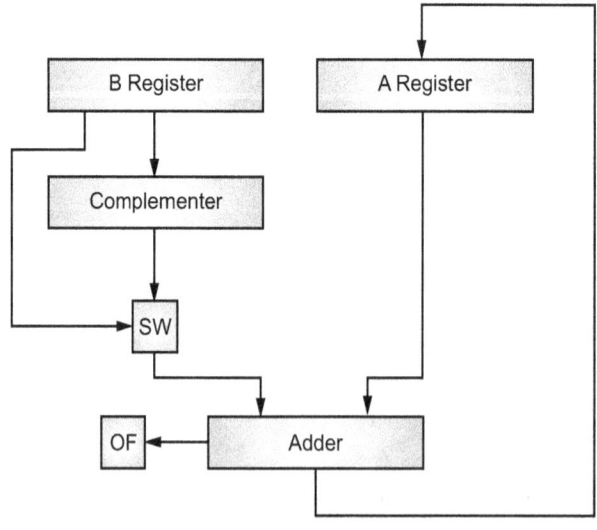

OF = Overflow bit

SW = Switch (Select addition or Subtraction)

Fig. 1.19 : Addition and subtraction

The binary adder treats the two numbers as unsigned integers. For addition, the two numbers are presented to the adder from two registers, designated in this case as A and B registers.

The result may be stored in one of these registers or in a third. The overflow indication is stored in a 1–bit overflow flag (0 – no overflow 1 – overflow). For subtraction, the subtrahend (B register) is passed through a two's complementer so that its two's complement is presented to the adder.

The logic circuit performs addition of two binary digits and produces a sum and a carry output in half adder. The circuit which performs addition of three bits (two significant bits and a previous carry) is called full adder. Three inputs and 1 output. A and B input variables and third input is C i.e. carry from the previous lower significant bit and output as sum as shown in Fig. 1.20.

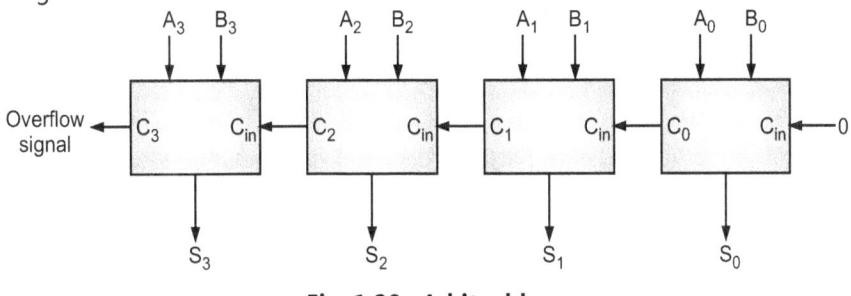

Fig. 1.20 : 4–bit adder

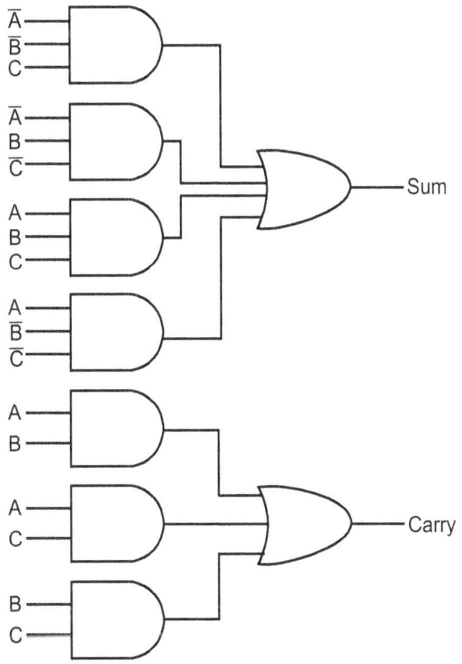

Fig. 1.21 : Implementation of adder

For multiple bit adder to work each of the single bit address must have three inputs. These implantation is shown in Fig. 1.21 which uses the AND, OR and NOT gates. Output from each adder depends upon carry from previous adder. There is an increasing delay from LSB to MSB. Each adder experiences certain amount of gate delay for lager adders the accumulated delay can become unacceptably high.

If the carry values could be determined without having to ripple through all the previous stages, then each single bit adder could function independently, and delay would not accumulate. This can be achieved with an approach known as **carry lookahead**.

1.13 2'S COMPLEMENT MULTIPLICATION

1.13.1 Basic of Multiplication

- The multiplication is complex operation. It can be performed by hardware and software. Multiplication process involves generation of partial products one for each digit in the multiplier. These partial products are then summed to produce the final products.

- In the binary system, the partial products are easily defined. When multiplier bit is 0 the partial product is 0 and when the multiplier is 1 the partial product is multiplicand.

- The final product is produced by addition of partial products. Each successive bit is shifted one position to the left relative to proceeding partial product.

- The product of two n digit numbers can be accommodated in 2n digits so product of 4 bit number is 8–bit number.

Example :

				0	1	0	1			multiplicand (5)
		×	0	1	0	0				multiplier (4)
0	0	0	0	0	0	0	0			as 8-bit product take 8 bit
0	0	0	0	0	0	0	+			left shift by 1 bit
0	0	0	1	0	1	+	+			multiplicand × 1
0	0	0	0	0	+	+	+			left shift by one
0	0	0	1	0	1	0	0			final product (20)

1.13.2 2's Complement Multiplication

We will discuss multiplication of 2's complement signed operand, also we apply partial product strategy by adding multiplicand (+ve and –ve) as selected by multiplier bit.

Note that when we add negative multiplicand we must extend the sign bit value of the multiplicand to the left as far as product will extend. The technique for 2's complement method known as Booth's algorithm.

1.14 BOOTH'S ALGORITHM

Booth's multiplication algorithm is an multiplication algorithm that multiplies two signed binary numbers in a two's complement notations. For signed number multiplication booths algorithm is used. It treats both positive and negative numbers. Three method for booths algorithm.

1. Using recoded multiplier.
2. Hardware implementation.
3. Modified booth algorithm.

1. Using recoded multiplier :

The product can be computed by adding 24 times the multiplicand to the 2's complement of 1 times of the multiplicand sequence of operations by recoding the proceeding multiplier as

$0 +1 0 0 -1 0$

–1 times the shifted multiplicand is selected when moving from 0 to 1.

+1 times the shifted multiplicand is selected when moving from 1 to 0.

0 times the shifted multiplicand is selected for none of above cases, as multiplier is scanned from right to left.

Example 1 : Recode the multiplier 0100 (4) for booths algorithm.

       0 1 0 0   ⓪   implied zero at end

       ◄────────   scan from right to left

       └┘└┘└┘└──┘   make pairs

       +1 –1 0   0   recoded multiplier.

Example 2 : Recode the multiplier 1100 (–4) for booths algorithm.

       1 1 0 0   ⓪   implied zero at end

       ◄────────   scan from right to left

       └┘└┘└┘└──┘   make pairs

       0 –1 0   0   recoded multiplier.

Whenever multiplicand is multiplied by –1. Its 2's complement is taken as a partial result.

Example 3 : Multiply 0 1 0 1 (5) and 0 1 0 0 (4) using booth's algorithm (5 × 4).

Solution :

0	1	0	0	0					multiplier with implied zero at end
+1	−1	0	0						recoded multiplier
0	1	0	1						multiplicand + 5
× +1	−1	0	0						recoded multiplier
0	0	0	0	0	0	0	0	as 8-bit product
0	0	0	0	0	0	0	+	
1	1	1	0	1	1	+	+	multiply by −1 take 2's complement
0	0	1	0	1	+	+	+	
0	0	0	1	0	1	0	0	final answer +20

When we multiply by −1 we will take 2's compliment of multiplicand and assign remaining bit to 1. Because product is negative.

Example 4 : Multiply 1 0 1 1 (−5) and 1 1 0 0 (−4) using booth's algorithm (−5 × −4).

Solution :

1	1	0	0	0					multiplier with implied zero at end
1	−1	0	0						recoded multiplier
1	0	1	1						multiplicand −5
× 0	−1	0	0						recoded multiplier
0	0	0	0	0	0	0	0	as 8-bit product
0	0	0	0	0	0	0	+	
0	0	1	0	0	1	+	+	multiply by −1 take 2's complement
0	0	0	0	1	+	+	+	
0	0	0	1	0	1	0	0	final answer +20

Here 1011(−5) is 2's complement of 0101(5) so multiplying by −1 it again calculates 2's complement but already its 2's complement of 5. So we take original number 0101 (5). We get result as +20.

Example 5 : Multiply 1011(–5) and 0100(4) using booth's algorithm (–5 × 4).

Solution : Recode the multiplier 0100.

1	0	1	1	0	multiplier with implied zero at end
+1	–1	0	0		recoded multiplier
1	0	1	1		multiplicand – 5
× +1	–1	0	0		recoded multiplier

0	0	0	0	0	0	0	0	as 8-bit product
0	0	0	0	0	0	0	+	
0	0	0	1	0	1	+	+	multiply by –1 take 2's complement
1	1	0	1	1	+	+	+	
1	1	1	0	1	1	0	0	final answer – 20 (2's complement of 20)

The Booth algorithm examines adjacent pair of bits of n bit multiplier y in signed two's complement.

2. Hardware implementation booths algorithm :

- The circuit consist of n bit adder, shift add subtract control logic and four registers A, B, Q, and Q–1.

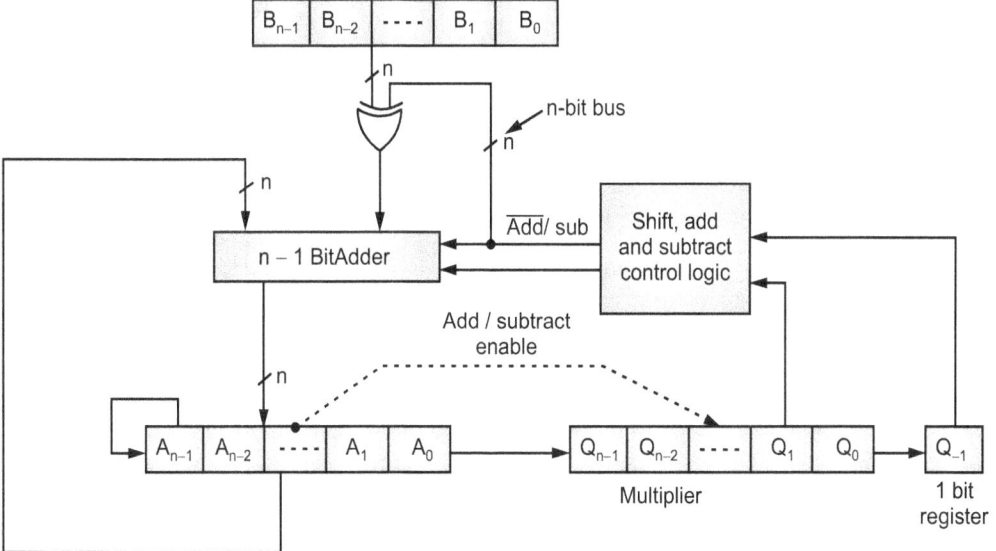

Fig. 1.22 : Hardware Implementation for Booth's algorithm

- Multiplier and multiplicand are loaded into register Q and register B respectively.

- Register A and Q–1 are initially set to 0.

- One input is A and other is multiplicand the shift, add, and subtract control logic scans bits Q and Q–1 one at a time and generate control signal. If two bits are same 1–1 or 0–0 then all of bits of A, Q and Q–1.

(1)   The Booth's algorithm can be implemented as shown in Fig. 1.22. The circuit is similar to circuit of positive number multiplication.

(2)   It consist of n–bit adder, shift, add subtract control logic and four registers. A, B, Q and Q – 1.

(3)   The multiplier is loaded in register Q and multiplicand in A.

(4)   The n–bit adder performs addition of two inputs. One input is the A register and other input is multiplicand.

(5)   In case of addition, $\overline{Add}$ /sub line is 0, therefore cin = 0 and multiplicand is directly applied as the second input to the n–bit adder.

(6)   In case of subtraction. $\overline{Add}$ /sub line is 1, and multiplicand is complemented form is applied to the n–bit adder.

(7)   The shift, add and subtract control logic scans bits Q_0 and Q_1 and generates the signal as follows :

Q_0	Q – 1	Add/Sub	Add/subtract enable	Shift
0	0	X	0	1
0	1	0	1	1
1	0	1	1	1
1	1	X	0	1

(8)   If the two bits are (0–0 or 1–1) then all registers are shifted to right with adding or subtracting.

(9)   If the two bits are (0–1) the multiplicand is added.

(10) If bits are (1–0) then multiplicand is subtracted.

Following Fig. 1.23 explains the sequence of events in Booths algorithm.

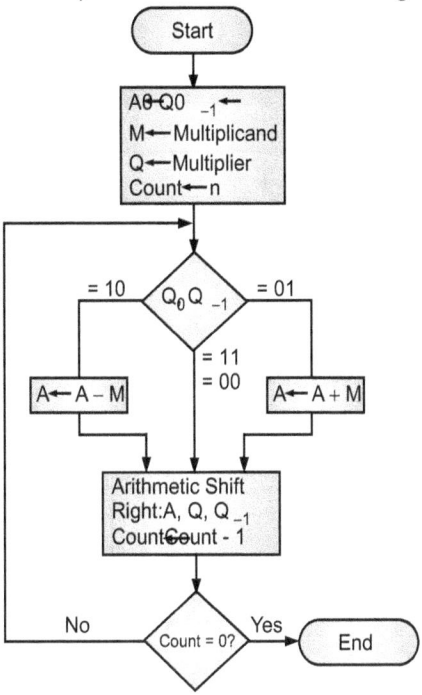

Fig 1.23 : Flowchart for booth's algorithm

Examples on Booth's Algorithm :

Example 1 : Both positive numbers (5 × 4)

Multiplicand (B) = 0101 (5) Multiplier (Q) = 0100 (4)

STEPS	A	Q	Q - 1	OPERATION
	0 0 0 0	0 1 0 0	0	Initial
Step 1	0 0 0 0	0 0 1 0	0	Arithmetic shift right
Step 2	0 0 0 0	0 0 0 1	0	Arithmetic shift right
Step 3	1 0 1 1	0 0 0 1	0	A ← A + B
	1 1 0 1	1 0 0 0	1	Arithmetic shift right
Step 4	0 0 1 0	1 0 0 0	1	A ← A + B
	0 0 0 1	0 1 0 0	0	Arithmetic shift right
Anwser : 0 0 0 1 01 00 = + 20				

Example 2 : Negative multiplier (5 × −4)

Multiplicand (B) = 0101(5)   Multiplier (Q) 1100(–4 2's complement of 4)

STEPS	A	Q	Q – 1	OPERATION
	0 0 0 0	1 1 0 0	0	Initial
Step 1	0 0 0 0	0 1 1 0	0	Arithmetic shift right
Step 2	0 0 0 0	0 0 1 1	0	Arithmetic shift right
Step 3	1 0 1 1	0 0 1 1	0	A ← A + B
	1 1 0 1	1 0 0 1	1	Arithmetic shift right
Step 4	1 1 1 0	1 1 0 0	1	Arithmetic shift right
Anwser : 1110 1100 = –20 (2 complement of 20)				

Example 3 : Negative multiplicand (–5 × 4)

Multiplicand (B) = 1011 (–5, 2's complement of 5)   Multiplier (Q) = 0100 (4)

STEPS	A	Q	Q – 1	OPERATION
	0 0 0 0	0 1 0 0	0	Initial
Step 1	0 0 0 0	0 0 1 0	0	Arithmetic shift right
Step 2	0 0 0 0	0 0 0 1	0	Arithmetic shift right
Step 3	0 1 0 1	0 0 0 1	0	A ← A + B
	0 0 1 0	1 0 0 0	1	Arithmetic shift right
Step 4	1 1 0 1	1 0 0 0	1	A ← A + B
	1 1 1 0	1 1 0 0	0	Arithmetic shift right
Answer = 1110 1100 = –20(2 complement of 20)				

Example 4 : Both negative (–5 × –4)

Multiplicand (B) = 1011 (–5, 2's complement of 5) Multiplier (Q) = 1100 (–4 2's complement of 4).

STEPS	A	Q	Q – 1	OPERATION
	0 0 0 0	1 1 0 0	0	Initial
Step 1	0 0 0 0	0 1 1 0	0	Arithmetic shift right
Step 2	0 0 0 0	0 0 1 1	0	Arithmetic shift right
Step 3	0 1 0 1	0 0 1 1	0	A ← A + B
	0 0 1 0	1 0 0 1	1	Arithmetic shift right
Step 4	0 0 0 1	0 1 0 0	1	Arithmetic shift right
Answer = 0001 0100 = +20				

SOLVED EXAMPLES ON BOOTH'S ALGORITHM

Example 5 : Explain Booth's Algorithm to multiply the following pair of signed two's complement numbers :

A = 110011 Multiplicand B = 101100 Multiplier

Also, implement the above using Bit–pair recording and explain how it achieves faster multiplication. **[May 05, 09, Dec. 06, Dec. 09, Dec. 10, 10 Marks]**

Solution : Both are – ve case 4 (Refer page 1–34)

Multiplicand (B)110011 (– 13)   Multiplier (Q) ← 101100 (– 20)

STEPS	A	Q	Q – 1	OPERATION
	000000	101100	0	Initial
1.	000000	010110	0	Shift right
2.	000000	001011	0	Shift right
3.	001101	001011	0	A ← A + B
	000110	100101	1	Shift right
4.	000011	010010	1	Shift right
5.	110110	010010	1	A ← A + B
	111011	001001	0	Shift right
6.	001000	001001	0	A ← A – B
	000100	000100	1	Shift right

Result 000100 000100 = + 260

Check Q_0 and Q – 1 bit. It is 00 then shift right operation. If 11 then shift right.

If 10 — then perform A ← A – B.

and if 01 — then perform A ← A – B.

Perform right shift operation for each step.

Implementation with bit pair recording .

Multiplier : 1 100 10 1 1 00 (–20)

Booth's algorithm may need the summation at each step and number of steps required in Booth's algorithm are equal to length of multiplier in bits. The bit pair recording halves the maximum number of summations. Hence, it achieves faster multiplication.

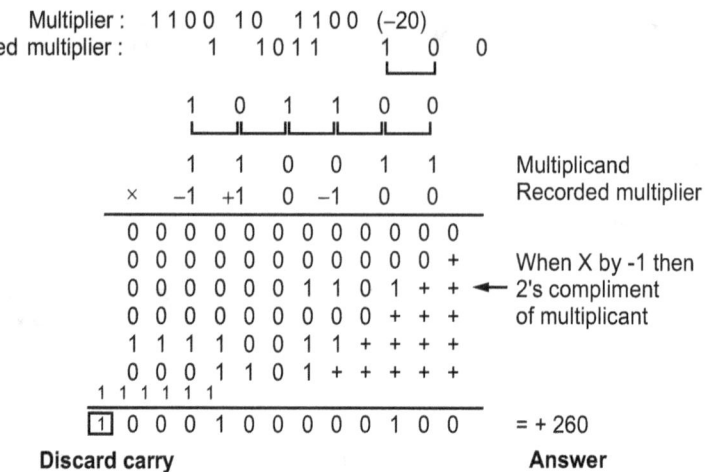

Example 6 : Using Booth's algorithm multiply the following :

Multiplicand = + 15

Multiplier = – 6   **[Dec. 05, 8 Marks]**

Solution : Multiplicand (B) ← 01111 multiplier (Q) ← 1010 (–6)

STEPS	A	Q	Q – 1	OPERATION
	000000	1010	0	Initial
1.	000000	0101	0	Shift right
2.	10001	0101	0	A ← A – B
	11000	1010	1	Shift right
3.	00111	1010	1	A ← A + B
	00011	1101	0	Shift right
4.	10100	1101	0	A ← A – B
	11010	0110	1	Shift right

Result : 11010 0 110 = – 90 (2's complement of 90)

Example 7 : Draw the hardware implementation of Booth's Algorithm. Using Booth's Algorithm multiplicand = + 22

Multiplier = – 5   **[Dec. 07, 7 Marks]**

Solution :

Refer Fig. 1.22 For Hardware Implementation of Booth's Algorithm

Multiplicand : 22 and

Multiplier : – 5

Take 2's complement of multiplier as it is – ve

111011 → 5

Recoded multiplier is

$$1 \quad 1 \quad 1 \quad 0 \quad 1 \quad 0$$
$$\leftarrow \leftarrow \leftarrow \leftarrow \leftarrow \leftarrow$$
$$0 \quad 0 \;-1 \quad 1 \quad 0 \;-1$$

When −1 is multiplied the 2's complement of the multiplicand is written and when 1 is multiplied the multiplicand is written as it is.

2's complement of 0 1 1 1 1 0 → 1 0 1 0 1 0

		0	1	0	1	1	0						
×		0	0	−1	1	0	−1						
	1	1	1	1	1	1	1	0	1	0	1	0	
	0	0	0	0	0	0	0	0	0	0	0	+	When × by −1 then
	0	0	0	0	0	1	0	1	1	0	+	+	← 2's compliment
	1	1	1	1	0	1	0	1	0	+	+	+	of multiplicand
	0	0	0	0	0	0	0	0	+	+	+	+	
	0	0	0	0	0	0	0	+	+	+	+	+	
	1	1	1	1	1	1	1	1					

$\boxed{1}$ 1 1 1 1 1 0 0 1 0 1 1 0 (−110)

ignore

1 1 1 1 1 0 0 1 0 0 1 0 is negative

Verify the result. Take 2's complement

0 0 0 0 0 1 1 0 1 1 0 1

+ _____ 1

1 1 0 1 1 1 0 (+ 110)

So the result is 2's complement of + 110 i.e. − 110 is verified.

3. Modified Booth's algorithm :

Bit pair recoding is used to speed up the multiplication process in Booth's algorithm. It have maximum number of summands.

In this technique, the Booth's recoded multiplier bits are grouped in the pairs. Then each pair is represented by its equivalent single bit multiplier reducing total number of multiplier bits to half. Example pair (+1 −1) is equivalent to pair (0 +1).

That is instead of adding −1 times multiplicand at shifted position i to +1 times the multiplicand at position i + 1, the same result is obtained by adding +1 times multiplicand at position i similarly (+1 0) is equivalent to (0 +2), (−1 +1) is equivalent to (0 − 1) and so on.

By replacing pairs with their equipments we can get bit pair–recoded multiplier. But instead of deriving bit pair recoded multiplier from booth recoded multiplier one can directly derive it pair recoded multiplier. The bit–pair recoding of multiplier can be directly derived from table.

Table shows the bit–pair code for all possible multiplier bit options.

Table 1.4 : Bit pair recode

Multiplier bit pair		Multiplier bit on the right	Bit pair recoded multiplier bit at position 1
i + 1	i	i − 1	.
0	0	0	0
0	0	1	+1
0	1	0	+1
0	1	1	+2
1	0	0	−2
1	0	1	−1
1	1	0	−1
1	1	1	0

Example 1 : Solve following using bit pair recoding method.

Multiplicand 0 1 1 1 1

Multiplier   1 0 1 1 0

2's complement of multiplicand = 1 0 0 0 1

Bit pair code for multiplier = sign extension

1 1 0 1 1 0 ① Implied zero end

 −1 2 −2   Recorded multiplier

By referring the table of modified Booths algorithm we determine the bit pair code.

```
      0   1   1   1   1                             Multiplicand
  ×  −1       2      −2                             recoded multiplier
     ─────────────────────────────────────
      1   1   1   1   1   0   0   0   1   0
      0   0   0   1   1   1   1   0   +   +
      0   1   0   0   0   1   +   +   +   +
     ─────────────────────────────────────
  1   0   1   0   1   1   0   1   0   1   0   Final Answer
```

Modified Booth's Algorithm :

Example 2 : Solve following using bit pair recoding method.

Multiplicand – 110101 (–11)

Multiplier - 011011 (27)

2's complement of multiplicand

   110101

   001010

+   1

_____

   001011   2's compliment

Bit pair code for multiplier 011010

```
0 1  1 0 1   1  ⓪   Implied zero end
    +2   −1    −1        Recorded multiplier
```

           110101

         + 2 − 1 − 1

   _____

   000000001011   ...2's compliment of muplicant

   0000001011++

   11101010++++

   _____

   111011010111   (−297)

Example on modified Booth's algorithm :

Example 3 : Draw the flow chart for Booth's algorithm and solve the following using bit pair recording method.

   Multiplicand 01111   Multiplier 10110   **[May 07, 8 Marks]**

Solution :

   Refer Fig. 1.23 for flow chart of Booth's algorithm.

   Multiplicand   0 1 1 1 1

   Multiplier   1 0 1 1 0

2's complement of multiplicand. Refer example for modified Booth's algorithm.

1.15 DIVISIONS

The division is more complex than multiplication for simplicity we will see division for positive numbers. The usual algorithm for dividing positive numbers by hand. It shows examples of decimal division and binary recoded division of the same value.

49 is partial reminder. Binary division quotient bits are 0 and 1. The bits of dividend are examined from left to right until the set of bits examined represents a number greater than or equal to the divisor. This is referred to as the divisor being able to divide the number. Until this condition occurs 0's are placed in the quotient from left to right. When condition is satisfied, a 1 is placed in the quotient and the divisor is subtracted from the partial dividend.

The result is referred to as a partial remainder. From this point onwards, the division process follows repetition of steps. Each repetition cycle, additional bits from the dividend are brought down to the partial remainder until the result is greater than or equal to the divisor, and the divisor is subtracted from the result to produce a new partial remainder. The process continues until all bits of the dividend are brought down and result is still less than divisor.

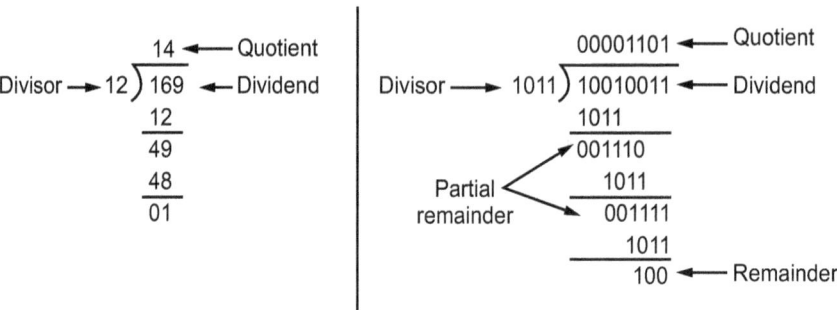

1.15.1 Restoring Division

Restoring division algorithm exist to perform division in digital designs restoring division operates on fixed point fractional number.

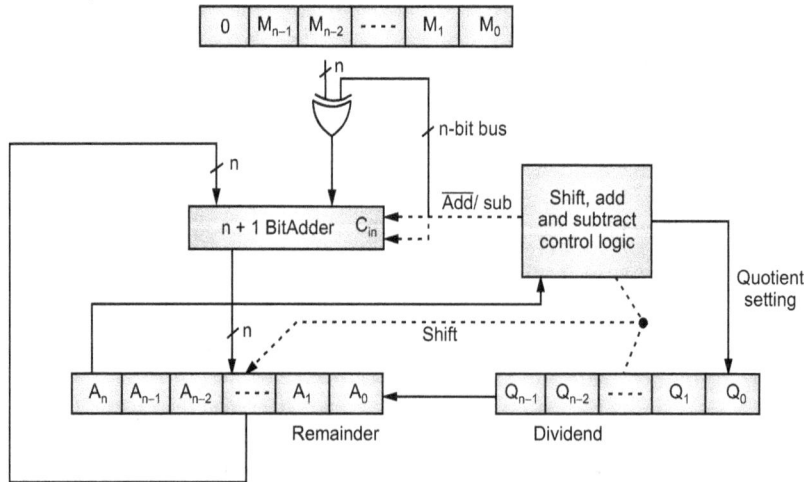

Fig 1.24 : Hardware to implement binary division

Hardware implementation of division consist of n + 1 bit binary adder, shift, add and subtract control logic registers A, M, and Q as shown in figure divisor and dividend are loaded into register M and register Q. Register A is initially set to zero. The division operation is then carried out. After the division is complete, the n–bit quotient is in register Q and the remainder is in register A. Operation include:

1. Shift A and Q left one binary position.

2. Subtract divisor from A and place answer back in A (M–A–M).

3. If the sign bit of A is 1, set Q0 to 0 and add divisor back to A(that is restore A) otherwise, set Q0 to 1.

4. Repeat steps 1, 2 and 3 times.

The division algorithm needs restoring A, after each unsuccessful subtraction. (Subtraction is said to be unsuccessful if the result is negative) therefore it is referred to as restoring division algorithm. This algorithm is improved, giving non–restoring division algorithm. Consider the sequence of operations that takes place after the subtraction operation in the restoring algorithm.

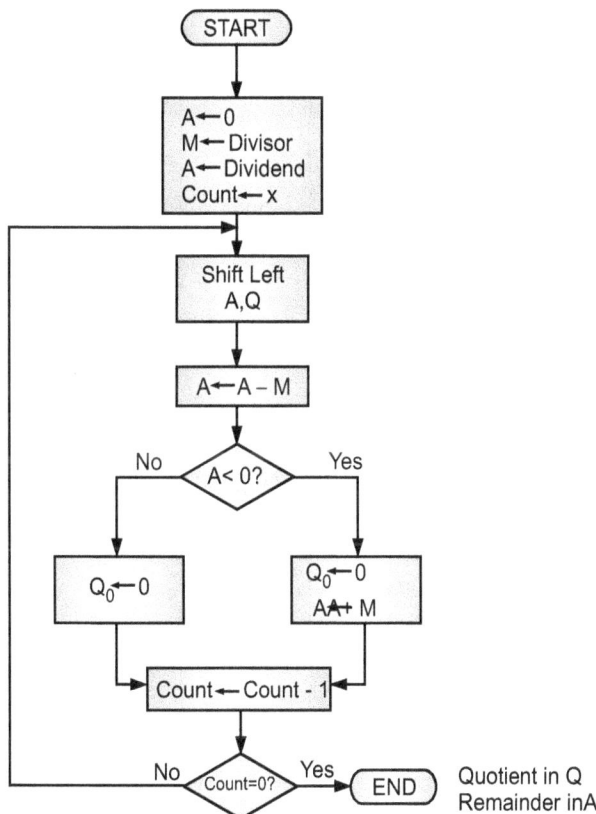

Fig. 1.25 : Flowchart for restoring division operation

Example for restoring division :

Dividend is 0 111 and divisor is 0011. Following figure shows (a), (b), (c), (d) all the four cases for signed restoring division. Where A consist of remainder and Q consist of Quotient. Consider subtract M means add M in 2's complement form.

If A is positive then shift left and subtract divisor 2A–M.

If A is negative then Restore A + M, Shift left and subtract divisor $->2(A + M)-M = 2A+M$

Consider following examples on restoring division.

A	Q	M = 0011	A	Q	M = 1101
0000	0111	Initial Value	0000	0111	Initial Value
0000	1110	Shift	0000	1110	Shift
1101		Subtract	1101		Add
0000	1110	Restore	0000	1110	Restore
0001	1100	Shift	0001	1100	Shift
1110		Subtract	1110		Add
0001	1100	Restore	0001	1100	Restore
0011	1000	Shift	0011	1000	Shift
0000		Subtract	0000		Add
0000	1001	Set $Q_0 = 1$	0000	1001	Set $Q_0 = 1$
0001	0010	Shift	0001	0010	Shift
1110		Subtract	1110		Add
0001	0010	Restore	0001	0010	Restore
(a) (7) ÷ (3)			(b) (7) ÷ (−3)		

A	Q	M = 0011	A	Q	M = 1101
1111	1001	Initial Value	1111	1001	Initial Value
1111	0010	Shift	1111	0010	Shift
0010		Add	0010		Subtract
1111	0010	Restore	1111	0010	Restore
1110	0100	Shift	1110	0100	Shift
0001		Add	0001		Subtract
1110	0100	Restore	1110	0100	Restore
1100	1000	Shift	1100	1000	Shift
1111		Add	1111		Subtract
1111	1001	Set $Q_0 = 1$	1111	1001	Set $Q_0 = 1$
1111	0010	Shift	1111	0010	Shift
0010		Add	0010		Subtract
1111	0010	Restore	1111	0010	Restore
(c) (−7) ÷ (3)			(d) (−7) ÷ (−3)		

1.15.2 Non-Restoring Division

Steps :

1. If the sign of A is 0, shift A and Q left one bit position and subtract divisor from A, therwise shift A and Q left and add divisor to A. if sign of A is 0,set Q_0 to 1; otherwise set Q_0 to 0.

2. Repeat steps 1 and 2 for n times.

3. If the sign of A is 1, add divisor to A.

Flowchart for non–restoring division

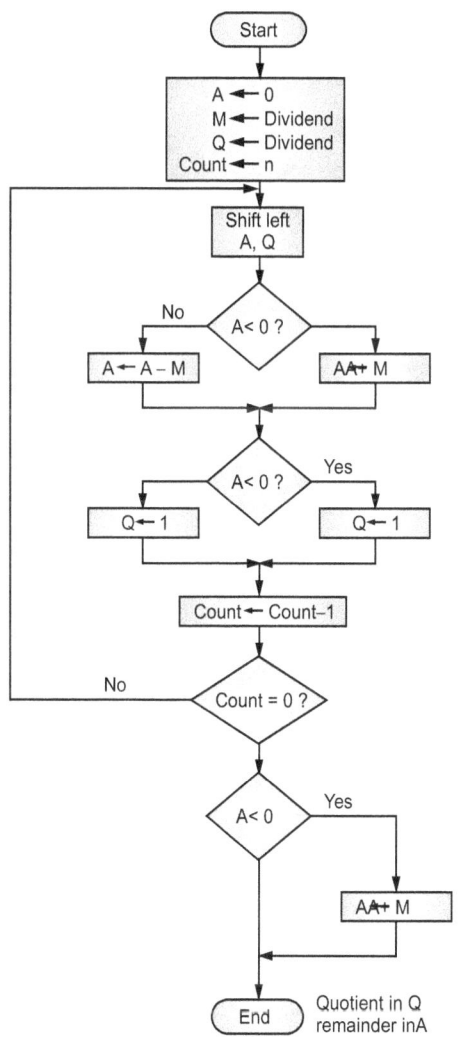

Fig 1.26 : Flowchart for non–restoring division

Step 3 is required to leave the proper positive number in A at the end of n cycles.

The hardware can also be used to perform non-restoring algorithm. There is no simple algorithm for signed division. The operand is preprocessed to transform them into positive values. Then using one of the algorithm just discussed quotients and remainders are calculated. The quotient and remainders are then transformed to the correct signed values.

Example 1 : For non-restoring division

Consider 4 bit dividend and 2 bit divisor

Dividend = 1010 (10)

Divisor = 0011 (3)   **[May 06]**

	A Register	Q Register	
	0 0 0 0 0	1 0 1 0	← Dividend
Subtract	0 0 0 0 0	1 0 1 ☐	First cycle
Set Q_0	1 1 1 0 1		
	① 1 1 1 0	0 1 0 ⓪	
Shift	1 1 1 0 0	1 0 0 ☐	Second cycle
Add	0 0 0 1 1		
Set Q_0	① 1 1 1 1	1 0 ⓪ ⓪	
Shift	1 1 1 1 1	0 ⓪ ⓪ ☐	Third cycle
Add	0 0 0 1 1		
Set Q_0	⓪ 0 0 1 0	0 ⓪ ⓪ ①	
Shift	0 0 1 0 0	⓪ ⓪ ① ☐	Fourth cycle
Subtract	1 1 1 0 1		
	⓪ 0 0 0 1	⓪ ⓪ ① ①	
	Remainder (1)	Quotient (3)	

In above example after 4 register A is positive and hence step 3 is not required. Let us see another examples in which step 3 is required.

Example 2 : Dividend = 1 0 1 1 (11)

Divisor = 0 1 0 1 (5)

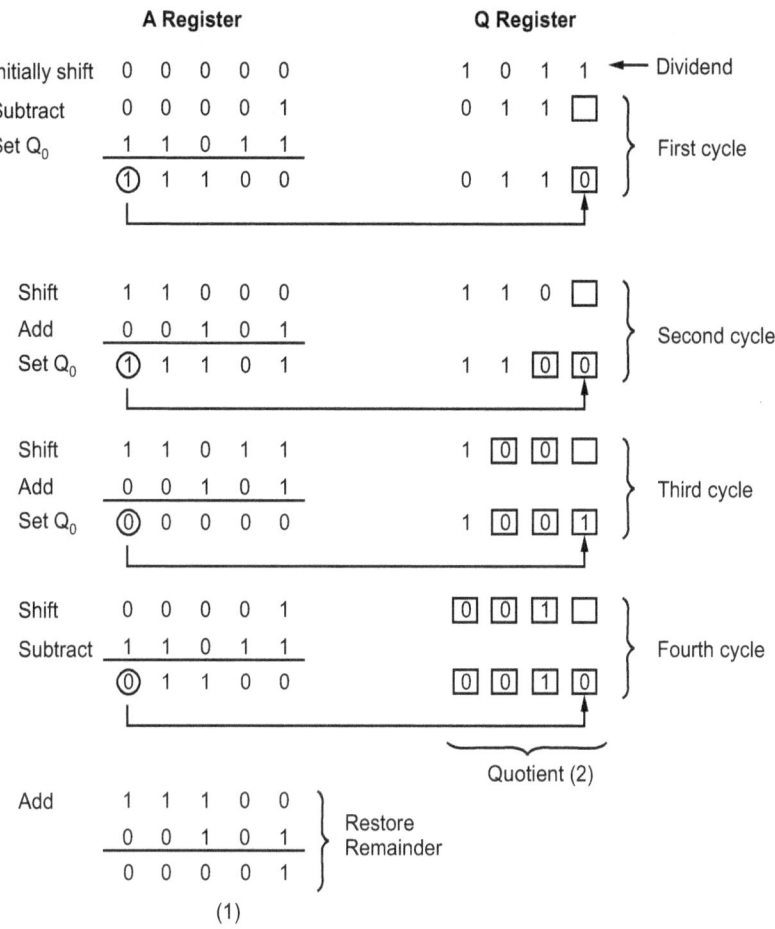

So, A consist of remainder 00001

and Quotient is 0010.

Table 1.5 : Comparison between Restoring and Non-Restoring Division Algorithm

No.	Restoring division Algorithm	Non-restoring division Algorithm
1.	Needs restoring of registers A if the result of subtraction is negative.	Does not need restoring.
2.	In such cycle content of register A is first shifted left and then divisor is subtracted from it.	In each cycle content of register A is first shifted left and then divisor is added or subtracted with the content of register A depending on the sign of A.
3.	Does not need restoring of remainder.	Needs restoring of remainder if remainder is negative.
4.	Slower algorithm.	Faster algorithm.

SOLVED QUESTIONS ON RESTORING AND NON-RESTORING DIVISION

Example 3 : Draw the flow chart for restoring division algorithm and solve the following using above algorithm.

　　　Dividend = 17　　　Divisor = 03

Solution :

Dividend = 17 = $(10001)_2 \to Q$　　Divisor = 03 – $(00011)_2 \to B$

For flow chart for restoring division refer Fig. 1.25.

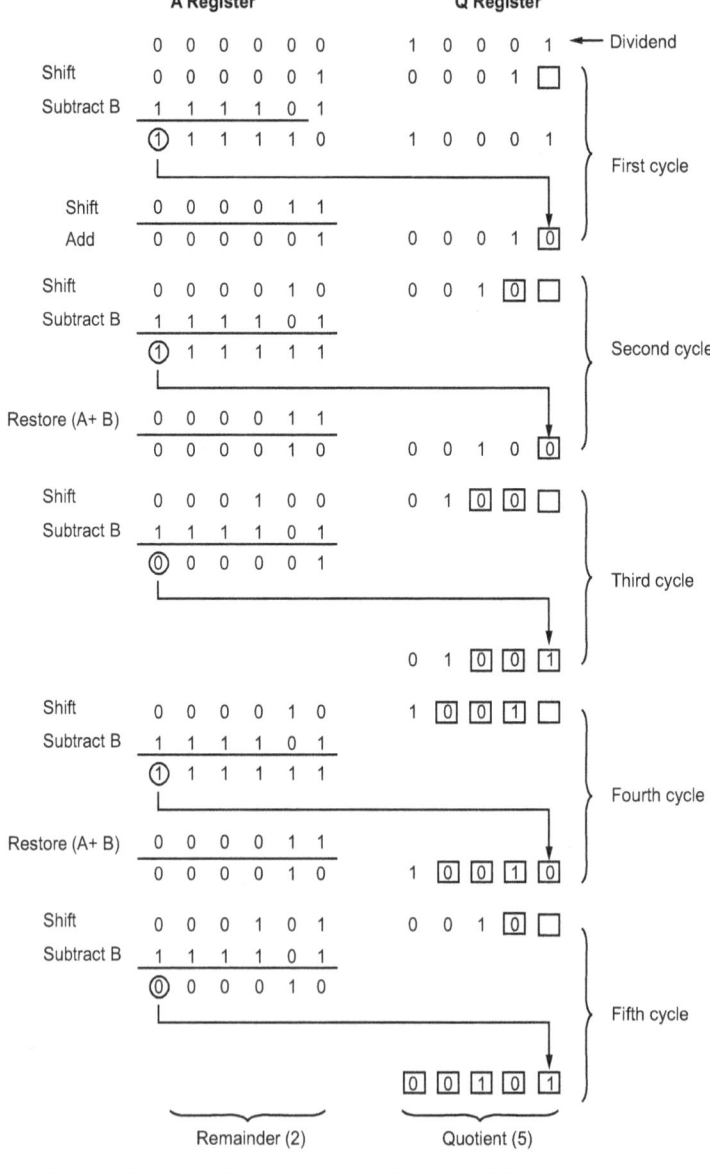

Remainder (2)　　　Quotient (5)

Example 4 : Draw the flow chart for non-restoring division algorithm and perform division of the following numbers using non-restoring.

Division algorithm :

    Dividend = 1011 (11)

    Divisor   = 0011 (3)   **[May 06, 10, Dec. 09, 10 Marks]**

Solution : Flowchart for non-restoring division refer Fig. 1.26.

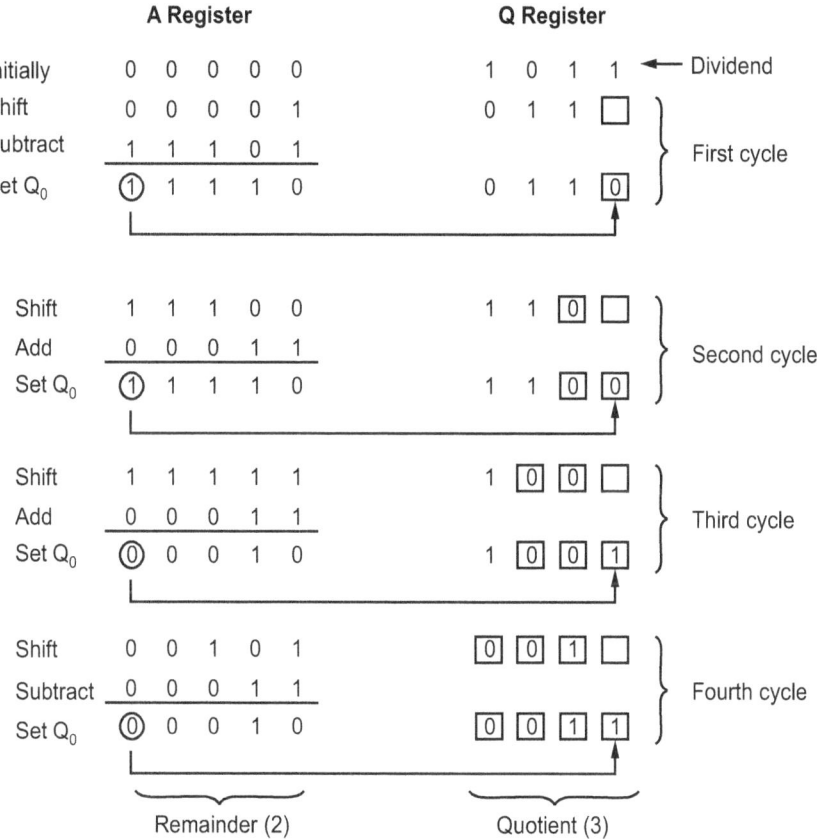

Example 5 : Compare restoring and non-restoring division algorithm. Perform division of the following numbers using restoring division algorithm.

Division algorithm :

    Dividend = 1101 (13)

    Divisor   = 11 (3)

Solution : For comparison refer table 1.5.

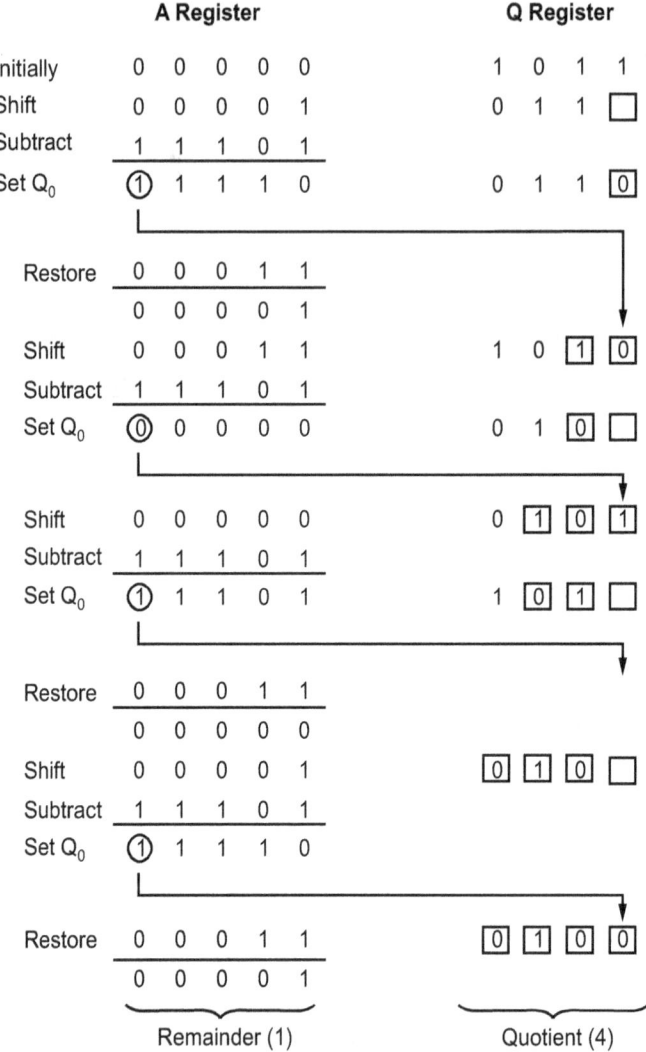

Example 6 : Draw flowchart for restoring division algorithm and perform division of the following numbers using restoring division algorithm. **(May 07, 10 Marks)**

    A : 1100 (12)

    B : 0100 (4)

Solution : Take 2's complement of divisor (B) = 1100

	A Register					Q Register			
A Register						**Q Register**			
Initially	0	0	0	0	0	1	1	0	0
Shift	0	0	0	0	1	1	0	0	☐
Subtract B	1	1	1	0	0				
Set Q_0	1	1	1	0	1	1	0	0	⓪
Restore (A+ B)	0	0	1	0	0				
	0	0	0	0	1	①⓪⓪⓪			
Shift	0	0	0	1	1	0	0	0	☐
Subtract B	1	1	1	0	0				
Set Q_0	1	1	1	1	1	0	0	0	⓪
Restore	0	0	1	0	0				
	0	0	0	1	1	0	0	0	0
Shift	0	0	1	1	0	0	0	0	☐
Subtract B	1	1	1	0	0				
Set Q_0	0	0	0	1	0	0	0	0	①
Shift	0	0	1	0	0	0	0	1	☐
Subtract B	1	1	1	0	0				
Set Q_0	0	0	0	0	0	0	0	1	①

    ⌣ Remainder   ⌣ Quotient (3)

Example 7 : Draw flowchart for non-restoring division operation. Perform the division of the following numbers using non-restoring division. **[Dec. 07, 14 Marks]**

    Dividend = 1101 (13)   Divisor = 0100 (4)

Solution : Refer Fig. 1.26 for flow chart

    Dividend : 1101   Divisor : 0100 (2's complement of divisior)

    Q → Dividend   B divisor   1100

    A → 00000

	A Register					Q Register				
Initially	0	0	0	0	0	1	1	0	1	← Dividend
Shift	0	0	0	0	1	1	0	1	☐	
Subtract	1	1	0	0	0					
Set Q_0	①	1	0	0	1	1	0	1	⓪	

First cycle
(Since sign bit ofAis
'0' subtract divisor i.e.
add two's comlement)

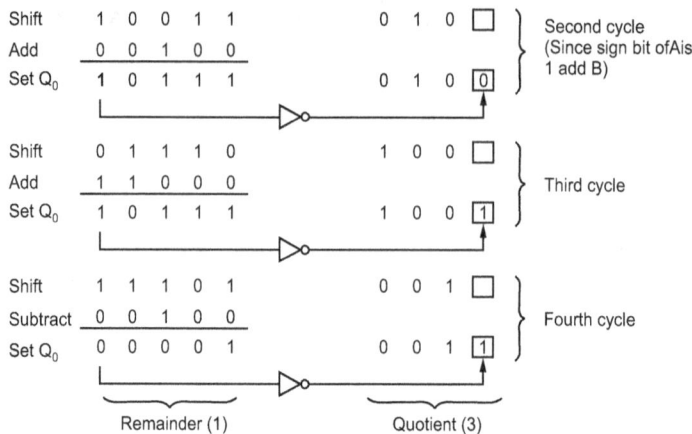

Example 8 : Perform the following division using restoring and non-restoring division algorithm.

Dividend = 1100 (12) Divisor = 0011 (3)   **[May 05, 06, 10 Marks]**

Solution : Restoring :

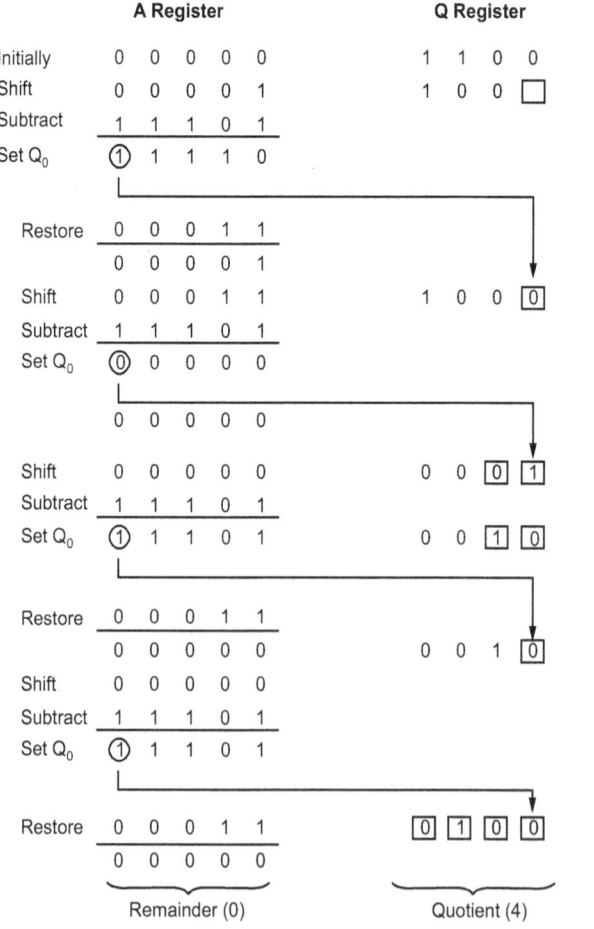

Non-Restoring :

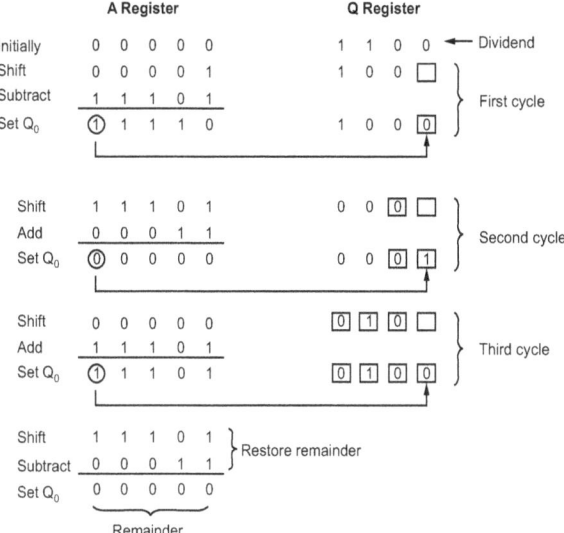

Example 9 : Perform the following division using restoring division algorithm :

Dividend = 1001 (9) Divisor = 0101 (5)   **[Dec. 08, 10, 8 Marks]**

Solution :

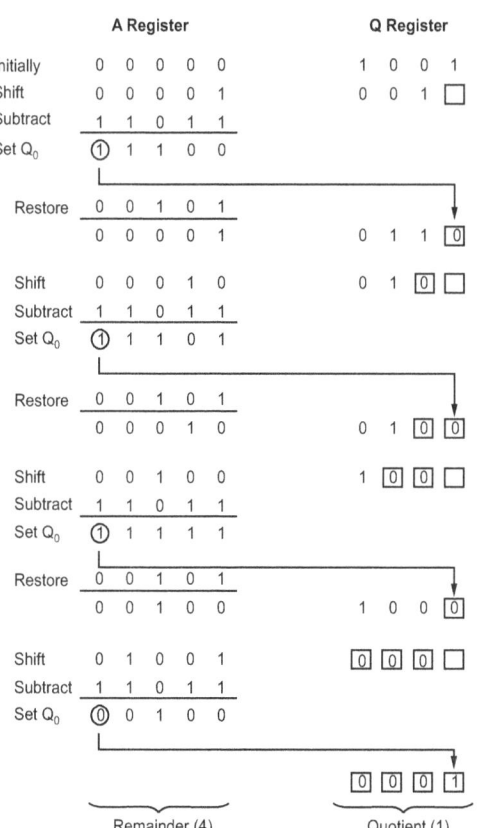

Example 10 : Perform the following division using restoring method :

Dividend = 1000 (8) and Divisor = 0010 (2)

Solution :

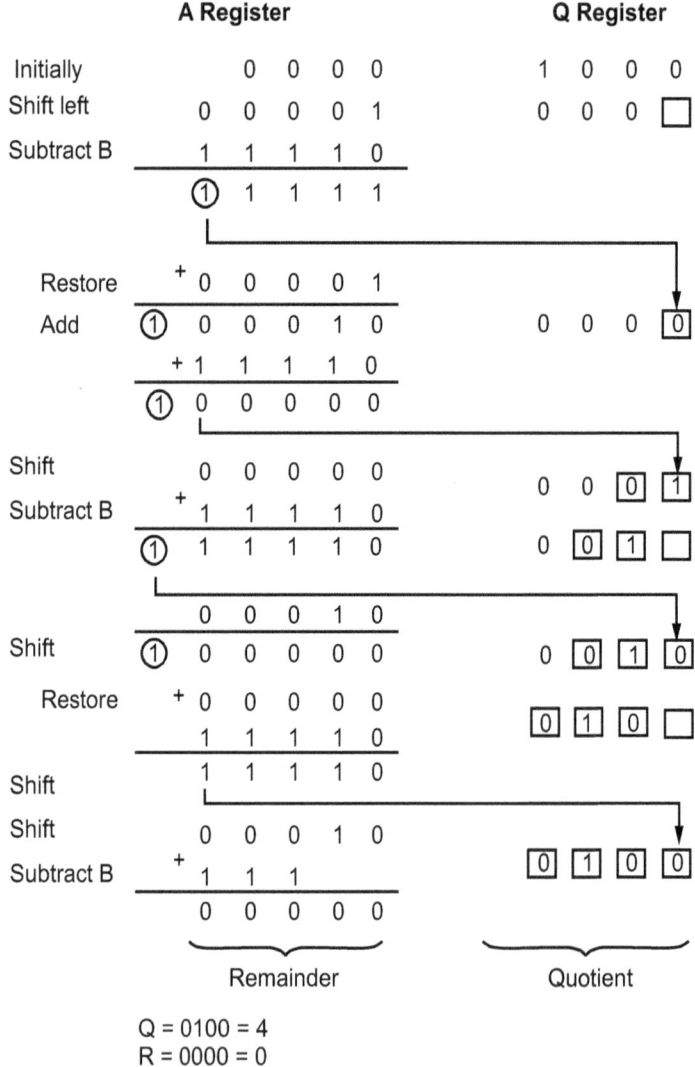

Q = 0100 = 4
R = 0000 = 0

Example 11 : Perform the following division using non-restoring method.

Dividend = 1000 (8) and Divisor = 0010 (2)

Solution : A → 0000, B → 0010 Q → 1000

```
            Sign          A              Q
             0        0 0 0 0       1 0 0 0

    Shift    0        0 0 0 0       0 0 0 □
 Subtract    1        1 1 1 0
   Set Q₀   [1]       1 1 1 1
                      1 1 1 1
                                   0 0 0 [0]
 Shift left  1        1 1 1 0      0 0 [0]□
  AddA+ B    0        0 0 1 0
             0        0 0 0 0

    Shift    0        0 0 0 0      0 0 [0][1]
 Subtract  + 1        1 1 1 0      0 [0][1]□
             1        1 1 1 0

    Shift    1        1 1 0 0      0 0 [1][0]
     Add     0        0 0 1 0      0 [1][0]□
             1        1 1 1 0

             1        1 1 1 0      [0][1][0][0]
     Add     0        0 0 1 0
             0        0 0 0 0
                      R (0)          Q (4)
```

1.16 Floating Point Representations

Integer fixed point schemes do not have the ability to represent very large or very small numbers. Need the ability to dynamically move the decimal point to a convenient location

$$\text{Format}: +/-M \times R +/-E$$

Mantissas are stored in a normalized format either 1xxxxx or 0.1xxxxx, Since the 1 is required, don't need to explicitly store it in the data word insert it for calculations only. Exponents can be positive or negative values. Use biasing (Excess coding) to avoid operating on negative exponents. Bias is added to all exponent positive numbers to represent fractional binary numbers it is necessary to consider binary point. If binary point is assumed to the right of the signed bit we can represent fractional binary number as.

$$B = (b_0 \times 2^0 + b_{-1} \times 2^{-1} + b_{-2} \times 2^{-2} + \ldots + b_{-[n-1]} \times 2^{(-n-1)})$$

With the fractional number system we can represent the fractional numbers in the following range.

$$2^{-(n-1)} \leq F \leq 1 - 2^{-(n-1)}$$

If n = 32 then value range is approximately

$$2^{-31} \leq F \leq 1 - 2^{-31} \, (1 - 2.3283 \times 10^{-10})$$

This range is not sufficient for representing fractional numbers. To accommodate very large integers and very small fractions, a computer must be able to represent numbers and operate on them in such a way that the position of binary point is variable and is automatically adjusted as computation proceeds.

The floating point representation has three fields: sign, significant digits, and exponent to represent the number in floating point format first binary point is shifted to right of the first bit and the number is multiplied by the correct scaling factor to get the same value. The number is said to be in the normalized form. It is given as

$$1\,1\,0\,1.1\,0\,0\,0\,1\,1\,0 \rightarrow 1.1\,1\,1\,0\,1\,1\,0\,0\,1\,1\,0 \times 2^5$$

base of scaling factor is fixed i.e. 2 and it does not need to appear explicitly in the machine representation 0 floating point number. Significant digits i.e. 1.11101100110 is known as mantissa. And exponent is 2's largest power value. i.e. 5.

Example 1 : Represent 1259. 125_{10} in single precision and double precision formats.

Solution : Step 1 : Convert decimal number in binary format.

$$
\begin{array}{ll}
78 & 4 \\
16\,)\,1259 & 16\,)\,78 \\
112 & 64 \\
0139 & 14 = E \\
128 & \\
011 = M &
\end{array}
$$

$$= 4\ EBH = \frac{100}{4} = \frac{1110}{E} = \frac{1011}{B}$$

Fractional part :

$$
\begin{array}{lll}
0.125 \times 2 & = & 0.25\ 0 \\
0.25 \times 2 & = & 0.5\ \ 0 \\
0.5 \times 2 & = & 1.0\ \ 1 \\
& & 0 \\
& = & 0.001 \\
\text{Binary number} & = & 10011101011 + 0.001 \\
& = & 10011101011.001
\end{array}
$$

Step 2 : Normalize the number

$$10011101011.001 = 1.0011101011001 \times 2^{10}$$

Now we will see the representation of the numbers in single precision and double precision formats.

Step 3 : Single precision representation for a given number S = 0. E = 10 and

M = 00111 01011 001

Bias for single precision format is = 127

$$E' = E + 127 = 10 + 127 = 137_{10} = 10001001_2$$

∴ Number in double precision format is given as

0	1000 1001	0011101011001...0
Sign	Exponent	Mantissa (23 bits)

Step 4 : Double precision representation for a given number

S = 0, E = 10, and M = 0011101011001

Bias for double precision format is = 1023

$$E' = E + 1023 = 10 + 1023 = 1033_{10}$$
$$= 10000001001_2$$

∴ Number in double precision format is given as

0	1000 1001	0011101011001...0
Sign	Exponent	Mantissa (52 bits)

Example 2 : Represent–307.1875$_{10}$ in single precision and double precision formats.

Solution : Step 1 : Convert decimal number in binary format integer part.

Integer part :

$$16 \overline{)307} \qquad 16 \overline{)19}$$
$$\underline{16} \qquad\qquad \underline{16}$$
$$147 \qquad\qquad 3$$
$$\underline{144}$$
$$3 = 3$$

$$=133 \ H= \ \frac{1}{1} = \frac{0011}{3} = \frac{0011}{3}$$

Fractional part :

$$0.1875 \times 2 = 0.3750 \qquad 0$$
$$0.3750 \times 2 = 0.750 \qquad 0$$
$$0.750 \times 2 = 1.5 \qquad 1$$

$$0.5 \times 2 = 1.0 \qquad 10$$
$$= 0.0011$$
$$\text{Binary number} = -100110011 + 0.0011$$
$$= -100110011.0011$$

Step 2 : Normalize the number -100110011.0011

$$= -1.001100110011 \times 2^8$$

Now we will see the representation of the numbers in single precision and double precision formats.

Step 3 : Single precision representation for a given number

S = 1, E = 8, and M = 0011 0011 0011

Bias for single precision format is = 127

$$E' = E + 127 = 8 + 127 = 135_{10}$$
$$= 10000111_2$$

Number in single precision format is given as

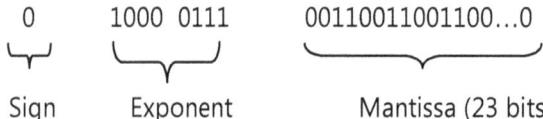

0	1000 0111	00110011001100...0
Sign	Exponent	Mantissa (23 bits)

Step 4 : Double precision representation for a given number

S = 1, E = 8, andM = 0011 0011 0011

Bias for double precision format is = 1023

$$E' = E + 1023 = 8 + 1023 = 1031_{10}$$
$$= 10000100111_2$$

∴ Number in double precision format is given as

1	100 0000 0111	0011001100110011000...0
Sign	Exponent	Mantissa (52 bits)

SOLVED QUESTIONS ON REPRESENTATIONS

Example 3 : Explain IEEE floating point number formats.   **[May 05, 4 Marks]**

Solution :

Represent $(178.1875)_{10}$ in single and double precision floating point format.

Step 1 : Convert decimal number in binary format integer part first

$$11 \rightarrow B$$

$$16 \overline{)178}$$
$$\frac{16}{18}$$
$$\frac{16}{2}$$

$$(178)_{10}\,(B2) = (1\ 0\ 1\ 1\ \underbrace{0\ 0\ 1\ 0}_{})_2$$
$$\underbrace{}_{B}\ \underbrace{}_{2}$$

$$(178)_{10} = (B2)_{16} = (1\ 0\ 1\ 1\ 0\ 0\ 1\ 0)_2$$
$$\underbrace{}_{B}\ \underbrace{}_{2}$$

Fractional Part :

$$0.1875 \times 2 = 0.3750 \quad 0$$
$$0.3750 \times 2 = 0.750 \quad 0$$
$$0.750 \times 2 = 1.51$$
$$0.5 \times 2 = 1.01$$
$$0 \quad 0$$
$$= 0.0011$$

$$\text{Binary number} = 1011\ 0010 + 0.0011 = 1011\ 0010.0011$$

Step 2 : Normalize the number

$$1011\ 0010.0011 = 1.01100100011 \times 2^7$$

Step 3 : Representation in signal precision for given number

$S = 0$, $E = 7$ and $M = 011\ 001\ 000\ 11$

Bias for single precision format is $= 127$

$$E' = E + 127 = 7 + 127 = 134_{10}$$
$$= 10000110_2$$

∴ Number in single precision format is given as

$$\begin{array}{ccc} 0 & 1000\ 0110 & 011001\ 000110...0 \\ \underbrace{} & \underbrace{} & \underbrace{} \\ \text{Sign} & \text{Exponent} & \text{Mantissa (23 bits)} \end{array}$$

Step 4 : Representation in double precision bias for double precision format is 1023.

$$E' = 7 + 1023 = 1030_{10}$$
$$= 100001000110_2$$

Number in double precession format

0	100001000110	01100100010...0
sign	Exponent	Mantissa (32 bits)

Example 4 : Represent the following numbers in single precision floating point format.

[May 08, Dec. 08, 5 Marks]

(a) 100.125   (b) 42.625   (c) 17.125   (d) 12.5

Solution :

(a) 100.125

Convert it into binary

$$(100)_{10} = (1100100)_2$$

Fractional part

$$0.125 \times 2 = 0.250$$
$$0.25 \times 2 = 0.50$$
$$0.50 \times 2 = 1.00$$
$$(100.125)_{10} = (1100100.001)_2$$

To convert above number in single precession format we will convert it into the form $N \times 2^{E-127}$

$$1100100.001 = 1.100\ 100001 \times 2^6$$
$$= 1.100100001 \times 2^{133-127}$$

0	1000101	1001 100000 100000
sign	E	Mantissa (B)

(b) 42.625

$$(42)_{10} = (101010)_2$$
$$0.625 \times 2 = 1.350$$
$$0.350 \times 2 = 0.70$$
$$0.70 \times 2 = 1.40$$
$$0.40 \times 2 = 0.80$$
$$0.80 \times 2 = 1.60$$
$$0.60 \times 2 = 1.20$$
$$0.20 \times 2 = 0.40$$
$$(0.625)10 = 101011001100110$$

$$42.625 = 101010. 101\ 0110\ 0110\ 0110$$

Convert it into $1.N \times 2^{E-127}$

$$1.0101010101100110 \ldots \times 2^5 = 1.01010101\ 0110\ 0110 \times 2^{132-127}$$

0	10000100	010 10 101 011 0110 0110 011

sign bit   Exponent   Mantissa

(c) 17.25

$$(17)_{10} = (10001)_2$$
$$0.125 \times 2 = 0.50$$
$$0.50 \times 2 = 1.00$$

$(17.125)_{10}$ $(10001.01)_2$

Convert it into the form $(1.N) \times 2^{E-127}$

$$10001.01 = 1.000101 \times 2^4$$
$$= 1.000101 \times 2^{131-127}$$

0	10000011	0001 0100 0000 0000 0000 0000

sign   Exponent   Mantissa (M)

(d) 12.5

$$(12.5)_{10} = (110.1)_2$$

Convert it into the form $1.N \times 2^{E-127}$

$$11001.1 = 1.10011 \times 2^4$$
$$= 1.10011 \times 2^{131-127}$$

0	10000011	1001 1000 0000 0000 0000 0000

sign   Exponent   mantissa

Example 5 : Represent 309.1975_{10} in single precesion and double precesion formats.

2	309	1
2	154	0
2	77	1
2	38	1
2	19	1
2	9	0

2	4	0
2	2	1
2	1	
	0	

$$309 = 10011010$$

Fractional part

$$0.1975 \times 2 = 0.3950$$
$$0.3950 \times 2 = 0.7900$$
$$.7900 \times 2 = 1.58$$
$$.58 \times 2 = 1.16$$
$$= 0.0011$$
$$(309.1975) = 100110101.0011$$

Normalize $\dfrac{1.001101010011 \times 2^8}{M}$

$$E = 8, S = 0$$

(1) Single precesion $\qquad E' = 8 + 127 = 135_{10}$

$$= 10000111_2$$

0	1000 0111	001101010011

23 bit

sign   Exponent   M

(2) Double precession

$$S = 0, E = 8, M = 001101010011$$

Bias for double precession format is 1023

$$E' = E + 1023 = 8 + 1023 = 1031_{10}$$
$$= 100001000111_2$$

0	1000000 0111	001101010011

sign   Exponent   mantissa (52 bit)

1.17 FLOATING POINT ARITHMETIC

1.17.1 Floating Point Addition and Subtraction Rules

Step 1 : Select the number with smaller exponent and shift its mantissa right, a number of steps equal to difference in exponents | e2 - e1|, for examples, if the number are 1.75×10^2 and 6.8×10^4 then the number 1.75×10^2 is selected and converted to 0.0175×10^4.

Step 2 : Set the exponent of the result equal to the larger exponent.

Step 3 : Perform addition/subtraction on the mantissas and determine the sign of the result.

Step 4 : Normalize the result, if necessary.

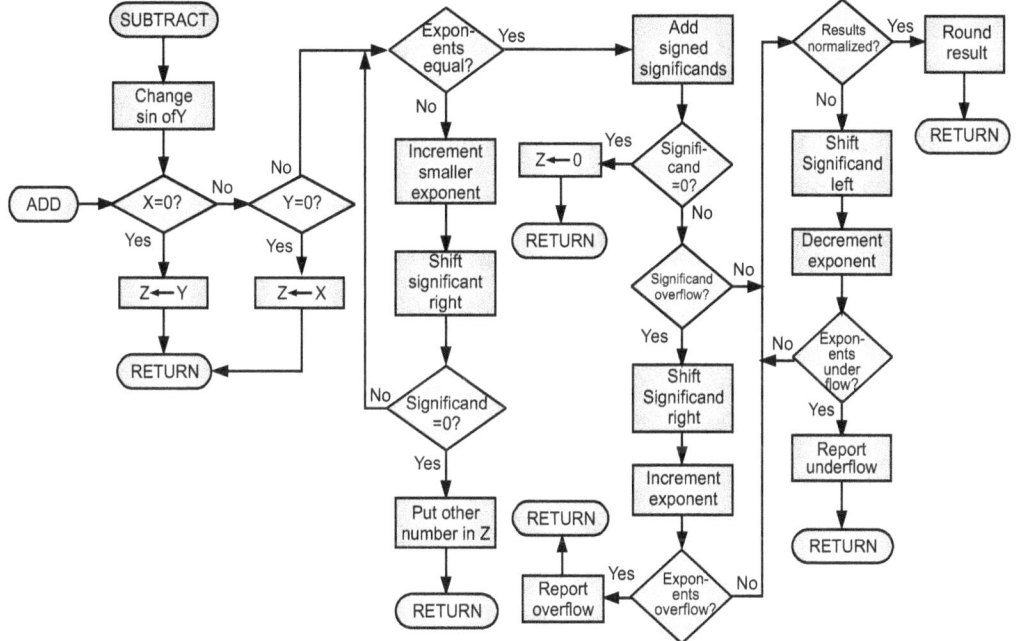

Fig. 1.27 : Floating point addition and subtraction

Example 1 : Add single precision floating point numbers A and B where

A = 44900000 H and B = 42 A 00000 H.

Solution : Step 1 : Represent numbers in single precision format

$$A = 0 \quad 1000 \quad 1001 \quad 0010000 \quad ......0$$
$$B = 0 \quad 1000 \quad 0101 \quad 010000 \quad ......0$$

$$\text{Exponent for A} = 1000\ 1001 = 137$$
$$\text{Actual exponent} = 137 - 127\ (\text{Bias}) = 10$$
$$\text{Exponent for B} = 1000\ 0101 = 133$$
$$\text{Actual exponent} = 133 - 127\ (\text{Bias}) = 6$$

Therefore. number B has smaller exponent with difference 4. Hence its mantissa is shifted right by 4-bits as shown below.

Step 2 : Shift mantissa

    Shifted mantissa of B = 00000100 0

Step 3 : Add mantissas

$$
\begin{array}{rll}
\text{Mantissa of A} = & 001\ 00\ 000 & ......0 \\
\text{Mantissa of B} = & 000\ 00\ 100 & ......0 \\
\hline
\text{Mantissa of Result} = & 001\ 00\ 100 & 0
\end{array}
$$

Both numbers are positive, sign of the result is positive

$$
\begin{array}{rll}
\text{Result} = & 01000\ 1001\ 00100\ 100 & ......0 \\
= & 44920000\ H
\end{array}
$$

Example 2 : Subtract single point precision floating point numbers A and B where A = 449 00 000 H and B = 42 A 00000 H.

Solution : Step 1 : Represent numbers in single precision format

$$
\begin{array}{rll}
A = & 0\ 10001001\ 0010000 & ......0 \\
B = & 0\ 10000101\ 010000 & ......0 \\
\text{Exponent for A} = & 10001001 = 137 \\
\text{Actual exponent} = & 137 - 127\ \text{(bias)} = 10 \\
\text{Exponent for B} = & 1000\ 0101 = 133 \\
\text{Actual exponent} = & 133 - 127\ \text{(Bias)} \\
= & 6
\end{array}
$$

Therefore, number B has smaller exponent with difference. Hence, its mantissa is shifted right by 4 bits as shown below.

Step 2 : Shift mantissa

    Shifted mantissa of B = 0000 0 100 0

Step 3 : Subtract mantissa

$$
\begin{array}{rll}
\text{Mantissa of A} = & 001\ 000\ 00 & ......0 \\
\text{Mantissa of B} = & 000\ 001\ 00 & ......0 \\
\hline
& 000\ 111\ 00 & 0
\end{array}
$$

Mantissa for A is greater than mantissa for B therefore sign of result is sign of A.

$$
\begin{array}{rll}
\text{Result} = & 0\ 1000\ 1001\ 00011100 & ......0 \\
= & 448E\ 0000\ H
\end{array}
$$

1.17.2 Hardware Implementation of Floating Point Addition and Subtraction

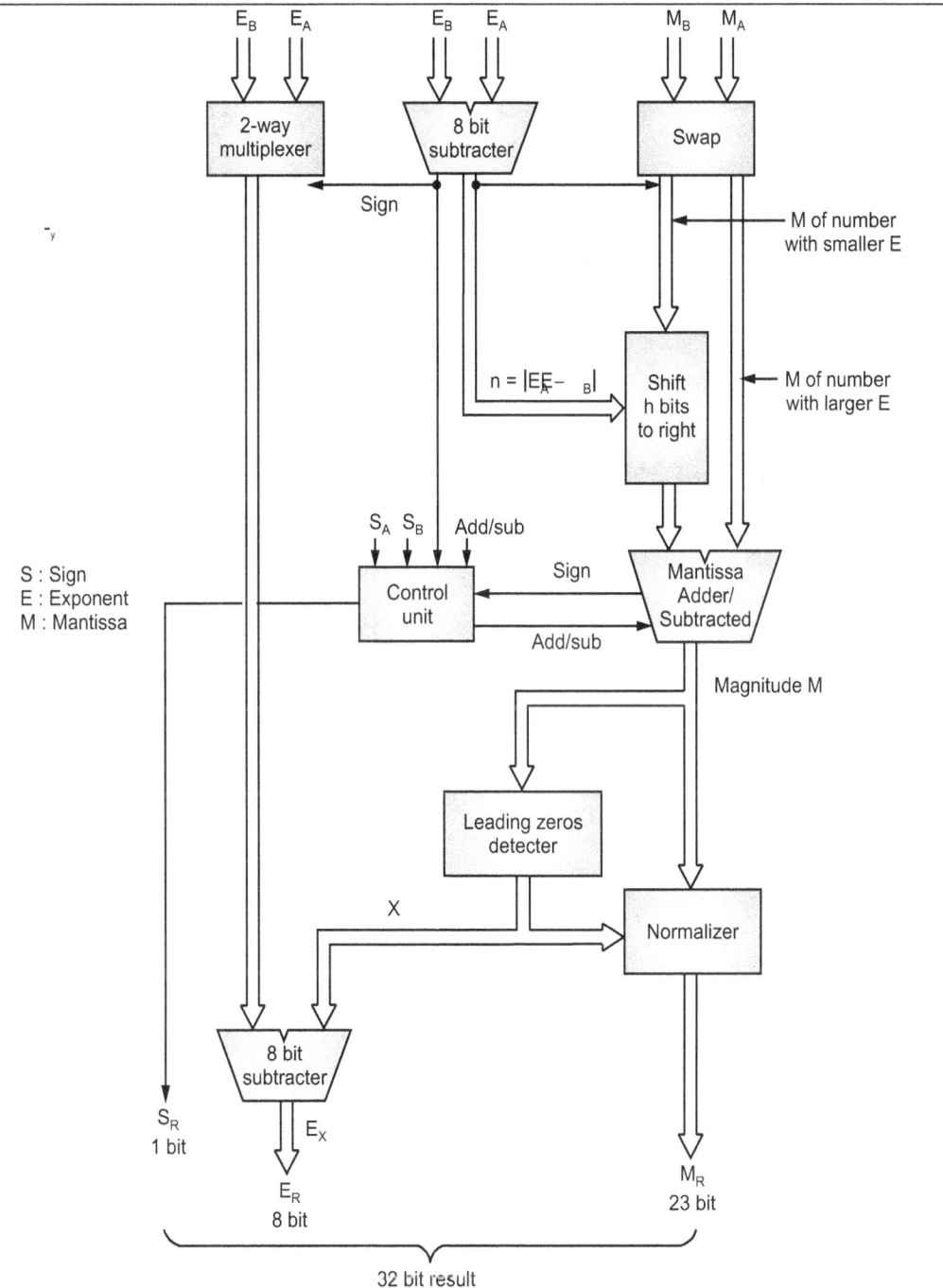

Fig. 1.28 : Hardware implementation of floating point addition and subtraction

Fig. 1.28 shows hardware implementation for the addition and subtraction of 32-bit floating point operands that have single precision format. 1 bit for sign, 8-bits for signed exponent and 23-bit for mantissa.

- As per addition or subtraction rule we have to first compare the exponents of numbers to determine a number with a smaller exponent or then to determine how for to shift the mantissa of that number so that its exponent matches with the other number.

- The shift count value n, is determined by the 8 bit subtractor. The inputs for the 8 bit subtractor are exponent values of two numbers and the operation performed is E_A - E_B. The subtraction gives the difference n.

- This difference is sent to the shifter unit. The sign of the difference that results from comparing exponents determines which mantissa is to be shifted.

- If the sign is 0, then $E_A \geq E$. and input to SWAP network is 0. This disables swapping and mantissa M_B is sent to the shifter.

- If the sign is 1, then E_A - E_B and input to SWAP network is 1. In this case, swapping is enabled and mantissa M_A is sent to the shifter. The shifter unit shifts the given mantissa n positions to the right.

- The two way multiplexer is used to set the exponent of the result (E) equal to the larger exponent i.e. step 5. Multiplexer has two inputs E_A and E_B and its output is based on the sign of the difference resulting from comparing exponents in step 1.

- The output of multiplexer is

$$E = E_A \quad \text{if } E_A \geq E_B$$
$$\text{or} \quad E = E_B \quad E_A < E_B$$

- The third step is to perform addition or subtraction on the mantissas and determine the sign of the result.

- The control logic is used to determine whether the mantissas are to be added or subtracted. It decides this by checking the signs of the operands (S_A and S_B) or the operation (Add or subtract) that is to be performed on the operands. The control logic is also responsible for determining the sign of the result (S_R).

- The control logic determines the sign of the result by checking the resulted sign of mantissa adder/ subtracted, sign from the exponent comparison signs of the operands and then operation to be performed.

- In step 4, the result of mantissa (M) is normalised, the normalized value is truncated to generate the 23 bit mantissa MR, of the result.

- The leading zeros detector determines the number of bits shifts, X to be applied to mantissa (M). The value X is then subtracted from the tentative resulted exponent E to generate the true result exponent, E_R.

1.17.3 Floating Point Multiplication/Division   [Dec. 10, 10 Marks]

For floating point multiplication and division first check for zero. Then add and subtract exponents.

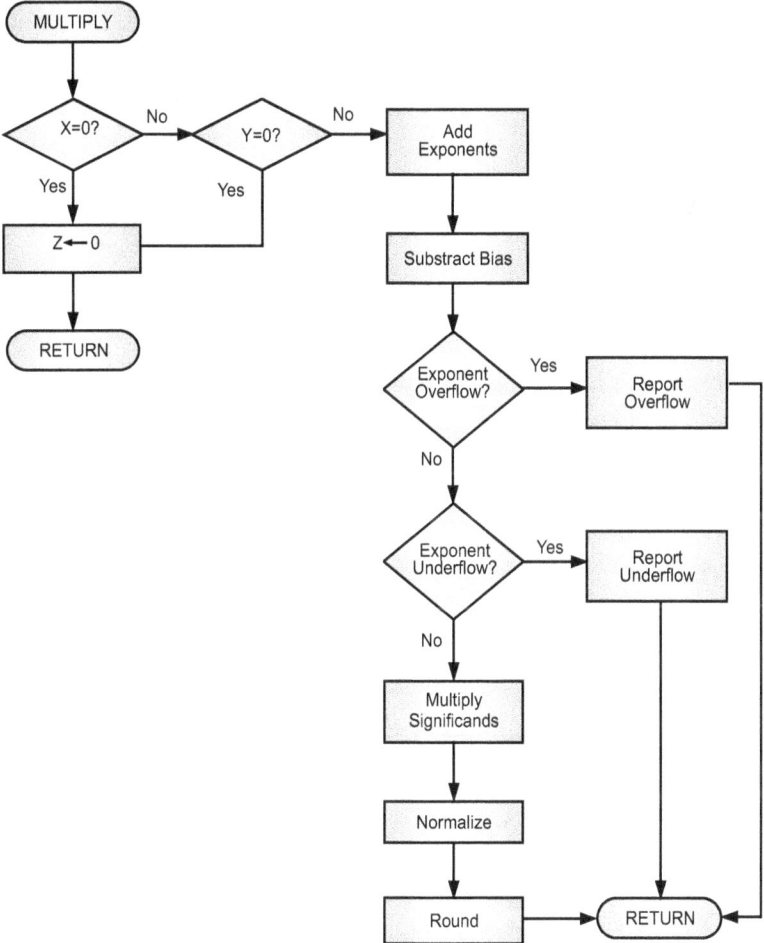

Fig. 1.29 : Floating point multiplication

Multiply or divide significant. Take care of sign of the bits. Then normalize the values. Round the values. All the intermediate results are in double length storage. Both the figures explain the steps involved in floating point multiplication and division.

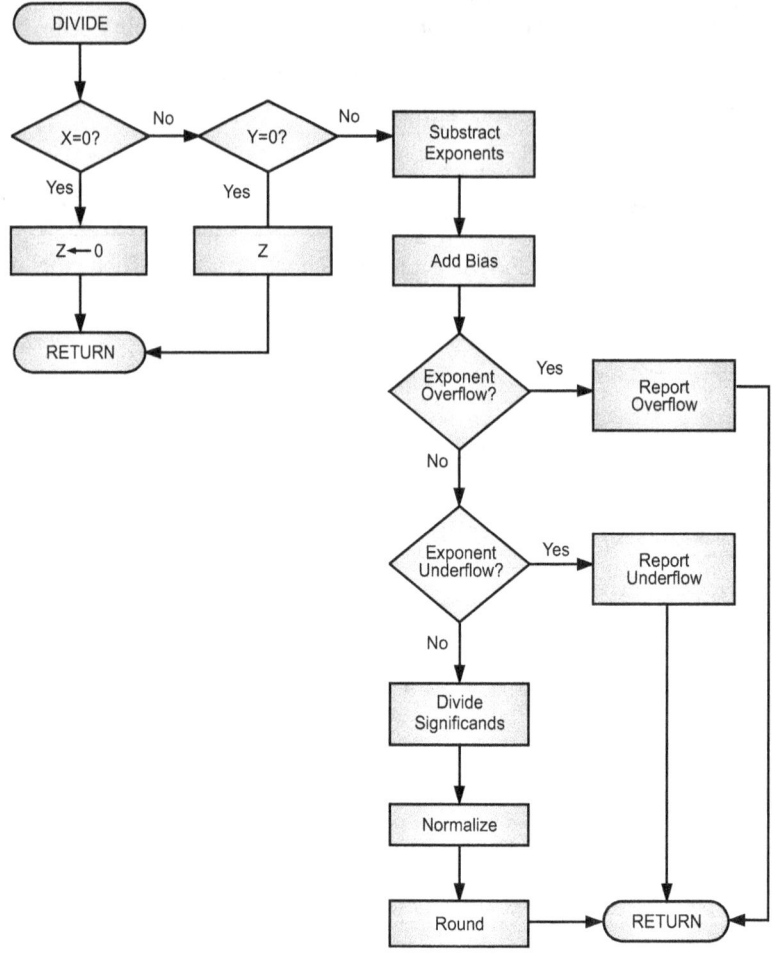

Fig. 1.30 : Floating point division

MULTIPLE CHOICE QUESTIONS (MCQ'S)

1. What was the name of the government funded computer used during world war II to compute firing tables?

   (a) VAX computer   (b) IBM computer

   (c) Colossus computer   (d) ENIAC computer

2. The fundamental conceptual unit in a computer is

   (a) CPU   (b) Hard Drive

   (c) Operating system   (d) Transister

3. First electronic computer was ......

    (a) EDVAC   (b) ENIAC

    (c) IAS   (d) None of these

4. ENIAC means ......

    (a) Electronic Numerical Integrator and Computation

    (b) Electrical Numerical Integrator and Computing

    (c) Electronic Numerical Integration and Computing

    (d) Electronic Numerical Integrator and Computing

5. EDVAC means ......

    (a) Electronic Discrete Variable and Computer

    (b) Electronic Discrete Variable and Computing

    (c) Electronic Discrete Variable and Computer

    (d) Electronic Discrete Variable and Computation

6. ENIAC was a ...... machine.

    (a) binary   (b) decimal

    (c) hexadecimal   (d) octal

7. ...... uses stored program concept.

    (a) EDVAC   (b) ENIAC

    (c) Ins   (d) None of these

8. ENIAC data memory consists of ...... accumulators and capable of storing ...... digits
    decimal number.

    (a)   10 and 20   (b)   20 and 10

    (c)   20 and 20   (d)   10 and 10

9. In EDVAC programs and their data were located in the ...... memory.

    (a) external   (b) separate

    (c) additional   (d) same

10. ...... invented an influential mechanical calculator.

    (a) Eckert and Mauchly   (b) Blaise Pascal

    (c) Von-Neumann   (d) Charles Babbage

11. ...... designed the first mechanical computer that can perform multistep operations automatically.

    (a) Charles Babbage   (b) Von-Neumann

    (c) Blaise pascal   (d) Harvard

12. Calculator invented by Pascal could do ...... operations on decimal numbers.

    (a) multiply and add   (b) subtract and multiply

    (c) compare and add   (d) add and subtract

13. First generation uses......

    (a) transistors   (b) Integrated circuits

    (c) vaccum tubes   (d) VLSI

14. Second generation had remarkable feature of use of ......

    (a) vaccum tubes   (b) Transistors

    (c) stored programs   (d) Integrated circuits

15. Integrated circuits were the features of ...... generation.

    (a) first   (b) second

    (c) third   (d) form

16. VLSI technology is used in ...... generation.

    (a) first   (b) second

    (c) third   (d) forth

17. In third generation, magnetic cone memories were replaced by ...... memories.

    (a) magnetic tape   (b) optical

    (c) IC   (d) magnetic disk

18. ...... was introduction of first minicomputer

    (a) IBM system 1360   (b) POP 8

    (c) POP 6   (d) IBM system 1340

19. ...... introduction bus structures.

    (a) IBM system 1360   (b) POP-8

    (c) POD 6   (d) IBM system 1340

20. First computer family was ......

    (a) IBM system 1360   (b) POP 8

    (c) POP – 6   (d) IBM system 1340

21. ...... invented IAS. (Institute for Advanced studies)

    (a) Von-Numann and Gold stine

    (b) Von-Neumann and Pascal

    (c) Von-Neumann and Charles Babbage

    (d) Eckert and Mauchly

22. In original IAS machine, storage location was referred to as ......

    (a) byte   (b) word

    (c) digit   (d) number

23. In IAS computer ...... fetches and interprets the instructions in memory and causes them to be executed.

    (a) ALU   (b) control unit

    (c) accumulator   (d) program counter

24. Von-Neumann architecture is

    (a) SISD   (b) SIMD

    (c) MIMD   (d) MISD

25. In original von-Neumann machine memory unit consists of ...... storage locations of ...... bits each.

    (a) 2048, 16   (b) 4096, 20

    (c) 4096, 60   (d) 4096, 40

26. In von-Neumann machine ...... feature was responsible for performance bottleneek.

    (a) stored program   (b) separate memory for data and wide

    (c) I/O access   (d) none of these

27. Which of the following operations are involved in an instruction cycle ?

    (a) opcode decoding   (b) Instruction execution

    (c) Instruction fetching   (d) all of these

28. ...... stores address of next instruction to be executed.

    (a) AR   (b) AC   (c) PC   (d) IR

29. AR in IAS is ...... wide.

    (a) 12 bit   (b) 14 bit   (c) 16 bit   (d) 48 bit

30. Data register in IAS is ...... wide.

    (a) 16 bit   (b) 20 bit   (c) 40 bit   (d) 48 bit

31. Accumulator and MQ (multiplier Quotient) register in IAS is ...... wide.

    (a) 16 bit   (b) 20 bit   (c) 40 bit   (d) 48 bit

32. ...... used to store an operand during the execution of an instruction.

    (a) AR   (b) DR   (c) IR   (d) IBR

33. Program control unit of IAS fetches ...... instructions simultaneously.

    (a) two   (b) three   (c) four   (d) six

34. IR stores ...... instruction.

    (a) immediately executable   (b) later executable

    (c) currently executing   (d) aborted type

35. IBR stores ...... instruction.

    (a) immediately executable   (b) later executable

    (c) currently executing   (d) aborted type

36. Data transfer instruction ...... transfer contents of register MQ to the accumulator AC.

    (a) AC ← MQ   (b) AC ← AC + MQ

    (c) AC ↔ MQ   (d) MQ ← AC

37. ...... architecture shows separate memory banks for data and program.

    (a) Princeton   (b) Harvard

    (c) Von Neumann   (d) Rockwell

38. Harvard architectures shows feature of executing instructions in ...... instruction cycles than von Neumann.

    (a) more   (b) double   (c) reduced   (d) exactly half

39. ...... is the example of Harvard architecture.

    (a) Microprocessor   (b) Microcontroller

    (c) Complier   (d) Assembler

40. ...... is the example of Von-Neumann architecture.

    (a) Microprocessor   (b) Microcontroller

    (c) Complier   (d) Assembler

41. ...... architecture uses both RISC and CISC architectures.

    (a) Von-Neumann   (b) Harvard

    (c) Babbage   (d) None of these

42. ...... architecture uses only RISE architecture.

    (a) Von-Neumann   (b) Hardvard

    (c) Babbage   (d) None of these

43. ...... bus is unidirectional.

    (a) Data   (b) Address

    (c) Control   (d) None of these

44. Use of ...... isolates CPU from frequent accesses to main memory.

    (a) local I/O controller   (b) expansion bus interface

    (c) cache structure   (d) system bus

45. In Harvard machine instruction are executed in ...... instruction cycles than von Neumann machine.

    (a) fever   (b) more

    (c) two   (d) none of these

46. In Harvard machine, greater amount of instruction parallelism is achieved due to separate ......

    (a) processing units   (b) execution units

    (c) memory banks   (d) none of these

47. The instruction suffer register stores ......

    (a) data   (b) address

    (c) instruction opcode   (d) operand

48. The first generation computer was designated and constructed by ......
    - (a) Von Neumann
    - (b) Eckert and Mauchly
    - (c) Blaise Pascal
    - (d) Charles Babbage

49. The first generation computer was a ...... machine.
    - (a) decimal
    - (b) binary
    - (c) octal
    - (d) hexadecimal

50. ...... timing involves a clock line.
    - (a) Synchronous
    - (b) Asynehronous
    - (c) Asymmetric
    - (d) None of these

51. ...... more data between system modules.
    - (a) Data bus
    - (b) Address Bus
    - (c) Control bus
    - (d) None of these

52. ...... designate source or destination of data of the data bus.
    - (a) Data bus
    - (b) Address bus
    - (c) Control bus
    - (d) None of these

53. ...... control access to and use of the data and address lines.
    - (a) Data bus
    - (b) Address bus
    - (c) Control bus
    - (d) None of these

54. ...... timing takes advantage of mixture of slow and fast devices, sharing the same bus.
    - (a) Synchronous
    - (b) Asynchronous
    - (c) Asymmetric
    - (d) None of these

55. Second generation computers can handle ...... operations.
    - (a) fixed point
    - (b) floating point
    - (c) both (a) and (b)
    - (d) none of these

56. The opcode fetched from memory is placed in ...... of processor.
    - (a) accumulator
    - (b) instruction register
    - (c) instruction decoder
    - (d) data register

57. ...... bus is used to connect major computer components.

  (a) Address   (b) Data

  (c) Control   (d) System

58. Data bus is ......

  (a) unidirectional   (b) Bidirectional

  (c) unidirectional or bidirectional (d) none of these

59. ...... bus width decides the number of bits transformed at one time.

  (a) Data   (b) Address

  (c) Control   (d) System

60. ...... bus width decides the range of locations that can be accessed.

  (a) Data   (b) Address

  (c) Control   (d) System

61. Assembly language ......

  (a) uses alphabetic codes in place of binary numbers used in machine language

  (b) is the eariest language to write programs

  (c) need not be translated into machine language

  (d) none of these

62. Any computer must at least consist of......

  (a) Data bus   (b) Address bus

  (c) control bus   (d) all of the above

63. A binary digit is called a......

  (a) Bit   (b) Byte   (c) Number   (d) Character

64. Floating point representation is used to store......

  (a) boolean valves   (b) whole numbers

  (c) real numbers   (d) integers

65. In computers, subtraction is generally carried out by......

  (a) 9's complement   (b) 10's complement

  (c) 1's complement   (d) 2's complement'

66. The highest positive decimal number represented in signed binary numbers is ......
    the highest positive decimal number for unsigned binary numbers of a fixed number
    of bits.

    (a) double   (b) equal   (c) half   (d) triple

67. 1's complement representation is nothing but bit by bit ...... operation.

    (a) OR   (b) AND   (c) Ex-OR   (d) NOT

68. Binary numbers can be used to represent......

    (a) integers only   (b) fractions only

    (c) both fractions and integers   (d) none of above

69. The two's complement representation of – 10 is......

    (a) 11110110   (b) 11011001

    (c) 00001010   (d) 11111100

70. 1's complement + ... = 2's complement.

    (a) 1   (b) 2   (c) 3   (d) – 1

71. In 2's complement subtraction when carry is generated it is......

    (a) ignored

    (b) added to final result

    (c) subtracted from final result

    (d) ignored and 1's complement of final result is done

72. (–27)10 can be represented in a signed magnitude format and in a 1's complement
    format as

    (a) 111011 and 100100   (b) 100100 and 111011

    (c) 011011 and 100100   (d) 100100 and 011011

73. (–64)10 can be represented in a signed magnitude format as

    (a) 1101 0000   (b) 1100 0000

    (c) 1000 1100   (d) 1110 1100

74. The binary representation of 15 is

    (a) 01010   (b) 01111

    (c) 10011   (d) 00101

75. Two's complement notation is frequently used for internal representation of

    (a) fractions   (b) Integers

    (c) true and false   (d) floating point numbers

76. The ...... bit in the binary number represents sign of the number.

    (a) leftmost   (b) right most

    (c) both (a) and (b)   (d) none of these

77. To solve problem of representation of negative exponent in floating point numbers ...... is added to the true exponent.

    (a) packed bias valve   (b)unpacked bias valve

    (c) bias valve   (d) slating factor

78. 1's complement of (11010100) is ......

    (a) 00101011   (b) 11001011

    (c) 01010111   (d) none of these

79. 2's complement of (11000100)2 is ......

    (a) 00111100   (b) 0011011

    (c) 11001100   (d) 10111101

80. 1's complement of (01011011)2 is ......

    (a) 10100100   (b) 00111100

    (c) 10111011   (d) none of these

81. For unsigned 8 bit binary numbers the decimal range is ......

    (a) 0 to 127   (b) 255 to 127

    (c) 0 to 255   (d) none of these

82. Which is the recoded multiplier at 101100 for Booth's multiplication ?

    (a) −1 + 1 0 − 1 00   (b) 10 − 10 + 1 − 1

    (c) Both (a) and (b)   (d) None of these

83. Recoded multiplier of 011001 per Booth's multiplication is......

    (a) −1 + 1 0 − 1 0 0   (b) 1 0 − 1 0 + 1 − 1

    (c) 1 − 1 0 + 1 − 1 0   (d) none of these

84. Find the bit pair code for multiplier 11010......

   (a) 0 –1 –2   (b) 2 –1 –1

   (c) –2 + 1 0   (d) none of these

85. Single procession representation occupies a single ...... word.

   (a) 16 bit   (b) 32 bit

   (c) 64 bit   (d) 8 bit

86. Double precession representation occupies a ...... word.

   (a) 16 bit   (b) 32 bit

   (c) 64 bit   (d) 8 bit

87. The 32 bit floating point system, bias value is ......

   (a) 126   (b) 1023

   (c) 127   (d) none of these

88. In 64 bit floating point system bias valve is ......

   (a) 127   (b) 1024

   (c) 1023   (d) none of these

89. Range of E' for normal values in double precision is ......

   (a) $0 < E' < 2047$ (b) $-127 < E' < 127$

   (c) $-1022 \leq E \leq 2047$ (d) none of these

90. In 2's complement subtraction of binary numbers if carry is generated then the result is ......

   (a) positive   (b) negative

   (c) zero   (d) none of these

91. In 2's complement subtraction of binary numbers if carry is not generated then the result is ......

   (a) positive   (b) negative

   (c) zero   (d) none of these

92. In Booth's algorithm , when addition is performed. Add /sub line = ... and cin = ...

   (a) 0 1   (b) 0 0

   (c) 1 0   (d) 1 1

93. In Booth's algorithm, when subtraction is performed. Add / sub line = ... and cin = ...

    (a) 0 1

    (b) 0 0

    (c) 1 0

    (d) 1 1

94. In signed division the operands are preprocessed to transform them into ...... values.

    (a) positive

    (b) negative

    (c) both (a) and (b)

    (d) none of these

95. In floating point arithmetic incase of division if the dividend is zero then result is ......

    (a) one

    (b) zero

    (c) ∞

    (d) none of these

96. In floating point arithmetic incase of division if the divider is zero, result is ......

    (a) one

    (b) zero

    (c) ∞

    (d) none of these

97. In single precession format ...... bit for sign ...... bit for exponent and ...... bits for mantissa.

    (a) 1, 8, 23

    (b) 8, 23, 1

    (c) 1, 1, 52

    (d) none of these

98. In double precesion format ...... bit for sing, ... bit for exponent and ......bits for mantissa.

    (a) 1, 8, 52

    (b) 1, 1, 52

    (c) 1, 8, 1023

    (d) none of these

99. In division process of binary numbers, first bits of dividend are checked from left to right until the set of bits examined represents a number ...... the divisor.

    (a) equal to

    (b) grater than or equal to

    (c) less than or equal to

    (d) none of these

100. In restoring division algorithm, if the result of subtraction is ...... then it needs restering of register A.

    (a) positive

    (b) negative

    (c) both (a) and (b)

    (d) none of these

101. Non-restoring division algorithm needs restoring of remainder if remainder is ......

   (a) positive   (b) negative

   (c) both (a) and (b)   (d) none of these

102. A bit pair recoding technique used in Booth's algorithm ...... the multiplication process.

   (a) speeds up   (b) slows-down

   (c) stops   (d) none of these

103. Maximum positive number of sign magnitude 8 bit format is ......

   (a) + 127   (b) + 128

   (c) + 255   (d) + 256

104. Maximum negative number for sign magnitude 8 bit format is ......

   (a) − 255   (b) −127

   (c) −256   (d) − 128

105. In sign-magnitude representation of the number if MSB is 1, number is ......

   (a) positive   (b) negative

   (c) integer   (d) fraction

106. In sign-magnitude representation of number if MSB is 0, number is ......

   (a) positive   (b) negative

   (c) integer   (d) fractions

107. Techniques to represent signed integer numbers are ......

   (a) sign magnitude representation   (b) 1's complement

   (c) 2's complement   (d) all of these

108. IEEE 754 standard for a single pression representation includes ...... bits.

   (a) 16   (b) 32

   (c) 48   (d) 64

109. IEEE 754 standard for double precesion representation includes ...... bits.

   (a) 16   (b) 32

   (c) 48   (d) 64

110. ...... bits are reserved for singed exponent in IEEE 754 standard for a single precesion representation of floating point numbers.

(a) 8   (b) 16

(c) 12   (d) 18

111. ...... bits are reserved for signal exponent in IEEE 754 standard for a double precesion representation of floating point numbers

(a) 8   (b) 16

(c) 12   (d) 18

112. ......bits are reserved for mantissa in single precesion format of floating point.

(a) 16   (b) 20

(c) 23   (d) 32

113. ......bits are reserved for mantissa in double precesion format of floating point.

(a) 16   (b) 32

(c)   52   (d) 64

114. In integer numbers, radix point is assumed to be to the ...... of the right most digit.

(a)   right   (b) left

(c) A or B   (d) none of these

115. Floating point number system allows the representation of numbers having ......

(a) integer part   (b) fractional part

(c) integer and fractional part   (d) integer or fractional part

116. (2FAOC)16 is equivalent to

(a) (195 084)10

(b) (0 0 1 0 1 1 1 1 1 0 1 0 0 0 0 0 0 1 1 0 0)2

(c) Both (a) and (b)

(d) none of these

117. A floating point number that has a 0 in the MSB of mantissa is said to have

(a) overflow   (b) underflow

(c) important   (d) undcrfinal

118. In signed magnitude binary division if the divided is (11100)2 2 divisior is (10011)2 then result is

   (a) (00100)2   (b) (10100)2

   (c) (11001)2   (d) (01100)2

ANSWERS

1.	d	2.	d	3.	b	4.	d	5.	c
6.	b	7.	a	8.	b	9.	d	10.	b
11.	a	12.	d	13.	c	14.	b	15.	c
16.	d	17.	c	18.	b	19.	c	20.	a
21.	a	22.	b	23.	b	24.	a	25.	d
26.	a	27.	d	28.	c	29.	a	30.	c
31.	c	32.	b	33.	a	34.	a	35.	b
36.	a	37.	b	38.	c	39.	b	40.	a
41.	a	42.	b	43.	b	44.	c	45.	a
46.	c	47.	c	48.	b	49.	a	50.	a
51.	a	52.	b	53.	c	54.	b	55.	c
56.	a	57.	d	58.	b	59.	a	60.	b
61.	c	62.	d	63.	a	64.	c	65.	d
66.	c	67.	d	68.	c	69.	a	70.	a
71.	a	72.	a	73.	b	74.	b	75.	b
76.	a	77.	c	78.	a	79.	c	80.	a
81.	c	82.	a	83.	b	84.	a	85.	b
86.	c	87.	c	88.	c	89.	a	90.	a
91.	b	92.	b	93.	d	94.	a	95.	b
96.	c	97.	a	98.	b	99.	b	100.	b

101.	b	102.	a	103.	a	104.	d	105.	b
106.	a	107.	d	108.	b	109.	d	110.	a
111.	c	112.	c	113.	c	114.	a	115.	c
116.	b	117.	b	118.	b				

QUESTIONS

1. Write note on electronic computer.   **[Dec. 05, 08, 09, 11, 12, May 07, 10, 11, 12, 13]**

2. Explain Hardware components.

3. Write a note on system bus.

4. Explain Bus timings.

5. Explain single line bus structure.

6. List the elements of the bus design

7. Explain IAs computer structure.

8. Write a note on IEEE floating point representation.

    [Dec. 07, 08, 09, 10, May 06, 10, 11, 12, 13]

9. Represent -309.1875_{10} in single precision and double precision format.

    [May 06, Dec. 09]

10. Represent $(778, 1875)_{10}$ in single and double precision floating point format.   **[May 11]**

11. Represent following number in single precision floating point format.   **[May 06]**

12. Represent $(335.2350)_{10}$ in single precision and double precision format. **[May 06, Dec. 09]**

13. Represent the following in single precision floating point format as well as double precision format. (i) 17.125 (ii) 125   **[Dec. 08, May 12]**

14. Represent $- (127.1075)_{10}$ in single precision format.   **[Dec. 07]**

15. Represent the following number in single precision floating point format

    (i) 101.25 (ii) 41.625   **[May 10]**

16. Explain Booth's algorithm for signed operand multiplication.

    [Dec. 07, 10, 11, 12, May 05, 07, 09, 10, 11, 12]

17. Explain the following pair of signed 2's complement numbers.

Multiplicand : 110011 (–13)

Multiplier : 101100 (–20)   **[Dec. 20]**

18. Using Booth's algorithm multiply the following multiplicand + 22, multiplier – 5. **[Dec. 07]**

19. Explain Booth's algorithm to multiply the following pair of number.

Multiplicand (A) = 13, Multiplier (B) = – 11   **[Dec. 12]**

20. Solve the following using bit pair recording method

Multiplicand = 01111 (15)

Multiplier = 10110   **[May 07]**

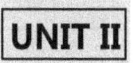

PROCESSOR ORGANIZATION

2.1 PROCESSOR BASICS

Fetching of instruction from memory/register, decoding, reading, executing and finally storing of that instruction is done by a processor. All the issues related to processor are discussed in this chapter.

2.1.1 CPU Organization   [May 10, 12, (10 Marks)]

CPU is nothing but processor program execution is carried out as follows :

1. CPU transfers instructions and operands from main memory to registers in CPU.
2. CPU executes the instructions in their stored sequence except when execution sequence is explicitly altered by a branch instruction.
3. Whenever required, CPU transfers output data (results) from the CPU registers to main memory.

Simultaneously, streams of instructions and data flow between the external memory and set of registers forms the CPU's internal memory. The efficient management of these instructions and data streams is basic function of CPU.

2.1.1.1 External Communication

Communication between CPU and main memory is of two types :

  (i) without cache memory
  (ii) with cache memory

As shown in Fig. 2.1, no cache memory is present; the CPU directly communicates with main memory (RAM). CPU is much more faster than main memory (RAM). It can read/write data to its register 5-10 times faster than it read/write data from/to main memory (RAM).

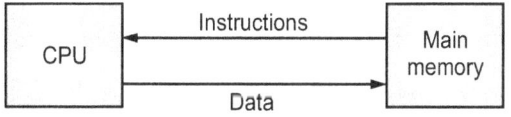

Fig. 2.1 : Without Cache

To overcome this speed difference between CPU and main memory concept of cache memory has been designed, which is positioned between CPU and main memory. Cache memory is smaller and faster than main memory and resides (located) on same chip of CPU. Cache memory is designed to bring compatibility between speed of CPU and main memory. The instructions whose load/store requires more time for CPU to fetch from main memory will be stored in cache only. CPU will read those instructions from cache. Cache memory gets flushed when CPU is restarted. Typical such organization is shown in Fig. 2.2.

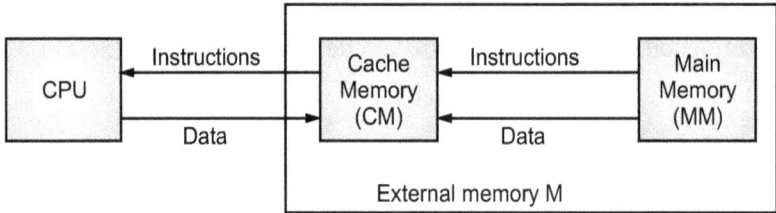

Fig. 2.2 : With Cache Memory

The CPU communicates with I/O devices in much similar way as that of external memory. I/O devices has addressable registers called I/O ports to which CPU can store a word or from which it can load a word. Some computers uses an approach in which all I/O data transfers are implemented by memory referencing instruction this approach is called **memory mapped I/O.** In this approach memory locations and I/O ports share the same set of addresses. Another approach employ I/O instructions that are distinct from memory referencing instructions. These instructions produce control signals to which I/O ports only respond not memory locations. This approach is called memory mopped I/O.

2.1.1.2 User and Supervisor Modes

Programs executed by CPU falls in to two categories :

    (i)   User programs   (ii) Supervisor programs

User or application program handles a specific application such as word processing. A supervisor program, on the other hand, manages various routine aspects of computer system on behalf of its user e.g. controlling a graphics interface and transferring data between secondary and main memory.

It is useful to design a CPU so that it can receive requests for supervisor services directly from secondary memory units and other I/O devices. Such a request is called an interrupt. During interrupt, CPU suspends execution of the currently executing program and transfers it to an appropriate interrupt handling program.

2.1.1.3 CPU Operation

Sequence of operations performed by the CPU in processing an instruction constitutes an **instruction cycle.** All instructions require two major steps, a **fetch step** and **execution step**. Fig. 2.3 explains main functions of CPU.

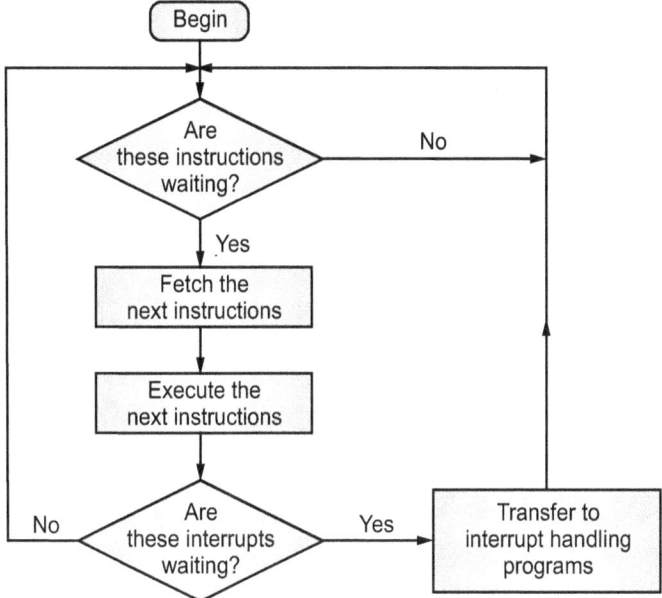

Fig. 2.3 : Overview of CPU behaviour

The actions of CPU during an instruction cycle are defined by a sequence of micro operations, each of which typically involves register transfer operation. The time required for shortest well defined CPU operation is CPU **Cycle time/clock period T_{clock}**.

Note : f, the CPU clock frequency (in MHz) is related to T_{clock} in use as

$$T_{clock} = 1/F$$

2.1.1.4 Accumulator Based CPU

With the advances in IC technology CPU design was expected to become as fast as possible. The CPU design proposed by van-Neumann comprises a small set of registers and circuits needed to execute a functionally complete set of instructions. In many designs, one of the CPU registers, the accumulator played a vital role being used to store an input or output operand in the execution of many instructions.

Fig. 2.4 shows at the register level the essential structure of a small accumulator based CPU.

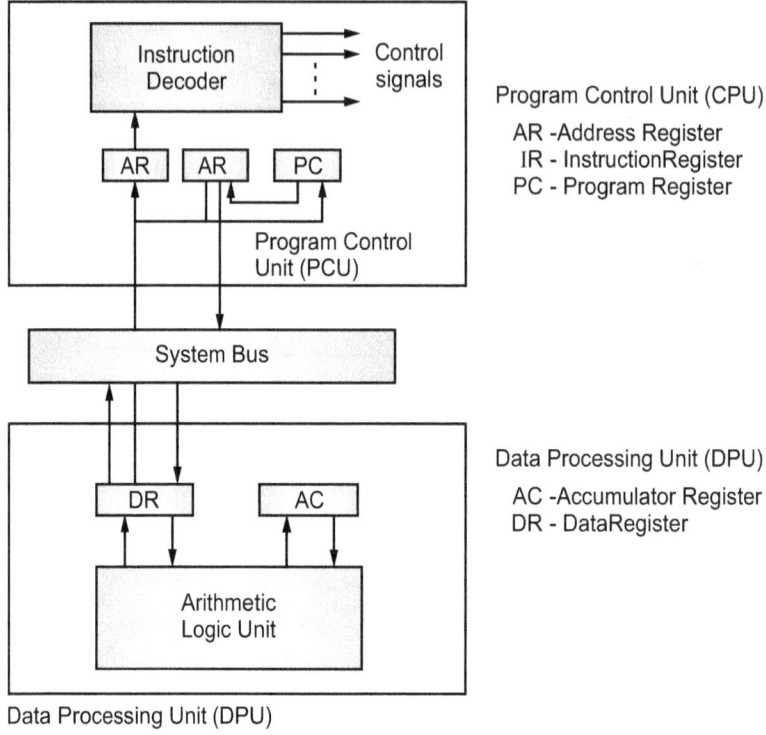

Program Control Unit (CPU)

AR -Address Register
IR - InstructionRegister
PC - Program Register

Data Processing Unit (DPU)

AC -Accumulator Register
DR - DataRegister

Fig. 2.4 : Accumulator based CPU

Here, most instructions perform operations of the form

$$X_1 = fi(X_1, X_2)$$

Where, X_1, X_2 denote a CPU register (AC, DR or PC) or an external memory location M(adr). Operations fi performed by the ALU are limited to fixed point (integer) addition and subtraction shifting and logical operations.

Two essential memory addressing instructions are called load and store. The load instruction for our sample CPU is

$$AC = M(adr)$$

which transfers a word from memory location with address adr to the accumulator. The corresponding store instruction is

$$M(adr) = AC$$

Which transfers a word from AC to M and may be written as ST adr.

2.1.1.5 Instruction Set

[Dec. 01, 03, 05, 08, 09, 11, 12 May 03, 05, 07, 08, 09, 11, 12, 13 8 Marks]

Table 2.1 gives a possible instruction set for accumulator based CPU.

Type	HDL format	Assembly lang format	Comment
1. Data transfor	AC = m(x)	LD x	Load x from M into AC
	M(x) = AC	ST x	Store contents of AC in M as x
	DR = AC	mov DR,AC	Copy content of AC to DR
	AC = DR	mov AC,DR	Copy content of DR to AC
2. Data processing	AC = AC + DR	ADD	Add DR to AC
	AC = AC − DR	SUB	Subtract DR from AC
	AC = AC and DR	AND	And bitwise DR to AC
	AC = not AC	NOT	Complement contents of AC
3. Program control	PC = M(adr)	BRAadr	Jump to instruction with address adr
	if AC = 0 then PC = M(adr)	BZadr	Jump to instruction adr it AC = 0

Example : The arithmetic operation negation for which many CPUs have a single instruction of the type AC = −AC

Table 2.2 : Illustrate the same

HDL format	Assembly language format	Comment
DR = AC	mov DR, AC	Copy contents x of AC to DR
AC = AC − DR	SUB	Compute AC = x − x = 0
AC = AC − DR	SUB	Compute AC = 0 − x = − x

Table 2.2 Arithmetic operation negation

2.2 ADDITIONAL FEATURES

Most recent CPU's contain the following extensions which significantly improve their performance and ease of programming.

(i) Multipurpose register set for storing data and addresses :

These replace the accumulator AC and the auxiliary register DR and AR of our basic CPU.

(ii) Additional data, instruction and address types :

Some microprocessors have only add and subtract instructions in arithmetic category, relatively little extra circuitry is required for multiply and divide instructions which simplify many programming tasks.

(iii) Register to indicate computation status :

A status register (also called a condition code or flag register) indicates infrequent or exceptional conditions resulting from the instruction execution.

(iv) Program control stack :

Many CPU's use a flexible scheme for program control transfer which employs part of the external memory M as a push down stack. A CPU address register called a stack pointer automatically keeps track of stack's entry point.

2.2.1 RISC and CISC

The computer systems in use today have evolved over years. Every new era of evolution was dominated by introduction of a new innovation at that particular time. For example, introduction of microprogrammed control units as suggested by Wilkies in 1951 and introduced by IBM on S/360 line in 1964.

In 1968, cache memories were introduced, to revolutenarize the computer architecture altogether. Later pipelining and multiple processors were introduced.

The computers of today are complex in design with large instruction sets. These instructions support a variety of addressing modes. The individual instructions are more powerful and require more than one machine cycles to execute. These type of instruction sets are known as complex instruction sets and the computers implementing them are known as **Complex Instruction Set Computers (CISC)**.

The architecture of such a computer is thus, inherently complex. These computers are designed around a microprogrammed control unit and normally have more sophisticated registers.

But such rich instructions are not required by most of the general purpose computer applications. So the cost of such computers is not justified for these applications.

To avoid these problems, the concept of **Reduced Instruction Set Computers (RISC)** was introduced. The RISC computers support only a few simple instructions that are very often needed. Most of these instructions execute in one machine cycle only. The RISC design emphasizes simplicity and efficiency. The RISC design begins with necessary and sufficient instruction sets. Most of the instructions support only a small number of addressing modes. So the hardware of the RISC computers is relatively simple. .

2.2.1.1 Goals of the RISC Architecture

Following are the goals of RISC architecture

1. To keep the hardware simple.
2. To maximize the effective speed of a design by performing the functions that are not often needed, in software rather than implementing such functions in the form of machine language instructions.
3. As the hardware is kept simple, the costs are brought down. This is one of the major goals of a RISC design.

2.2.1.2 Characteristics of RISC architecture

The following are the characteristics of a RISC architecture.

1. **Simple fixed format instructions with few addressing modes :** All the instructions are of the same length (typically 32-bit).
2. **Single cycle execution :** Most of the instructions are executed in a single machine cycle.
3. **Hardwired control** with little or no microcode. Microcode adds a level of complexity and increases the number of cycles per instruction.
4. **Load/Store register-to-register design :** All computational instructions involve registers. Memory accesses are made with only load and store instructions.
5. **Pipelining :** The instruction set design allows for the processing of several instructions at a time.
6. **High performance memory :** RISC machines have atleast 32 general purpose registers and large cache memories.

7. **Migration of functions to software :** Only those features that measurably improve performance are implemented in hardware. Software contains sequences of simple instructions for executing complex functions rather than complex instructions themselves, which improve system efficiency.

2.2.1.3 A Comparison between RISC and CISC

The table 2.3 compares RISC and CISC on the basis of various architectural features :

Table 2.3

Architectural feature	Complex Instruction Set Computer (CISC)	Reduced Instruction Set Computer (RISC)
Instruction set	• Variable format instructions • Powerful instructions • Instructions involve memory references • Instructions support a variety of addressing modes (12 – 24)	• Fixed format instructions • Simple instructions • Most of the instructions (except load/store) do not involve memory references. • Instructions support only a few addressing modes (3 – 5)
Register organisation	A small number of general purpose registers (8 – 24) are provided.	A large register file containing 32 to 192 general purpose registers are provided.
Cache design	A single unified cache for instructions and data.	Split data cache and instruction cache.
Control unit	Microprogrammed control using a control memory (ROM), but a few modern CISC also use hardwired control.	Mostly hardwired control is used.
Support for HLL	Many HLL features are implemented as machine instructions.	Only a few HLL features are implemented at machine level.
Clock and CPI (Cycles per instruction)	33 – 50 MHz in 1992 with a CPI between 2 and 15.	50 – 150 MHz in 1993 with one cycle for almost all instructions and an average CPI < 1.5.

Let us see the differences in the architecture of RISC and CISC.

Fig. 2.5 depicts the architectural differences between RISC and CISC designs.

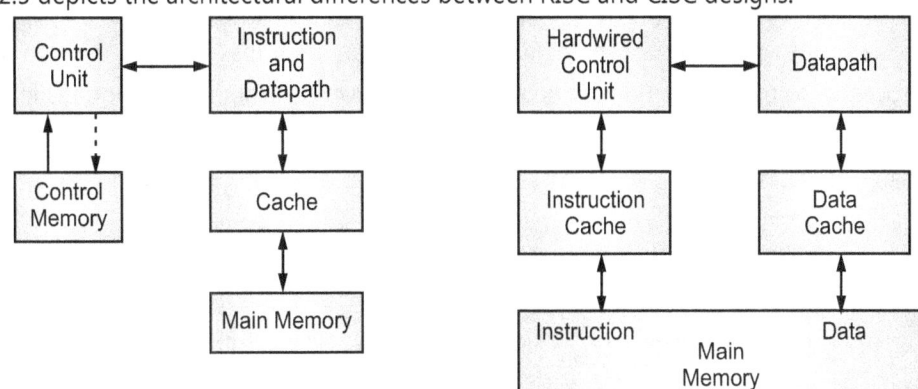

Fig. 2.5 : RISC and CISC Architecture

There are various distinctions apparent from the diagram. The CISC architecture uses a microprogrammed control unit, in contrast, the RISC architecture uses a hardwired control unit.

The cache used in CISC architecture is unified instruction and data cache; while RISC uses split data and instruction cache. The control memory is absent in the RISC architecture as it is hardwired.

A hardwired control unit provides a better performance in terms of CPI than a microprogrammed control.

2.2.1.4 Advantages of RISC

The RISC architecture has the following advantages :

1. **Simple fixed format instructions with few addressing modes :** All the instructions are of the same length (typically 32-bit).

2. **Single cycle execution :** Most of the instructions are executed in a single machine cycle.

3. **Hardwired control** with little or no microcode. Microcode adds a level of complexity and increases the number of cycles per instruction.

4. **Load/Store register-to-register design :** All computational instructions involve registers. Memory accesses are made with only load and store instructions.

5. **Pipelining :** The instruction set design allows for the processing of several instructions at a time.

6. **High performance memory :** RISC machines have atleast 32 general purpose registers and large cache memories.

2.2.2 Co-Processors

A co-processor P is a specialized instruction execution unit that can be coupled to a microprocessor so that instructions to be executed by P can be included in programs fetched by the microprocessor. Co-processor serves as an extention to the microprocessor and forms part of the CPU.

Fig. 2.6 shows 68020 based microcomputer with floating point co-processor.

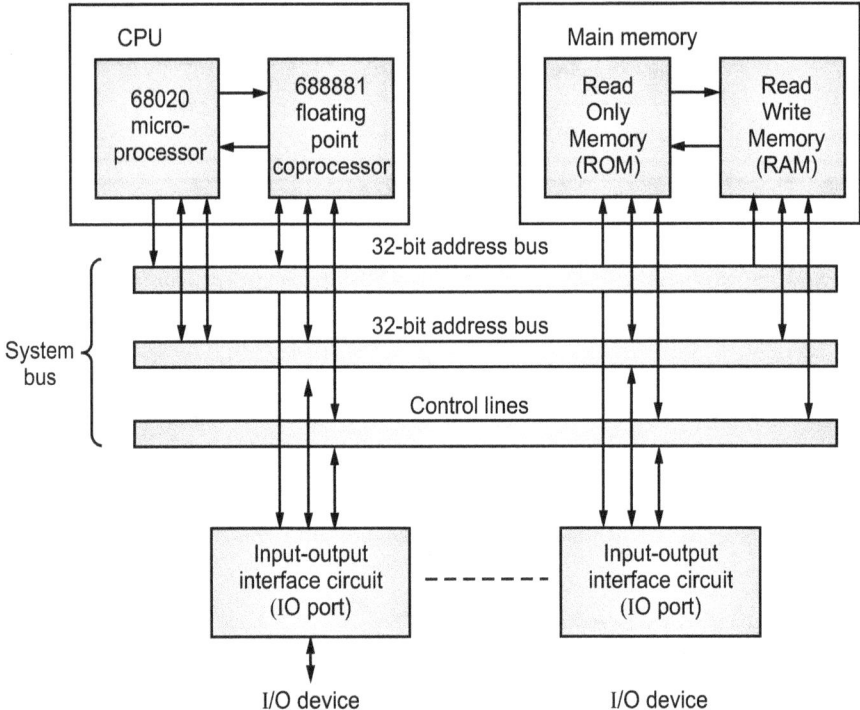

Fig. 2.6 : 68020 based microcomputer with floating point co-processor

The 68881 contains a set of eight 80 bit registers for storing floating point numbers of various formats including 32 and 64 bit numbers conforming to the standard IEEE 754 format. The commands executed by 68881 include the basic arithmetic operations, (add, subtract, multiply and devide), square root, logarithms and trigonometric functions.

2.2.3 Data Representation

As shown in Fig. 2.7 division of information is done.

Fundamental division of data is within instructions and data. Data is further subdivided into numerical and non-numerical. Here two main number formats fixed point and floating point are evolved which are subdivided as binary and decimal.

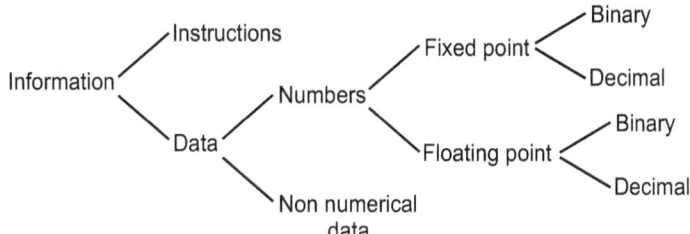

Fig. 2.7 : Basic information types

2.2.3.1 Word Length

Information is represented in terms of binary words. Where 'n' is length of word. An n bit word allows upto 2^n different items to be represented.

e.g. with n = 4, we can encode 10 decimal digits

0 = 0000   1 = 0001   2 = 0010   3 = 0011   4 = 0100

5 = 0101   6 = 0110   7 = 0111   8 = 1000   9 = 1001

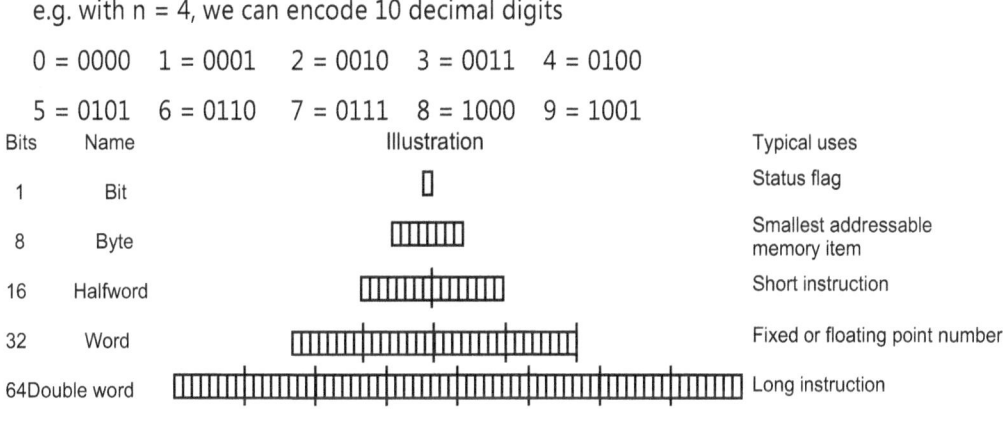

Fig. 2.8

No single word length is suitable for representing every kind of information encountered in a typical computer. Even within a single domain such as a computers instruction set we find several different word sizes.

e.g. instructions such as load and store that reference memory need long address fields.

Fig. 2.8 shows some of the information format of Motorola 680 × 0 microprocessor series.

2.2.3.2 Storage Order

This is important aspect, the way in which the bits of a word are indexed. As shown in Fig. 2.9, the right most bit is assigned the index 0 and the bits are labelled in increasing order from right to left. Advantage of this conception is that when the word is interpreted as an unsigned binary integer, the low-order indexes correspond to numerically less significant bits and high-order indexes correspond to the numerically more significant bits.

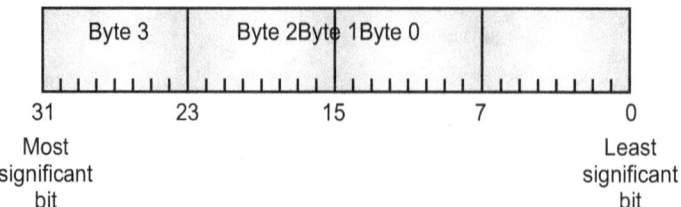

Fig. 2.9 : Indexing conventional of bits and bytes or word

There are two main storage sequences

(i) Big endian and (ii) Little endian

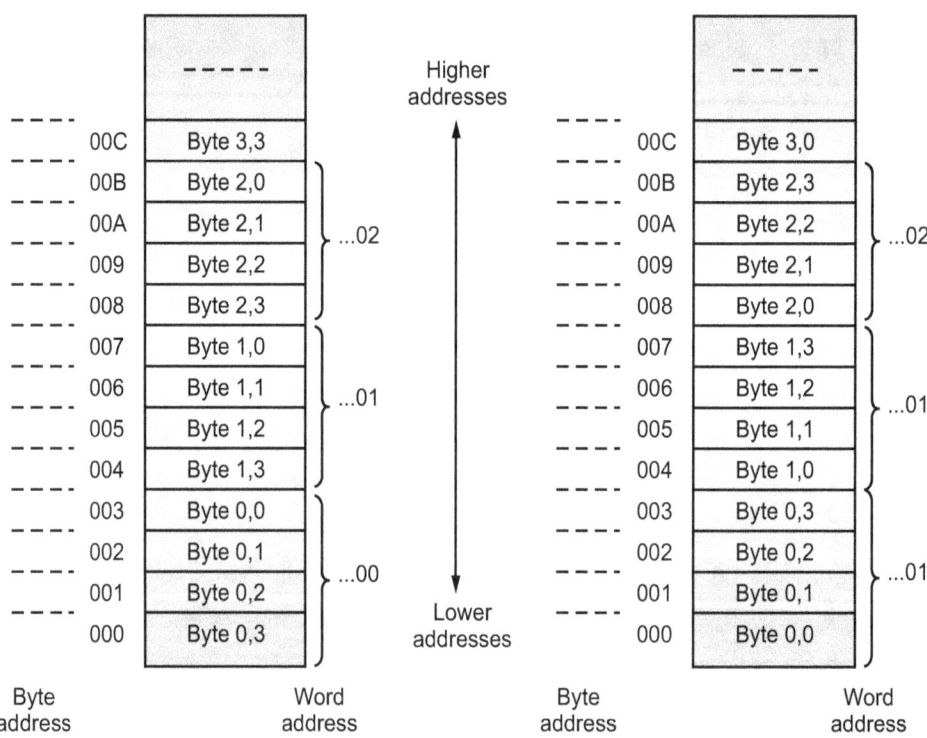

Fig. 2.10 : Storage methods (a) big endian (b) little endian

As shown in Fig. 2.10, a byte storage convention is called **big endian**. It is named so because most significant byte Bi,3 of word wi is assigned the lowest address and the least significant byte Bi,0 is assigned the highest address. In short, the big endian scheme assigns the highest address to byte 0.

The alternative byte storage scheme called little endian assigns the lowest address to byte 0 as shown in Fig. 2.10.

2.3   MACHINE INSTRUCTION CHARACTERISTICS

The operation of the CPU is determined by the instructions it executes, is referred to as machine instructions or computer instructions. The collection of different instructions that the CPU can execute is referred to as the CPU's instruction set.

2.3.1 Elements of Machine Instructions

Each instruction must contain the information required by the CPU for execution. Fig. 2.11 shows the steps involved in instruction execution and define the elements of a machine instruction. The essential elements of a computer instruction are :

1. **Operation code/opcode :** Specifies the operation to be performed. The operation is specified by a binary code, known as the operation code or opcode. Opcode specify operation in one of the following general categories: arithmetic and logical operations and data transfer operations. We will discuss these types in detail in the next section.

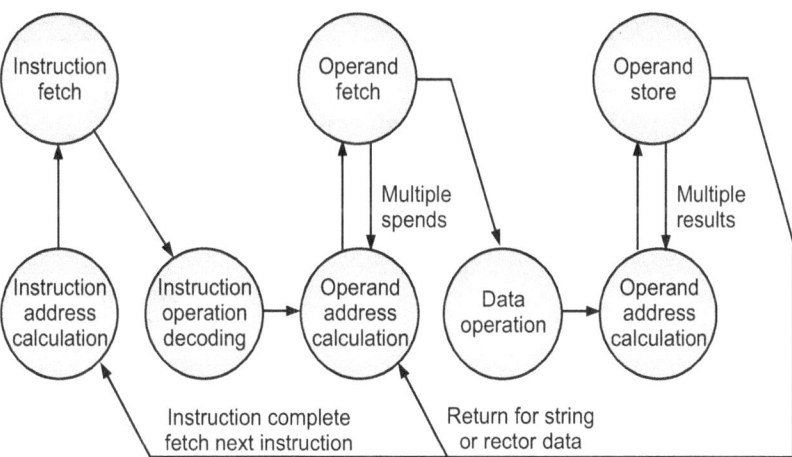

Fig 2.11 : Instruction Cycle State Diagram

2. **Source operand :** The operation may involve one or more source operands, which are inputs for the operation. This field specifies the input location for the operation.

3. **Destination operand :** The operation produces result in destination operand. This field specifies the output location for the operation.

4. **Next instruction reference :** This field tells CPU where to switch after the execution of current instruction. The next instruction to be fetched is located either in main memory or in secondary memory (disk).

A common architectural feature in processors is the use of a stack, which may or may not be visible to the programmer. Stacks are used to manage procedure calls and returns. The basic stack operations are PUSH and POP.

Source and result operands can be in one of three areas:

1. Main or virtual memory   2. CPU Register

3. I/O device

2.3.2 Instruction Representation

In the computer system, each instruction is represented by a sequence of bits. The instruction is divided into fields, corresponding to the elements of the instruction. A simple example of an instruction format is shown in Fig. 2.12. During instruction execution an instruction is read into an instruction register (IR). The CPU must be able to extract data from the various instruction fields to perform the required operation.

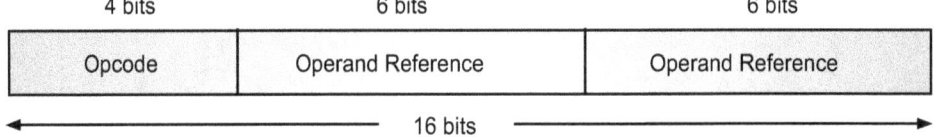

Fig. 2.12 : Instruction Representation

Opcodes are represented by abbreviations, called mnemonics that indicates the operation. Common examples include.

Table 2.4

Sr. No.	Opcode	Operation performed
1.	ADD	Add
2.	SUB	Subtract
3.	MUL	Multiply
4.	DIV	Divide
5.	LOAD	Load data from memory
6.	STOR	Store data to memeory

Operands may represent symbolically.

For example: ADD R, Y

This instruction adds the value contained at location Y to the contents of register R. In this example Y refers to the location in memory and R refers to a register. Note that the operation is performed on the contents of location not on its address.

2.3.3 Instruction Types

Instructions are categorized into the different types according to Data processing, Data storage, Data movement and Data control as follows:

A. Arithmetic and logical instructions

B. Memory instructions

C. I/O instructions

D. Test and branch instructions

- Arithmetic instructions provide computational capabilities for processing numeric data.

- Logical (Boolean) instructions operate on bits rather than numbers. These operations are performed primarily on data in CPU registers.

- Memory instructions are used for data transfer between memory and registers.

- I/O instructions are needed to transfer programs and data into memory and the results of computations back out to the user.

- Test instructions are used to test the value of data word or the status of a computation.

- Branch instructions are used to branch to a different set of instruction depending on the decision made.

We will study these types in detail in the next session.

2.3.4 Number of Addresses

One of the traditional ways of describing processor architecture is the number of addresses contained in each instruction.

Length of instruction can be reduced by having less number of operands or addresses in an instruction. Most of the instructions require three operands, some instructions require two operands and some instructions require only one operand.

Arithmetic and logic instructions require the most operands. Virtually all arithmetic and logic operations are either unary (one operand) or binary (two operands). Thus, we need a maximum of two addresses to reference operands. The result of an operation must be stored, suggesting a third address. Finally, after completion of an instruction the next instruction must be fetched, and its address is needed. That means an instruction requires four address references: two operands, one result, and the address of next instruction. In practice, four-address instructions are extremely rare. Most instructions have one, two, or three operand addresses, with the address of the next instruction being implicit (obtained from the program counter).

Instructions may be of

1. Zero address instructions
2. One address instructions
3. Two address instructions
4. Three address instructions

Following Fig.s gives description of number of addresses that can be used to compute $Y = (A - B)/(C + D*E)$.

(a) Three Address Instructions

Instruction	Comment
SUB Y,A,B	Y ← A-B
MPY T,D,E	T ← D*E
ADD T,T,C	T ← T+C
DIV Y,Y,T	Y ← Y+T

(b) Two Address Instructions

Instruction	Comment
MOVE Y,A	Y ← A
SUB Y,B	Y ← Y − B
MOVE T,D	T ← D
MPY Y,E	T ← T * E
ADD T,C	T ← T + C
DIV Y,T	Y ← Y + T

(c) One Address Instructions

Instruction	Comment
LOAD D	AC ← D
MPY E	AC ← AC * E

ADD	C	AC ← AC + C
STOR	Y	Y ← AC
LOAD	A	AC ← A
SUB	B	AC ← AC – B
DIV	Y	AC ← AC+Y
STOR	Y	Y ← AC

Fig. 2.13 : Program to compute Y = (A – B)/(C + D*E)

The one-address instruction is simpler. Second address must be implicit. The implied address is in a CPU register known as the accumulator or AC. The accumulator contains one of the operands and is used to store the result. In our example, eight instructions are needed to accomplish the task.

Zero address instructions are applicable to a special memory organization called stack. A stack is last-in-first-out set of locations. Zero address instructions referes the top of stack elements.

Table 2.5 : Instruction Addresses

No. of Addresses	Symbolic Representation	Interpretation
0	OP	T←(T – 1)OP T
1	OP A	AC ← AC OP A
2	OP A,B	A ← A OP B
3	OP A,B,C	A ← B OP C

In above table it is assumed that the address of the next instruction is implicit.

2.4   TYPES OF OPERANDS

Machine instructions operate on data. Most important general categories of data are :

- Addresses
- Numbers
- Characters
- Logical data

2.4.1 Addresses

Addresses are form of data. In many cases, some calculation must be performed on the operand reference to determine the main or virtual memory addresses. In this context addresses can be considered as unsigned integers.

2.4.2 Number

All computers support numeric data types. The common numeric data types are

1. Integer or fixed point data
2. Floating point data
3. Decimal data

Although all internal computer operations are binary in nature, users of system deal with decimal numbers. Thus, there is a necessity to convert a decimal number to binary number after input and from binary to decimal at the time of output. Each decimal digit is represented by a 4-bit code. So 0 = 0000, 1 = 0001, ...and 9 = 1001.

2.4.3 Characters

A common form of data is text or character strings. Characters are represented by a sequence of bits. The characters are encoded in bits by using ASCII values, IRA (International Reference Alphabet) and Extended Binary Coded Decimal Interchange Code (EBCDIC).

2.4.4 Logical data

Normally, each word or other addressable unit (bit, byte, word, double word, quad word, and ten words) is treated as a single unit of data. It is sometimes useful. However, to consider an n-bit unit consisting of n-1 bit items of data, each item having the value 0 or 1. When data are viewed in this way, they are considered to be Logical Data.

There are two advantages to the bit-oriented view. Logical data is used to store an array of Boolean or binary data items, in which each item can take only the values 1 (true) and 0 (false). With logical data, memory can be used most efficiently for this storage. Second, to manipulate the bits of data item.

2.5   TYPES OF OPERATIONS

Types of operations are as follows

*   Data transfer operations
*   Arithmetic operations
*   Logical operations
*   Conversion operations
*   I/O operations
*   System control operations
*   Transfer of control operations

Table 2.6 : Common instruction set operations

Sr. No.	Type	Operation Name	Description
1.	Data transfer	Move (transfer)	Transfer word or block from source to destination
		Store	Transfer word from processor to memory
		Load(fetch)	Transfer word from memory to processor
		Exchange	Swap contents of source and destination
		Clear(reset)	Transfer word 0s to destination
		Set	Transfer word 1s to destination
		Push	Transfer word from source to top of stack
		Pop	Transfer word from top of stack to destination
2.	Arithmetic	Add	Compute sum of two operands
		Substract	Compute difference of two operands
		Multiply	Compute product of two operands
		Divide	Compute quotient of two operands
		Absolute	Replace operand by its absolute value
		Negate	Change sign of operand
		Increment	Add 1 to operand
		Decrement	Substract 1 to operand
3.	Logical	AND OR NOT	Perform the specified logical operation bitwise
		Exclusive-OR Test	Test specified operation
		Compare	Make logical or arithmetic comparison
		Shift	Left/right shift operand introducing constants at end
		Rotate	Left/right shift operand, with wrap around end
4.	Transfer of control	Jump(branch)	Unconditional transfer
		Jump conditional	Conditional transfer
		Jump to	Place current PC information in known

		subroutine	location; jump to specified address
		Return	Replace contents of PC and other register from known location
		Execute	Fetch operand from specified location and execute as instruction; do not modify PC.
		Skip	Increment PC to skip next instruction
		Skip conditional	Check condition
		Halt	Stop program execution
		Wait(hold)	Stop program execution; check condition; resume execution when condition is satisfied.
		No operation	No operation is performed but program execution is continued.
5.	I/O	Input(read)	Transfer data from specified I/O port or device to destination (e.g. main memory or processor register)
		Output(write)	Transfer data from specified source to I/O port or device
		Start I/O	Transfer instruction to I/O processor to initiate I/O operation
		Test I	Transfer status information from I/O system to specified destination
6.	Conversions	Translate	Translate values in a section of memory based on a table of correspondences
		Convert	Convert the contents of a word from one form to another.

2.5.1 Data Transfer Operations

The most fundamental type of machine instruction is the data transfer instruction. The data transfer instruction must specify several things. First, the location of the source and destination operands must be specified. Each location should be memory, a register, or the top of the stack. Second, the length of data to be transferred must be indicated, third, addressing mode for each operand must be specified.

Since the arithmetic and logic operations are normally performed on the data stored in CPU registers; we need instructions to bring data to/from memory to/from registers. We identify a memory location by a name.

For example names for memory locations may be I, j, x, y.

Registers names may be R0, R1, R2, R3, AX, BX, CX, etc.

The contents of memory locations or register are denoted as given below.

    R1 ← X   contents of memory location X are transferred into register R1.

    R1 ← R2   contents of register R2 are transferred into a register R1.

    X ← R1   contents of register R1 are transferred into memory location X.

2.5.2 Arithmetic and Logic Operations

These instructions are used for arithmetic and logic operations in machine.

Example :

    R1 ← R2+R1   contents of register R1 and R2 are added and the result is stored in register R1.

    X ← R1+Y   contents of register R1 and memory location Y are added and the result is stored in memory location X.

Table 2.7 Basic Logical Operations

P	Q	NOT P	P AND Q	P OR Q	P XOR Q	P = Q
0	0	1	0	0	0	1
0	1	1	0	1	1	0
1	0	0	0	1	1	0
1	1	0	1	1	0	1

2.5.3 Shift and Rotate Operations

These operations shift or rotate the bits of the operand right or left by some specified number of bit positions.

• **Logical shift :** There are two logical shift instructions logical shift left and logical shift right. These instructions shift an operand by a number of the positions specified in a count operand in an instructions.

Syntax

      SHL dest, count

      SHR dest, count

Fig. 2.14 shows the operation of left shift and right shift instructions. The shifted bits of the operand are lost except for last bit shifted out which is retained in the carry flag (c).

e.g. AL = 23 (00100011)

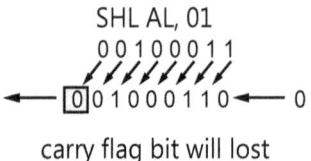

carry flag bit will lost

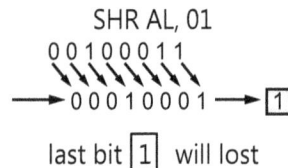

last bit [1] will lost

Fig. 2.14 : Shift operations

- **Rotate Operations**

Moves the bits that are shifted out of end of the operand back into the other end. Two basic types of rotate operations are Rotate Left and Rotate Right.

    Syntax   ROL   dest, count

                            ROR   dest, count

                            RCL   dest, count

                            RCR   dest, count

    e.g.   AL = 23 (0010 0011)

(a) RoL AL, 01   Rotate Left (without carry)

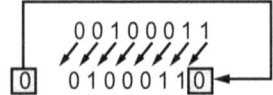

(b) ROR AL, 01   Rotate Right (without carry)

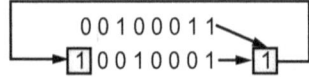

Rotate instructions Rotate the last shifted bit to the first shifted bit either with carry bit or without carry bit.

   (c)   RCL AL, 01 Rotate left (with carry)

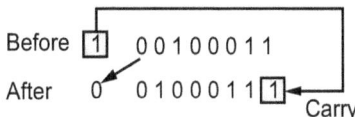

   (d)   RCR AL, 01 Rotate Right (with carry)

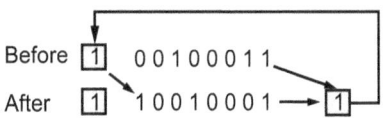

Fig. 2.15 : Rotate operations

2.5.4 Control Transfer Instructions

These instructions are conditional and unconditional branching operations. It includes-

   If - then - else statement.

   While loop,

   For loop

   Jump instructions.

Processor keeps the track of some information regarding the result of various arithmetic and logic operations. This result is used by subsequent conditional branching instructions. This information stores in a special register known as status (flag) register. Every bit of the status register stands for a condition. Commonly used condition flags are :

N (Negative) - Set to 1 if the result is negative.

Z (Zero) - Set to 1 if the result is zero.

O (Overflow) - Set to 1 if the arithmetic overflow has occurred.

C (Carry) - Set to 1 if carry out or borrow in results from an operation.

In arithmetic and logic operations

Fig 2.16 shows Logical Shift and rotates operations.

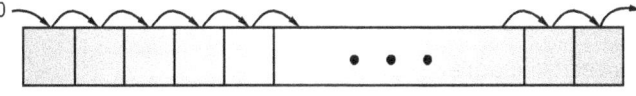

(a) Logical right shift

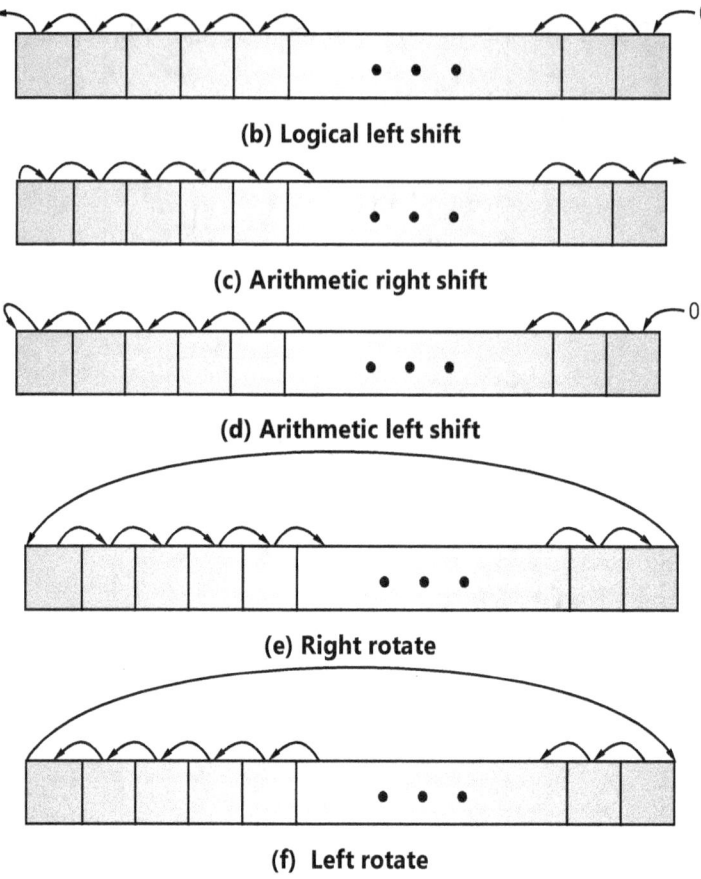

(b) Logical left shift

(c) Arithmetic right shift

(d) Arithmetic left shift

(e) Right rotate

(f) Left rotate

Fig. 2.16 : Logical shift and rotate operations

2.6 ADDRESSING MODES

The way in which an operand is specified is called the *Addressing Mode*. Different addressing modes may take different amount of time to compute the effective address.

Every processor supports the following addressing modes :

- The register addressing mode
- The immediate addressing mode
- The direct addressing mode
- The indirect addressing mode
- The base plus index addressing mode
- The register relative addressing mode
- The base relative plus index addressing mode
- The memory addressing mode

Before going to start the addressing modes let's see the syntax of MOV instruction

MOV Destination operand, Source Operand.

The MOV instruction transfers the contents of source operand to destination operand.

2.6.1 The Register Addressing Mode

Instructions using the registers are shorter and faster than those that access memory. In register addressing mode both the source operand and destination operand are registers.

e.g. MOV R1, R2

This instruction copies the data from the source operand R1 to the destination operand R2. The 8 bit, 16 bit, 32 bit, or 64 bit registers are certainly valid operands for this instruction. The only restriction is that both operands must be of the same size.

2.6.2 The Immediate Addressing Mode

The term immediate implies that the data immediately follow the hexadecimal opcode in the memory. Immediate are constant data. The MOV immediate instruction transfers a copy of the immediate data into a register or a memory location. The source data (sometimes preceded by #) overwrite the destination data. The instruction copies the 1345H into register AX

e.g. MOV AX, 1345 H

2.6.3 The Direct Addressing Mode

The most common addressing mode, and the one that's easiest to understand, is the displacement-only (or direct) addressing mode. The displacement-only addressing mode consists of a constant that specifies the address of the target location. The displacement-only addressing mode is perfect for accessing simple variables.

Intel named this the displacement-only addressing mode because a constant (displacement) follows the MOV opcode in memory. A direct address is a displacement from address zero. The displacement is an offset from the base address.

E.g. MOV DX, [1234]

In this instruction direct address is specified. 1234 is a memory location. The instruction copies contents of memory location 1234 to a register DX.

E.g. MOV DX, DATA

In this instruction direct address is specified by a variable. DATA is a variable name indicating memory location. The instruction copies contents of memory location DATA to a register DX.

2.6.4 The Register Indirect Addressing Modes

The addressing mode specifies the memory location indirectly through a register. Either base register or index register is used to hold the address of variable.

It allows data to be addressed at any memory location through an offset address held in any of the following register: BP, BX, DI and SI. Data segment is used by default with register.

E.g. MOV AL, [BX]

MOV AL, [SI]

The instruction reference the byte at the offset found in the BX, SI register and copies contents to the AL register.

2.6.5 Indexed Addressing Modes

In Indexed Addressing mode the address is available in any index register SI, DI

MOV AX, [SI]

The instruction copies contents of memory location to AX register. The offset is available in SI.

2.6.6 Based Indexed Addressing Modes

The based indexed addressing modes are simply combinations of the register indirect addressing modes. These addressing modes form the offset by adding together a base register (BX or BP) and an index register (SI or DI). The allowable forms for these addressing modes are

MOV   AL, [BX] [SI]

MOV   AL, [BX] [DI]

MOV   AL, [BP] [SI]

MOV   AL, [BP] [DI]

Suppose that BX contains 1000h and SI contains 880h. Then the instruction

MOV   AL, [BX][SI]

would load AL from location DS : 1880h. Likewise, if BP contains 1598h and DI contains 1004, MOV AX, [BP+DI] will load the 16 bits in AX from locations SS:259C and SS:259D.

The addressing modes that do not involve BP use the data segment by default. Those that have BP as an operand use the stack segment by default.

2.6.7 Register Relative Addressing Mode

In its, the data in a segment of memory are addressed by adding the displacement to the contents of a base register and index register (BP, BX, DI, or SI)

Eg. MOV AX, [BX + 1000 H]

- The displacement can be a number added to the register within the [ ], as in MOV AL, [DI+2], or it can be a displacement substracted from the register, as in MOV AL, [SI-1]
- It is possible to address array data with register relative addressing such as one does with base-plus-index addressing.

2.6.8 Based Indexed Plus Displacement Addressing Mode

These addressing modes are a slight modification of the base/indexed addressing modes with the addition of an eight bit or sixteen bit constant. The following are some examples of these addressing modes:

E.g. MOV AL, 10H [BX+SI]

MOV CH, 125H [BP+DI]

Suppose BP contains 1000h, BX contains 2000h, SI contains 120h, and DI contains 5.

Then MOV AL, 10H [BX+SI]   Loads AL from address DS : 2130;

MOV CH, 125H [BP+DI]   Loads CH from location SS : 112A; and

MOV BX, CS: 2[BX][DI]   Loads BX from location CS :2007.

2.6.9 Memory Addressing Modes

The 8086 provides 17 different ways to access memory. The key to good assembly language programming is the proper use of memory addressing modes.

The addressing modes provided by the 8086 family include displacement-only, base, displacement plus base, base plus indexed, and displacement plus base plus indexed. Variations on these five forms provide the 17 different addressing modes on the 8086.

2.7   INSTRUCTION FORMAT

An instruction format defines the layout of the bits of an instruction it must include opcode, zero or more operands and addressing mode for each operand. The instruction length is usually 8-bits.

Once the instruction length is fixed, it is necessary to allocate number of bits for opcode, operands and addressing modes. For an instruction format of a given length, if more number of bits are allocated to opcode field then less number of bits available for addressing. The bits allocation for addressing can be determined by the following factors.

- number of addressing modes
- number of operands
- number of CPU register
- number of register sets
- address range or number of address lines
- address granularity

Fig 2.17 shows the general IA – 32 instruction format, the format consists of four fields. Opcode field, Addressing mode field, displacement field and immediate field.

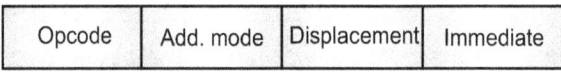

| Opcode | Add. mode | Displacement | Immediate |

1/2 bytes1/2 bytes1 or 4 bytes1 or 4 bytes

Fig. 2.17 : IA - 32 Instruction format

For instruction that involve the use of only one register in generating the effective address of an operand, only one byte is needed for two register to generate effective address two bytes are needed.

If displacement value is used in computing an effective address it requires one or four bytes.

If one of the operand is an immediate value, then it is placed in the last field of an instruction and it occupies either one or four bytes.

Fig. 2.18 shows Pentium instruction format it consists of six fields. Instruction prefixes, Opcode, Mod/RM, SIB, displacement and immediate.

1. Instruction prefixes : The field is divided further into four subfields. Instruction prefix, segment override, operand size override and address size override.

(a) Instruction Prefixes : If present consists of either lock prefix or one of the repeat prefixes such as RED, REPE, REPZ, REPNE and REPNZ. The lock prefix is used to ensure exclusive use or shared memory in multiprocessing environment. The repeat prefixes specify repeated operations of string.

(b) Segment override : Specifies which segment register an instruction should use rather than default segment register.

(c) Operand size override : Specifies which operand size an instruction should use.

(d) Address size override : Specifies the address size that instruction should use to access memory either 16 bit or 32 bit.

2. **Opcode :** The opcode fields is always present. It consists of one or two byte opcode.

3. **Mod R/M :** This field provides addressing information it specifies whether an operand is in memory or in register it consists of three subfields :

mod, Reg / Opcode and R/M

Mod field specifies mode, Reg/opcode field specifies either a register number or opcode information and R/M field specifies a register as the location of operand or it can form part of the address mode.

4. **SIB (Scaled, Index Based) :** This field specifies an 8, 16 or 32 bit signed integer displacement, it specified by an addressing mode.

5. **Immediate :** This field provides the value of an 8, 16, or 32 bit operand.

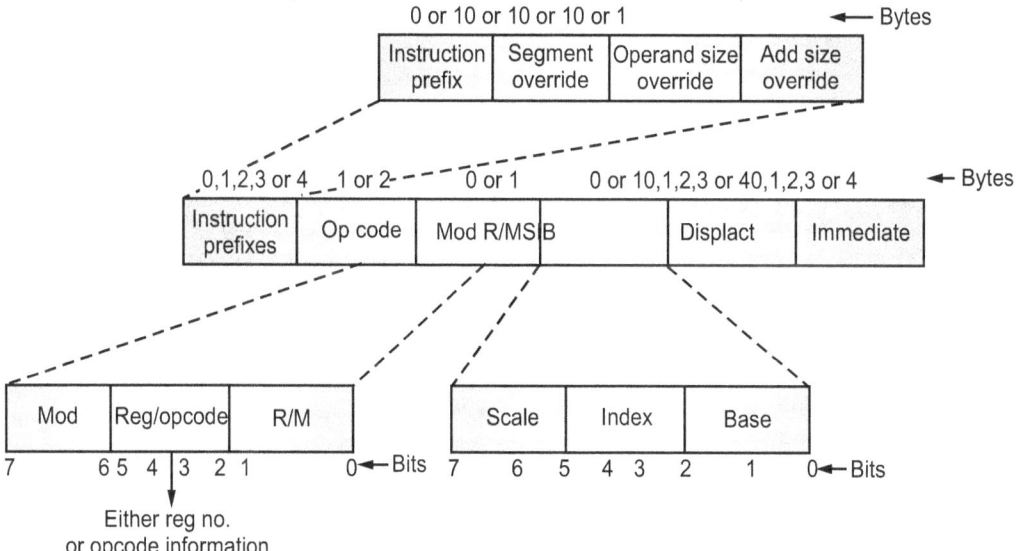

Fig. 2.18 : Pentium instruction format

2.8 INSTRUCTION TYPES

Instructions are classified into seven types as :

1. **Data Transfer Instructions :**

Instructions used to perform data transfer between source and destination operand. e.g. MOV, XCHG, LOAD, LEA, LDS.

2. Arithmetic Instructions :

The instructions used to perform arithmetic operations. e.g. ADD, SUB, MUL, DIV.

3. Logical Instructions :

The instructions used to perform Logical operations. e.g. AND OR, XOR.

4. Control Instructions :

The instructions used to control the flow of operation execution. e.g. JMP instructions.

5. Processor Control Instructions :

The instructions used to control the flow of processor operations.

6. String Manipulation Instructions :

The instructions used to perform string operations. e.g. MOVSB MOVW, CMPSB, CMPSW, SCANS.

7. Interrupt Control Instructions :

These instructions are discussed in section 2.5.

2.9 PROCESSOR ORGANIZATION: 8086 MICROPROCESSOR

2.9.1 History of Intel Microprocessor

In 1957, the company Fairchild Semiconductors invented the first IC. In 1968, Robert Noyce, Gordan Moore, Andrew Grove resigned from Fairchild Semiconductors. They founded their own company Intel (Integrated Electronics). Intel grown from 3 man start-up in 1968. And then it had over 20,000 employees and over $188 million revenue.

Fig. 2.19 : INTEL 4004

Intel Introduced the first microprocessor in 1971. It was a 4-bit µP. Its clock speed was 740 kHz. It had 2,300 transistors. It could execute around 60,000 instructions per second.

Fig. 2.20 : INTEL 4040

Intel Introduced 4040 in 1974. It was also 4-bit μP.

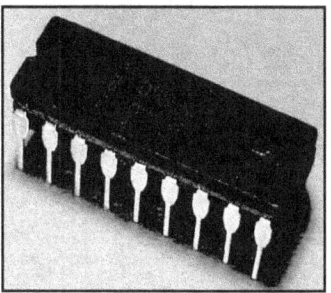

Fig. 2.21 : INTEL 8008

Intel Introduced 8008 in 1972. It was first 8-bit μP. Its clock speed was 500 KHz. It could execute 50,000 instructions per second.

Fig. 2.22 : INTEL 8080

Intel 8080 is Introduced in 1974. It was also 8-bit μP. Its clock speed was 2MHz. It had 6,000 transistors. It was 10 times faster than 8008. It could execute 5,00,000 instructions per second.

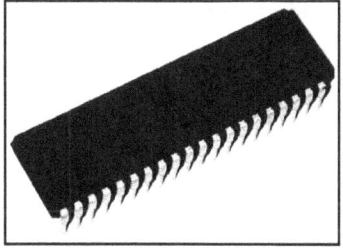

Fig. 2.23 : INTEL 8085

Intel 8085 is Introduced in 1976. It was also 8-bit µP. Its clock speed was 3 MHz. Its data bus is 8-bit and address bus is 16-bit. It had 6,500 transistors. It could execute 7,69,230 instructions per second. It could access 64 KB of memory. It had 246 instructions.

Fig. 2.24 : Intel 8086

Intel 8086 is Introduced in 1978. It was first 16-bit µP.

Its clock speed is 4.77 MHz, 8MHz and 10 MHz, depending on the version. Its data bus is 16-bit and address bus is 20-bit. It had 29,000 transistors. It could execute 2.5 million instructions per second. It could access 1 MB of memory. It had 22,000 instructions.

It had **Multiply** and **Divide** instructions.

8088 is Introduced in 1979. It was also 16-bit microprocessor. It was created as a cheaper version of Intel's 8086. It was a 16-bit processor with an 8-bit external bus. It could execute 2.5 million instructions per second. This chip became the most popular in the computer industry when IBM used it for its first PC.

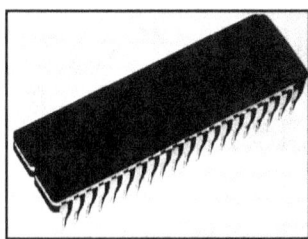

Fig. 2.25 : Intel 8088

Then intel has introduced a series of Microprocessors 80186 / 188,80286,80386DX / SX / SL / SLC/EX, 80486 DX/SX/dx2/sl/dx4, Pentium, PentiumPro, Pentium MMX, Pentium II, Celeron, Pentium III, Pentium II/III Xeon, Pentium 4, Itanium, Xeon, Itanium 2 and Itanium 3 and So on.

2.9.2 Introduction to Microprocessor

A processor is a circuitry that processes the data.

Data is raw facts or raw information after processing, data becomes meaningful and we call it as information.

e.g. Dipak 32 MBA this data is not meaningful. We can not understand what the other user want to say after processing we get

My name is Dipak. I am 32 years old. I have completed MBA.

which is meaningful data and so it is called information.

The processor takes input as data process the data and provides o/p as result.

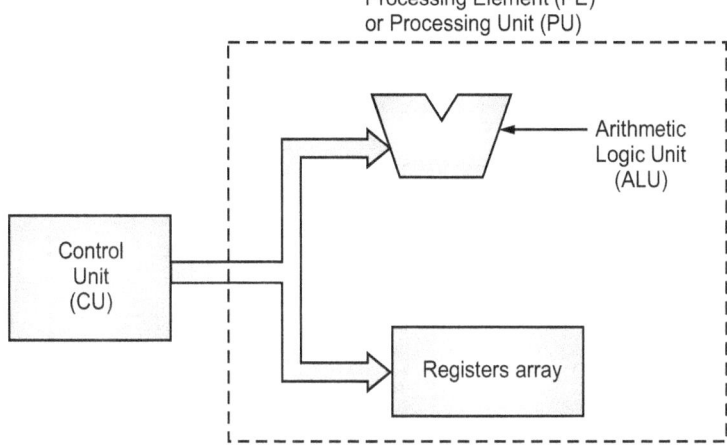

Fig. 2.26 : Processor

The components of processor are arithmetic logic unit (ALU), register array and control unit (CU).

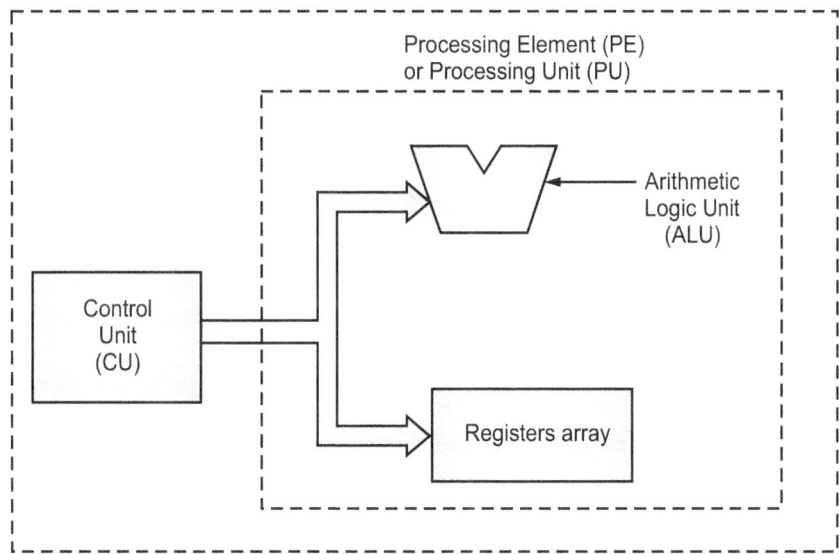

Fig. 2.27 : Microprocessor

ALU and Register array together form the Processing Element (PE) or Processing Unit (PU). As shown in Fig. 2.26. If all components of processor (ALU, register array and CU) register present on a single chip, the size of the processor reduces and the processor is called a **Microprocessor**. The microprocessor is as shown in Fig. 2.27.

When the processor is interfaced with memory and/or input/output (I/O) or pheripheral, the combination is called a computer. A computer is shown in Fig. 2.28.

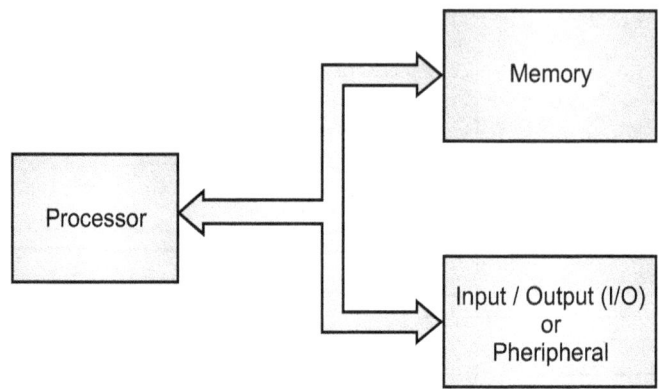

Fig. 2.28 : Computer

If the processor in the computer is a microprocessor the computer is called a Microcomputer or a Microprocessor based system.

A microcomputer or a microprocessor based system is shown in Fig. 2.29.

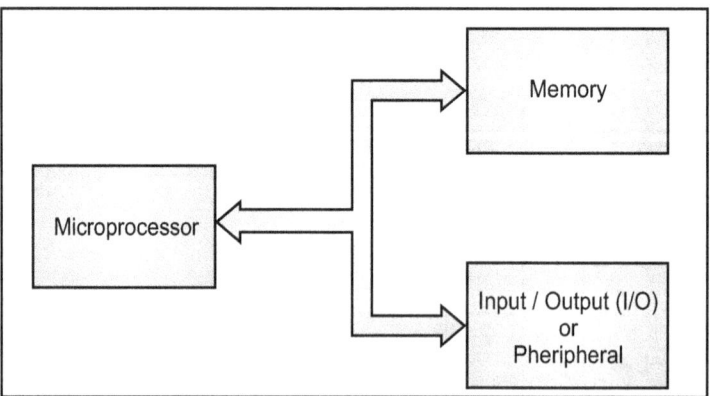

Fig. 2.29 : Microcomputers or microprocessor based system

When the microprocessor, memory and input/output (I/O) or peripherial are present on single chip it is called a single-chip microcomputer or microcontroller, when chip memory is not sufficient, the additional memory can be interfaced externally to the microcontroller Fig. 2.30 shows microcontroller.

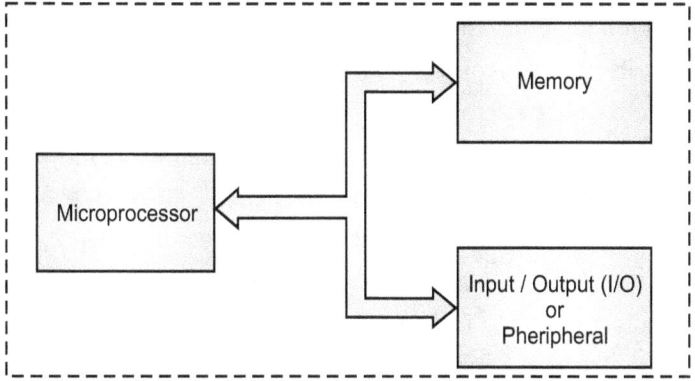

Fig. 2.30 : Microcontroller

2.9.3 Features of 8086 Microprocessor

- It was the first 16-bit microprocessor.

- It is available as 40-pin Dual-Inline-Package (DIP).

- It consists of 29,000 transistors.

- 8086 has 16-bit ALU; this means 16-bit numbers are directly processed by 8086.

- It has 16-bit data bus, so it can read data or write data to memory or I/O ports either 16 bits or 8 bits at a time.

- It has 20 address lines, so it can address up to 2^{20} i.e. 1048576 = 1M bytes of memory (words i.e. 16 bit numbers are stored in consecutive memory locations). Due to the 1 Mbytes memory size multiprogramming is made feasible as well as several multiprogramming features have been incorporated in 8086 design.

- 8086 includes few features, which enhance multiprocessing capability (it can be used with math coprocessors like 8087, I/O processor 8089 etc.

- Operates on +5V supply and single phase (single line) clock frequency. (Clock is generated by separate peripheral chip 8284).

- 8086 comes with different versions. 8086 runs at 5 MHz, 8086-2 runs at 8 MHz, 8086-1 runs at 10 MHz.

- It has multiplexed address and data bus like 8085 due to which the pin count is reduced considerably.

- Higher Throughput (Speed) (This is achieved by a concept called pipelining. Fetching the next instruction while current instruction is under execution is called pipelining.)

8086 is the first 16-bit microprocessor from INTEL, released in the year 1978. The term 16 bit means that it's ALU, its internal registers and most of the instructions are designed to work with 16 bit binary words. 8086 microprocessor has a 16-bit data bus and 20-bit address bus. So, it can address any one of 2^{20} = 1048576 = 1 mega byte memory locations. INTEL 8088 has the same ALU, same registers and same instruction set as the 8086. But the only difference is 8088 has only 8-bit data bus and 20-bit address bus. Hence, the 8088 can only read/write/ports of only 8-bit data at a time. The 8088 was used as the CPU in the original IBM personal computers [IBMPC/XT]. The 8086 microprocessor can work in two modes of operations. They are Minimum mode and Maximum mode. In the minimum mode of operation the microprocessors do not associate with any co-processors and cannot be used for multiprocessor systems. But in the maximum mode the 8086 can work in multi-processor or co-processor configuration. This minimum or maximum operations are decided by the pin MN/ MX(Active low). When this pin is high 8086 operates in minimum mode otherwise it operates in Maximium mode.

2.9.4 Differences between 8086 and 8088 Microprocessors

Though the architecture and instruction set of both 8086 and 8088 processors are same, still we find certain differences between them. They are

(i)   8086 has 16-bit data bus lines whereas 8088 has 8-data lines.

(ii)   8086 is available in three clock speds namely 5 MHz, 8MHz (8086-2) and 10 MHz (8086-1) whereas 8088 is available is only available only in two speeds namely 5 MHz and 8MHz.

(iii)   The memory address space of 8086 is organized as two 512 kB banks whereas 8088 memory space is implemented as a single 1 MX 8 memory bank.

(iv)   8086 has a 6-byte instruction queue whereas 8088 has a 4 byte instruction queue. The reason for this is that 8088 can fetch only one byte at a time.

(v)   In 8086 the memory control pin (M/ IO) signal is complement of the 8088 equivalent signal (IO/M).

(vi)   The 8086 has BHE (Bank High Enable) whereas 8088 has SSO status signal.

(vii)   The byte and word data operations of 8086 are different from 8088.

(viii) 8086 can read or write either 8-bit or 16-bit word at a time, whereas 8088 can read only 8-bit data at a time.

(ix)   The I/O voltage levels for 8086 are, Vol is measured at 2.5 mA and for 8088 it is measured at 2.0 mA.

(x)   8086 draws a maximum supply current of 360 mA and the 8088 draws a maximum of
       340 mA.

Now-a-days 8086 are no longer used. But the concept of its principles and structures is very
useful for understanding other advanced Intel microprocessors.

2.10 ARCHITECTURE OF 8086/8088

The microprocessors functions as the CPU digital computer. Its job is to generate all system
timing signals and synchronize the transfer of data between memory, I/O and itself. It
accomplishes this task via the three-bus system architecture previously discussed.

The microprocessor also has a S/W function. It must recognize, decode, and execute program
instructions fetched from the memory unit. This requires an Arithmetic-Logic Unit (ALU)
within the CPU to perform arithmetic and logical (AND, OR, NOT, compare, etc) functions.

To improve the performance by implementing the parallel processing concept, the
8086/8088 CPU is organized as two separate units-

   1.   Bus Interface Unit (BIU) and

   2.   Execution Unit (EU).

Fig. 2.31 shows the Architecture of 8086 Microprocessor.

The BIU provides H/W functions, including generation of the memory and I/O addresses for
the transfer of data between the outside world, outside the CPU, and the EU.

The BIU sends addresses, fetches instructions, read data from ports and memory and writes
data to ports and memory. The BIU handles all transfers data and addresses on the buses
required by the execution unit. Whereas the Execution Unit decodes the instructions and
executes the instructions. The EU receives program instruction codes and data from the BIU,
executes these instructions and store the results in the general registers. By passing the data
back to the BIU, data can also be stored in a memory location or written to an output device.
Note that the EU has no connection to the system buses. It receives and outputs all its data
through the BIU.

2.10.1 The Execution Unit

The Execution Unit consists of a control system, a 16-bit ALU, 16-bit Flag register and four
general purpose registers namely AX, BX, CX and DX, pointer registers SP, BP and Index
registers SI, DI of each 16-bits.

The control unit controls all the internal operations. The instruction decoder in the execution
unit decodes the instructions fetched from the memory into a series of actions. The ALU

performs the operations like add, subtract, AND, OR, XOR, increment, decrement, complement, and shifting the binary numbers.

2.10.2 Bus Interface Unit

The BIU consists of a 6-byte long instruction register called Instruction Queue.

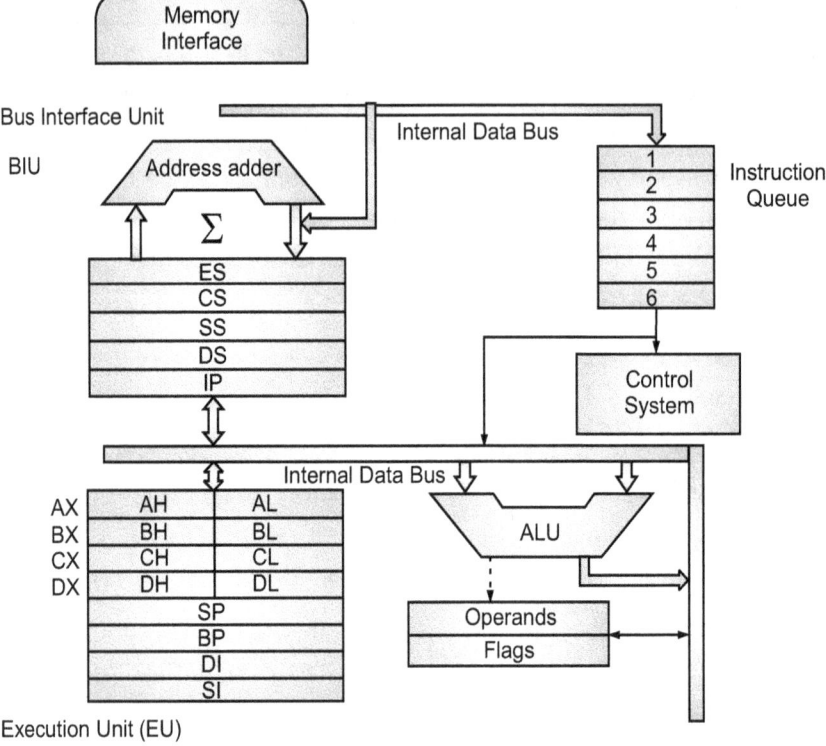

Fig. 2.31 : Architecture of 8086 Microprocessor

And four segment registers as Extra segment register ES, Code segment register CS, Stack Segment Register SS and Data Segment Register DS, one Instruction Pointer IP and an adder circuit to calculate the 20 bit physical address of a location. This bus interface unit performs all the external bus operations like fetching the instructions from the memory, read/write data from/into memory or port and also supporting the instruction Queue etc. The BIU fetches up to six instruction bytes from the memory and stores these pre-fetched bytes in a first-in first out register set called Instruction Queue. When the execution unit is ready for the execution of the instruction, it reads the byte from the Queue instead of fetching the byte/word from the memory. This will increase the overall speed of microprocessor. Fetching the next instruction while the current instruction executes is called pipelining or parallel processing.

The important point to note, however, is that because the EU is the same for each processor (8086/8088), the programming instructions are exactly the same for each. Programs written for the 8086 can be run on the 8088 without any changes.

2.10.3 Fetch and Execute

Although the 8086/88 still functions as a stored program computer, organization of the CPU into a separate BIU and EU allows the fetch and execute cycles to overlap. To see this, consider what happens when the 8086 or 8088 is first started.

1. The BIU outputs the contents of the instruction pointer register (IP) onto the address bus, causing the selected byte or word to be read into the BIU.

2. Register IP is incremented by 1 to prepare for the next instruction fetch.

3. Once inside the BIU, the instruction is passed to the queue. This is a first-in, first-out storage register sometimes likened to a "pipeline".

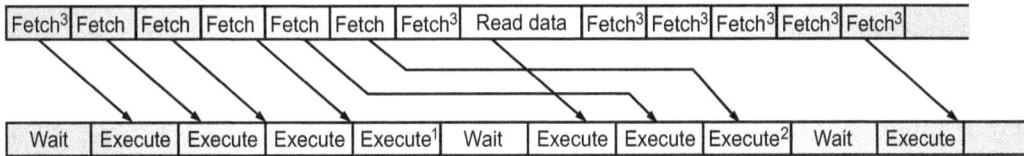

[1] This instruction requires a request for data not in the queue
[2] Jump instruction occurs
[3] These bytes are discarded

Fig. 2.32 : Fetch and Execute cycle of 8086

4. Assuming that the queue is initially empty, the EU immediately draws this instruction from the queue and begins execution.

5. While the EU is executing this instruction, the BIU proceeds to fetch a new instruction. Depending on the execution time of the first instruction, the BIU may fill the queue with several new instructions before the EU is ready to draw its next instruction.

The BIU is programmed to fetch a new instruction whenever the queue has room for one (with the 8088) or two (with the 8086) additional bytes. The advantage of this pipelined architecture is that the EU can execute instructions almost continually instead of having to wait for the BIU to fetch a new instruction.

There are three conditions that will cause the EU to enter a "wait" mode :

1. The first occurs when an instruction requires access to a memory location not in the queue. The BIU must suspend fetching instructions and output the address of this

memory location. After waiting for the memory access, the EU can resume executing instruction codes from the queue (and the BIU can resume filling the queue).

2. The second condition occurs when the instruction to be executed is a "jump" instruction. In this case, control is to be transferred to a new (non-sequential) address. The queue, however, assumes that instructions will always be executed in sequence and thus will be holding the "wrong" instruction codes. The EU must wait while the instruction at the jump address is fetched. Note that any bytes presently in the queue must be discarded (they are overwritten).

3. One other condition can cause the BIU to suspend fetching instructions. This occurs during execution of instructions that are slow to execute. For example, the instruction AAM (ASCII Adjust for Multiplication) requires 83 clock cycles to complete. At four cycles per instruction fetch, the queue will be completely filled during the execution of this single instruction. The BIU will thus have to wait for the EU to pull over one or two bytes from the queue before resuming the fetch cycle.

A subtle advantage to the pipelined architecture should be mentioned. Because the next several instructions are usually in the queue, the BIU can access memory at a somewhat "leisurely" pace. This means that slow-mem parts can be used without affecting overall system performance.

2.10.4 Register Organization

Total 14 registers are available in 8086 microprocessor are these are categorized into four groups. They are General purpose data registers, Pointer & Index registers, Segment registers and Flag register as shown in the table below.

Table 2.8 : 8086 Microprocessor Register

Sr. No	Type	Register width	Name of the Registers
1	General purpose Registers(4)	16-bit	AX,BX,CX,DX
		8-bit	AL,AH,BL,BH,CL,CH,DL,DH
2	Pointer Registers	16-bit	Stack Pointer(SP) Base Pointer(BP)
3	Index Registers	16-bit	Source Index(SI) Destination Index(DI)

4	Segment Registers	16-bit	Code Segment(CS)
			Data Segment(DS)
			Stack Segment(SS)
			Extra Segment(ES)
5	Instruction	16-bit	Instruction Pointer (IP)
6	Flag (PSW)	16-bit	Flag Register

- **General purpose registers :** There are four 16-bit 4 general purpose registers namely (AH, AL);(BH,BL); (CH,CL); (and DH,DL) which are part of Execution unit. These registers can be used individually for storing 16-bit data temporarily. The AL register is also called the accumulator. The pairs of registers can be used together to store 16-bit data words.

It is always advantageous to store the data in these registers because the data can be accessed much more easily as these registers are already in the execution unit. Here L indicates the lower byte and H indicates the higher byte. X indicates the extended register. The general purpose data registers are used for data manipulations. The use of these registers is more dependent on the mode of addressing also.

8086 CPU has 8 general purpose registers, each register has its own name:

AX - the accumulator register (divided into **AH / AL**) :

1.   Generates shortest machine code

2.   Arithmetic, logic and data transfer

3.   One number must be in AL or AX

4.   Multiplication & Division

5.   Input & Output

BX - the base address register (divided into **BH / BL**).

CX - the count register (divided into **CH / CL**) :

1.   Iterative code segments using the LOOP instruction

2.   Repetitive operations on strings with the REP command

3.   Count (in CL) of bits to shift and rotate

DX - the data register (divided into **DH / DL**) :

1.   DX:AX concatenated into 32-bit register for some MUL and DIV operations

2.   Specifying ports in some IN and OUT operations

The other four registers of EU are referred to as index / pointer registers. They are Stack Pointer register, Base Pointer register, Source Index register and Destination Index registers. The pointer registers contain the offset within a particular segment.

SI - source index register:

1. Can be used for pointer addressing of data

2. Used as source in some string processing instructions

3. Offset address relative to DS

DI - destination index register:

1. Can be used for pointer addressing of data

2. Used as destination in some string processing instructions

3. Offset address relative to ES

BP - base pointer:

1. Primarily used to access parameters passed via the stack

2. Offset address relative to SS

SP - stack pointer:

1. Always points to top item on the stack

2. Offset address relative to SS

3. Always points to word (byte at even address)

4. An empty stack will had SP = FFFEh

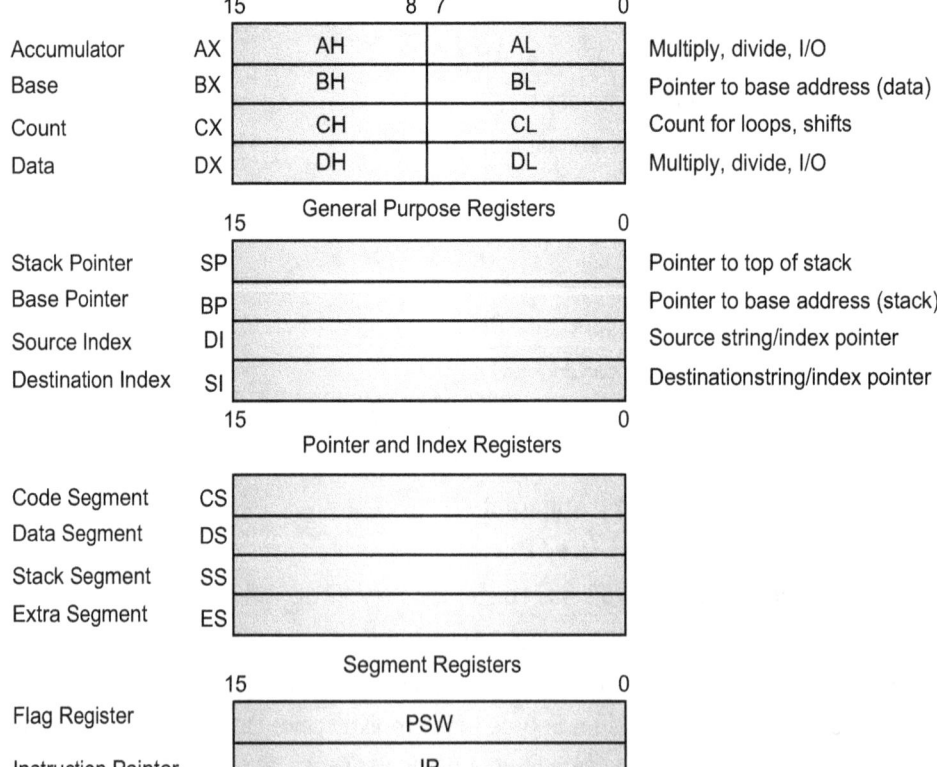

Fig. 2.33 : Register Organisation

The BP & SP registers holds the offsets within the data and stack segments respectively. The Index registers are used as general purpose registers as well as for holding the offset in case of indexed based and relative indexed addressing modes. The source Index register is generally used to store the offset of source data in data segment while the Destination Index register used to store the offset of destination in data or extra segment. These index registers are specifically used in string manipulations.

- **Segment Registers :** There are four 16-bit segment registers namely code segment register (CS), Stack segment register (SS),Data segment register (DS) and Extra segment register(ES). The code segment register is used for addressing the 64 kB memory location in the code segment of the memory, where the code of the executable program is stored. Similarly, the DS register points to the data segment of the 64 kB memory where the data is stored. The Extra segment register also refers to essentially another data segment of the memory space. The SS register is useful for addressing stack segment of memory. So, the CS, DS, SS and ES segment registers respectively contains the segment addresses for the code, data, stack and extra segments of the memory.

CS - points at the segment containing the current program.

DS - generally points at segment where variables are defined.

ES - extra segment register, it's up to a coder to define its usage.

SS - points at the segment containing the stack.

Although it is possible to store any data in the segment registers, this is never a good idea. The segment registers have a very special purpose - pointing at accessible blocks of memory. Segment registers work together with general purpose register to access any memory value. For example, if we would like to access memory at the physical address **12345h** (hexadecimal), we could set the **DS = 1230h and SI = 0045h**. This way we can access much more memory than with a single register, which is limited to 16 bit values.

The CPU makes a calculation of the physical address by multiplying the segment register by 10h and adding the general purpose register to it (1230h * 10h + 45h = 12345h):

$$12300$$
$$+0045$$
$$\overline{12345}$$

The address formed with 2 registers is called an **effective address**. By default **BX, SI** and **DI** registers work with **DS** segment register; **BP** and **SP** work with **SS** segment register. Other general purpose registers cannot form an effective address. Also, although **BX** can form an effective address, **BH** and **BL** cannot.

- **Instruction Pointer Register :** It is a 16-bit register which always points to the next instruction to be executed within the currently executing code segment. So, this register contains the 16-bit offset address pointing to the next instruction code within the 64 kB of the code segment area. Its content is automatically incremented as the execution of the next instruction takes place.

IP - the instruction pointer:

1. Always points to next instruction to be executed
2. Offset address relative to CS

IP register always works together with **CS** segment register and it points to currently executing instruction.

- **Flag Register :** This register is also called status register. It is a 16 bit register which contains six status flags and three control flags. So, only nine bits of the 16 bit register are defined and the remaining seven bits are undefined. Normally, this status flag bits indicate the status of the ALU after the arithmetic or logical operations. Each bit of the status register is a flip/flop. The Flag register contains Carry flag, Parity flag, Auxiliary flag, Zero flag, Sign flag, Trap flag, Interrupt flag, Direction flag and overflow flag as shown in the diagram. The CF, PF, AF, ZF, SF, OF are the status flags and the TF, IF and CF are the control flags.

X	X	X	X	OF	DF	IF	TF	SF	ZF	X	AF	X	PF	X	CF

Fig. 2.34 : Flag Register

CF- **Carry Flag :** This flag is set to 1, when there is a carry out of MSB in case of addition or a borrow in case of subtraction. Otherwise this bit sets to 0.

PF - **Parity Flag :** This flag is set to 1, if the lower byte of the result contains even number of 1's and for odd number of 1s in result the bit set to zero.

AF- **Auxilary Carry Flag :** This bit is set to 1, if there is a carry from the lowest nibble, i.e, bit three to bit four during addition, or borrow for the lowest nibble, i.e, bit three, during subtraction. (bits 0 to bit 7 take in consideration)

ZF- **Zero Flag :** This flag is set to 1, if the result of the computation or comparison performed by the previous instruction is zero otherwise bit is set to 0 indicating that result is non-zero.

SF- **Sign Flag :** This flag is set to 1, when the result of any computation (MSB is 1) is negative and set to 0 if result is positive (MSB is 0).

TF - **Tarp Flag :** If this flag is set 1, the processor enters the single step execution mode.

IF- **Interrupt Flag :** If this flag is set to 1, the maskable interrupt INTR of 8086 is enabled and if it is zero, the interrupt is disabled. It can be set by using the STI instruction and can be cleared by executing CLI instruction.

DF- **Direction Flag :** This is used by string manipulation instructions. If this flag bit is '0', the string is processed beginning from the lowest address to the highest address, i.e., auto incrementing mode. Otherwise, the string is processed from the highest address towards the lowest address, i.e., auto decrementing mode.

OF- **Over flow Flag :** This flag is set, if an overflow occurs, i.e, if the result of a signed operation is large enough to accommodate in a destination register. The result is of more than 7-bits in size in case of 8-bit signed operation and more than 15-bits in size in case of 16-bit sign operations, then the overflow will be set.

2.11 PIN DIAGRAM OF 8086

Fig. 2.35 shows signal description of 8086 microprocessor.

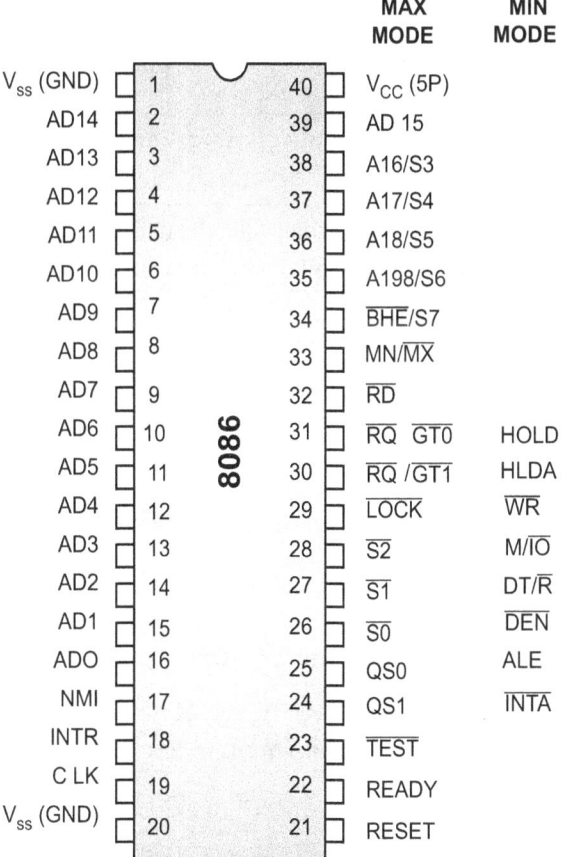

Fig. 2.35 : Pin Diagram of 8086

Intel 8086 is a 16-bit microprocessor. It is available in 40 pin DIP chip. It uses a 5 V d.c. supply for its operation. The 8086 uses 20-line address bus. It uses a 16-line data bus. The 20 lines of the address bus operate in multiplexed mode. The 16-low order address bus lines are multiplexed with data and 4 high-order address bus lines are multiplexed with status signals.

AD_0-AD_{15} (Bidirectional) : Address/Data bus. These are low order address bus. They are multiplexed with data. When AD lines are used to transmit memory address the symbol A is used instead of AD, for example, A_0-A_{15}. When data are transmitted over AD lines the symbol D is used in place of AD, for example, D_0-D_7, D_8-D_{15} or D_0-D_{15}.

A_{16}-A_{19} (Output) : High order address bus. These are multiplexed with status signals.

Table 2.9 : Common Pins of 8086

AD_7-AD_0	The 8086/8088 **address/data bus** lines compose the multiplexed address data bus of the 8086/8088.
A_{15}-A_8	The 8086/8088 **address bus** provides the upper-half memory address.
AD_{15}-AD_8	The 8086 **address/data bus** lines compose the upper multiplexed address/data bus on the 8086.
A_{19}-S_6 A_{16}/S_3	The **address/status bus** bits are multiplexed to provide address signals A19-A16 and also status bits S6-S3.
$\overline{RD}$	Whenever the read signal is a logic 0, the data bus is receptive to data from the memory or I/O devices connected to the system.
INTR	Interrupt request is used to request a hardware interrupt.
NMI	The non-maskable interrupt.
RESET	The reset input causes the microprocessor to reset.
CLK	The clock pin provides the basic timing signal to the microprocessor.
MN/$\overline{MX}$	The minimum/maximum mode pin selects either minimum mode or maximum mode operation for the microprocessor.
$\overline{BHE}$ /S7	The bus high enable pin is used in the 8086 to enable the most significant data bus bits (D15-D8) during a read or a write operation. The state of S7 of always a logic 1.

Table 2.10 : Minimum Mode Pins

IO/$\overline{M}$ or M/$\overline{IO}$	The IO/$\overline{M}$ (8088) or the M/$\overline{IO}$ (8086) pin selects memory or I/O.
$\overline{WR}$	The write line is a strobe that indicates the 8086/8088 is outputting data to a memory or I/O device.
$\overline{INTA}$	The interrupt acknowledge signal is a response to the INTR input pin.

ALE	Address latch enable shows that the 8086/8088 address / data bus contains address information.
DT/$\overline{\text{R}}$	The data transmit/receive signal shows that the microprocessor data bus is transmitting (DT/R = 1) or receiving (DT/R = 0) data.
DEN	Data bus enable activates external data bus buffers.
HOLD	The hold input requests a direct memory access (DMA).
HLDA	Hold acknowledge indicates that the 8086/8088 has entered the hold state.
$\overline{\text{SS0}}$	The $\overline{\text{SS0}}$ status line is equivalent to the S0 pin in maximum mode operation of the microprocessor. This signal is combined with IO/$\overline{\text{M}}$ and DT/$\overline{\text{R}}$ to decode the function of the current bus cycle.

Table 2.11 : Maximum Mode Pins

Maximum mode signals (MN / $\overline{\text{MX}}$ = GND)		
Name	**Function**	**Type**
$\overline{\text{RQ/ GT1, 0}}$	Request / Grant Bus Access Control	Bidirectional
$\overline{\text{LOCK}}$	Bus Priority Lock Control	Output, 3-State
$\overline{\text{S}_2}$ – $\overline{\text{S}_0}$	Bus Cycle Status	Output, 3-State
QS1, QS0	Instruction Queue Status	Output

A_{16}/S_3, A_{17}/S_4, A_{18}/S_5, A_{19}/S_6 : The specified address lines are multiplexed with corresponding status signals.

BHE (Active Low)/S7 (Output) : Bus High Enable/Status. During T1 it is low. It is used to enable data onto the most significant half of data bus, D8-D15. 8-bit device connected to upper half of the data bus use BHE (Active Low) signal. It is multiplexed with status signal S7. S7 signal is available during T2, T3 and T4.

RD (Read) (Active Low) : The signal is used for read operation. It is an output signal. It is active when low.

READY : This is the acknowledgement from the slow device or memory that they have completed the data transfer. The signal made available by the devices is synchronized by the 8284A clock generator to provide ready input to the 8086. The signal is active high.

INTR-Interrupt Request : This is a triggered input. This is sampled during the last clock cycles of each instruction to determine the availability of the request. If any interrupt request is pending, the processor enters the interrupt acknowledge cycle. This can be internally masked by resulting the interrupt enable flag. This signal is active high and internally synchronized.

NMI (Input) – Non-Maskable Interrupt : It is an edge triggered input which causes a type 2 interrupt. A subroutine is vectored to via an interrupt vector lookup table located in system memory. NMI is not maskable internally by software. A transition from LOW to HIGH initiates the interrupt at the end of the current instruction. This input is internally synchronized.

INTA : Interrupt acknowledge. It is active LOW during T_2 ,T_3 and T_w of each interrupt acknowledge cycle.

MN/ MX MINIMUM / MAXIMUM : This pin signal indicates what mode the processor is to operate in.

RQ/GT RQ/GT0 : REQUEST/GRANT : These pins are used by other local bus masters to force the processor to release the local bus at the end of the processor's current bus cycle. Each pin is bidirectional with RQ/GT having higher priority than RQ /GT1.

LOCK : Its an active low pin. It indicates that other system bus masters are not to allowed to gain control of the system bus while LOCK is active LOW. The LOCK signal   remains active until the completion of the next instruction.

TEST : This input is examined by a 'WAIT' instruction. If the TEST pin goes low, execution will continue, else the processor remains in an idle state. The input is synchronized internally during each clock cycle on leading edge of clock.

CLK - Clock Input : The clock input provides the basic timing for processor operation and bus control activity. Its an asymmetric square wave with 33% duty cycle.

RESET (Input) : RESET : causes the processor to immediately terminate its present activity. The signal must be active HIGH for at least four clock cycles.

Vcc – Power Supply (+5 V D.C.)

GND – Ground

QS_1, QS_0 (Queue Status) : These signals indicate the status of the internal 8086 instruction queue according to the table shown below

Table 2.12

QSI	QS0	Status
0 (LOW)	0	No Operation
0	1	First Byte of Op Code from Queue
1 (HIGH)	0	Empty the Queue
1	1	Subsequent Byte from Queue

DT/R : DATA TRANSMIT/RECEIVE : This pin is needed in minimum system that desires to use an 8086/8087 data bus transceiver. It is used to control the direction of data flow through the transceiver.

DEN : DATA ENABLE : This pin is provided as an output enable for the 8086/8087 in a minimum system which uses the transceiver. DEN is active LOW during each memory and I/O access and for INTA cycles.

HOLD/HLDA : HOLD indicates that another master is requesting a local bus. This is an active HIGH. The processor receiving the "hold" request will issue HLDA (HIGH) as an acknowledgement in the middle of a T_4 or T_1 clock cycle.

2.12 INSTRUCTION CYCLES

The complete instruction cycle involves three operations. Instruction fetching, opcode decoding and instruction execution.

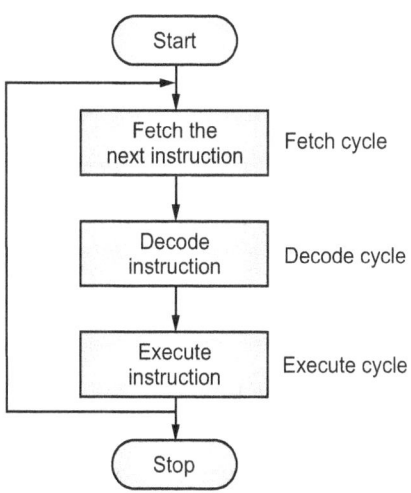

Fig. 2.36 (a) : Basic instruction cycle

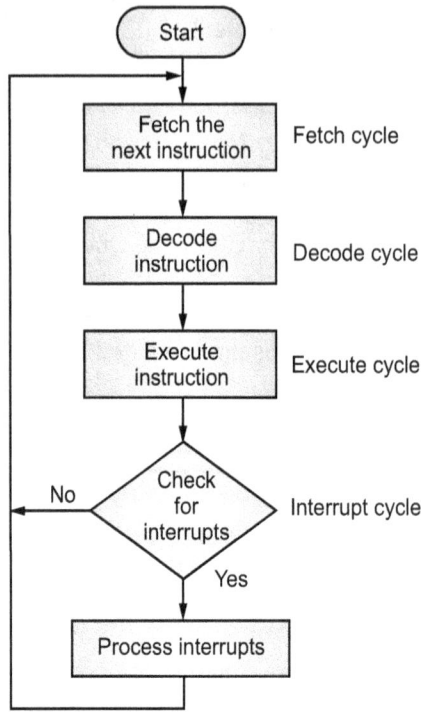

Fig. 2.36 (b) : Basic instruction cycle with interrupt

Fig. 2.36 (a) shows the basic instruction cycle. After each instruction cycle, CPU checks for any valid interrupt request. If so, CPU fetches the instruction from the interrupt service routine and after completion of interrupt service routine, CPU starts the new instruction cycle from where it has been interrupted. Fig. 2.36 (b) shows instruction cycle with interrupt cycle.

The fetch and execute cycles of 8086 have discussed in detail in section

CPU Bus Cycle :

T-State is the One clock period is referred to as a T-State.

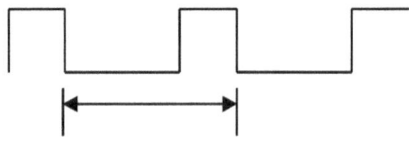

Fig. 2.37 : T-state

An operation takes an integer number of T-States. A bus cycle is broken into four states or T periods:

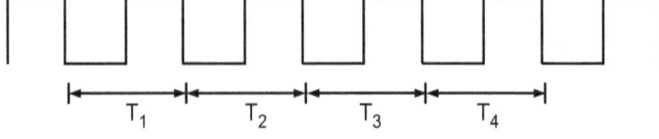

Fig. 2.38 : Bus cycle

During T$_1$: The address is placed on the Address/Data bus Control signals M/ IO, ALE and DT/ R specify memory or I/O, latch the address onto the address bus and set the direction of data transfer on data bus.

During T$_2$: 8086 issues the RD or WR signal, DEN, to read or write data. DEN enables the memory or I/O device to receive the data for writes and the 8086 to receive the data for reads.

During T$_3$: This cycle is provided to allow memory to access data. READY is sampled at the end of T$_2$. If low, T$_3$ becomes a wait state. Otherwise, the data bus is sampled at the end of T$_3$.

During T$_4$: All bus signals are deactivated, in preparation for next bus cycle. Data is sampled for reads, writes occur for writes.

Each BUS CYCLE on the 8086 equals **four** system clocking periods (T states). The clock rate is **5 MHz** , therefore one Bus Cycle is 800ns. The transfer rate is **1.25 MHz**.

2.13 MINIMUM AND MAXIMUM MODE OF 8086

8086/8088 microprocessor operates in two modes one is Minimum mode and other is Maximum mode. Mode selection is accomplished by how the chip is hard-wired in the circuit. Specifically, pin #33 (MN/MX) is used to select the mode, depending on whether it is wired to voltage or to ground. Changing the state of pin #33 changes the function of certain other pins. Mode cannot be changed by software.

Maximum mode is for large applications such as multiprocessing. The mode is hard-wired into the circuit and cannot be changed by software. Specifically, pin #33 (MN/MX) is either wired to voltage or to ground to determine the mode. Changing the state of pin #33 changes the function of certain other pins, most of which have to do with how the CPU handles the (local) bus. The IBM PC and PC/XT use an Intel 8088 running in maximum mode.

2.13.1 Minimum Mode 8086 system

In a minimum mode 8086 system, the microprocessor.8086 is operated in minimum mode by strapping its MN/MX pin to logic 1. There is a single microprocessor in the minimum mode system. The remaining components in the system are latches, transreceivers, clock generator, memory and I/O devices. The **clock generator** also synchronizes some external signal with the system clock. It has 20 address lines and 16 data lines, the 8086 CPU requires three octal address latches and two octal data buffers for the complete address and data separation. **Latches** are generally buffered output **D-type flip-flops** like 74LS373 or 8282. They are used for separating the valid address from the multiplexed address/data signals and **are controlled by the ALE signal generated by 8086. Transreceivers are the bidirectional buffers** and some times they are called as data amplifiers. They are **required to separate the valid data** from the time multiplexed address/data signals. They **are controlled by two signals namely, DEN and DT/R**. The DEN signal indicates the availability of valid data over the address/data lines. The DT/R signal indicates direction of data, i.e. from or to the processor.

The timing diagram can be categorized in two parts,

    (a) Minimum mode read cycle

    (b) Minimum mode write cycle.

(a) Minimum Mode – READ Cycle :

- The **read cycle** begins in T_1 with the assertion of address latch enable (ALE) signal and also M / IO signal. During the negative going edge of this signal, the valid address is latched on the local bus. The BHE and A0 signals address low, high or both bytes.

- From T_1 to T_4 , the M/IO signal indicates a memory or I/O operation.

- At T_2, the address is removed from the local bus and is sent to the output. The read (RD) control signal is also activated in T_2. The read (RD) signal causes the address device to enable its data bus drivers. After RD goes low, the valid data is available on the data bus.The addressed device will drive the READY line high. When the processor returns the read signal to high level, the addressed device will again tristate its bus drivers.

- Dump address on address bus.

- Issue a read (RD) and set M/ IO to 1.

- Wait for memory access cycle.

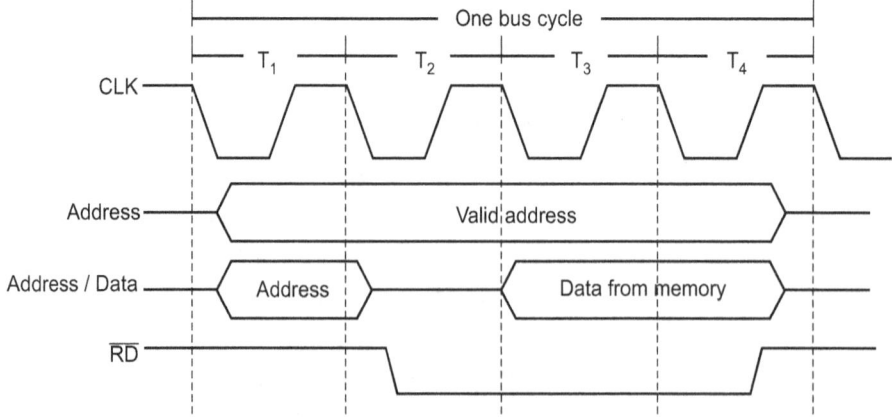

Fig. 2.39 : Simplified 8086 Read Bus Cycle

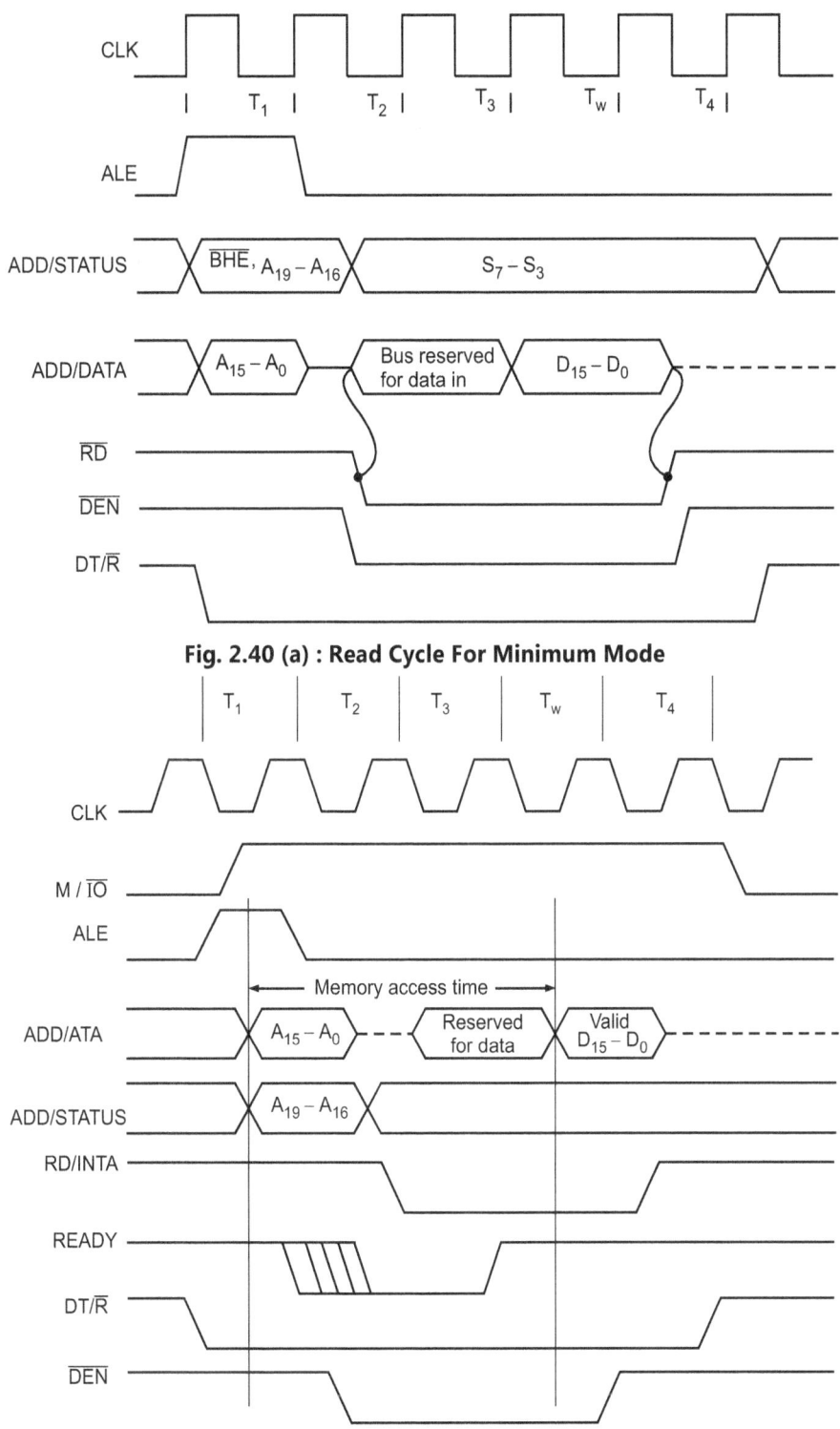

Fig. 2.40 (a) : Read Cycle For Minimum Mode

Fig. 2.40 (b) : Memory I/O read cycle for minimum mode

(b) Minimum Mode-Write cycle :

- A write cycle also begins with the assertion of ALE and the emission of the address. The M/IO signal is again asserted to indicate a memory or I/O operation.

- In T_2, after sending the address in T_1, the processor sends the data to be written to the addressed location. The data remains on the bus until middle of T_4 state. The WR becomes active at the beginning of T_2. The BHE signal is used to select the proper byte or bytes of memory or I/O word to be read or write.

- The M/IO, RD and WR signals indicate the type of data transfer as specified in table below.

Table 2.13

M/$\overline{\text{IO}}$	$\overline{\text{RD}}$	$\overline{\text{WR}}$	Transfer	Type
0	0	1	IO	Read
0	1	0	IO	Write
1	0	1	Memory	Read
1	1	0	Memory	Write

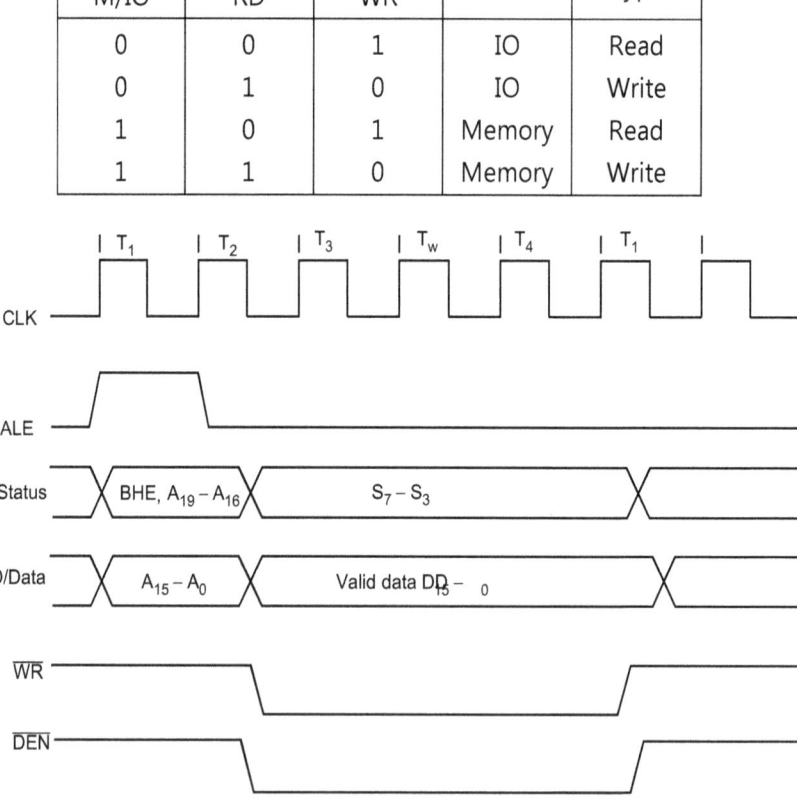

Fig. 2.41 (a) : Write Cycle in Minimum Mode

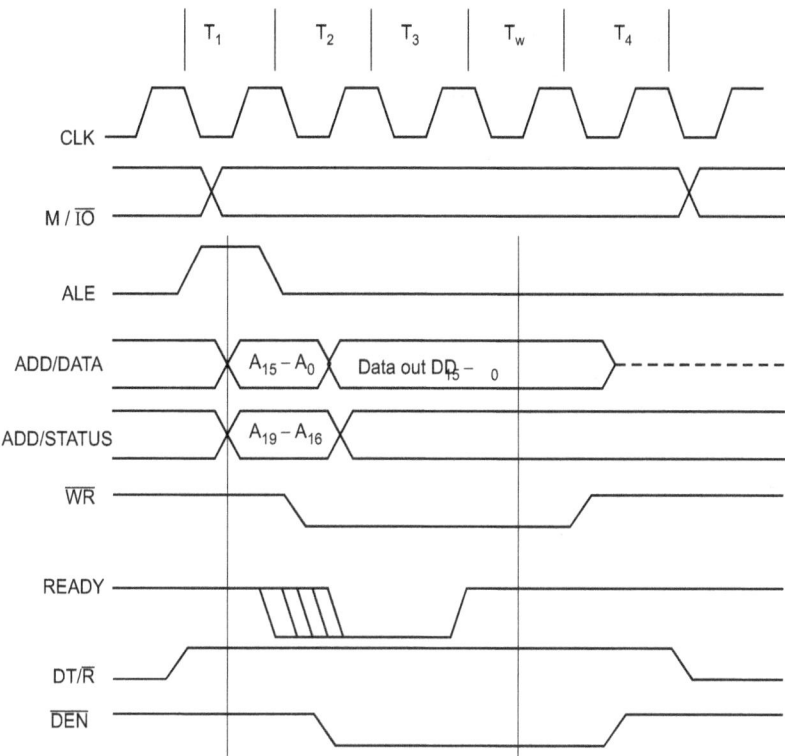

Fig. 2.41 (b) : Memory I/O write cycle in minimum mode

2.13.2 Maximum Mode 8086

In the maximum mode, the 8086 is operated by strapping the MN/MX pin to ground. In this mode, the processor derives the status signal S_2, S_1, S_0. Another chip called bus controller derives the control signal using this status information. In the maximum mode, there may be more than one microprocessor in the system configuration. The components in the system are same as in the minimum mode system. The basic function of the bus controller chip IC8288, is to derive control signals like RD and WR (for memory and I/O devices), DEN, DT/R, ALE etc. using the information by the processor on the status lines.

The bus controller chip has input lines S_2, S_1, S_0 and CLK. These inputs to 8288 are driven by CPU

It derives the outputs ALE, DEN, DT/R, MRDC, MWTC, AMWC, IORC, IOWC and AIOWC. The AEN, IOB and CEN pins are specially useful for multiprocessor systems.

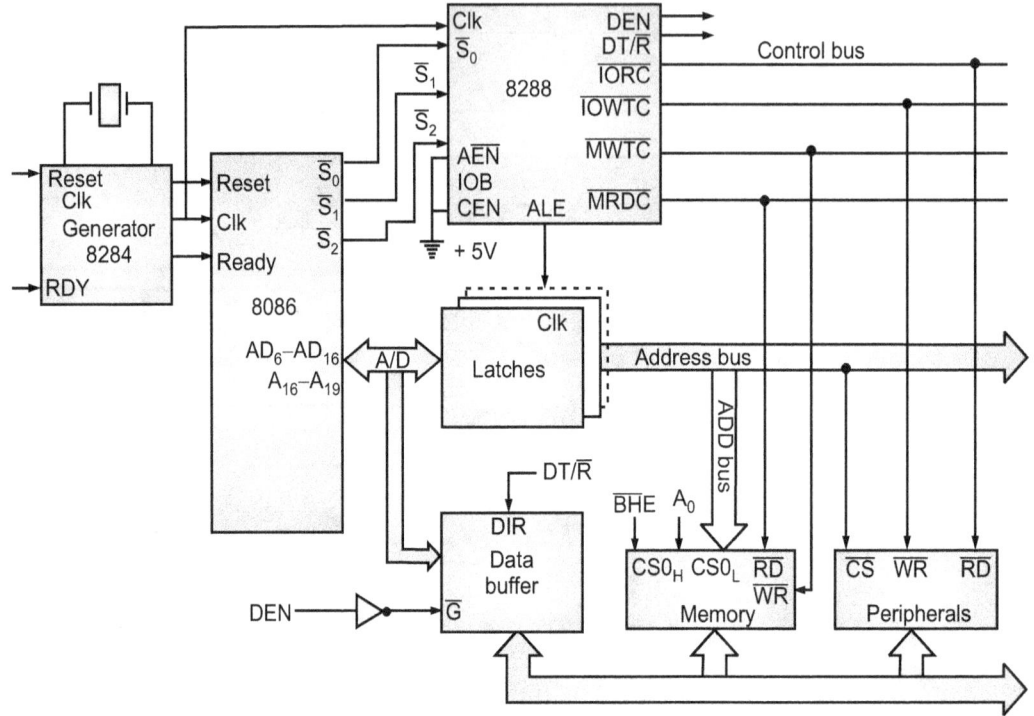

Fig. 2.42 : Maximum Mode 8086 Microprocessor

AEN and IOB are generally grounded. CEN pin is usually tied to +5 V. The significance of the MCE/PDEN output depends upon the status of the IOB pin. If IOB is grounded, it acts as master cascade enable to control cascade 8259A, else it acts as peripheral data enable used in the multiple bus configurations. INTA pin used to issue two interrupt acknowledge pulses to the interrupt controller or to an interrupting device. IORC, IOWC are I/O read command and I/O write command signals respectively. These signals enable an IO interface to read or write the data from or to the address port.

The MRDC, MWTC are memory read command and memory write command signals respectively and may be used as memory read or write signals.

All these command signals instructs the memory to accept or send data from or to the bus.

For both of these write command signals, the advanced signals namely AIOWC and AMWTC are available.

(a) Maximum Mode-Read Cycle :

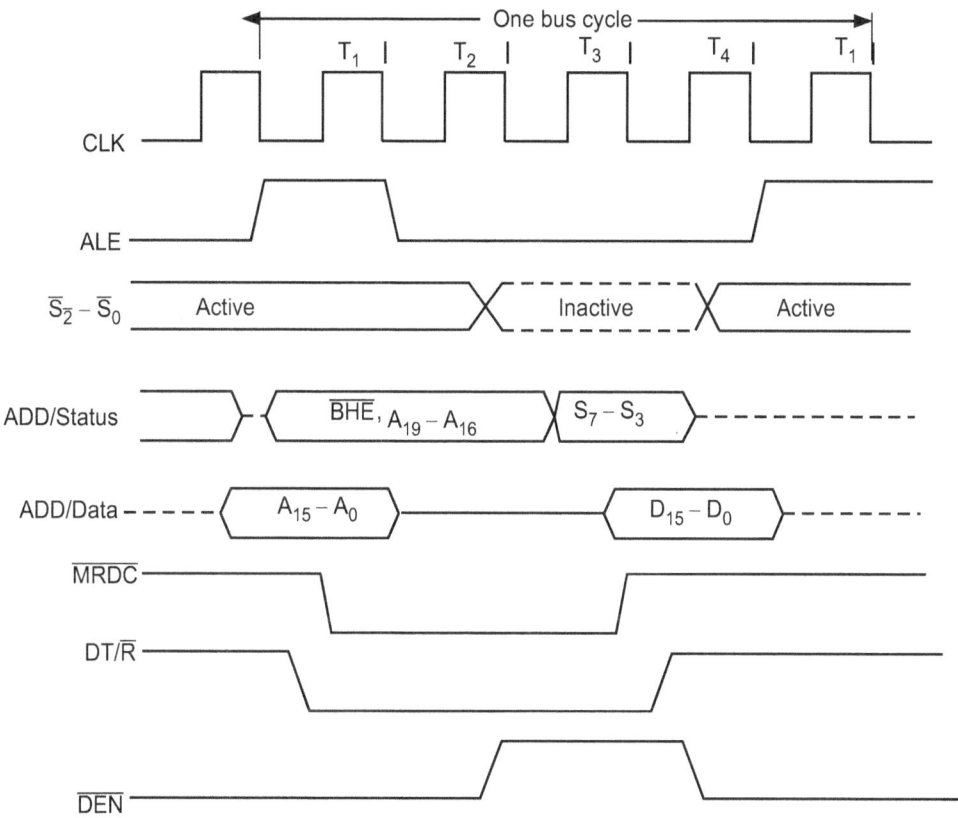

Fig. 2.43 : Memory Read in Maximum Mode

(b) Maximum Mode-Write Cycle :

The request/grant response sequence contains a series of three pulses. The request/grant pins are checked at each rising pulse of clock input. When a request is detected and if the condition for HOLD request are satisfied, the processor issues a grant pulse over the RQ/GT pin immediately during T_4 (current) or T_1 (next) state. When the requesting master receives this pulse, it accepts the control of the bus, it sends a release pulse to the processor using RQ/GT pin.

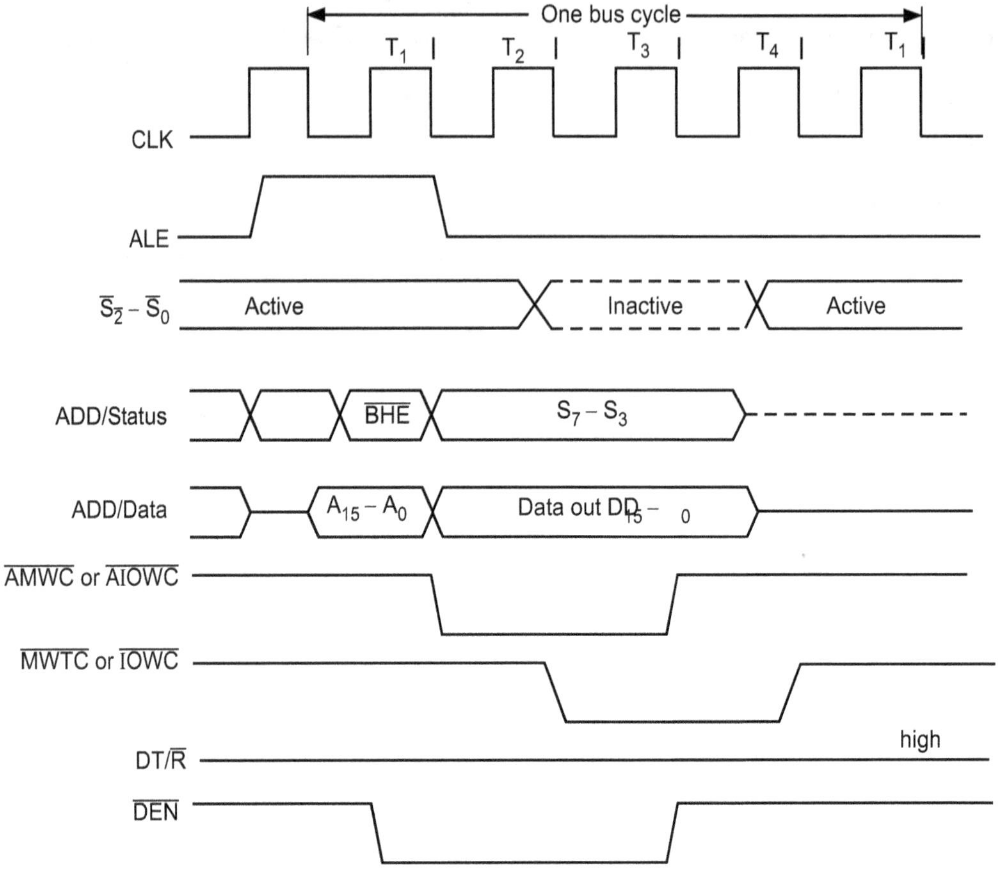

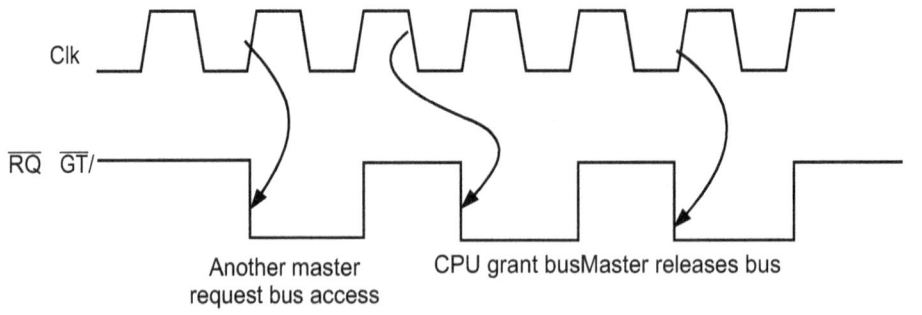

One bus cycle

CLK

ALE

$\overline{S_2} - \overline{S_0}$ Active   Inactive   Active

ADD/Status $\overline{BHE}$ $S_7 - S_3$

ADD/Data $A_{15} - A_0$ Data out $D_{15} - D_0$

$\overline{AMWC}$ or $\overline{AIOWC}$

$\overline{MWTC}$ or $\overline{IOWC}$

DT/$\overline{R}$ high

$\overline{DEN}$

Fig. 2.44 : Memory Write Maximum Mode

Clk

$\overline{RQ}$ $\overline{GT/}$

Another master   CPU grant busMaster releases bus
request bus access

Fig. 2.45 : Request / grant cycle

2.14 PROGRAMMERS MODEL OF 8086

As a programmer of the 8086 or 8088 you must become familiar with the various registers in the EU and BIU of 8086.

The detail Register organization we seen in the section 2.10

The data group consists of the accumulator and the BX, CX, and DX registers. Note that each can be accessed as a byte or a word. Thus, BX refers to the 16-bit base register but BH refers only to the higher 8 bits of this register. The data registers are normally used for storing temporary results that will be acted on by subsequent instructions.

The pointer and index group are all 16-bit registers (you cannot access the low or high bytes alone). These registers are used as memory pointers. Sometimes a pointer register will be interpreted as pointing to a memory byte and at other times a memory word. As you will see, the 8086/88 always stores words with the high-order byte in the high-order word address.

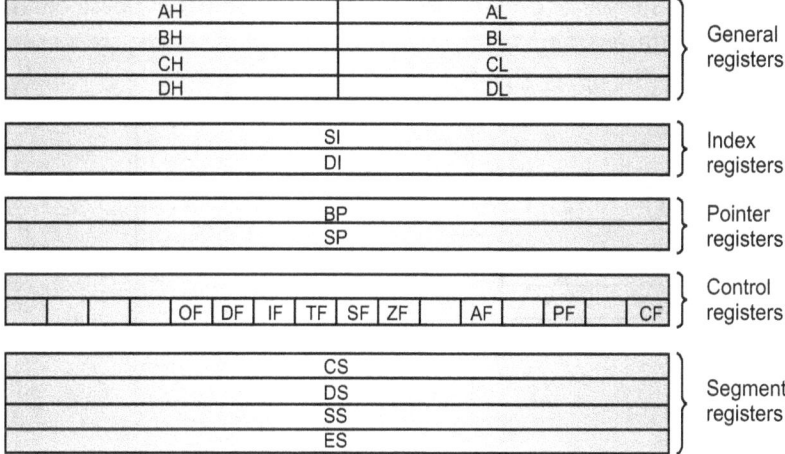

Fig. 2.46 : Programmers model of 8086

Register IP could be considered in the previous group, but this register has only one function to point to the next instruction to be fetched in to the BIU. Register IP is physically part of the BIU and not under direct control of the programmer as are the other pointer registers.

Six of the flags are status indicators, reflecting properties of the result of the last arithmetic or logical instructions. The 8086/88 has several instructions that can be used to transfer program control to a new memory location based on the state of the flags.

Three of the flags can be set or reset directly by the programmer and are used to control the operation of the processor. These are TF, IF, and DF.

The final group of registers is called the segment group. These registers are used by the BIU to determine the memory address output by the CPU when it is reading or writing from the memory unit. To fully understand these registers, we must first study the way the 8086/88 divides its memory into segments.

2.15 MEMORY SEGMENTATION

- The total memory size is divided into segments of various sizes. A segment is just an area in memory. The process of dividing memory this way is called Segmentation.
- In memory, data is stored as bytes. Each byte has a specific address. Intel 8086 has 20 lines address bus. With 20 address lines, the memory that can be addressed is 2^{20} bytes 2^{20} = 1,048,576 bytes (1 MB).
- The 8086 processor provides a 20-bit address to access any location of the 1 MB memory space. The memory is organized as a linear array of 1 million bytes, addressed as 00000(H) to FFFFF(H).
- The memory is logically divided into code, data, extra data, and stack segments of up to 64 K bytes each .
- Each of these segments are addressed by an address stored in corresponding segment register. These registers are 16-bit in size. Each register stores the base address (starting address) of the corresponding segment. Because the segment registers cannot store 20 bits, they only store the upper 16 bits.

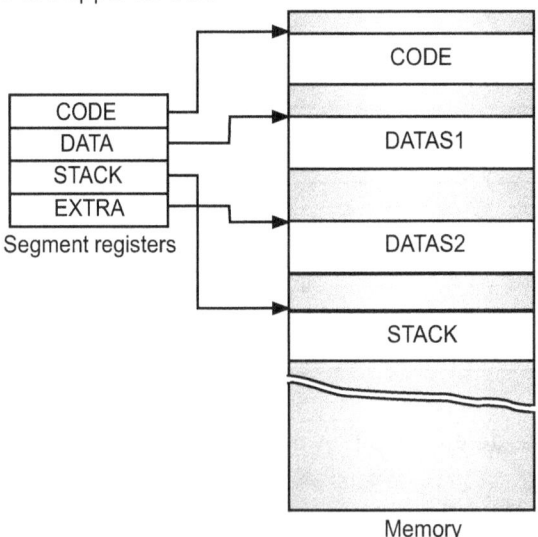

Fig. 2.47 : Segment Registers

Physical memory address pointed by segment:offset pair is calculated as:

address = (* 16) + <offset>

The memory is divided as follows :

- **Program memory :** Program can be located anywhere in memory. Jump and call instructions can be used for short jumps within currently selected 64 kB code segment, as well as for far jumps anywhere within 1 MB of memory. All conditional jump instructions can be used to jump within approximately +127 to –127 bytes from current instruction.

- **Data memory :** The processor can access data in any one out of four available segments, which limits the size of accessible memory to 256 kB (if all four segments point to different 64 kB blocks). Accessing data from the Data, Code, Stack or Extra segments can be usually done by prefixing instructions with the DS:, CS:, SS: or ES: (some registers and instructions by default may use the ES or SS segments instead of DS segment).

Word data can be located at odd or even byte boundaries. The processor uses two memory accesses to read 16-bit word located at odd byte boundaries. Reading word data from even byte boundaries requires only one memory access.

- **Stack memory :** can be placed anywhere in memory. The stack can be located at odd memory addresses, but it is not recommended for performance reasons

- **Reserved locations :**
    - 0000h - 03FFh are reserved for interrupt vectors. Each interrupt vector is a 32-bit pointer in format segment: offset.

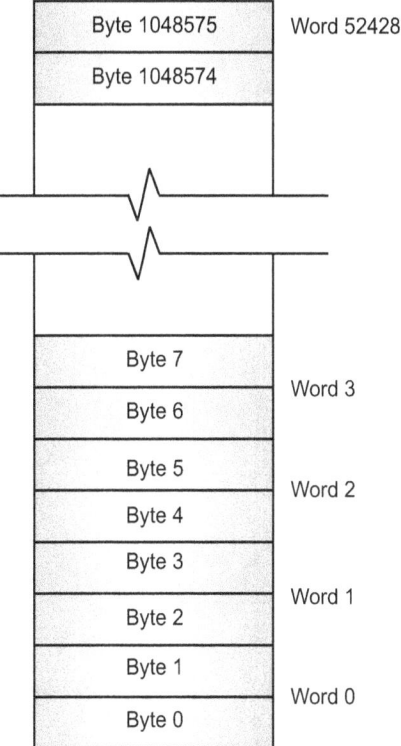

Fig. 2.48 : Memory layout

FFFF0h - FFFFFh - after RESET the processor always starts program execution at the FFFF0h address.

- With 20 bits, 1,048,576 different combinations are available. Each memory location is assigned a different combination. Each memory location is 1 byte wide. Therefore, the memory space of the 8086 consists of 1,048,576 bytes or 524,288 16-bit words.
- The 8086 has a 20-bit address bus. Therefore, it can access 1,048,576 bytes of memory. How many bits and how many HEX digits are required to access 1 M memory?

$2^N = 1M$ (where N is in bits)

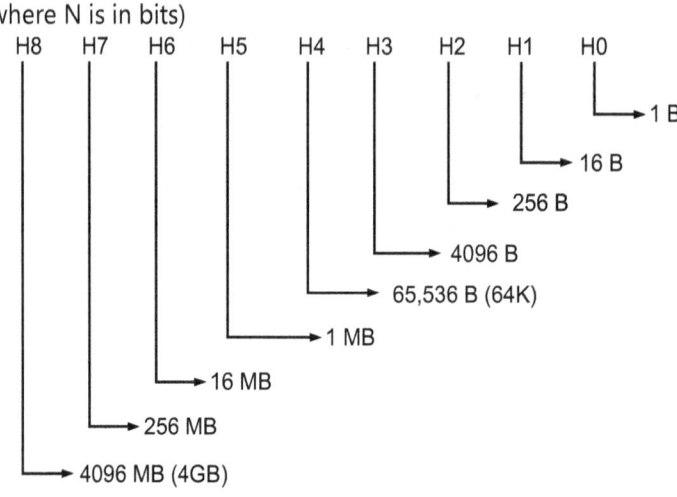

N = 20 bits   20/4 = 5 HEX digits

Fig. 2.49 : Positional Notation (Hex Digits)

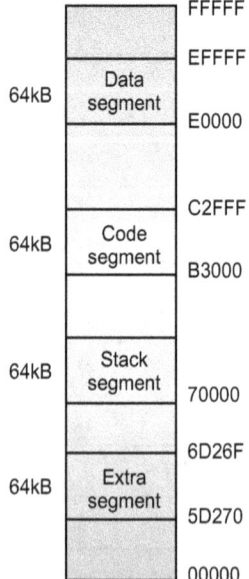

Fig. 2.50 : Segmented Memory

N = 20 bits = 20/4 = 5 HEX digits

- Within the 1 MB of memory, the 8086 defines 4 64 kB memory blocks. The segment registers point to location 0 of each segment. (The base address)
- Segments are variable-sized areas of memory used by a program containing either code or data.
- Segmentation provides a way to isolate memory segments from each other. This permits multiple programs to run simultaneously without interfering with each other. A segment selector is a 16-bit value stored in a segment register. A logical address is a combination of a segment selector and an offset(16-bit for 8086).

How is a 20-bit address obtained if there are only 16- bit registers?

- The 20-bit address of a byte is called its **Physical Address**. But, it is specified as a **Logical Address**. Logical address is in the form of: **Base Address : Offset**.

Offset is the displacement of the memory location from the starting location of the segment.

Example :

The value of Data Segment Register (DS) is 2222 H. To convert this 16-bit address into 20-bit, the BIU appends 0H to the LSBs of the address. After appending, the starting address of the Data Segment becomes 22220H. If the data at any location has a logical address specified as: 2222 H : 0016 H. Then, the number 0016 H is the offset. 2222 H is the value of DS.

To calculate the effective address of the memory, BIU uses the following formula :

Effective Address = Starting Address of Segment + Offset

To find the starting address of the segment, BIU appends the contents of Segment Register with 0H. Then, it adds offset to it. Therefore :

$$
\begin{aligned}
EA &= 22220\ H \\
&+ 0016\ H \\
\hline
&\ 22236\ H
\end{aligned}
$$

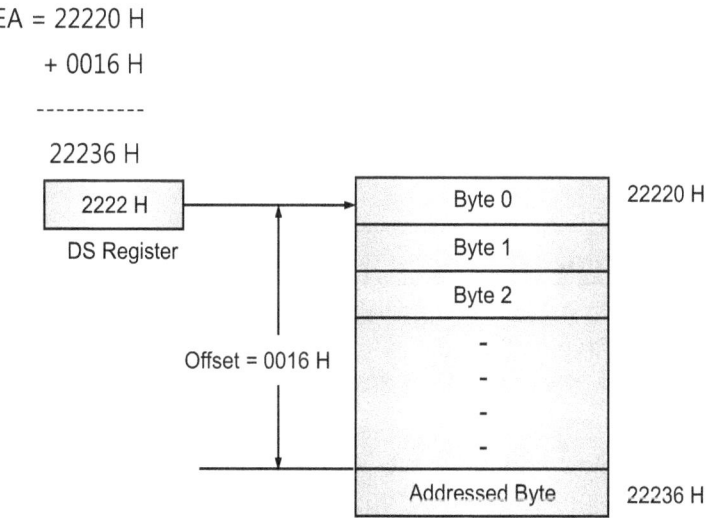

Fig. 2.51 : Memory layout for example

All offsets are limited to 16-bits. It means that the maximum size possible for segment is 216 = 65,535 bytes (64 kB). The offset of the first location within the segment is 0000 H. The offset of the last location in the segment is FFFF H.

Table 2.14

Segment	Offset Registers	Function
CS	IP	Address of the next instruction
DS	BX, DI, SI	Address of data
SS	SP, BP	Address in the stack
ES	BX, DI, SI	Address of destination data (for string operations)

e.g. The contents of the following registers are :

$$CS = 1111 \text{ H}$$
$$DS = 3333 \text{ H}$$
$$SS = 2526 \text{ H}$$
$$IP = 1232 \text{ H}$$
$$SP = 1100 \text{ H}$$
$$DI = 0020 \text{ H}$$

Calculate the corresponding physical addresses for the address bytes in CS, DS and SS.

1. CS = 1111 H

The base address of the code segment is 11110 H.

Effective address of memory is given by 11110H + 1232H = 12342H.

2. DS = 3333 H

The base address of the data segment is 33330 H.

Effective address of memory is given by 33330H + 0020H = 33350H.

3. SS = 2526 H

The base address of the stack segment is 25260 H.

Effective address of memory is given by 25260H + 1100H = 26350H.

2.16 MEMORY ORGANIZATION

We know that the 8086 has a 20 bit Address bus. So it can address 2^{20} or 1,048576 address. At each address we can store an 8 bit data i.e. 1 byte. Hence the total memory capacity of 8086 is 1M byte. However the data bus of 8086 is 16 bit and the processor is capable of processing 16 bit data i.e. words.

The question is how to write a word i.e. 16 bit data into segmented memory.

The answer is that a word is written into two consecutive memory addresses. That means the lower byte is writeen into the specified memory address.

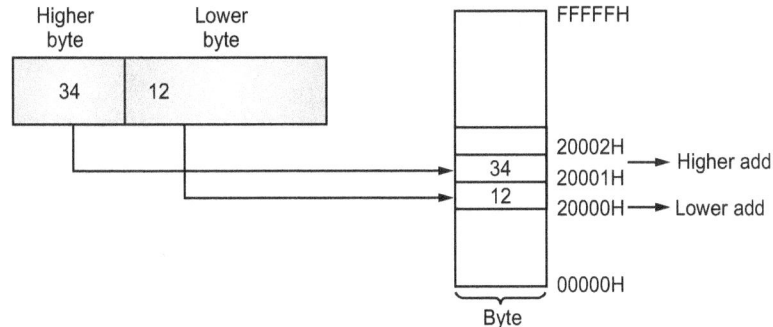

Fig. 2.52 : Data storage in 8086 memory

To read or write a word with one machine cycle; the memory of 8086 is divided into two bank of upto 524, 288 bytes. i.e. 50014 bytes each as shown in Fig. 2.53.

The two memory banks are known as

(1) The even addressed memory bank

(2) The odd addressed memory bank

The even addressed memory bank contains all the bytes which have even addresses such as 00000, 00002, 00004 etc. The odd addressed memory bank, contains all the bytes which have odd addresses such as 00001, 00003, 00005 etc.

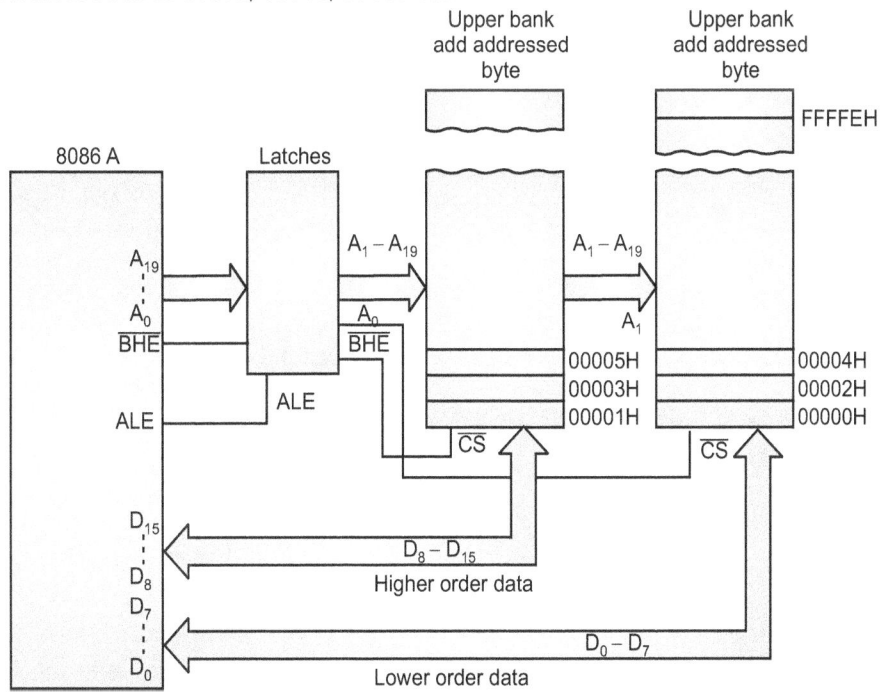

Fig. 2.53 : 8086 Memory Banks Block diagram

- The even addressed bank is also called as lower bank and the data present on the lines $D_0 - D_7$ of 8086.

- The odd addressed bank is also called as the upper bank is also called as the upper bank and the data lines of this bank are D_8-D_{15} of 8086. Address line A_0 is used to enable the lower memory bank and $\overline{BHE}$ BHE is used to enable the higher memory bank.

- Add lines A_1-A_{19} are used for selecting the desired memory address in the lower and upper memory bank.

- ALE signal is used to strobe in the address into the external latch. The same latch stores the $\overline{BHE}$ signal.

Table 2.15 : Signals for the byte and word operations

Add	Data type	$\overline{BHE}$	A_0	Bus Cycle	Data lines
0000	Byte	1	0	one	D_0-D_7
0000	Word	0	0	one	D_0-D_{15}
0001	Byte	0	1	one	D_8-D_{15}
0001	Word	0	1	first	D_0-D_7
		1	0	Second	D_8-$1D_{15}$

(I) Accessing even addressed byte :

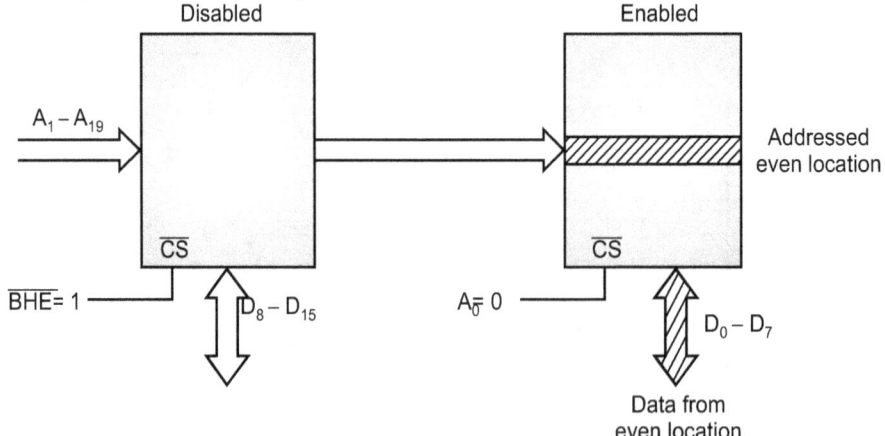

Fig. 2.54 : Accessing an even addressed byte

Fig. 2.54 shows the process to access an even addressed byte.

The 8086 forces A_0 line to low and $\overline{BHE}$ high. This will enable the lower memory bank and disable the higher memory bank. The 8086 outputs the address of the desired even memory location on the address lines A_1 to A_{19}. The data stored at even memory location will appear on D_0-D_7 lines.

(II) Accessing the odd addressed byte : Fig. 2.55 shows the process involved in accessing the odd addressed byte.

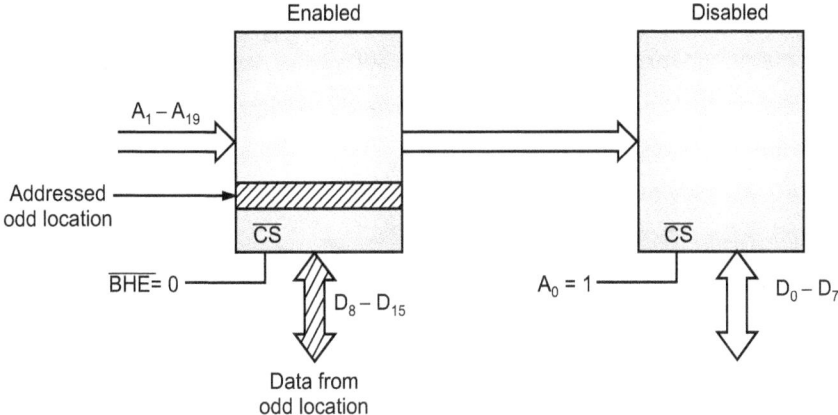

Fig. 2.55 : Accessing an odd addressed byte

The 8086 forces A_0 = 1 (High) and $\overline{BHE}$ = 0 (low). This will disable the lower memory bank and enable the upper memory bank.

The 8086 will output the address of desired memory, location on A_1-A_{19} Address lines.

The data byte from odd location will appear on D_8-D_{15} data lines.

(III) Accessing even addressed word :

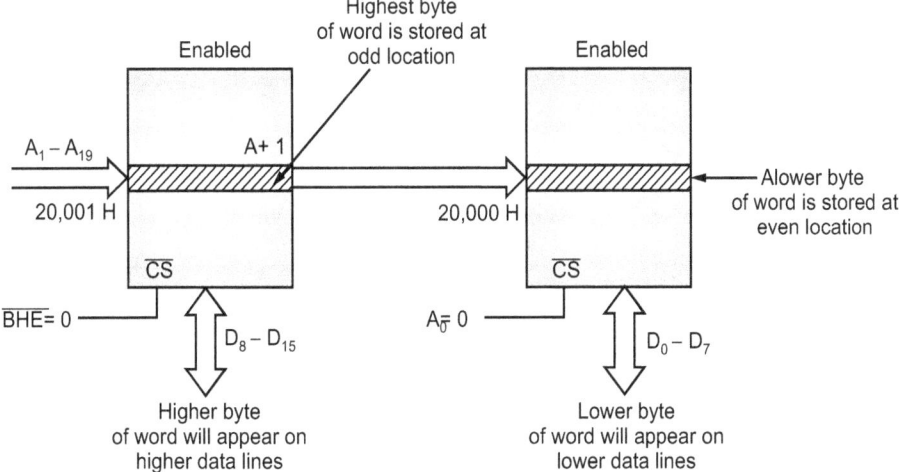

Fig. 2.56 : Accessing an even addressed word

* The lower byte of this word is stored first and the higher byte is stored first and the higher byte is stored at the next higher.

- The lower byte of the word has been stored at the even memory location 20,000 H and the higher byte of the same word has been stored at the next location 20,001 H which is odd location.
- Both the memory banks are enabled because 8086 will force A_0 and $\overline{BHE}$ to low.
- The address on the lines A_1-A_{19} will point towards the locations 20,000 H and 20,001 H simultaneously.
- The lower byte of word will appear on the data lines D_0-D_7 and the higher byte will appear on D_8-D_{15} simultaneously.
- To read a word from even address the 8086 needs only one bus cycle.

(IV) Accessing an odd addressed word :

- To access odd addressed word 8086 required two bus cycles. Because the lower byte is stored at odd address and the upper byte of the word is at even address. Fig. 2.57 shows the situation.

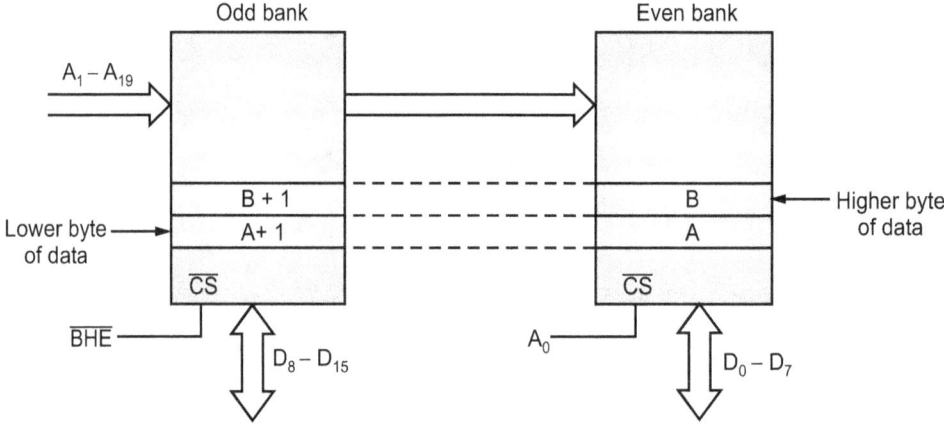

Fig. 2.57 : Accessing odd addressed word

The locations A + 1 and B are not at the same level.

Therefore, the 8086 cannot use the same address for both these locations, A+ 1 and B.

Therefore, for it is not possible for 8086 to read all 16 bits of word at same time.

Hence, the 8086 needs two bus cycles to read the 16 bit word. One bus cycle is required to read the contents of locations (A + 1) and other to read the contents of location B.

(a) First bus cycle :

In first cycle the 8086 forces A_0 = 1 and $\overline{BHE}$ = 0 to enable the odd bank.

It then outputs the A_1-A_{19} lines to point to location A + 1.

The contents of A + 1 location will appear on the data lines D_8 – D_{15}.

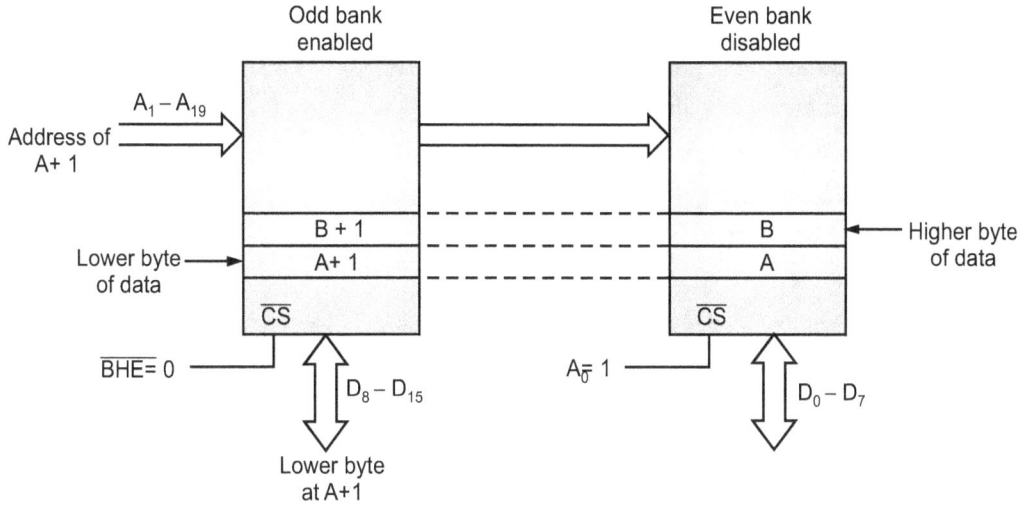

Fig. 2.58 : First bus cycle

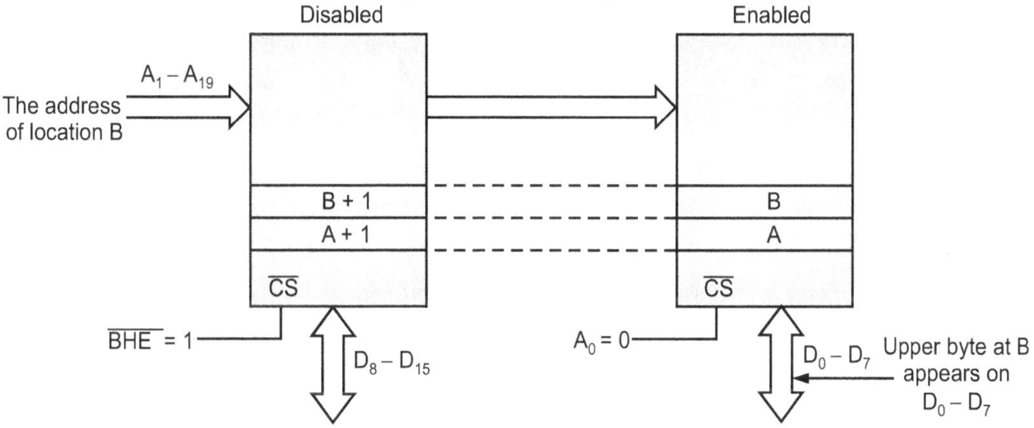

Fig. 2.59 : Second bus cycle

In the second bus cycle the 8086 forces. A_0 = 0 and $\overline{BHE}$ = 1 to enable the lower i.e. even bank.

Then it outputs the new address on the A_1–A_{19} lines to put at location B.

Then the contents of location B will appear on D_0–D_7 data line.

2.17 8086 ADDRESSING MODES

The way in which an operand is specified is called the *Addressing Mode*. Different addressing modes may take different amount of time to compute the effective address.

The x86 instructions use five different operand types : registers, constants, and three memory addressing schemes. Each form is called an addressing mode.

The x86 processors support :

- The register addressing mode.
- The immediate addressing mode.
- The direct addressing mode.
- The indirect addressing mode.
- The base plus index addressing mode.
- The register relative addressing mode.
- The base relative plus index addressing mode.
- The memory addressing mode.

2.17.1 The Register Addressing Mode

Instructions using the registers are shorter and faster than those that access memory.

Most 8086 instructions can operate on the 8086's general purpose register set. By specifying the name of the register as an operand to the instruction, you may access the contents of that register. Consider the 8086 MOV (move) instruction:

      MOV   destination, source

This instruction copies the data from the source operand to the destination operand. The 8 and 16 bit registers are certainly valid operands for this instruction. The only restriction is that both operands must be the same size. Now let's look at some actual 8086 MOV instructions:

      MOV   AX, BX ; Copies the value from BX into AX
      MOV   DL, AL ; Copies the value from AL into DL
      MOV   SI, DX ; Copies the value from DX into SI
      MOV   SP, BP ; Copies the value from BP into SP
      MOV   DH, CL ; Copies the value from CL into DH
      MOV   AX, AX ; Yes, this is legal!

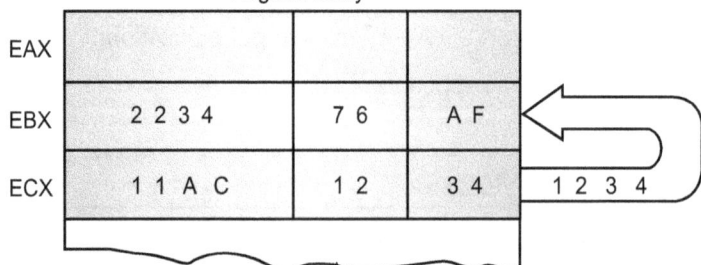

Fig. 2.60 : Register Addressing Mode e.g. MOV BX, CX

You should never use the segment registers as data registers to hold arbitrary values. They should only contain segment addresses.

2.17.2 The Immediate Addressing Mode

The term immediate implies that the data immediately follow the hexadecimal opcode in the memory. Immediate are constant data. The MOV immediate instruction transfers a copy of the immediate data into a register or a memory location

Fig. 2.61 shows the source data (sometimes preceded by #) overwrite the destination data. The instruction copies the 1345H into register AX.

e.g. MOV AX, 1345 H

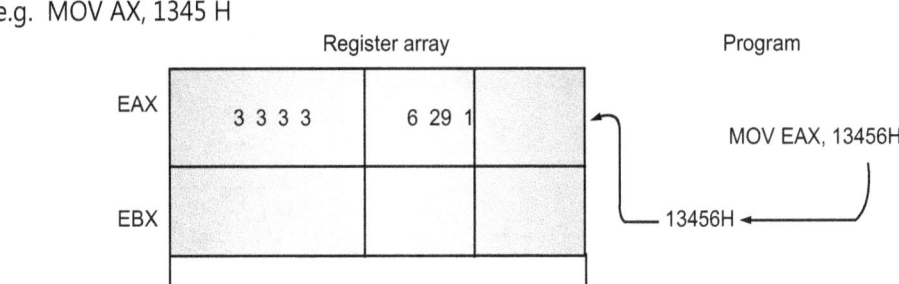

Fig. 2.61 : Immediate Addressing Mode. e.g.MOV EAX,13456H

TYPE	INSTRUCTION	SOURCE	ADDRESS GENERATION	DESTINATION
(1) REGISTER	MOV AX, BX	REGISTER BX		REGISTER AX
(2) IMMEDIATE	MOV CH, 3AH	DATA 3AH		REGISTER CH
(3) DIRECT	MOV (1234],AX	REGISTER AX	(DS x 10H) + DISPLACEMENT 10000H + 1234	MEMORY 11234H
(4) REGISTER INDIRECT	MOV [BX], CL	REGISTER CL	(DS x 10H) + BX 10000H + 0300H	MEMORY 10300H
(5) BASE PLUS INDEX	MOV [BX + SI], BP	REGISTER BP	(DS x 10H) + BX + SI 10000H + 0300H + 0200H	MEMORY 10500H
(6) REGISTER RELATIVE	MOV CL, [BX 44]	MEMORY 10304H	(DS x 10H) + BX + 4 10000H + 0300H + 4	REGISTER CL
(7) BASE RELATIVE PLUS INDEX	MOVARRAY(BX + SI], DX	REGISTER DX	(DS x 10H) +ARRAY+ BX + SI 10000H + 1000H + 0300H + 0200H	MEMORY 11500H

Fig. 2.62 : Addressing modes

2.17.3 The Direct Addressing Mode

The most common addressing mode, and the one that's easiest to understand, is the displacement-only (or direct) addressing mode. The displacement-only addressing mode consists of a 16 bit constant that specifies the address of the target location. The displacement-only addressing mode is perfect for accessing simple variables.

Intel named this the displacement-only addressing mode because a 16 bit constant (displacement) follows the MOV opcode in memory. On the x86, a direct address can be thought of as a displacement from address zero. On the 80x86 processors, this displacement is an offset from the beginning of a segment.

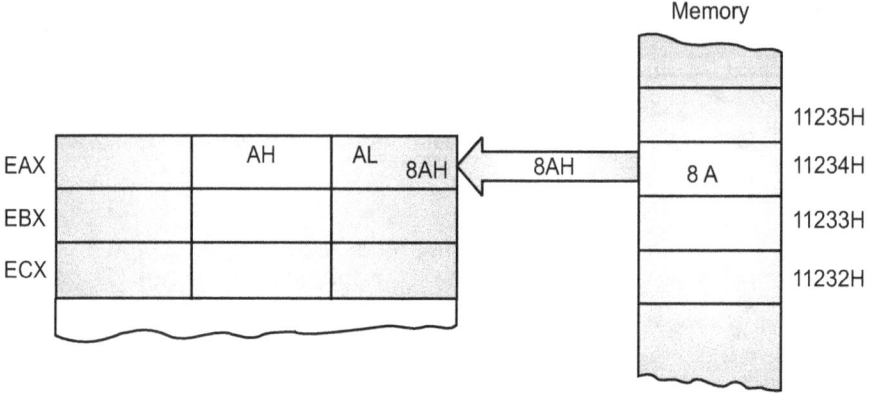

Fig. 2.63 : Direct /Displacement Addressing Mode e.g. MOV AL, [11234H]

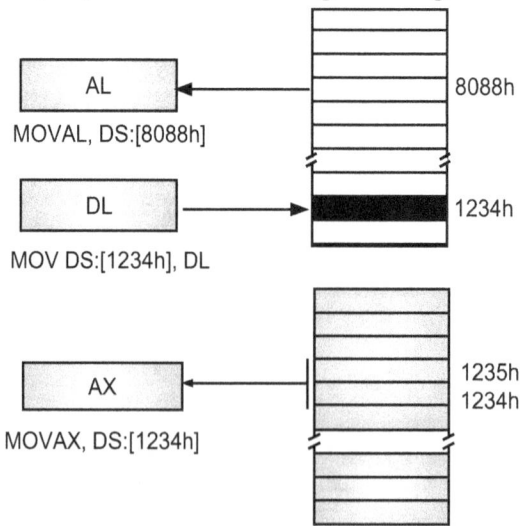

Fig. 2.64 : The direct addressing mode

There are two basic forms of direct data addressing :

*   Direct addressing, which applies to a MOV between a memory location and AL, AX or EAX.

- Displacement addressing, which applies to almost any instruction in the instruction set.

e.g. Dierct Addressing: MOV AL, DATA ; MOV instruction is 3-byte long instruction.

Displacement Addressing: MOV CL, DATA almost identical with direct addressing except that the instruction is four bytes wide.

2.17.4 The Register Indirect Addressing Modes

The 80x86 CPUs let you access memory indirectly through a register using the register indirect addressing modes. There are four forms of this addressing mode on the 8086, best demonstrated by the following instructions:

```
MOV   AL, [BX]
MOV   AL, [BP]
MOV   AL, [SI]
MOV   AL, [DI]
```

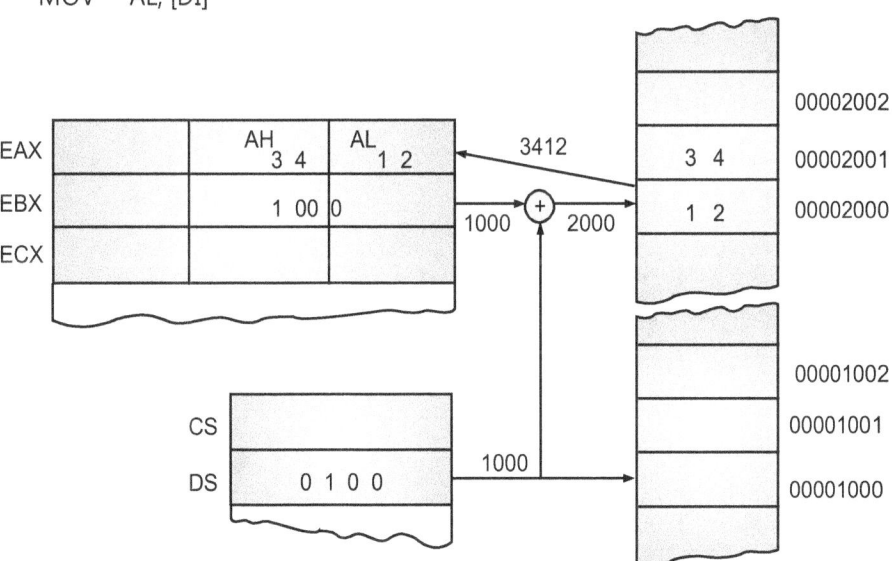

Fig. 2.65 : Register Indirect Addressing Modes

This addressing modes reference the byte at the offset found in the BX, BP, SI, or DI register, respectively. The [BX], [SI], and [DI] modes use the DS segment by default. The [BP] addressing mode uses the stack segment (SS) by default.

You can use the segment override prefix symbols if you wish to access data in different segments. The following instructions demonstrate the use of these

```
MOV   AL, CS:[BX]
MOV   AL, DS:[BP]
```

MOV   AL, SS:[SI]

MOV   AL, ES:[DI]

Fig. 2.65 shows the operation of instruction MOV AX, [BX]   when BX = 1000H and DS = 0100H.

2.17.5 Indexed Addressing Modes

Indexed Addressing mode: address is available in any index register SI, DI

MOV AX, [SI]

2.17.6 Based Indexed Addressing Modes

The based indexed addressing modes are simply combinations of the register indirect addressing modes. These addressing modes form the offset by adding together a base register (BX OR BP) and an index register (SI OR DI). The allowable forms for these addressing modes are

MOV   AL, [BX][SI]

MOV   AL, [BX][DI]

MOV   AL, [BP][SI]

MOV   AL, [BP][DI]

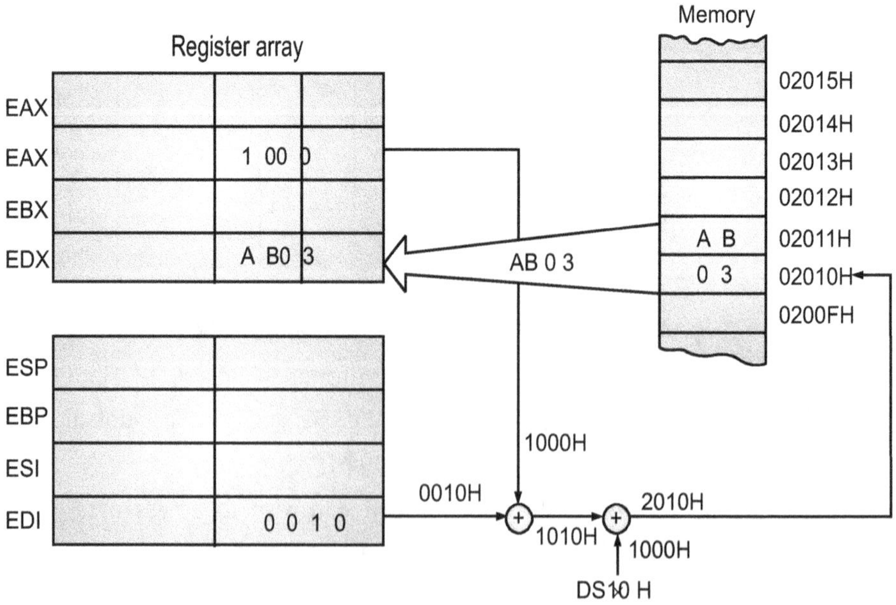

Fig. 2.66 : Based Indexed Addressing Modes

Suppose that BX contains 1000h and SI contains 880h. Then the instruction

     MOV   AL, [BX] [SI]

would load AL from location DS:1880h. Likewise, if BP contains 1598h and DI contains 1004, MOV AX,[BP+DI] will load the 16 bits in AX from locations SS:259C and SS:259D.

The addressing modes that do not involve BP use the data segment by default. Those that have BP as an operand use the stack segment by default.

Fig. 2.66 shows the operation of Instruction MOV DX, [BX+DI]   where DS = 0100H, BX = 1000H and DI=0010H

2.17.7 Register Relative Addressing Mode

In its, the data in a segment of memory are addressed by adding the displacement to the contents of a base ro and index register (BP, BX, DI, or SI)

e.g. MOV AX,[BX+ 1000H]. The displacement can be a number added to the register within the [ ], as in MOV AL,[DI+2], or it can be a displacement substracted from the register, as in MOV AL,[SI-1]. It is possible to address array data with register relative addressing such as one does with base-plus-index addressing. Fig. 2.67 shows the operation of instruction

     MOV AX, [BX+1000H] when BX = 0100H and DS = 0200H

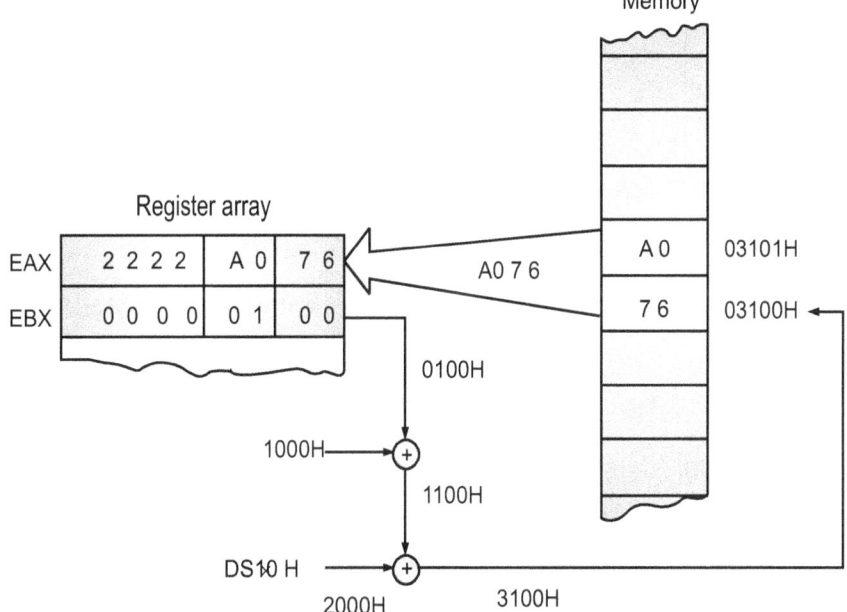

Fig. 2.67 : Register Relative Addressing Mode

2.17.8 Based Indexed Plus Displacement (Relative) Addressing Mode

These addressing modes are a slight modification of the base/indexed addressing modes with the addition of an eight bit or sixteen bit constant. The following are some examples of these addressing modes:

        MOV   AL, DISP[BX][SI]

        MOV   AL, DISP[BX+DI]

        MOV   AL, [BP+SI+DISP]

        MOV   AL, [BP][DI][DISP]

Fig. 2.68 shows the operation of instruction MOV AX, [BX+SI+100H] when DS = 1000H.

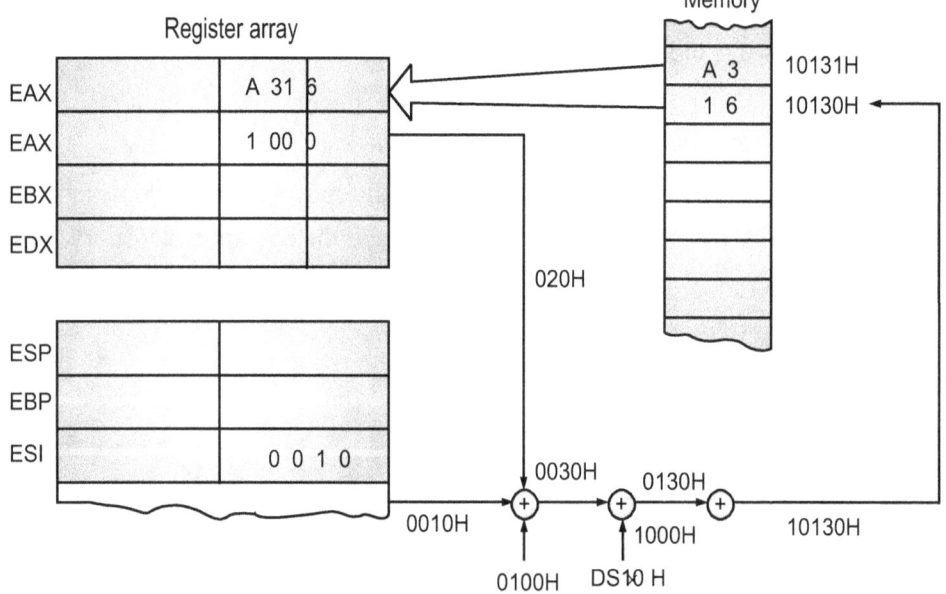

Fig. 2.68 : Based Indexed Plus Displacement Addressing Mode

2.17.9 Memory Addressing Modes

The 8086 provides 17 different ways to access memory. The key to good assembly language programming is the proper use of memory addressing modes.

The addressing modes provided by the 8086 family include displacement-only, base, displacement plus base, base plus indexed, and displacement plus base plus indexed. Variations on these five forms provide the 17 different addressing modes on the 8086.

2.18 INSTRUCTION PIPELING

- Pipelining is used by virtually all modern microprocessors to enhance performance by overlapping the execution of instructions.
- A common analogue for a pipeline is a factory assembly line. Assume that there are three stages:
  - Welding
  - Painting
  - Polishing
- For simplicity, assume that each task takes one hour.
- If a single person has to work on the product it would take three hours to produce one product.
- If we had three people, one person could work on each stage, upon completing their stage they could pass their product on to the next person (since each stage takes one hour there will be no waiting).
- We could then produce one product per hour assuming the assembly line has been filled.

  Instruction Pipelining is a technique used in advanced microprocessors where the microprocessor begins executing a second instruction before the first has been completed. A Pipeline is a series of stages, where some work is done at each stage. The work is not finished until it has passed through all stages.

  With pipelining, the computer architecture allows the next instructions to be fetched while the processor is performing arithmetic operations, holding them in a buffer close to the processor until each instruction operation can perform.

- If the stages of a pipeline are not balanced and one stage is slower than another, the entire throughput of the pipeline is affected.
- In terms of a pipeline within a CPU, each instruction is broken up into different stages. Ideally if each stage is balanced (all stages are ready to start at the same time and take an equal amount of time to execute.) the time taken per instruction (pipelined) is defined as: *Time per instruction (unpipelined) / Number of stages.*

2.18.1   How Pipelines Works

The pipeline is divided into segments and each segment can execute it operation concurrently with the other segments. Once a segment completes an operations, it passes the result to the next segment in the pipeline and fetches the next operations from the preceding segment.

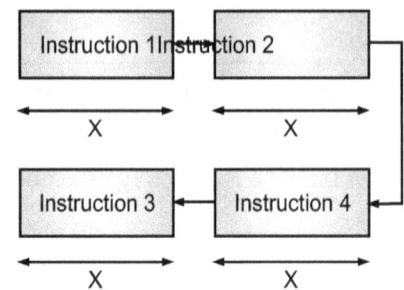

Fig. 2.69 : Four sample instructions, executed linearly

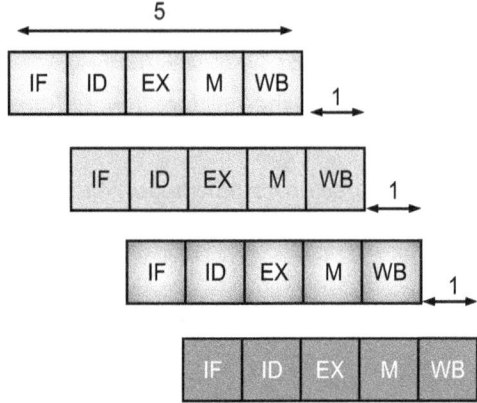

Fig. 2.70 : Four pipelined instructions

(a) The Instruction Fetch (IF) stage is responsible for obtaining the requested instruction from memory. The instruction and the program counter (which is incremented to the next instruction) are stored in the IF/ID pipeline register as temporary storage so that may be used in the next stage at the start of the next clock cycle.

- The value in the PC represents an address in memory. The MIPS64 instructions are all 32-bits in length.
- First we load the 4 bytes in memory into the CPU.

Second we increment the PC by 4 because memory addresses are arranged in byte ordering. This will now represent the next instruction. (Is this certain???)

(b) The Instruction Decode (ID) stage is responsible for decoding the instruction and sending out the various control lines to the other parts of the processor. The instruction is sent to the control unit where it is decoded and the registers are fetched from the register file.

- This stage decodes the instruction and at the same time read in the values of the register involved. As the registers are being read, do equality test incase the instruction decodes as a branch or jump.

- The offset field of the instruction is sign-extended incase it is needed. The possible branch effective address is computed by adding the sign-extended offset to the incremented PC. The branch can be completed at this stage if the equality test is true and the instruction decoded as a branch.
- Instruction can be decoded in parallel with reading the registers because the register addresses are at fixed locations.

(c) The Execution (EX) stage is where any calculations are performed. The main component in this stage is the ALU. The ALU is made up of arithmetic, logic and capabilities.

- If a branch or jump did not occur in the previous cycle, the arithmetic logic unit (ALU) can execute the instruction.
- At this point the instruction falls into three different types :

(a) Memory Reference : ALU adds the base register and the offset to form the effective address.

(b) Register-Register : ALU performs the arithmetic, logical, etc... operation as per the opcode.

(c) Register-Immediate : ALU performs operation based on the register and the immediate value (sign extended).

(d) The Memory and IO (MEM) stage is responsible for storing and loading values to and from memory. It also responsible for input or output from the processor. If the current instruction is not of Memory or IO type than the result from the ALU is passed through to the write back stage.

- If a load, the effective address computed from the previous cycle is referenced and the memory is read. The actual data transfer to the register does not occur until the next cycle.

If a store, the data from the register is written to the effective address in memory.

(e) The Write Back (WB) stage is responsible for writing the result of a calculation, memory access or input into the register file.

- Occurs with Register-Register ALU instructions or load instructions.
- Simple operation whether the operation is a register-register operation or a memory load operation, the resulting data is written to the appropriate register.

2.18.2 Advantages/Disadvantages

Advantages :

- More efficient use of processor.
- Quicker time of execution of large number of instructions.

Disadvantages :

- Pipelining involves adding hardware to the chip.
- Inability to continuously run the pipeline at full speed because of pipeline hazards which disrupt the smooth execution of the pipeline.

2.18.3 Pipeline Hazards

- The performance gain from using pipelining occurs because we can start the execution of a new instruction each clock cycle. In a real implementation this is not always possible.
- Another important note is that in a pipelined processor, a particular instruction still takes at least as long to execute as non-pipelined.
- Pipeline hazards prevent the execution of the next instruction during the appropriate clock cycle.

There are three types of hazards in a pipeline, they are as follows:

1. **Structural Hazards :** Are created when the data path hardware in the pipeline cannot support all of the overlapped instructions in the pipeline. Two instructions need to access the same resource.

2. **Data Hazards :** When there is an instruction in the pipeline that affects the result of another instruction in the pipeline. An instruction uses the result of the previous instruction. A hazard occurs exactly when an instruction tries to read a register in its ID stage that an earlier instruction intends to write in its WB stage.

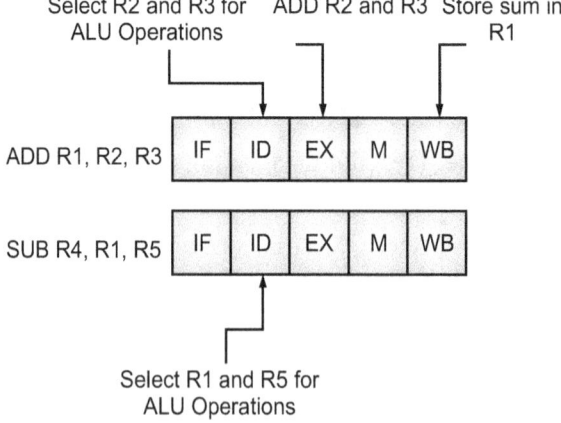

Fig. 2.71 : Data Hazards

3. **Control Hazards :** The PC causes these due to the pipelining of branches and other instructions that change the PC. the location of an instruction depends on previous instruction.

2.18.4 Stalling

Hazards in pipeline can make the pipeline to stall. Eliminating a hazard often requires that some instructions in the pipeline to be allowed to proceed while others are delayed. When an instruction is stalled, instructions issued latter than the stalled instruction are stopped, while the ones issued earlier must continue. No new instructions are fetched during the stall. Stalling involves halting the flow of instructions until the required result is ready to be used. However stalling wastes processor time by doing nothing while waiting for the result.

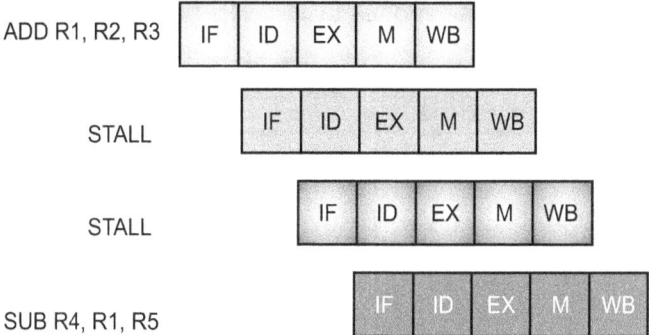

Fig. 2.72 : Instruction Stalling

- Software Pipelining
    (1) Can Handle Complex Instructions.
    (2) Allows programs to be reused.
- Hardware Pipelining
    (1) Help designer manage complexity – a complex task can be divided into smaller, more manageable pieces.
    (2) Hardware pipelining offers higher Performance.

2.18.5 Type of Hardware Pipelines

1. Instruction Pipeline : An instruction pipeline is very similar to a manufacturing assembly line.

- First stage receives some parts, performs its assembly task, and passes the results to the second stage;
- Second stage takes the partially assembled product from the first stage, performs its task, and passes its work to the third stage;
- Third stage does its work, passing the results to the last stage, which completes the task and outputs its results.

Instruction Pipelines Conflict :

It divided into two categories :

- Data Conflicts
- Branch Conflicts
- When the current instruction changes a register that the next one needed, data conflicts happens.
- When the current instruction make a jump, branch conflicts happens.

2. **Data Pipeline** : data pipeline is designed to pass data from stage to stage.

2.19 INSTRUCTION SET OF 8086

8086 instruction set is classified into seven categories :

1. Data Transfer Instruction
2. Arithmetic Instruction
3. Logical Instruction
4. Control Instruction
5. Processor Control Instructions
6. String Manipulation Instruction
7. Interrupt Control Instruction

Table 2.16 : 8086 Instructions

Type	Instruction	Comment
Data Transfer	[1] **MOV**dest, src	Transfers contents from source location destination location. Note that source and destination cannot be memory location. Also source and destination must be same type
	[2] **PUSH** Src	Copies word on stack.
	[3] **POP** dest	Copies word from stack into dest. Reg.
	[4] **IN** acc, port	Copies 8 or 16 bit data from port to accumulator.
		a) Fixed Port
		b) Variable Port
	[5] **OUT**port, acc	Copies 8 or 16 bit data from accumulator to port

	[6] **LES** Reg, Mem	Load register and extra segment register with words from memory.
	[7] **LDS** Reg, Mem	Load register and data segment register with words from memory
	[8] **LEA**Reg, Src	Load Effective address.
		(Offset is loaded in specified register)
	[9] **LAHF**	Copy lower byte of flag register into AH register.
	[10] **SAHF**	Copy AH register to lower byte of flag
	[11] **XCHG** dest, src	Exchange contains of source and destination.
	[12] **XLAT**	Translate a byte in AL. This instruction replaces the byte in AL with byte pointed by BX.
Arithmetic	[1]**ADD** dest, src	Add source operand to destination operand.
	[2] **ADC** dest, src	Add with carry
	[3] **AAA** : ASCII adjust after addition.	Add two ASCII numbers directly and use AAA after addition so as to get result directly in BCD. (Works with AL only)
	[4] **DAA** : Decimal adjust accumulator.	Adds two decimal numbers and used DAA to get result.
	[5] **SUB** dest, src	Subtract source operand from destination operand.
	[6] **SBB** dest, src	Subtract with borrow.
	[7] **AAS**	ASCII adjust for subtraction
	[8] **DAS**	Decimal adjust after Subtraction.
	[9] **MUL** src	Multiplication of unsigned byte.
	[10] **IMUL** src	Multiplication of signed byte.
	[11] **AAM** : BCD	Adjust after multiply.
	[12] **DIV**src	Division of unsigned numbers.
	[13] **IDIV**	Division of signed numbers

	[14] **AAD**	BCD to Binary convert before Division.
	[15] **DEC**dest	Decrements by 1
	[16] **INC**dest	Increments by 1
	[17] **CWD**:	Convert signed word to signed double word.
	[18] **CBW**	Convert signed byte to signed word
	[19] **NEG** dest	Forms Twos complement.
Logical	[1] **AND** dest, src	Bitwise multiplication of source and destination operand.
	[2] **NOT** dest	Invert each bit in destination
	[3] **OR** dest, src	Bitwise addition of sources and destination operand.
	[4] **XOR** dest, src	Bitwise substraction
	[5] **RCL** dest, count	Rotate left through Carry
	[[6] **RCR** dest, count	Rotate right through carry
	[7] **ROL** dest, count	Rotate left
	[8] **ROR** dest, Count	Rotate right
	[9] **SAL/ SHL** dest, count	Shift left and put 0in LSB.
	[10] **SAR**dest,count	Shift right New MSB = Old MSB
	[11]**SHR**dest,count	Shift right .MSB is filled with 0's.
	[12] **TEST**dest,src:	Compares source and destination operand EX. TEST CX, BX
	[13] **CMP**dest,src	CF, ZF and SF are used Ex .CMP CX,BX
Control Transfer	[1] **CALL** :	Call a procedure
		Two types of calls
		(i) Near Call (Intrasegment)
		(ii) Far Call (Intersegment)
	[2] **RET** :	Return execution from procedure
	[3] **JMP** :	Unconditional Jump to specified destination. Two types near and Far

	[4] **JA / JNBE**:	Jump if above / Jump if not below
		The terms above and below are used when we refer to the magnitude of Unsigned number. Used normally after CMP.
	[5] **JAE / JNB / JNC**	Jump if above or equal/jump if not below
	[6] **JB / JC / JNAE**	Jump if below/carry not above or equal
	[7] **JBE / JNA**	Jump if below and equal / not above
	[8] **JE/ JZ**	Jump if equal / zero.
	[9] **JCXZ**:	Jump if CX is Zero.
	[10] **JG / JNLE**:	Jump if Greater /Jump if not less than or equal. The term greater than or less than is used in connection with two signed numbers.
	[11] **JGE / JNL**:	Jump if grater or equal / not less than
	[12] **JL / JNGE** :	Jump if less / not greater or equal
	[13] **JLE / JNG** :	Jump if less or equal / not greater
	[14] **JNE / JNZ** :	Jump if not equal / not zero
	[15] **JNO** :	Jump if no overflow
	[16] **JNS** :	Jump if no sign
	[17] **JS**	Jump if sign
	[18] **JO**	Jump if overflow
	[19] **JNP / JPO**	Jump if parity
	[20] **JP / JPE**	In all above conditional instructions the destination of jump is in the range of -128 to + 127 bytes from the address after jump.
	[21] **LOOP**	Loop while CX not equal to zero and ZF =0
	[22] **LOOPE/ LOOPZ**	Loop if equal / zero.
	[23] **LOOPNE / LOOPNZ**	Loop if not equal not zero. In all above LOOP instructions the destination of jump is in the range of -128 to + 127 bytes from the address after LOOP.
Processor Control	[1] **CLC**	Clear Carry flag.

Instructions		
	[2] **STC**	Set carry Flag
	[3] **CMC**	Complement Carry Flag
	[4] **CLD**	Clear Direction Flag
	[5] **STD**	Set Direction Flag
	[6] **CLI**	Clear Interrupt Flag.
	[7] **STI**	Set Interrupt Flag.
	[8] **HLT**	Halt Processing.
	[9] **NOP**	No Operation
	[10] **ESC**	Executed by Co-processors and actions are performed according to 6 bit coding in the instruction.
	[11] **LOCK**	Assert bus lock Signal This is prefix instruction.
String Manipulation	[12] **WAIT**	Wait for test or Interrupt Signal. Assert wait states.
	[1] **MOVS/ MOVSB/ MOVSW**	This instruction moves data byte or word from location in DS to location in ES.
	[2] **REP / REPE / REPZ / REPNE / REPNZ**	Repeat string instructions until specified conditions exist. This is prefix instruction
	[3] **CMPS / CMPSB / CMPSW**	Compare string bytes or string words. Scan a string byte or string word.
	[4] **SCAS / SCASB / SCASW**	Compares byte in AL or word in AX. String address is to be loaded in DI.
	[5] **STOS / STOSB / STOSW**	Store byte or word in a string. Copies a byte or word in AL or AX to memory location pointed by DI.
	[6] **LODS / LODSB /LODSW**	Load a byte or word in AL or AX. Copies byte or word from memory location pointed by SI into AL or AX register
Interrupt Control	[1] **INT** Type	Interrupt
	[2] **INTO**	Interrupt on overflow
	[3] **IRET**	Interrupt return

Along with this instruction set let's discuss some instructions.

1. ADC   Add with carry flag

Syntax :

         ADC   DEST, SRC

         DEST: memory or register

         SRC: memory, register, or immediate

Action : DEST = DEST + SRC + CF

Flags Affected: OF, SF, ZF, AF, PF, CF

Notes : This instruction is used to perform 32-bit addition.

2. ADD   Add two numbers

Syntax :

         ADD   DEST, SRC

         DEST : register or memory

         SRC : register, memory, or immediate

Action : DEST = DEST + SRC

Flags Affected: OF, SF, ZF, AF, PF, CF

Notes : Works for both signed and unsigned numbers.

3. AND   Bitwise logical AND

Syntax :

         AND   DEST, SRC

         DEST : register or memory

         SRC : register, memory, or immediate

Action : DEST = DEST & SRC

Flags Affected : OF=0, SF, ZF, AF=?, PF, CF=0

4. CALL   Call procedure or function

Syntax :

         CALL   ADDRESS

         ADDRESS : register, memory or immediate

Action : Push IP onto stack, set IP to ADDRESS

Flags Affected: None

5. CBW   Convert byte to word (signed)

Syntax :

         CBW

Action : Sign extend AL to create a word in AX.

Flags Affected : None

Notes : For unsigned numbers use "MOV AH, 0".

6. CLI   Clear interrupt flag (disable interrupts)

Syntax :

Cli

Action : Clear IF

Flags Affected : IF=0

7. CMP Compare two operands

Syntax :

CMP OP1, OP2

OP1 : register or memory

OP2 : register, memory, or immediate

Action : Perform OP1-OP2, discarding the result but setting the flags.

Flags Affected : OF, SF, ZF, AF, PF, CF

Notes : Usually used before a conditional jump instruction.

8. CWD Convert word to doubleword (signed)

Syntax :

CWD

Action : Sign extend AX to fill DX, creating a dword contained in DX::AX.

Flags Affected : None

Notes : For unsigned numbers use "XOR DX, DX" to clear DX.

9. DEC   Decrement by 1

Syntax :

DEC   OP

OP: register or memory

Action: OP = OP - 1

Flags Affected: OF, SF, ZF, AF, PF

10.   DIV   Unsigned divide

Syntax :

DIV   OP8

DIV   OP16

OP8 : 8-bit register or memory

OP16: 16-bit register or memory

Action : If operand is OP8, unsigned AL = AX / OP8 and AH = AX % OP8

If operand is OP16, unsigned AX = DX::AX / op16 and DX = DX::AX % OP16

Flags Affected: OF=?, SF=?, ZF=?, AF=?, PF=?, CF=?

Notes : Performs both division and modulus operations in one instruction.

11. IDIV Signed divide

Syntax :

IDIV   OP8

IDIV   OP16

OP8: 8-bit register or memory

OP16: 16-bit register or memory

Action : If operand is OP8, signed AL = AX / OP8 and AH = AX % OP8

If operand is op16, signed AX = DX::AX / op16 and DX = DX::AX % OP16

Flags Affected: OF=?, SF=?, ZF=?, AF=?, PF=?, CF=?

Notes : Performs both division and modulus operations in one instruction.

12. IMUL   Signed multiply

Syntax :

IMUL   OP8

IMUL   OP16

OP8 : 8-bit register or memory

OP16: 16-bit register or memory

Action: If operand is OP 8, signed AX = AL * OP 8

If operand is OP 16, signed DX::AX = AX * OP 16

Flags Affected: OF, SF=?, ZF=?, AF=?, PF=?, CF

13. IN Input (read) from port

Syntax :

IN   AL, OP 8

IN   AX, OP 8

OP 8: 8-bit immediate or DX

Action: If destination is AL, read byte from 8-bit port OP 8.

If destination is AX, read word from 16-bit port OP 8

Flags Affected: None

14. INC   Increment by 1

Syntax :

INC   OP

OP : register or memory

Action : OP = OP + 1

Flags Affected: OF, SF, ZF, AF, PF

15. INT   Call to interrupt procedure

Syntax :

INT   imm8

imm8: 8-bit unsigned immediate

Action : Push flags, CS, and IP; clear IF and TF (disabling interrupts); load word at address (imm8*4) into IP and word at (imm8*4 + 2) into CS.

Flags Affected: IF=0, TF=0

Notes : This instruction is usually used to call system routines.

16. IRET   Interrupt return

Syntax :

IRET

Action: Pop IP, CS, and flags (in that order).

Flags Affected: All

Notes : This instruction is used at the end of ISRs.

17. J?? Jump if ?? condition met

Syntax :

J??   REL8

rel8: 8-bit signed immediate

Action: If condition ?? met, IP = IP + REL8 (sign extends REL8)

Flags Affected: None

Notes : Use the cmp instruction to compare two operands then j?? to jump conditionally. The ?? of the instruction name represents the jump condition, allowing for the following instructions :

JA   jump if above, unsigned >

JAE   jump if above or equal, unsigned >=

JB   jump if below, unsigned <

JBE   jump if below or equal, unsigned <=

JE   jump if equal, ==

JNE   jump if not equal, !=

JG   jump if greater than, signed >

JGE   jump if greater than or equal, signed > =

JL   jump if less than, signed <

JLE   jump if less than or equal, signed <=

All of the ?? suffixes can also be of the form n?? (e.g., jna for jump if not above). An assembler label should be used in place of the REL8 operand. The assembler will then calculate the relative distance to jump.

Note also that REL8 operand greatly limits conditional jump distance (−127 to +128 bytes from IP). Use the jmp instruction in combination with j?? to overcome this barrier.

18. JMP   Unconditional jump

Syntax :

JMP   REL

JMP   OP16

JMP   SEG:OFF

REL: 8 or 16-bit signed immediate

OP16 : 16-bit register or memory

SEG:OFF : Immediate 16-bit segment and 16-bit offset

Action : If operand is REL, IP = IP + REL

If operand is OP16, IP = OP16

If operand is SEG:OFF, CS = seg, IP = off

Flags Affected: None

Notes : An assembler label should be used in place of the REL8 operand. The assembler will then calculate the relative distance to jump.

19. LEA   Load effective address offset

Syntax :

LEA REG16, MEMREF

REG16: 16-bit register

memref: An effective memory address (e.g., [bx+2])

Action : REG16 = address offset of memref

Flags Affected: None

Notes : This instruction is used to easily calculate the address of data in memory.

It does not actually access memory.

20. MOV   Move data

Syntax :

MOV   DEST, SRC

DEST: register or memory

SRC: register, memory, or immediate

Action: DEST = SRC

Flags Affected: None

21. MUL Unsigned multiply

Syntax :

MUL   OP8

MUL   OP16

OP8: 8-bit register or memory

OP 16: 16-bit register or memory

Action : If operand is OP 8, unsigned AX = AL * OP 8

If operand is OP 16, unsigned DX::AX = AX * OP 16

Flags Affected: OF, SF=?, ZF=?, AF=?, PF=?, CF

22. NEG Two's complement negate

Syntax :

NEG   OP

OP : register or memory

Action: OP = 0 - op

Flags Affected : OF, SF, ZF, AF, PF, CF

23. NOP No operation

Syntax :

NOP

Action: None

Flags Affected: None

24. NOT   One's complement negate

Syntax :

NOT   OP

OP : register or memory

Action: OP = ~OP

Flags Affected: None

25. OR   Bitwise logical OR

Syntax :

OR   DEST, SRC

DEST : register or memory

SRC: register, memory, or immediate

Action : DEST = DEST | SRC

Flags Affected: OF=0, SF, ZF, AF=?, PF, CF=0

26. OUT Output (write) to port

Syntax :

OUT OP, AL

OUT OP, AX

OP : 8-bit immediate or DX

Action: If source is AL, write byte in AL to 8-bit port op.

If source is AX, write word in AX to 16-bit port op.

Flags Affected: None

27. POP Pop word from stack

Syntax :

POP OP16

REG16 : 16-bit register or memory

Action : POP word off the stack and place it in OP16 (i.e., OP16 = [SS:SP] then SP = SP + 2).

Flags Affected : None

Notes : Pushing and popping of SS and SP are allowed but strongly discouraged.

28. POPF Pop flags from stack

Syntax :

POPF

Action: Pop word from stack and place it in flags register.

Flags Affected: All

29. PUSH   Push word onto stack

Syntax :

PUSH   OP16

OP16 : 16-bit register or memory

Action : PUSH OP16 onto the stack (i.e., SP = SP - 2 then [SS:SP] = OP16).

Flags Affected: None

Notes : Pushing and popping of SS and SP are allowed but strongly discouraged.

30. PUSHF   Push flags onto stack

Syntax :

PUSHF

Action: Push flags onto stack as a word.

Flags Affected: None

31. RET   Return from procedure or function

Syntax :

RET

Action : Pop word from stack and place it in IP.

Flags Affected: None

32. SAL   Bitwise arithmetic left shift (same as shl)

Syntax :

SALOP, 1

SALOP, CL

OP : register or memory

Action: If operand is 1, OP = OP << 1

If operand is CL, OP = OP << CL

Flags Affected: OF, SF, ZF, AF=?, PF, CF

33. SAR   Bitwise arithmetic right shift (signed)

Syntax :

SAR   OP, 1

SAR   OP, CL

op: register or memory

Action : If operand is 1, signed op = op >> 1 (sign extends op)

If operand is CL, signed op = op >> CL (sign extends op)

Flags Affected: OF, SF, ZF, AF=?, PF, CF

34. SBB   Subtract with borrow

Syntax :

SBB   DEST, SRC

DEST : register or memory

SRC : register, memory, or immediate

Action : DEST = DEST – (SRC + CF)

Flags Affected: OF, SF, ZF, AF, PF, CF

Notes : This instruction is used to perform 32-bit subtraction.

35. SHL   Bitwise left shift (same as sal)

Syntax :

SHL   OP, 1

SHL   OP, CL

OP : register or memory

Action : If operand is 1, OP = OP << 1

If operand is CL, OP = OP << CL

Flags Affected: OF, SF, ZF, AF=?, PF, CF

36. SHR   Bitwise right shift (unsigned)

Syntax :

SHR   OP, 1

SHR   OP, CL

op : register or memory

Action : If operand is 1, OP = (unsigned)OP >> 1

If operand is CL, OP = (unsigned)OP >> CL

Flags Affected: OF, SF, ZF, AF=?, PF, CF

37. STI   Set interrupt flag (enable interrupts)

Syntax :

STI

Action: Set IF

Flags Affected: IF=1

38. SUB   Subtract two numbers

Syntax :

SUB   DEST, SRC

DEST : regsiter or memory

SRC : register, memory, or immediate

Action : DEST = DEST - SRC

Flags Affected: OF, SF, ZF, AF, PF, CF

Notes : Works for both signed and unsigned numbers.

39. TEST Bitwise logical compare

Syntax :

TEST OP1, OP2

OP1: register, memory, or immediate

OP2: register, memory, or immediate

Action : Perform OP1 & OP2, discarding the result but setting the flags.

Flags Affected: OF=0, SF, ZF, AF=?, PF, CF=0

Notes : This instruction is used to test if bits of a value are set.

40. XOR   Bitwise logical XOR

Syntax :

XOR   DEST, SRC

DEST : register or memory

SRC : register, memory, or immediate

Action: DEST = DEST ^ SRC

Flags Affected: OF=0, SF, ZF, AF=?, PF, CF=0

2.20 INTRODUCTION TO 8086 ASSEMBLY LANGUAGE PROGRAMMING

The 8086 microprocessor is one of the family of 8086, 80286, 80386, 80486, Pentium, Pentium I, II, III ....also referred to as the X86 family.

Learning any imperative programming language involves concepts:

- **Variables :** declaration/definition
- **Assignment :** assigning values to variables
- **Input/Output :** displaying messages, displaying variable values
- **Control flow :** if-then Loops
- **Subprograms :** Definition and Usage

Programming in assembly language involves the same concepts and a few other issues.

- **Variables**

Are considered as registers. The 8086 has 14 registers. Each of these is a 16-bit register.Initially, we will use four of them –so called the general purpose registers:

AX, BX, CX, DX

These four 16-bit registers can also be treated as eight 8-bit registers:

AH, AL, BH, BL, CH, CL, DH, DL

- **Assignment**

In Java, assignment takes the form:

x = 42;

y = 24;

z = x + y;

In assembly language we carry out the same operation but we use an instruction to denote the assignment operator ("=" in Java). The above assignments would be carried out in 8086 assembly langauge as follows

MOV X, 42

MOV Y, 24

ADD Z, X

ADD Z, Y

The **mov** instruction carries out assignment.It which allows us place a number in a register or in a memory location (a variable) i.e. it assigns a value to a register or variable.

Example: Store the ASCII code for the letter A in register bx.

MOV BX, 'A'

The mov instruction also allows you to copy the contents of one register into another register.

Example:

MOV BX, 2

MOV CX, BX

The first instruction loads the value 2 into bx where it is stored as a binary number. [a number such as 2 is called an integer constant.] The MOV instruction takes two operands, representing the destination where data is to be placed and the source of that data.

General Form of Mov Instruction

mov destination, source

where destination must be either a register or memory location and source may be a constant, another register or a memory location.

Note : The comma is essential. It is used to separate the two operands.

A missing comma is a common syntax error.

- **Comments**

Anything that follows semi-colon (;) is ignored by the assembler. It is called a **comment**. Comments are used to

- **Implementing a loop :**

The **JMP** instruction

LABEL_X: ADD   AX,   2

            ADD   BX,   3

            JMP   LABEL_X

The jmp instruction causes the program to start executing from the position in the program indicated by the label Label_X. This is an example of an endless loop. We could implement a while loop using a conditional jump instruction such as JL which means jumi-if-less-than. It is used in combination with a comparision instruction – CMP.

            MOV   AX,   0

LABEL_X :   ADD   AX,   2

            ADD   BX,   3

            CMP   AX,   10

            JL LABEL_X

The above loop continues while the value of ax is less than 10. The CMP instruction compares AX to 0 and records the result. The JL instruction uses this result to determine whether to jump to the point indicated by LABEL_X.

- **Complete Programming :**

We will write a complete 8086 program. You must use an **editor** to enter the program into a file. The process of using the editor (**editing**) is a basic form of word processing. We use Microsoft's MASM and LINK programs for assembling and linking 8086 assembly language programs. MASM program files should have names with the **extension** (3 characters after period) **asm**. We will call our first program *prog1.asm*, it displays the letter 'a' on the screen. Having entered and saved the program using an editor, you must then use the MASM and LINK commands to translate it to machine code so that it may be executed as follows:

C> **masm** prog1

If you have syntax errors, you will get error messages at this point. You then have to edit your program, correct them and repeat the above command, otherwise proceed to the link command, pressing Return in response to prompts for file names from masm or link.

H:\> **link** prog1

To execute the program, simply enter the program name and press the Return key:

H:\> prog1

a

H:\>

Example : Write a program to display the letter 'a' on the screen

```
; PROG1.ASM: DISPLAYS THE CHARACTER 'A' ON THE SCREEN
      .MODEL SMALL
      .STACK 100H
      .CODE
START:
      MOV  DL,  'A'         ; STORE ASCII CODE OF 'A' IN DL
      MOV  AH,  2H          ; MS-DOS CHARACTER OUTPUT FUNCTION
      INT  21H              ; DISPLAYS CHARACTER IN DL REGISTER
      MOV  AX,  4C00H       ; RETURN TO MS-DOS
      INT  21H
END START
```

The first three lines of the program are comments to give the name of the file containing the program, explain its purpose, give the name of the author and the date the program was written. The first two are directives, **.model** and **.stack**. They are concerned with how your program will be stored in memory and how large a stack it requires. The third directive, **.code**, indicates where the program instructions (i.e. the program code) begin.

You must also specify where your program starts, i.e. which is the **first** instruction to be executed. This is the purpose of the label, **start**. You could use any label, e.g. begin in place of start.

This same label is also used by the **end** directive.

When a program has finished, we return to the operating system. Like carrying out an I/O operation, this is also accomplished by using the int instruction. This time MS-DOS subprogram number **4c00h** is used. It is the subprogram to terminate a program and return to MSDOS.

Hence, the instructions:

        MOV AX, 4C00H   ; Code for return to MS-DOS
        INT   21H   ; Terminates program

terminate a program and return you to MS-DOS.

Assembler Directives

Assembler directives are preprocessor directives which are used to tell the assembler to perform the specified operation. Following are some of the assembler directive.

- **ASSUME :** Used to tell assembler the name of logical segment. Ex. ASSUME CS: Code here
- **EXTRN :** Tells the assembler that the names or labels following this directive is in some other assembly module
- **SHORT :** Operator that tells assembler about short displacement.
- **EVEN :** Align on even memory address.
- **DD :** Define Double Word.
- **DQ :** Define Quad Word.
- **DT :** Define Ten Bytes.
- **PROC :** Procedure PROC DELAY NEAR.
- **PUBLIC :** Links modules together.
- **INCLUDE :** Include source code from file.
- **NAME :** To give specific name to module.

- **GROUP :** Grouping of logical segments.
- **TYPE :** Type of variable whether byte or word.
- **END , ENDP, ENDS**
- **EQU, ORG , OFFSET**
- **DB, DW**
- PTR Pointer, **LABEL , SEGMENT**

THE FORM OF AN ASSEMBLY LANGUAGE PROGRAM

NOTE : USING SIMPLIFIED SEGMENT DEFINITION

```
    .MODEL SMALL
    .STACK 64
    .DATA
DATA1    DB    52H
DATA2    DB    29H
SUM      DB    ?
.CODE
MAIN  PROC   FAR         ;this is the program entry point
      MOV    AX,@DATA    ;load the data segment address
      MOV    DS,AX       ;assign value to DS
      MOV    AL,DATA1    ;get the first operand
      MOV    BL,DATA2    ;get the second operand
      ADD    AL,BL       ;add the operands
      MOV    SUM,AL      ;store the result in location SUM
      MOV    AH,4CH      ;set up to
      INT    21H         ;return to DOS
      MAIN   ENDP
      END    MAIN        ;this is the program exit point
```

2.21 8086 INTERRUPT STRUCTURE

Computer Interrupt is a signal indicating that an event, needing immediate attention. An interrupt is an external event which informs the CPU that a device needs its service.

Interrupts are useful when interfacing I/O devices at relatively low data transfer rates, such as keyboard inputs. Interrupt processing allows the processor to execute other software while the keyboard operator is thinking about what to type next. When a key is pressed, the keyboard encoder debounces the switch and puts out one pulse that interrupts the microprocessor.

- **Types of Interrupts :**

There are two main types of interrupts in the 8086 microprocessor, **internal and external interrupts**. External interrupts occur when a peripheral device asserts an interrupt input pin of the microprocessor. Whereas internal interrupts are initiated by the state of the CPU (e.g. divide by zero error) or by an instruction.

(1) External - generated outside the CPU by other hardware

(2) Internal - generated within the CPU as a result of an instruction or operation

X86 has internal interrupts: INT, INTO, Divide Error and Single Step. The internal and external interrupts of X86 comes in the following types:

(1) Hardware Interrupt

(2) Software Interrupt

(3) Processor Interrupt

- Intel processors include two hardware pins (INTR and NMI) that request interrupts...
- And one hardware pin (INTA) to acknowledge the interrupt requested through INTR.
- The processor also has software interrupts INT, INTO, INT 3, and BOUND.
- Flag bits IF (interrupt flag) and TF (trap flag), are also used with the interrupt structure and special return instruction IRET, IRETD in the 80386, 80486, or Pentium.

The 8086/88 microprocessors allow normal program execution to be interrupted by external signals or by special instructions embedded in the program code. When the microprocessor is interrupted, it stops executing the current program and **calls** a procedure which **services** the interrupt. At the end of the **interrupt service routine**, the code execution sequence is returned to the original, interrupted program.

An interrupt can be generated by one of three sources. First, an interrupt can be generated as a result of a processor state violation, called an exception. An example would be a divide-by-zero interrupt produced when the DIV instruction is interpreted to have a zero divisor. Program execution is automatically interrupted and control transferred to an interrupt handler. Conditional interrupts such as this are referred to as internal interrupts.

An interrupt can also be generated by an external device requesting service. This happens when a device signals its request on either the non-maskable interrupt (NMI) or on the INTR interrupts input lines of the processor. The NMI interrupt is generally used to signal the occurrence of a catastrophic event, such as the immanent loss of power. The INTR interrupt is used by all other devices. An interrupt caused by a signal applied to either the NMI or INTR input is referred to as **hardware interrupt**.

Since there is only one INTR input, and multiple devices may have an interrupt capability, an Intel 8259A Programmable Interrupt Controller (PIC) can be used to manage multiple interrupt requests. The PIC receives requests from peripheral equipment, decides which request has the highest priority and issues an interrupt request to the CPU.

Finally, interrupts may be generated as a result of executing the INT instruction. This is referred to as **software interrupt**.

- In 8086/8088 there are a total of 256 interrupts: INT 00, INT 01,..., INT FF.
- When an interrupt is executed, the microprocessor automatically saves
    - Flag register
    - Instruction pointer
    - Code segment register
- On the stack and goes to a fixed memory location

2.21.1 Interrupt Vector Table

- Interrupt vectors and the vector table are crucial to an understanding of hardware and software interrupts.
- The **interrupt vector table** is located in the first 1024 bytes of memory at addresses 000000H–0003FFH.
    - Contains 256 different four-byte interrupt vectors.
    - An interrupt vector contains the address (segment and offset) of the interrupt service procedure.
    - The first five interrupt vectors are identical in all Intel processors.
    - Intel reserves the first 32 interrupt vectors.
    - The last 224 vectors are user-available.
    - Each is four bytes long in real mode and contains the starting address of the interrupt service procedure.
    - The first two bytes contain the offset address.
    - The last two contain the segment address.

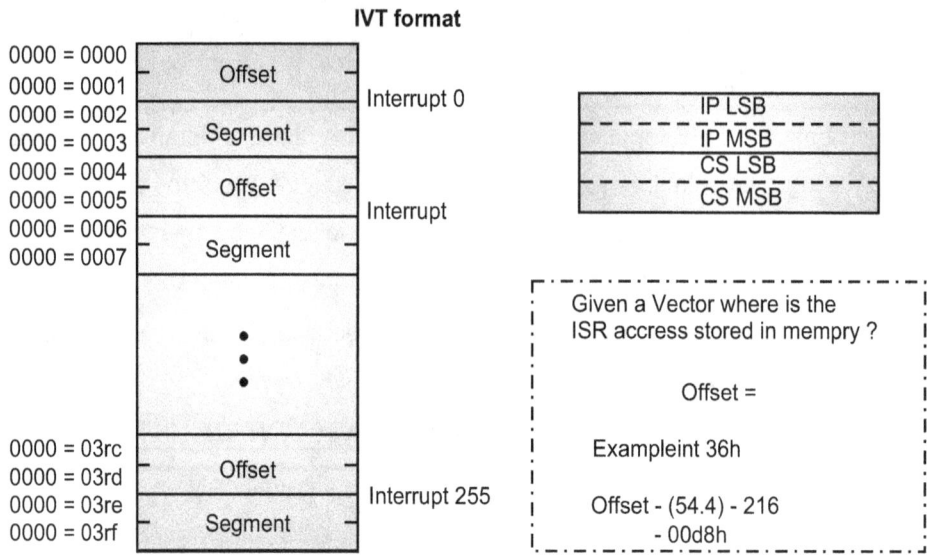

Fig. 2.73 : IVT format

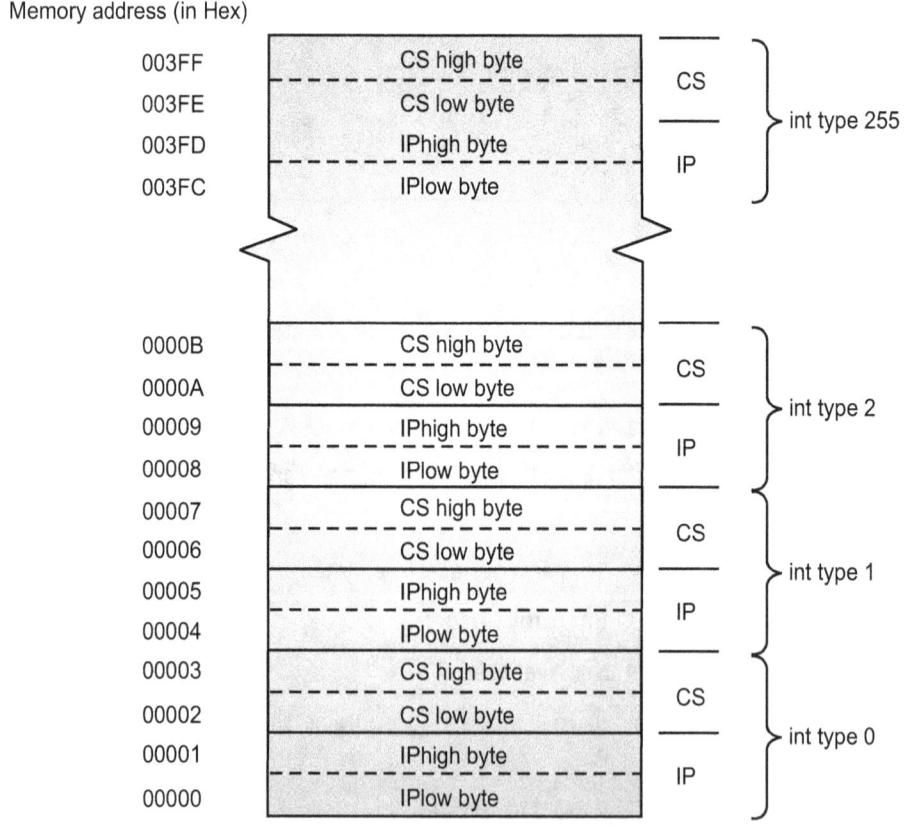

Fig. 2.74 : Interrupt vector table

256 Interrupts of 8086 are Divided into three groups :

- Type 0 to type 4 interrupts : These are used for fixed operations and hence are called **dedicated interrupts.**
- Type 5 to type 31 interrupts not used by 8086, **reserved** for higher processors like 80286, 80386 etc.
- Type 32 to 255 interrupts available for user, called **user defined interrupts** these can be h/w interrupts and activated through intr line or can be s/w interrupts

(a) Dedicated Interrupts :

Type 0 : divide error interrupt occurs whenever the result from a division overflows or an attempt is made to divide by zero that is quotient is large can't be fit in AL/AX or divide by zero

Type 1 : single step interrupt used for executing the program in single step mode by setting trap flag to set trap flag. Single-step or trap occurs after execution of each instruction if the trap (TF) flag bit is set. Upon accepting this interrupt, TF bit is cleared.

Type 2 : non-maskable interrupt occurs when a logic 1 is placed on the NMI input pin to the microprocessor.

- non-maskable-it cannot be disabled

Type 3 : break point interrupt used for providing break points in the program.

A special one-byte instruction (INT 3) that uses this vector to access its interrupt-service procedure.

Type 4 : over flow interrupt used to handle any overflow error after signed arithmetic. Overflow is a special vector used with the INTO instruction. The INTO instruction interrupts the program if an overflow condition exists.

(b) Intel Reserved Interrupts :

Type 5 : The **BOUND** instruction compares a register with boundaries stored in the memory. If the contents of the register are greater than or equal to the first word in memory and less than or equal to the second word, no interrupt occurs because the contents of the register are within bounds.

- if the contents of the register are out of bounds,a type 5 interrupt ensues

Type 6 : An **invalid opcode** interrupt occurs when an undefined opcode is encountered in a program.

Type 7 : The **coprocessor not available** interrupt occurs when a coprocessor is not found, as dictated by the machine status word (MSW or CR0) coprocessor control bits.

- if an ESC or WAIT instruction executes and no coprocessor is found, a type 7 exception or interrupt occurs

Type 8 : A **double fault** interrupt is activated when two separate interrupts occur during the same instruction.

Type 9 : The **coprocessor segment overrun** occurs if the ESC instruction (coprocessor opcode) memory operand extends beyond offset address FFFFH in real mode.

Type 10 : An **invalid task state** segment interrupt occurs in the protected mode if the TSS is invalid because the segment limit field is not 002BH or higher.

- usually because the TSS is not initialized

Type 11 : The **segment not present** interrupt occurs when the protected mode P bit (P = 0) in a descriptor indicates that the segment is not present or not valid.

Type 12 : A **stack segment overrun** occurs if the stack segment is not present (P = 0) in the protected mode or if the limit of the stack segment is exceeded

Type 13 : The **general protection fault** occurs for most protection violations in 80286–Core2 in protected mode system.

Type 14 : Page fault interrupts occur for any page fault memory or code access in 80386, 80486, and Pentium–Core2 processors.

Type 16 : Coprocessor error takes effect when a coprocessor error (ERROR = 0) occurs for ESCape or WAIT instructions for 80386, 80486, and Pentium–Core2 only.

Type 17 : Alignment checks indicate word and doubleword data are addressed at
an odd memory location (or incorrect location, in the case of a doubleword).

- interrupt is active in 80486 and Pentium–Core2

Type 18 : A machine check activates a system memory management mode interrupt in Pentium–Core2

These interrupts may be -

1. Edge or Level sensitive Interrupts :

- Edge level interrupts are recognized on the falling or rising edge of the input signal. They are generally used for high priority interrupts and are latched internally inside the processor. If this latching was not done, the processor could easily miss the falling edge (due to its short duration) and thus not respond to the interrupt request.
- Level sensitive interrupts overcome the problem of latching, in that the requesting device holds the interrupt line at a specified logic state (normally logic zero) till the processor acknowledges the interrupt. This type of interrupt can be shared by other

devices in a wired 'OR' configuration, which is commonly used to support daisy chaining and other techniques.

- The interrupt request input (INTR) is level-sensitive, which means that it must be held at a logic 1 level until it is recognized.
    - INTR is set by an external event and cleared inside the interrupt service procedure
    - INTR is automatically disabled once accepted.
    - re-enabled by IRET at the end of the interrupt service procedure.

2. Maskable Interrupts :

The processor can inhibit certain types of interrupts by use of a special interrupt mask bit. This mask bit is part of the flags/condition code register, or a special interrupt register. In the 8086 microprocessor if this bit is clear, and an interrupt request occurs on the Interrupt Request input, it is ignored.

3. Non-Maskable Interrupts :

There are some interrupts which cannot be masked out or ignored by the processor. These are associated with high priority tasks which cannot be ignored (like memory parity or bus faults). In general, most processors support the Non-Maskable Interrupt (NMI). This interrupt has absolute priority, and when it occurs, the processor will finish the current memory cycle, and then branch to a special routine written to handle the interrupt request.

The **non-maskable interrupt** (NMI) is an edge-triggered input that requests an interrupt on the positive edge (0-to-1 transition).

- After a positive edge, the NMI pin must remain logic 1 until recognized by the microprocessor.
- Before the positive edge is recognized, NMI pin must be logic 0 for at least two clocking periods.
- The NMI input is often used for parity errors and other major faults, such as power failures.

Power failures are easily detected by monitoring the AC power line and causing an NMI interrupt whenever AC power drops out.

2.21.2 Advantages of Interrupts

Interrupts are used to ensure adequate service response times by the processing. Sometimes, with software polling routines, service times by the processor cannot be guaranteed, and data may be lost. The use of interrupts guarantees that the processor will service the request within a specified time period, reducing the likelihood of lost data.

2.21.3 The Operation of an Interrupt Sequence on the 8086 Microprocessor

1. External interface sends an interrupt signal, to the Interrupt Request (INTR) pin, or an internal interrupt occurs.

2. The CPU finishes the present instruction (for a hardware interrupt) and sends Interrupt Acknowledge (INTA) to hardware interface.

3. The interrupt type N is sent to the Central Processor Unit (CPU) via the Data bus from the hardware interface.

4. The contents of the flag registers are pushed onto the stack.

5. Both the interrupt (IF) and (TF) flags are cleared. This disables the INTR pin and the trap or single-step feature.

6. The contents of the code segment register (CS) are pushed onto the Stack.

7. The contents of the instruction pointer (IP) are pushed onto the Stack.

8. The interrupt vector contents are fetched, from (4 x N) and then placed into the IP and from (4 x N +2) into the CS so that the next instruction executes at the interrupt service procedure addressed by the interrupt vector.

9. While returning from the interrupt-service routine by the Interrupt Return (IRET) instruction, the IP, CS and Flag registers are popped from the Stack and return to their state prior to the interrupt.

MULTIPLE CHOICE QUESTIONS (MCQ's)

1. The load instruction is mostly used to designate a transfer from memory to a processor register known as ......

   (a) accumulator   (b) instruction register
   (c) program counter   (d) memory address register

2. In which addressing mode the operand is given explicitly in the instruction......

   (a) Absolute   (b) Immediate
   (c) Indirect   (d) Direct

3. Assembly language......

   (a) uses alphabetic codes in place of binary numbers used in machine language

   (b) is the easiest language to write programs

   (c) need not be translated into machine language

   (d) none of these

4. When CPU is executing a Program that is part of the Operating System, it is said to be in......

    (a) interrupt mode   (b) system mode

    (c) half mode   (d) simplex mode

5. The communication between the components in a microcomputer takes place via the address and......

    (a) i/o bus   (b) data bus

    (c) address bus   (d) control lines

6. An instruction pipeline can be implemented by means of......

    (a) LIFO buffer   (b) FIFO buffer

    (c) Stack   (d) None of these

7. Data input command is just the opposite of a......

    (a) Test command   (b) Control command

    (c) Data output   (d) Data channel

8. What is the content of Stack Pointer (SP)?

    (a) Address of the current instruction

    (b) Address of the next instruction

    (c) Address of the top element of the stack

    (d) Size of the stack.

9. Which of the following interrupt is non-maskable ?

    (a) INTR   (b) RST 7.5

    (c) RST 6.5   (d) TRAP

10. Which of the following are not a machine instructions ?

    (a) MOV   (b) ORG

    (c) EN (d)   (d) (b) & (c)

11. In Assembly language programming, minimum number of operands required for an instruction is/are ......

    (a) zero   (b) one

    (c) two   (d) both (b) & (c)

12. The maximum addressing capacity of a microprocessor which uses 16 bit database and 32 bit address base is

(a) 64 k   (b) 4 gb

(c) both (a) and (b)   (d) none of these

13. The load instruction is mostly used to designate a transfer from memory to a processor register known as____.

(a) Accumulator   (b)   Instruction register

(c) Program counter   (d)   Memory address register

14. A group of bits that tell the computer to perform a specific operation is known as.......

(a) Instruction code   (b)   Micro-operation

(c) Accumulator   (d)   Register

15. The time interval between adjacent bits is called the......

(a) Word-time   (b) Bit-time

(c) Turn around time   (d) Slice time

16. A k-bit field can specify any one of......

(a) 3k registers   (b) 2k registers

(c) K2 registers   (d) K3 registers

17. MIMD stands for ......

(a) Multiple instruction multiple data

(b) Multiple instruction memory data

(c) Memory instruction multiple data

(d) Multiple information memory data

18. The BSA instruction is......

(a) Branch and store accumulator   (b) Branch and save return address

(c) Branch and shift address   (d) Branch and show accumulator

19. The instruction 'ORG O' is a......

(a) Machine Instruction   (b) Pseudo instruction

(c) High level instruction   (d) Memory instruction

20. 'Aging registers' are ......

(a) Counters which indicate how long ago their associated pages have been referenced.

(b) Registers which keep track of when the program was last accessed.

(c) Counters to keep track of last accessed instruction.

(d) Counters to keep track of the latest data structures referred.

21.   ......register keeps tracks of the instructions stored in program stored in memory.
       (a) AR (Address Register)   (b) XR (Index Register)
       (c) PC (Program Counter)   (d) AC (Accumulator)

22.   PSW is saved in stack when there is a ......
       (a) interrupt recognized   (b) execution of RST instruction
       (c) execution of CALL instruction   (d) all of these

23.   An n-bit microprocessor has......
       (a) n-bit program counter   (b) n-bit address register
       (c) n-bit ALU   (d) n-bit instruction register

24.   The register starting with E indicates that the register is ......bits wide
       (a) 8   (b) 16
       (c) 32   (d) 64

25.   A Stack-organised Computer uses instruction of ......
       (a) Indirect addressing   (b) Two-addressing
       (c) Zero addressing   (d) Index addressing

26.   In a program using subroutine call instruction, it is necessary......
       (a) Initialize program counter   (b) Clear the accumulator
       (c) Reset the microprocessor   (d) Clear the instruction register

27.   In a vectored interrupt.
       (a) the branch address is assigned to a fixed location in memory.
       (b) the interrupting source supplies the branch information to the processor through
           an interrupt vector.
       (c) the branch address is obtained from a register in the processor
       (d) none of the above

28.   An interface that provides a method for transferring binary information between
       internal storage and external devices is called......
       (a) I/O interface   (b) input interface
       (c) output interface   (d) I/O bus

29.   An interface that provides I/O transfer of data directly to and form the memory unit
       and peripheral is termed as......
       (a) DDA   (b) Serial interface
       (c) BR   (d) DMA

30. The addressing mode used in an instruction of the form ADD X Y, is ......

    (a) Absolute   (b) indirect

    (c) index   (d) none of these

31. ......register keeps track of the instructions stored in program stored in memory.

    (a) AR (Address Register)   (b) XR (Index Register)

    (c) PC (Program Counter)   (d) AC (Accumulator)

32. Computers use addressing mode techniques for ......

    (a) giving programming versatility to the user by providing facilities as pointers to memory counters for loop control

    (b) to reduce number of bits in the field of instruction

    (c) specifying rules for modifying or interpreting address field of the instruction

    (d) all the above

33. The register ending with L indicates that the register is ......bits wide

    (a) 8   (b) 16

    (c) 32   (d) 64

34. Suppose that a bus has 16 data lines and requires 4 cycles of 250 n secs each to transfer data.

    The bandwidth of this bus would be 2 Mega bytes/sec. If the cycle time of the bus was reduced to 125 nsecs and the number of cycles required for transfer stayed the same what would the bandwidth of the bus?

    (a) 1 Mega byte/sec   (b) 4 Mega bytes/sec

    (c) 8 Mega bytes/sec   (d) 2 Mega bytes/sec

35. Which of the following is a set of general purpose internal registers?

    (a) Stack   (b) Scratch pad

    (c) Address register   (d) Status register

36. P : "Program is a step by step execution of the instructions". Given P, which of the following is true ?

    (a) Program is a subset of an instruction set.

    (b) Program is a sequence of a subset of an instruction set.

    (c) Program is a partially ordered set of an instruction set.

    (d) All of the above

37. Interrupts which are initiated by an I/O drive are
    (a) Internal   (b) External
    (c) Software   (d) All of these

38. What is meant by a dedicated computer?
    (a) Which is used by one person only
    (b) Which is assigned to one and only one task
    (c) Which does one kind of software
    (d) Which is meant for application software only

39. In which addressing mode the operand is given explicitly in the instruction
    (a) Absolute   (b) Immediate
    (c) Indirect   (d) Direct

40. The program counter......
    (a) Is a register
    (b) During execution of the current instruction its content changes
    (c) Both (a) and (b)
    (d) None of these

41. A complete microcomputer system consists of ......
    (a) Microprocessor   (b) Memory
    (c) Peripheral equipment   (d) All of these

42. The addressing mode used in the instruction PUSH B is......
    (a) Direct   (b) Register
    (c) Register indirect   (d) Immediate

43. The register used as a working area in CPU is ......
    (a) Program counter   (b) Instruction register
    (c) Instruction decoder   (d) Accumulator

44. In which addressing mode the operand is given explicitly in the instruction itself?
    The register used as a working area in CPU is ......
    (a) Absolute mode   (b) Immediate mode
    (c) Indirect mode   (d) Index mode

45. A ......development system and an......are essential tools for writing large assembly
     language programs.

     (a) Microprocessor, assembler   (b) none of these

46. An instruction used to set the carry flag in a computer can be classified as......

     (a) Data transfer   (b) Process control

     (c) Logical   (d) Program control

47. The most relevant addressing mode to write position independent code......

     (a) Direct mode   (b) Indirect mode

     (c) Relative mode   (D) Indexed mode

48. A stack organized computer has ......

     (a) Three-address Instruction   (b) Two-address Instruction

     (c) One-address Instruction   (d) Zero-address Instruction

49. Zero address instruction format is used for ......

     (a) RISC architecture   (b) CISC architecture

     (c) Von-Neuman architecture   (d) Stack-organized architecture

Explanation : In stack organized architecture push and pop instruction is needs a address
field to specify the location of data for pushing into the stack and destination location during
pop operation but for logic and arithmetic operation the instruction does not need any
address field as it operates on the top two data available in the stack.

50. Interrupts which are initiated by an instruction are ......

     (a) Internal   (b) External

     (c) Hardware   (d) Software

51. The addressing mode used in an instruction of form ADD X,Y is ......

     (a) Absolute   (b) Immediate

     (c) Indirect   (d) Index

52. The device which is used to connect a peripheral to bus is called ......

     (a) Control register   (b) Interface

     (c) Communication protocol   (d) None of these

53. The process of fetching and executing instruction one at a time in order of increasing
     addresses is called ......

     (a) Instruction execution   (b) Straight line sequencing

     (c) Instruction fetch   (d) Random sequencing

54. The function of program counter holds......

(a) Temporary   (b) Address for memory

(c) Memory operand   (d) Address for instruction

55. When a subroutine is called, the address of the instruction following the CALL instructions stored in/on the ......

(a) Stack pointer   (b) Accumulator

(c) Program counter   (d) Stack

56. A stack pointer is ......

(a) A register that decodes and executes 16-bit arithmetic expression.

(b) A 16-bit register in the microprocessor that indicate the beginning of the stack memory.

(c) First memory location where a subroutine address is stored.

(d) A register in which flag bits are stored

57. Processors of all computers, whether micro, mini or mainframe must have ......

(a) ALU   (b) Primary Storage

(c) Control unit   (d) All of these

58. Which of the following registers is used to keep track of address of the memory location where the next instruction is located?

(a) Memory Address Register   (b) Memory Data Register

(c) Instruction Register   (d) Program Register

59. On receiving an interrupt from an I/O device, the CPU......

(a) halts for predetermined time

(b) branches off to the interrupt service routine after completion of the current instruction

(c) branches off to the interrupt service routine immediately

(d) hands over control of address bus and data bus to the interrupting device

60. The bus which is used to transfer data from main memory to peripheral device is......

(a) Data bus   (b) Input bus

(c) DMA bus   (d) Output bus

61.   An interrupt can be temporarily ignored by the counter is called......

(a) Vector interrupt   (b) Non maskable interrupt

(c) Maskable interrupt   (d) Low priority interrupt

62.   A CPU generally handles an interrupt by executing an interrupt service routine......

(a) as soon as an interrupt is raised

(b) by checking the interrupt register at the end of fetch cycle

(c) by checking the interrupt register after finishing the executing the current instruction

(d) by checking the interrupt register at fixed time intervals

63. The register ending with X indicates that the register is ......bits wide

(a) 8   (b) 16

(c) 32   (d) 64

64.   The concept of pipelining is most effective in improving performance if the tasks being performed in different stages ......

(a) Require different amount of time

(b) Require about the same amount of time

(c) Require different amount of time with time difference between any two tasks being same

(d) Require different amount with time difference between any two tasks being different

65.   Arithmetic shift left operation......

(a) Produces the same result as obtained with logical shift left operation

(b) Causes the sign bit to remain always unchanged

(c) Needs additional hardware to preserve the sign bit

(d) Is not applicable for signed 2s complement representation

66.   Register renaming is done in pipelined processors ......

(a) as an alternative to register allocation at compile time

(b) for efficient access to function parameters and local variables

(c) to handle certain kinds of hazards

(d) as part of address translation

67. Pipelining strategy is called implement ......

    (a) instruction execution   (b) instruction prefetch

    (c) instruction decoding   (d) instruction manipulation

68. In a non-vectored interrupt, the address of interrupt service routine is......

    (a) Obtained from interrupt address table

    (b) Supplied by the interrupting I/O device

    (c) Obtained through Vector address generator device

    (d) Assigned to a fixed memory location

Explanation : The source device that interrupted the processor supply the vector address which helps processor to find out the actual memory location where ISR is stored for the device.

69. Divide overflow is generated when......

    (a) Sign of the dividend is different from that of divisor.

    (b) Sign of the dividend is same as that of divisor.

    (c) The first part of the dividend is smaller than the divisor.

    (d) The first part of the dividend is greater than the divisor.

Explanation : If the first part of the dividend is greater than the deviser, then the result should be of greater length, then that can be hold in a register of the system. The registers are of fixed length in any processor.

70. An instruction pipeline can be implemented by means of ......

    (a) LIFO buffer   (b) FIFO buffer

    (c) Stack   (d) None of the above

71. Stack overflow causes ......

    (a) Hardware interrupt   (b) External interrupt

    (c) Internal interrupt   (d) Software interrupt

Explanation : Stack overflow occurs while execution of a program due to logical faults. So it is a program dependent, hence interrupt activate

72. Performance of a pipelined processor suffers if ......

    (a) The pipeline stages have different delays

    (b) Consecutive instructions are dependent on each other

    (c) The pipeline stages share hardware resources

    (d) All of these

73. A basic instruction that can be interpreted by computer generally has ......

    (a) An operand and an address   (b) A decoder and an accumulator

    (c) Sequence register and decoder   (d) An address and decoder

74. The ALU of a computer normally contains a number of high speed storage elements called ......

    (a) Semi conductor   (b) Register

    (c) Hard disk   (d) Magnetic disk

75. In immediate addressing the operand is placed ......

    (a) in the CPU register   (b) after OP code in the instruction

    (c) in memory   (d) in stack

76. In a virtual memory system, the addresses used by the programmer belongs to ......

    (a) Memory space.   (b) Physical addresses

    (c) Address space   (d) Main memory address

77. Combination of ......and......registers result in a 20-bit address that points to the top of stack.

    (a) SI and DI   (b) SS and SP

    (c) SS and BP   (d) CS and SP

Explanation : An address used by programmers in a system supporting virtual memory concept is called virtual address and the set of such addresses are called address space

78. Computers use addressing mode techniques for ....

    (a) giving programming versatility to the user by providing facilities as pointers to memory counters for loop control

    (b) to reduce no. of bits in the field of instruction

    (c) specifying rules for modifying or interpreting address field of the instruction

    (d) all the above

79. Choose the correct alternative A successive A/D converter is
    (a) a high-speed converter   (b) a low speed converter
    (c) a medium speed converter   (d) none of these

80. When necessary, the results are transferred from the CPU to main memory by
    (a) I/O devices   (b) CPU
    (c) shift registers   (d) none of these

81. The ...... is set when there is a carry out of the lowest nibble of the result.
    (a) carry flag   (b) auxillary carry flag
    (c) overflow flag   (d) sign flag

82. Which is default segment for instruction fetch ?
    (a) CS   (b) DS
    (c) ES   (d) SS

83. Which is the default segment for general data ?
    (a) CS   (b) DS
    (c) ES   (d) SS

84. Which is the default segment for string destination ?
    (a) CS   (b) DS
    (c) ES   (d) SS

85. What physical memory location is accessed by the instruction Mov (BP], AL if BP = 2C30 H and SS = SE7H
    (a) 5FEAOH   (b) 2C300H
    (c) 5D270H   (d) 1003cH

86. Segmentation provides ...... memory manage mechanism.
    (a) execution independent of physical address
    (b) relocation
    (c) both (a) and (b)
    (d) none of these

87. How can you increase the size of segment beyond 64 kB?
    (a) by increasing the size of IP
    (b) by increasing the size of CS

(c) both (a) and (b)

(d) by allooting more than one segment

88. The ...... design provides a way to start a new task before the previous one has been completed.

(a) segmentation   (b) pipelining

(c) banking   (d) none of these

89. The maximum speed-up in a pipeline system is ......

(a) k (where k is no. of stages)   (b) n (where n is no. of instructions)

(c) k – 1   (d) n – 1

90. If the following instructions are executed simultaneously will they cause data dependency problem ?

(1) x = y + z   (2) x1 = x + 1

(a) yes   (b) no

(c) can't say   (d) may be or may not

91. The BIU is programmed to fetch a new instruction whenever the queue has room for ...... additional bytes.

(a) 1   (b) 2

(c) 3   (d) 4

92. State addressing modes for the following instruction : Mov AY, [By], [SI]

(a) Based indexed   (b) Indexed

(d) Direct   (d) Based indexed relative

93. What is the addressing mode for Move CY, [DI] ?

(a) Based indexed   (b) Indexed

(d) Direct   (d) Based indexed relative

94. State addressing mode for instruction Mov DX, [123] ......

(a) Register   (b) Immediate

(c) direct   (d) Register Indirect

95. State addressing mode for follow instruction Mov By, [BP] [DI] [0045]

(a) Register   (b) Immediate

(c) Register Indirect   (d) Based Indexed Relative

96.   In AL, C8# uses ...... port add mode.
      (a) fixed   (b) variable
      (c) both (a) and (b)   (d) none of these

97.   Out DY, AL uses ...... port add mode same options as above.
      (a) fixed   (b) variable
      (c) both (a) and (b)   (d) none of these

98.   In case of push operation in 8086 the stack pointer (SP) is ......
      (a) incremented twice   (b) decremented twice
      (c) incremented once   (d) decremented once

99.   In case of POP instruction the SP is same option as above......
      (a) incremented twice   (b) decremented twice
      (c) incremented once   (d) decremented once

100. The ...... bytes are loaded from memory in case of the LDs instruction.
      (a) L   (b) 2
      (c) 3   (d) 4

101. The ...... bytes are loaded from memory in case of LES instruction.
      (a) 1   (b) 2
      (c) 3   (d) 4

102. Using IN instruction we can only read ...... data.
      (a) 8 bit   (b) 16 bit
      (c) 32 bit   (d) both (a) and (b)

103.   Using OUT instruction we can write ......
      (a) 8 bit   (b) 16 bit
      (c) both (a) and (b)   (d) 32 bit

104. IN and OUT instructions are for the no devices mapped in ...... mapped HO.
      (a) Ho   (b) memory
      (c) Bus   (d) All of these

105. DAA is used for......
      (a) decimal adjustment after addition   (b) decimal adjustment before addition
      (c) ASC II adjustment after addition   (d) ASC II adjustment before addition

106. DAS is used for......
   (a) decimal adjustment after subtraction   (b) decimal adjustment before subtraction
   (c) Agc II adjustment after subtraction   (d) Agc II adjustment before subtraction

107. ...... instruction is used to convert from unpacked BCD to hexadecimal.
   (a) AAA   (b) AAS
   (c) AAM   (d) AAD

108. ...... instruction is used to convert from hex to anpacked BCD.
   (a) AAA   (b) AAS
   (c) AAM   (d) AAD

109. ...... instruction is used for signed multiplex.
   (a) MUL   (b) IMUL
   (c) DIV   (d) IDIV

110. The difference between CMD instruction and SUB instruction is ......
   (a) both effective flag   (b) both store the result
   (c) CMP does not store the result   (d) both (a) and (b)

111. A collection of lines that connects several devices is called ....
   (a) bus   (b) peripheral connection wires
   (c) both (a) and (b)   (d) internal wires

112. A complete microcomputer system consist of ....
   (a) microprocessor   (b) memory
   (c) peripheral equipment   (d) all of these

113. PC Program Counter is also called ....
   (a) instruction pointer   (b) memory pointer
   (c) data counter   (d) file pointer

114. In a single byte how many bits will be there?
   (a) 8   (b) 16
   (c) 4   (d) 32

115. CPU does not perform the operation ....
   (a) data transfer   (b) logic operation
   (c) arithmetic operation   (d) all of these

116. The access time of memory is .... the time required for performing any single CPU operation.
    (a) longer than   (b) shorter than
    (c) negligible than   (d) same as

117. Memory address refers to the successive memory words and the machine is called as ....
    (a) word addressable   (b) byte addressable
    (c) bit addressable   (d) tera byte addressable

118. A microprogram written as string of 0's and 1's is a ....
    (a) symbolic microinstruction   (b) binary microinstruction
    (c) symbolic microinstruction   (d) binary microprogram

119. A pipeline is like ....
    (a) an automobile assembly line   (b) house pipeline
    (c) both (a) and (b)   (d) a gas line

120. Data hazards occur when ....
    (a) greater performance loss
    (b) pipeline changes the order of read/write access to operands
    (c) some functional unit is not fully pipelined
    (d) machine size is limited

121. Computers use addressing mode techniques for ....
    (a) giving programming versatility to the user by providing facilities as pointers to memory counters for loop control
    (b) to reduce number of bits in the field of instruction
    (c) specifying rules for modifying or interpreting address field of the instruction
    (d) all the above

122. ....register keeps track of the instructions stored in program stored in memory.
    (a) AR (Address Register)   (b) XR (Index Register)
    (c) PC (Program Counter)   (d) AC (Accumulator)

123. The addressing mode used in an instruction of the form ADD X Y, is

   (a) absolute   (b) indirect

   (c) index   (d) none of thes

124. In a vectored interrupt.

   (a) the branch address is assigned to a fixed location in memory.

   (b) the interrupting source supplies the branch information to the processor through an interrupt vector.

   (c) the branch address is obtained from a register in the processor

   (d) none of the above

125. The circuit used to store one bit of data is known as

   (a) Encoder   (b) OR gate

   (c) Flip Flop   (d) Decoder

126. In a program using subroutine call instruction, it is necessary

   (a) initialise program counter   (b) Clear the accumulator

   (c) Reset the microprocessor   (d) Clear the instruction register

127. A Stack-organised Computer uses instruction of

   (a) Indirect addressing   (b) Two-addressing

   (c) Zero addressing   (d) Index addressing

128. An n-bit microprocessor has

   (a) n-bit program counter   (b) n-bit address register

   (c) n-bit ALU   (d) n-bit instruction register

129. A group of bits that tell the computer to perform a specific operation is known as

   (a) Instruction code   (b) Micro-operation

   (c) Accumulator   (d) Register

130. A binary digit is called a......

   (a) Bit   (b) Byte

   (c) Number   (d) Character

131. Self-contained sequence of instructions that performs a given computational task is called......

    (a) Function   (b) Procedure

    (c) Subroutine   (d) Routine

132. Status bit is also called......

    (a) Binary bit   (b) Flag bit

    (c) Signed bit   (d) Unsigned bit

133. An address in main memory is called......

    (a) Physical address   (b) Logical address

    (c) Memory address   (d) Word address

134. If the value V(x) of the target operand is contained in the address field itself, the addressing mode is......

    (a) immediate   (b) direct

    (c) indirect   (d) implied

135. The instructions which copy information from one location to another either in the processor's internal register set or in the external main memory are called......

    (a) Data transfer instructions   (b) Program control instructions

    (c) Input-output instructions   (d) Logical instructions

136. A device/circuit that goes through a predefined sequence of states upon the application of input pulses is called......

    (a) register   (b) flip-flop

    (c) transistor   (d) counter

137. Content of the program counter is added to the address part of the instruction in order to obtain the effective address is called......

    (a) relative address mode   (b) index addressing mode

    (c) register mode   (d) implied mode

138. A register capable of shifting its binary information either to the right or the left is called a......

    (a) parallel register   (b) serial register

    (c) shift register   (d) storage register

139. A byte is a group of 16 bits.

   (a) True   (b) False

140. A nibble is a group of 16 bits.

   (a) True   (b) False

141. In an operation performed by the ALU, carry bit is set to 1 if the end carry C8 is ...... It is cleared to 0 (zero) if the carry is ......

   (a) One, two   (b) Zero, one

142. A stack organized computer has

   (a) Three-address Instruction.   (b) Two-address Instruction.

   (c) One-address Instruction.   (d) Zero-address Instruction.

143. A system program that translates and executes an instruction simultaneously is

   (a) Compiler   (b) Interpreter

   (c) Assembler   (d) Operating system

144. A 32-bit address bus allows access to a memory of capacity ......

   (a) 64 Mb   (b) 16 Mb

   (c) 1Gb   (d) 4 Gb

145. Which processor structure is pipelined?

   (a) all x80 processors   (b) all x85 processors

   (c) all x86 processors

146. In 8086 microprocessor one of the following statements is not true.

   (a) Coprocessor is interfaced in MAX mode

   (b) Coprocessor is interfaced in MIN mode

   (c) I/O can be interfaced in MAX / MIN mode

   (d) Supports pipelining

147. The ......ensures that only one IC is active at a time to avoid a bus conflict caused by two ICs writing different data to the same bus.

   (a) control bus   (b) control instructions

   (c) address decoder   (d) CPU

148. In an 8085 microprocessor, the instruction CMP B has been executed while the contents of accumulator is less than that of register. As a result carry flag and zero flag will be respectively......

    (a) set, reset   (n) reset, set

    (c) reset, reset   (d) set, set

149. To put the 8085 microprocessor in the wait state......

    (a) lower the HOLD input   (b) lower the READY input

    (c) raise the HOLD input   (d) raise the READY input

150. Registers, which are partially visible to users and used to hold conditional, are known as......

    (a) PC   (b) Memory address registers

    (c) General purpose register   (d) Flags

151. What type of control pins are needed in a microprocessor to regulate traffic on the bus, in order to prevent two devices from trying to use it at the same time?

    (a) Bus control   (b) Interrupts

    (c) Bus arbitration   (d) Status

152. Who invented the microprocessor?

    (a) Marcian E Huff   (b) Herman H Goldstein

    (c) Joseph Jacquard   (d) All of these

153. What does microprocessor speed depends on......

    (a) Clock   (b) Data bus width

    (c) Address bus width   (d) Size of register

154. The status that cannot be operated by direct instructions is......

    (a) Cy   (b) Z

    (c) P   (d) AC

155. The necessary steps carried out to perform the operation of accessing either memory or I/O Device, constitute a ......

    (a) fetch operation   (b) execute operation

    (c) machine cycle   (d) instruction cycle

156. Which is a 8 bit Microprocessor ......

    (a) Intel 4040   (b) Pentium – I

    (c) 8088   (d) Motorala MC-6801

157. Interfacing devices for DMA controller, programmable interval timer are respectively...

    (a) 8257, 8253   (b) 8253, 8257

    (c) 8257, 8251   (d) 8251, 8257

158. Consider the following set of 8085 instruction MVI A,82HORA AJP DSPLYXRA ADSPLY:OUT PORT1 HLT. The output at PORT1 is

    (a) 00H   (b) FFH

    (c) 92H   (d) 11H

159. The contents of accumulator before CMA instruction is A5H. Its content after instruction execution is

    (a) A5H   (b) 5AH

    (c) AAH   (d) 55H

160. How many transistors does the 8086 have?

    (a) 10,000   (b) 29,000

    (c) 110,000   (d) 129,000

161. What generation chip is the Pentium 4 for the Intel central processing units?

    (a) Seventh generation   (b) Eighth generation

    (c) Ninth generation   (d) Tenth Generation

162. The first processor to include Virtual memory in the Intel microprocessor family was:

    (a) 80286   (b) 80386

    (c) 80486   (d) Pentium

163. Intel Itanium processors are designed for ......

    (a) Servers and personal computers   (b) Servers only

    (c) Personal computers only   (d) Calculators

164. In 8086 microprocessor one of the following instructions is executed before an arithmetic co-operation......

    (a) , AAM   (b) AAD

    (c) DAS   (d) DAA

165. In 8051, after reset the SP register is initialized to address.........

    (a) 8H   (b) 9H

    (c) 7H   (d) 6H

166. Serial port interrupt is generated, if ....bits are set.

    (a) IE   (b) RI, IE

    (c) IP, TI   (d) RI, TI

167. In 8051 which interrupt has highest priority?

    (a) IE1   (b) TF0

    (c) IE0   (d) TF1

168. When the 8051 is reset and the line is LOW, the program counter points to the first program instruction in the ......

    (a) internal code memory   (b) external code memory

    (c) internal data memory   (d) external data memory

169. In 8051 an external interrupt 1 vector address is of ....and causes of interrupt if ....

    (a) 000BH, a high to low transition on pin INT1

    (b) 001BH, a low to high transition on pin INT1

    (c) 0013H, a high to low transition on pin INT1

    (d) 0023H, a low to high transition on pin INT1

170. In a microprocessor, the service routine for a certain interrupt starts from a fixed location of memory which cannot be externally set, but the interrupt can be delayed or rejected. Such an interrupt is

    (a) non-maskable and non-vectored   (b) maskable and non-vectored

    (c) non-maskable and vectored   (d) maskable and vectored

171. For the 8085 assembly language program given below, the content of the accumulator after the execution of the program is   3000 MVI A, 45H3002 MOV B, A3003 STC3004 CMC3005 RAR3006 XRA B

    (a) 00H   (b) 45H

    (c) 67H   (d) E7H

172. The TRAP is one of the interrupts available its INTEL 8085. Which one of the following statements is true of TRAP?

(a) It is level triggered

(b) It is negative edge triggered

(c) It is positive edge triggered

(d) It is both positive edge triggered and level triggered

173. In a 16-bit microprocessor, words are stored in two consecutive memory locations. The entire word can be read in one operation provided the first

(a) word is even   (b) word is odd

(c) memory location is odd   (d) memory address is even

174. The ESC instruction of 8086 may have two formats. In one of the formats, no memory operand is used. Under this format, the number of external op-codes (for the co-processor) which can be specified is?

(a) 64   (b) 128

(c) 256   (d) 512

175. DB, DW and DD directives are used to place data in particular location or to simply allocate space without preassigning anything to space. The DW and DD directories are used to generate

(a) offsets

(b) full address of variables

(c) full address of labels

(d) offsets of full address of labels and variables

176. When the RET instruction at the end of subroutine is executed,

(a) the information where the stack is iniatialized is transferred to the stack pointer

(b) the memory address of the RET instruction is transferred to the program counter

(c) two data bytes stored in the top two locations of the stack are transferred to the program counter

(d) two data bytes stored in the top two locations of the stack are transferred to the stack pointer

177. Feature of fetching the next instruction while current instruction is executing called

(a) Fetching   (b) Executing

(c) Pipelining   (d) Decoding

178. ......flag of 8086 is used for BCD operations.

   (a) ZF   (b)   TF

   (c) IF   (d) AF

179. In 8086, the segment can start at any memory address which is divisible by ......

   (a) 8   (b) 16

   (c)   20   (d) 24

180. ......allows to use separates memory area for program, data and stack.

   (a) Segmentation   (b) Pipelining

   (c) Main memory   (d) MMU

181. For 8086 ......bus is bidirectional and ......bus is unidirectional.

   (a) Address, data   (b) data , address

   (c) Control, data   (d) Address, control

182. The ALU of 8086 is ......bits.

   (a) 8   (b) 6

   (c) 20   (d) 24

183. The 8086 supports ......flags.

   (a) 5   (b) 6

   (c) 8   (d) 9

184. Length of double word is ......and quad word is ......

   (a) 2 words, 4/3 words   (b) 2 words, 4 words

   (c) 4 bits, 4 words   (d) 64 bits , 80 bits

185. The flags which reflects the state of a particular program are known as ......and flags which reflects status of machine are known as ......flags .

   (a) Status, system   (b) System, Status

   (c) Status, Control   (d) Status , status control

186. During physical address calculations segments register contents are shifted by ......
   (a) 2 bits left   (b) 4 bits left

   (c) 2 bits right   (d) 4 bits right .

187. The BIU of 8086 consists of ....

(a) segment registers   (b) instruction queue

(c) instruction pointer   (d) all of these.

188. During instruction fetch......and......register are used.

(a) IP, DS   (b) CS, IP

(c) SS, BP   (d) SS, IP

189. Which of the following is not an interrupt signal?

(a) INTR   (b) NMI

(c) NA#   (d) RESET

190. Number of segments in 8086 are ......

(a) 4,   (b) 6

(c) 3   (d) 2

191. ....was the first microprocessor to be used as a multi-user microcomputer.

(a) 8086   (b) 80186

(c) 80286   (d) 80386

192. 8080 needed ......power supplied.

(a) One   (b) Two

(c) Three   (d) Four

193. 8008 microprocessor has ......instruction.

(a) 32   (b) 45

(c) 48   (d) 54

194. 8088 Data bus is ......bit wide.

(a) 2   (b) 4

(c) 6   (d) 8

195. 8086 allows ......of addressing space.

(a) 4 GB   (b) 64 GB

(c) 1 MB   (d) 30 GB

196. The 8086 and 8088 processor would run at a speed ranging from ......

(a) 4 MHz to 16 MHz   (b) 5 to 20 MHz

(c) 1 to 4 MHz   (d) 10 to 12 MHZ

197. 80186/80188 processors running at a speed ranging between ......
    (a) 3 to 10 MHz   (b) 4 to 16 MHz
    (c) 6 to 40 MHz   (d) all of these

198. The 80286 has a ......bit address bus.
    (a) 24   (b) 12
    (c) 10   (d) 20

199. The 80286's speed could range between ......
    (a) 6 MHz to 25 MHz   (b) 5 to 20 MHz
    (c) 1 to 4 MHz   (d) 10 to 12 MHZ

200. 8086 has ......vectored interrupts.
    (a) 256   (b) 125
    (c) 124   (d) 254

201. The process of fetching of next instruction when the current instruction has been executed is called ......
    (a) execution   (b) decoding
    (c) fetching   (d) pipelining

202. The 8086 can access up to ......I/O ports.
    (a) 256   (b) 65536
    (c) 1024   (d) 4096

203. The segment register of 8086 is ......bit.
    (a) 32   (b) 16
    (c) 24   (d) 8

204. Each segment in the 8086 is of ......
    (a) 16 kB   (b) 1 MB
    (c) 4 kB   (d) 64 kB

205. ......unit is called the external world interface of the processor.
    (a) EU   (b) BIU
    (c) Both (a) and (b)   (d) None of these

206. ......unit taks care of performing operations on data.
    (a) BIU   (b) EU
    (c) Both (a) and (b)   (d) None of these

207. ......unit works in synchronous with T-states.

(a) Segmentation   (b) Paging

(c) Bus interface   (d) Execution

208. What is the minimum size of segment in 8086?

(a) 64 kbytes   (b) 16 bytes

(c) 1 Kbytes   (d) 256 bytes

209. The ...... pair gives the address of the next instruction to be executed in the program sequence.

(a) CS : IP   (b) DS : IP

(c) ES : IP   (d) SS : IP

210. The ...... pair is used as a pointer into the stack.

(a) CS : IP   (b) DS : IP

(c) ES : IP   (D) SS : BP

211. The ......pair gives the address of the top of the stack.

(a) SS : SP   (b) DS : IP

(c) ES : IP   (d) SS : BP

212. During physical address calculations the segment register contents are shifted by ......

(a) 2-bits left   (b) 4-bits left

(c) 2_bits right   (d) 4-bits right

213. ......is used for random access of the stack.

(a) BP   (b) AX

(c) IP   (d) BX

214. The ......pair is used as a source pointer for sting instructions.

(a) DS:SI   (b) DS:DI

(c) Both (a) and (b)   (d) None of these

215. The ......pair is used as a destination pointer for sting instructions.

(a) ES:SI   (b) ES:DI

(c) Both (a) and (b)   (d) None of these

216. A flag is a ......

(a) Flipflop   (b) Register

(c) Both (a) and (b)   (d) None

217. Flag register consists of ......active flags.

   (a) Nine   (b) Six

   (c) Four   (d) Two

218. ......flag of 8086 is specifically for string instructions.

   (a) SF   (b) IF

   (c) DF   (d) TF

219. ......flag of 8086 is used for BCD operations.

   (a) ZF   (b) IF

   (c) DF   (d) AF

220. Which of the following flag status is wrong after addition of (65D1) and (2359)?

   (a) SF=1   (b) PF=1

   (c) CF=1   (d) AF=0

221. Which of the following flag status is/are correct after addition of (65D1) and (2359)?

   (a) SF=1   (b) ZF=0

   (c) OF=1   (d) All of these

222. ......allows programmers to deviate from the default segment.

   (a) segment override prefix   (b) segment registers

   (c) segmentation   (d) paging

223. For undefined opcodes in 8086/8088 exception ......is generated

   (a) 8   (b) 2

   (c) 4   (d) 6

224. What is the status of W/R# and M/IO# signals to read data from memory ?

   (a) W/R#=0 & M/IO#=0   (b) W/R#=0 & M/IO#=1

   (c) W/R#=1 & M/IO#=0   (d) W/R#=1 & M/IO#=1

225. One common use of ......register is to reference parameters that were passed to a subroutine by way of the stack.

   (a) SI   (b) DI

   (c) SP   (d) BP

ANSWERS

1.	a	2.	b	3.	a	4.	b	5.	b
6.	b	7.	c	8.	c	9.	d	10.	d
11.	a	12.	b	13.	a	14.	a	15.	b
16.	b	17.	a	18.	b	19.	b	20.	a
21.	c	22.	a	23.	d	24.	d	25.	c
26.	d	27.	b	28.	a	29.	d	30.	c
31.	c	32.	d	33.	a	34.	d	35.	b
36.	b	37.	b	38.	b	39.	b	40.	c
41.	d	42.	c	43.	d	44.	b	45.	a
46.	b	47.	c	48.	d	49.	d	50.	d
51.	a	52.	b	53.	b	54.	d	55.	d
56.	b	57.	d	58.	b	59.	b	60.	c
61.	c	62.	c	63.	b	64.	b	65.	a
66.	c	67.	b	68.	d	69.	b	70.	b
71.	b	72.	d	73.	a	74.	b	75.	b
76.	c	77.	b	78.	d	79.	c	80.	b
81.	b	82.	a	83.	b	84.	b	85.	a
86.	c	87.	d	88.	b	89.	a	90.	a
91.	b	92.	a	93.	b	94.	c	95.	d
96.	a	97.	b	98.	b	99.	a	100.	d
101.	d	102.	b	103.	c	104.	a	105.	a
106.	a	107.	d	108.	c	109.	b	110.	d
111.	a	112.	d	113.	a	114.	a	115.	a
116.	a	117.	a	118.	d	119.	a	120.	b

121.	d	122.	c	123.	c	124.	b	125.	c
126.	d	127.	c	128.	d	129.	a	130.	a
131.	a	132.	b	133.	a	134.	b	135.	a
136.	d	137.	a	138.	c	139.	b	140.	b
141.	a	142.	d	143.	c	144.	d	145.	c
146.	b	147.	c	148.	a	149.	b	150.	c
151.	c	152.	a	153.	c	154.	d	155.	c
156.	d	157.	a	158.	a	159.	b	160.	b
161.	a	162.	a	163.	b	164.	b	165.	c
166.	d	167.	c	168.	b	169.	c	170.	d
171.	c	172.	d	173.	d	174.	b	175.	d
176.	c	177.	c	178.	d	179.	a	180.	a
181.	d	182.	a	183.	d	184.	b	185.	d
186.	b	187.	d	188.	b	189.	d	190.	a
191.	c	192.	c	193.	a	194.	d	195.	c
196.	a	197.	c	198.	a	199.	a	200.	a
201.	d	202.	b	203.	b	204.	d	205.	b
206.	b	207.	d	208.	b	209.	a	210.	d
211.	a	212.	b	213.	a	214.	a	215.	a
216.	c	217.	a	218.	c	219.	d	220.	c
221.	c	222.	a	223.	d	224.	b	225.	d

QUESTIONS

1. Write a note on CPU organization.   **[May 10, 12]**

2. Explain addressing modes with one example each.

[May 2000, 03, 04, 08, Dec. 01, 03, 05, 08, 09]

3. Explain following addressing modes with one example each

    (i)   Auto increment

    (ii) Auto decrement

    (iii) Immediate

    (iv) Register

    (v)   Direct addressing   **[May 08, 12, 13]**

4. Write a note on instruction cycle.   **[May 05, 07, 13]**

5. List the features of 8086 microprocessor.   **[Dec. 08, 09, 10, 11,12]**

6. Draw and explain functional block diagram of 8086.   **[May 11, Dec. 11]**

7. Draw and explain architecture of 8086.   **[Dec. 08, 09, 10, 12]**

8. Draw and explain programmers model of 8086.   **[May 08, 09, 10, 12, 13]**

DATA PATHS AND ALU

3.1 FIXED POINT ARITHMETIC

This includes addition, subtraction, multiplication and division through arithmetic of binary.

3.1.1 Addition and Subtraction

Addition and subtraction for binary numbers are part or instruction set of every computer. Addition and subtraction are used to implement multiplication and division also.

3.1.1.1 Basic Adders

To add two n-bits unsigned binary numbers. The fastest adder is a two level combinational circuit in which each of the n sum bits is expressed as a logical sum or product of sums of the n input variables. This circuit is feasible for very small values of n as it require $c(n)$ gates with fan-in $f(n)$, where both $c(n)$ and $f(n)$ grow exponentially with n.

Actually, the addition of two n-bit numbers x and y is performed by subdividing the numbers into stages x_i and y_i of length n_i where $n > n_i > 1$. The sum z_i, C_i of two 1-bit numbers x_i, y_i can be expressed by half adder logic equations.

$$z_i = x_i \oplus y_i$$

$$C_i = x_i y_i$$

where, z_i is the sum bit, C_i is the carry-out bit, $\oplus$ denotes EXCLUSIVE-OR and juxtaposition denotes AND. If we introduce third input bit C_{i-1} denoting carry in signal, it will give following full adder equations.

$$z_i = x_i \oplus y_i \oplus c_{i-1}$$

$$C_i = x_i y_i + x_i C_{i-1} + y_i C_{i-1}$$

A full adder, also called 1 bit adder can be directly implemented from these equations with AND-OR realization of 1-bit adder as shown in Fig. 3.1.

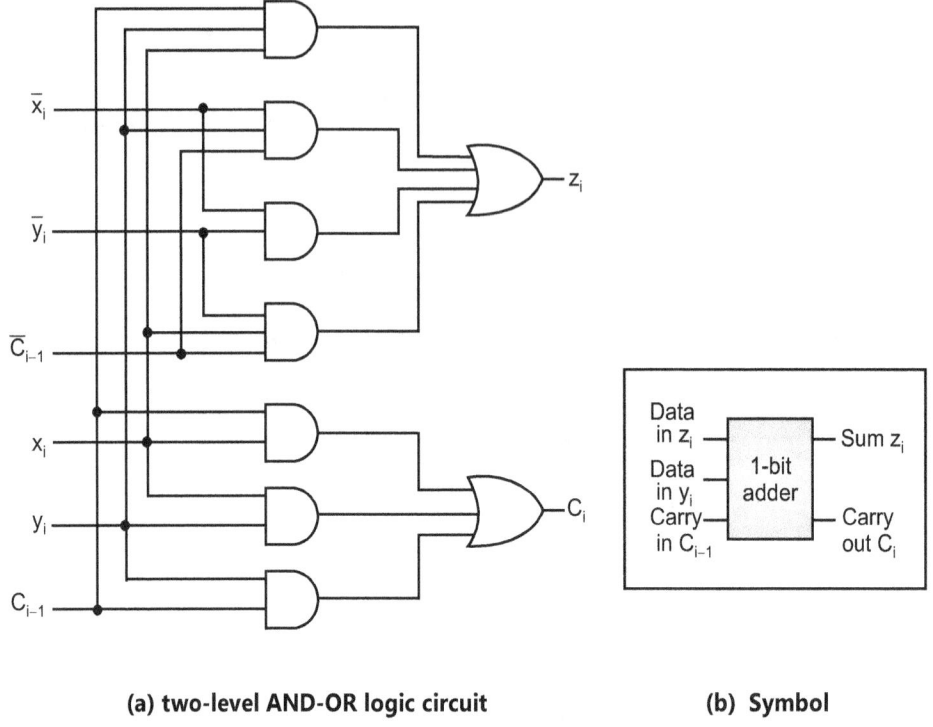

(a) two-level AND-OR logic circuit   (b) Symbol

Fig. 3.1 : 1bit full adder

In terms of Hardware cost, least expensive circuit for adding two n-bit binary numbers is serial adder. It adds numbers bit by bit and requires n-clock cycles. As shown in Fig. 3.2, a serial adder consists of full adder and a flip-flop to store C_i. One sum bit is generated in each clock cycle, a carry is also computed and stored for use during next clock-cycle.

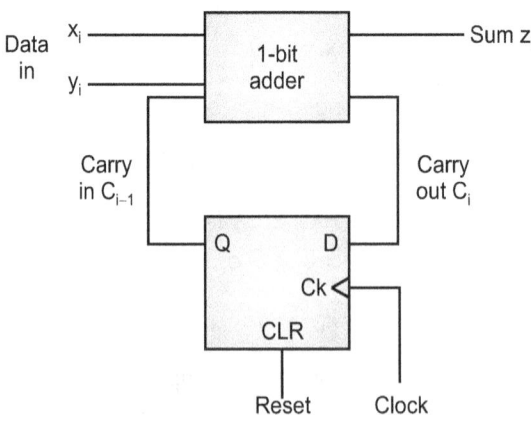

Fig. 3.2 : Serial binary adder

One more type of adder is formed by connected n full adders where, each 1-bit adder stage supplies a carry-bit to stage on its left. A 1 appearing on the carry-in line of a 1-bit adder can cause it to generate a1 on its carry-out line. Hence, carry signals propagate through the adder from right to left giving rise to name ripple-carry adder.

Fig. 3.3 illustrate n-bit ripple carry adder.

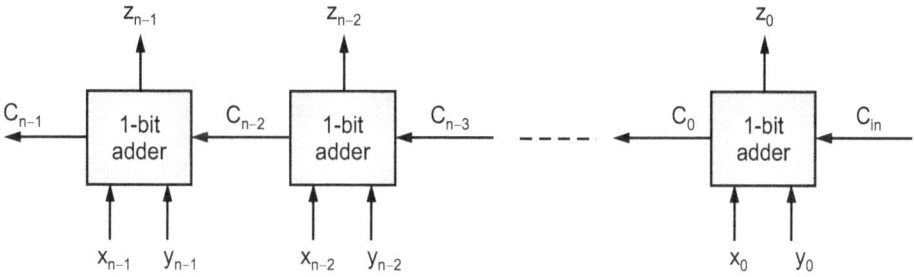

Fig. 3.3 : n-bit ripple carry adder composed of n-1-bit (full) address

3.1.1.2 Subtracters

Subtraction is relatively simple with two's-complement code because negation (changing x to −x) is very easy to implement. If $x = x_{n-1} x_{n-2} \ldots x_0$ is a two's complement integer, then negation is realized by

$$-x = \overline{x}_{n-1} \overline{x}_{n-2} \ldots \overline{x}_0 + 1$$

where , + denotes addition modulo 2^n. Efficient way to obtain one's complement portion

$\overline{x} = \overline{x}_{n-1} \overline{x}_{n-2} \ldots \overline{x}_0$ of −x uses the word based EXCLUSIVE-OR function x ⊕ s with a control variable s. When s = 0, x ⊕ s = X, but when s = 1, x ⊕ s = $\overline{x}$

Suppose, Y and x ⊕ s are now applied to the inputs of an n-bit adder. The addition of 1 by above equation acquired to change x to −x can be realized by applying s to the carry input line of the adder. In the resulting circuit as shown in Fig. 3.4, the control line s selects the addition operation Y + X when s = 0 and the subtraction operation Y − X = Y + $\overline{x}$ + 1 when s = 1. Thus, extending a parallel adder to perform two's complement subtraction as well as addition merely requires connecting n-two input EXCLUSIVE-OR gates to the adders inputs as shown in Fig. 3.4.

$$Z = Y \pm X$$

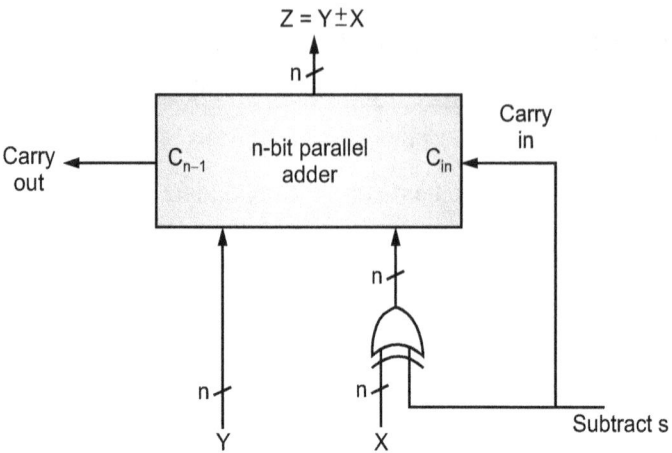

Fig. 3.4 : An n-bit two's complement adder subtracter

For example, Let x = 11101011 and y = 00101000, denoting -21_{10} and 40_{10} respectively in two's complement code. Bit-by-bit addition produces

$$Z = X + Y = 11101011 + 00101000 = 00010011 \quad ...(a)$$

which correspond to $-21_{10} + 40_{10} = +19_{10}$

To subtract X from Y, we first compute

$$-X = \overline{1}\,\overline{1}\,\overline{1}\,0\,\overline{1}\,0\,\overline{1}\,\overline{1} + 1 = 00010101$$

which correspond to $21_{10} + 40_{10} = +61_{10}$

3.1.1.3 Overflow

When the result of an arithmetic operation exceeds the standard word size n, overflow occurs with n-bit unsigned numbers, overflow is indicated by an output carry bit $C_{n-1} = 1$.

For example, adding the unsigned numbers x = 11101011 = 235_{10} and y = 00101010 = 42_{10} using an adder like that of Fig. 3.3 yields.

$$Z = X + Y = 11101011 + 00101010$$

$$= 00010101 \hspace{4cm} ...(b)$$

with $C_{n-1} = C_7 = 1$. Now 2 corresponds to 21_{10}, which is $235_{10} + 42_{10}$ (modulo 256) and is the result of addition that "wraps around" when the largest number $2^n - 1$, in this case 11111111 = 255_{10}, is exceeded. On oppending C_7 to z, we get C_7 to z, we get $C_7z = 100010101 = 277_{10}$ = $256_{11} + 21_{10}$ which is the sum in ordinary arithmetic. Unsigned arithmetic operations are often viewed as modulo 2^n operations only and overflow is not explicitly detected. This is the case when computing memory addresses in a computer, for instance, where addresses simply wrap around to zero after the highest address is reached.

3.1.2 Multiplication

Multiplication is usually implemented by some form of repeated addition. A method to compute $X \times Y$ is to add the multiplicand Y to itself X times, where X is multiplier. Example shown below explain this.

$$
\begin{array}{ll}
1010 & \text{Multiplicand Y} \\
\underline{1101} & \text{Multiplier } X = x_3\, x_2\, x_1\, x_0 \\
1010 & x_0\, y \\
0000 & x_1\, ZY \\
1010 & x_2 Z^2 Y \\
\underline{1010} & x_3\, Z^3 Y \\
10000010 & \\
\end{array}
$$

$$
\text{Product P} = \sum_{j=0}^{3} x_j\, Z\, Y^j
$$

But, this method is inefficient in that the 1-bit products $x_j Z^i Y$ must be stored until the final addition step is completed. For machine implementation it is desirable to add each $x_j ZY$ term as it is generated to the sum of the preceding terms to form a number P_{i+1} called a partial product.

Example shown below has the computation involved in one multiple bit x_j can be described by a register transfer statement of the form.

$$
P_{i+1} = P_i + x_j\, Z^i Y \qquad \qquad \qquad \text{...(1)}
$$

$$
\begin{array}{ll}
1010 & \text{Multiplicand Y} \\
\underline{1101} & \text{Multiplier } X = x_3\, x_2\, x_1\, x_0 \\
00000000 & P_0 = 0 \\
\underline{1010} & x_0\, Y \\
00001010 & p_1 = p_0 + x_0 Y \\
\underline{0000} & x_1\, ZY \\
00001010 & P_2 = P_1 + x_2 ZY \\
\underline{1010} & x_2\, Z^2 Y^3 \\
00110010 & p_3 = p_2 + x_2 Z^2 Y \\
\underline{1010} & x_3 Z^3 Y \\
10000010 & p_4 = p_3 + x_3 Z^3 Y = P \\
\end{array}
$$

where, $Z^i Y$ is equivalent to Y shifted i positions to the left. In the version of this multiplication algorithm presented, P_i is shifted right with respect to a fixed multiplicand Y so that equation (1) shown above can be replaced by the equivalent two operations.

$$P_i = P_i + x_j Y$$

$$P_{i+1} = Z^j P_i \qquad \qquad \text{...(2)}$$

3.1.2.1 Two's Complement Multipliers

The multiplication of two's complement numbers presents some difficulties in case of –ve operands.

For example when a negative P_i is right shifted as in equation (2), leading 1s rather than leading 0s must be introduced at the left end of the number.

A simple approach to two's complement multiplication is to negate all negative operands at the beginning, perform unsigned multiplication on the resulting (+ve) numbers and then negate the result if necessary.

Two's complement negation for an integer

$$X = x_{n-1} x_{n-2} x_{n-3} \dots x_1 x_0 \text{ is specified by}$$

$$-X = \overline{x}_{n-1} \overline{x}_{n-2} \overline{x}_{n-3} \dots \overline{x}_1 \overline{x}_0 + 000\dots01 \text{ (modulo } 2^n) \qquad \text{...(3)}$$

and can easily be implemented by on adder and an EXCLUSIVE-OR word gate as in Fig. 3.4. Several faster schemes have been proposed to handle negative operands. Since, these hinge on certain properties of the two's complement representation, we consider the latter first.

Clearly $\overline{x}_i = 1 - x_i$ (modulo 2), so we can write equation (3) as follows

$$-X = 111\dots1 - x_{n-1} x_{n-2} x_{n-3}\dots x_1 x_6 + 000\dots01 \text{ (modulo } 2^n) \text{ ...(4)}$$

Since, $Z^n = 111\dots11 + 000\dots01$, this equation is equivalent to $-x = Z^n - x$, which incidentally, indicates the origin of the term two's complement. Now, if x is positive ($x_{n-1} = 0$), we can express its value as

$$X = \sum_{i=0}^{n-2} Z^i x_i \qquad \qquad \text{...(5)}$$

if X is negative ($x_{n-1} = 1$) then equation (5), does not hold. However, we can retrieve equation 4 as

$$-X = 111\dots11 - (0x_{n-2}x_{n-3} \dots x_1 x_0 + 100 \dots 00) + 000\dots01$$

$$= Z^{n-1} - x_{n-2} x_{n-3} \dots x_1 x_0 \qquad \qquad \text{...(6)}$$

because $\qquad Z^{n-1} = 111...11...100...00 + 000 ... 0$

Hence, for negative X,

$$X = -Z^{n-1} + x_{n-2} \, x_{n-3} \, ... \, x_1 x_0$$

$$= -Z^{n-1} + \sum_{i=0}^{n-2} Z^i x_i \qquad\qquad ...(7)$$

Finally, we combine equations (5) and (7) into a single formula

$$X = -Z^{n-1} x_{n-1} + \sum_{i=0}^{n-2} Z^i x_i \qquad\qquad ...(8)$$

which is valid for both positive and negative n-bit integers.

For example : suppose, n = 6 and x = 101101,

evaluating X according to equation (8) yields

$$X = -2^5 \times 1 + 2^4 \times 0 + 2^3 \times 1 + 2^2 \times 1 + 2^1 \times 0 + 2^0 \times 1$$

$$= -32 + 8 + 4 + 1 = -19$$

Equation 8 implies that we can treat bits $x_{n-2} \, x_{n-3} \, ... \, x_1 x_0$ of a −ve two's complement integer in the same way as the corresponding bits of a +ve number, each bit x_i has the positive weight Z^i. Weight $+ Z^{n-1}$ is assigned to the sign bit x_{n-1} of a + ve number. However, since $x_{n-1} = 0$, its contribution to the number is zero.

If $X = x_{n-1} \, x_{n-2}...x_1 x_0$ is a two's complement fraction instead of an integer, then the negation formula equation (3) remains valid, but because bit i now has weight Z^{i-n+1} instead of Z^i equation (8) is replaced by

$$X = -Z^0 x_{n-1} + \sum_{i=0}^{n-2} 2^{i-n+1} x_i \qquad\qquad ...(9)$$

actually we have multiplied equation (8) by scaling factor $Z^{-(n-1)}$.

For example : let n = 4 and x = 1011, which represent the fraction -0.625_{10}. Application of equation (9) yields.

$$X = -2^0 \times 1 + 2^{-1} \times 0 + 2^{-2} \times 1 + 2^{-3} \times 1$$

$$= -1.000 + 0.250 + 0.125 = -0.625$$

Note : Another widely used scheme for two's complement multiplication was proposed by Booth which has been discussed in detail in Chapter 1.

3.1.3 Division

In fixed point division, two numbers, a divisor V and a dividend D are given. The object is to compute third number Q, the quotient, such that $Q \times V$ equals or is very close to D e.g. if unsigned integer formats are being used, Q is computed so that

$$D = Q \times V + R$$

$$R \text{ - remainder to be less than V}$$

We can then write

$$\frac{D}{V} = Q + \frac{R}{V}$$

...(10)

Here, $\frac{R}{V}$ is a small quantity representing the error in using Q alone to represent $\frac{D}{V}$, this error is zero if R = 0.

3.1.3.1 Preliminaries

The relationship $D \approx Q \times V$ represent that a close correspondence exist between division and multiplication. In multiplication, the shifted multiplier is added to the multiplicand to form the product. In division, the shifted divisor is subtracted from the dividend to form the quotient. One of the simpler binary division methods is a sequential digit by digit algorithm. Next example illustrate this approach for 3-bit divisor V = 101 and 6-bit dividend D = 100110. The dividend is scanned from left to right and the quotient is computed bit-by-bit.

$$
\begin{array}{r|ll}
 & 0111 & \text{Quotient } Q = a_3\, a_2\, a_1\, a_0 \\
\hline
101 & 100110 & \text{Dividend } D = R_0 \\
 & \underline{000} & a_3\, V \\
 & 100110 & R_1 \\
 & \underline{101} & a_2 Z^{-1} V \\
 & 10010 & R_2 \\
 & \underline{101} & a_1 Z^{-2} V \\
 & 1000 & R_3 \\
 & \underline{101} & \\
 & 011 & \\
\end{array}
$$

If the numbers appearing in the division calculation of previous example are unsigned binary integers of length six, then equation (10) becomes,

$$\frac{100110.}{000101.} = 000111. + 00011 \cdot \frac{000011.}{000101.}$$

corresponding to the decimal division $\frac{38}{5} = 7 + \frac{3}{5}$. If the numbers are unsigned 6-bit fractions, the example of division shown above is represented as

$$\frac{0.100110}{0.101000} = 0.111000 + \frac{.000011}{0.101000}$$

Corresponding to

$$\frac{0.59375}{0.625} = 0.875 + \frac{0.046875}{0.625}$$

In integer arithmetic Q and R always integers of the standard word size. If fraction formats are used, the number of bits of Q is not necessarily bounded.

For example $\frac{0.2000}{0.3000}$ might be required to yield a four digit quotient Q with truncation or rounding determining the final digit of Q. Another difficulty is if D is too large relation to U, then Q will not fit in the standard word size, resulting in quotient overflow.

3.2 FLOATING POINT ARITHMETIC

3.2.1 Floating Point Addition and Subtraction Rules

(Dec. 10, 10 Marks)

Step 1 : Select the number with smaller exponent and shift its mantissa right, a number of steps equal to difference in exponents |e2 - e1|, for examples, if the number are 1.75×10^2 and 6.8×10^4 then the number 1.75×10^2 is selected and converted to 0.0175×10^4.

Step 2 : Set the exponent of the result equal to the larger exponent.

Step 3 : Perform addition/ subtraction on the mantissas and determine the sign of the result.

Step 4 : Normalize the result, if necessary.

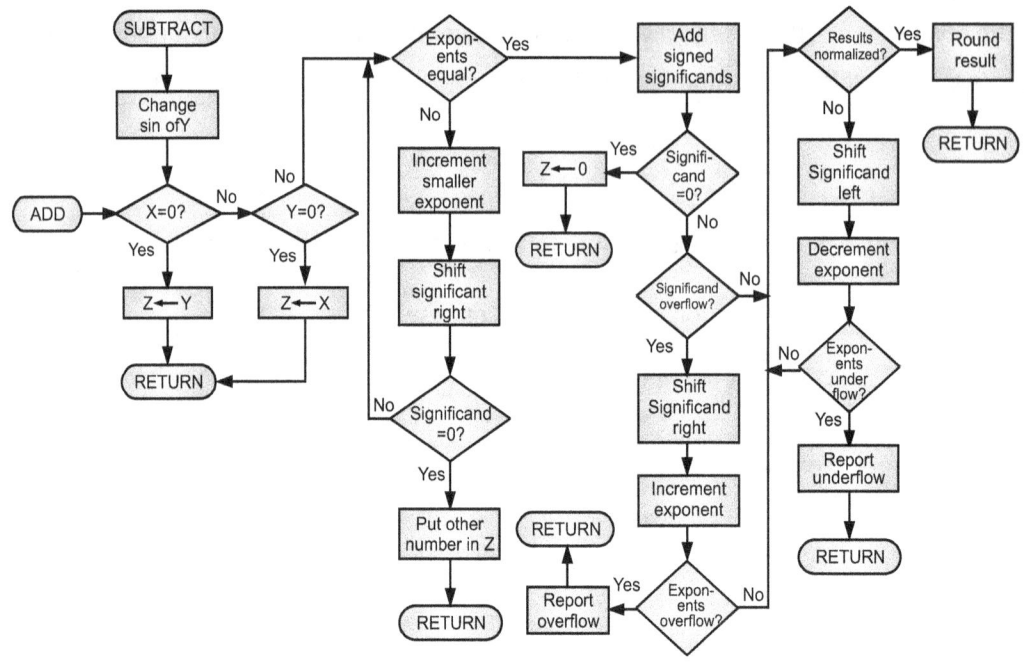

Fig. 3.5 : Floating point addition and subtraction

Example 1 : Add single precision floating point numbers A and B where

A = 44900000 H and B = 42 A 00000 H.

Solution : Step 1 : Represent numbers in single precision format

$$A = 0\ \ 1000\ \ 1001\ \ 0010000\ \ \ \ ......0$$

$$B = 0\ \ 1000\ \ 0101\ \ 010000\ \ \ \ ......0$$

Exponent for A = 1000 1001 = 137

Actual exponent = 137 − 127 (Bias) = 10

Exponent for B = 1000 0101 = 133

Actual exponent = 133 − 127 (Bias) = 6

∴ Number B has smaller exponent with difference 4. Hence, its mantissa is shifted right by 4-bits as shown below.

Step 2 : Shift mantissa

Shifted mantissa of B = 00000100 0

Step 3 : Add mantissas

$$\begin{array}{ll}
\text{Mantissa of A} = & 001\ 00\ 000 \qquad ......0 \\
\text{Mantissa of B} = & 000\ 00\ 100 \qquad ......0 \\
\hline
\text{Mantissa of Result} = & 001\ 00\ 100 \qquad 0
\end{array}$$

Both numbers are positive, sign of the result is positive

$$\begin{array}{ll}
\text{Result} = & 01000\ 1001\ 00100\ 100 \qquad ......0 \\
= & 44920000\ \text{H}
\end{array}$$

Example 2 : Subtract single point precision floating point numbers A and B where

A = 449 00 000 H and B = 42 A 00000 H.

Solution : Step 1 : Represent numbers in single precision format

$$\begin{array}{ll}
\text{A} = & 0\ 10001001\ 0010000 \qquad ......0 \\
\text{B} = & 0\ 10000101\ 010000 \qquad ......0 \\
\text{Exponent for A} = & 10001001 = 137 \\
\text{Actual exponent} = & 137 - 127\ (\text{bias}) = 10 \\
\text{Exponent for B} = & 1000\ 0101 = 133 \\
\text{Actual exponent} = & 133 - 127\ (\text{Bias}) \\
= & 6
\end{array}$$

∴ Number B has smaller exponent with difference. Hence, its mantissa is shifted right by 4 bits as shown below.

Step 2 : Shift mantissa

$$\text{Shifted mantissa of B} \ = \ 0000\ 0\ 100 \qquad ......0$$

Step 3 : Subtract mantissa

$$\begin{array}{ll}
\text{Mantissa of A} = & 001\ 000\ 00 \qquad ......0 \\
\text{Mantissa of B} = & 000\ 001\ 00 \qquad ......0 \\
\hline
& 000\ 111\ 00 \qquad 0
\end{array}$$

Mantissa for A is greater than mantissa for B therefore sign of result is sign of A.

$$\begin{array}{ll}
\text{Result} = & 0\ 1000\ 1001\ 00011100 \qquad ......0 \\
= & 448\text{E}\ 0000\ \text{H}
\end{array}$$

3.2.2 Hardware Implementation of Floating Point Addition and Subtraction

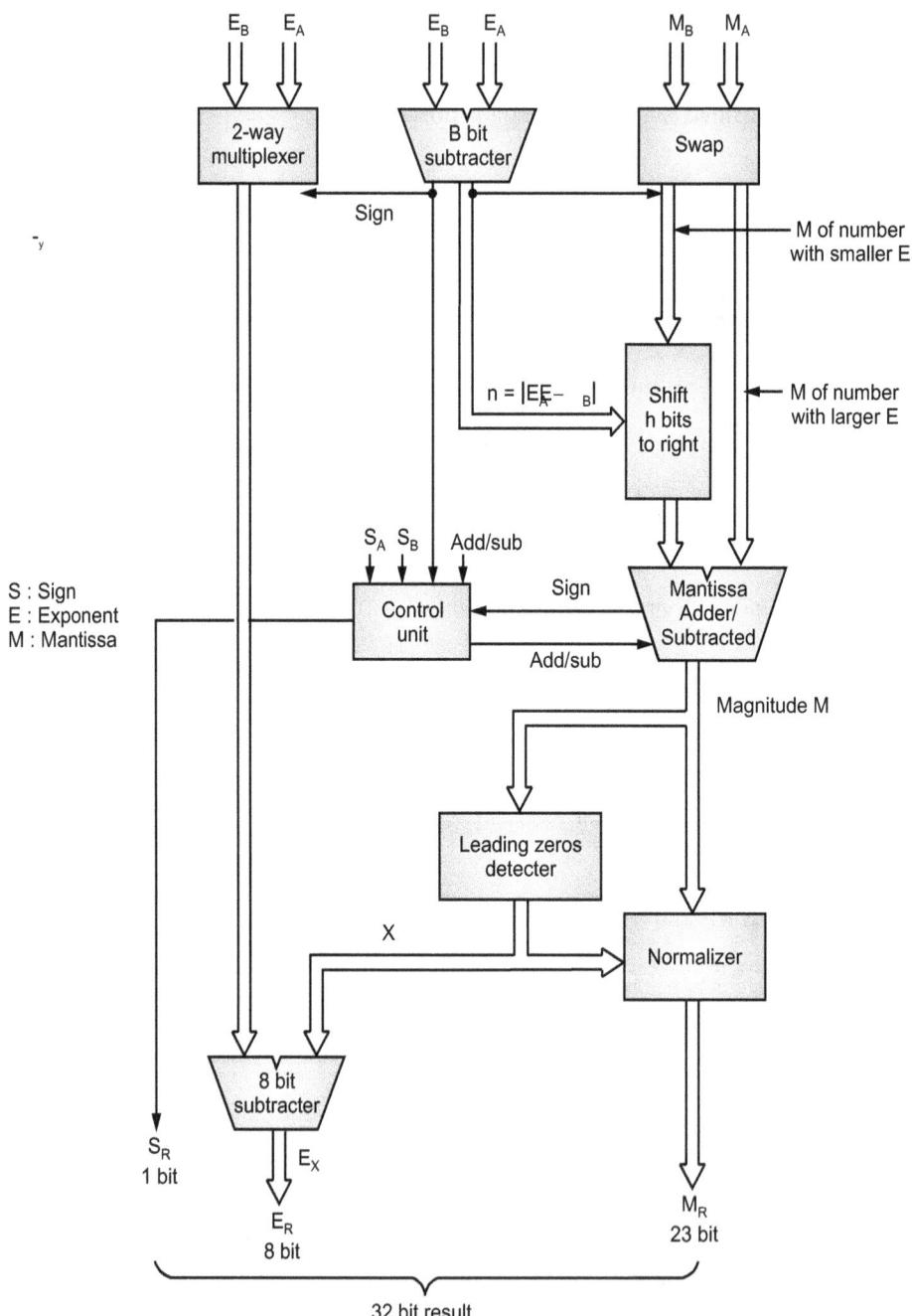

Fig. 3.6 : Hardware implementation of floating point addition and subtraction

Fig. 3.6 shows hardware implementation for the addition and subtraction of 32-bit floating point operands that have single precision format. 1 bit for sign, 8-bits for signed exponent and 23-bit for mantissa.

- As per addition or subtraction rule we have to first compare the exponents of numbers to determine a number with a smaller exponent or then to determine how for to shift the mantissa of that number so that its exponent matches with the other number.

- The shift count value n, is determined by the 8 bit subtractor. The inputs for the 8 bit subtractor are exponent values of two numbers and the operation performed is $E_A - E_B$. The subtraction gives the difference n.

- This difference is sent to the shifter unit. The sign of the difference that results from comparing exponents determines which mantissa is to be shifted.

- If the sign is 0, then $E_A \geq E$. and input to SWAP network is 0. This disables swapping and mantissa M_B is sent to the shifter.

- If the sign is 1, then $E_A - E_B$ and input to SWAP network is 1. In this case, swapping is enabled and mantissa M_A is sent to the shifter. The shifter unit shifts the given mantissa n positions to the right.

- The two way multiplexer is used to set the exponent of the result (E) equal to the larger exponent i.e. step 5. Multiplexer has two inputs E_A and E_B and its output is based on the sign of the difference resulting from comparing exponents in step 1.

- The output of multiplexer is

$$E = E_A \quad \text{if} \quad E_A \geq E_B$$

$$\text{or} \quad E = E_B \qquad E_A < E_B$$

- The third step is to perform addition or subtraction on the mantissas and determine the sign of the result.

- The control logic is used to determine whether the mantissa are to be added or subtracted. It decides this by checking the signs of the operands (S_A and S_B) or the operation (Add or subtract) that is to be performed on the operands. The control logic is also responsible for determining the sign of the result (S_R).

- The control logic determines the sign of the result by checking the resulted sign of mantissa adder/subtracted, sign from the exponent comparison signs of the operands and then operation to be performed.

- In step 4, the result of mantissa (M) is normalised, the normalized value is truncated to generate the 23 bit mantissa MR, of the result.

- The leading zeros detector determines the number of bits shifts, X to be applied to mantissa (M). The value X is then subtracted from the tentative resulted exponent E to generate the true result exponent, E_R.

3.2.3 Floating Point Multiplication/Division   (Dec. 10, 10 Marks)

For floating point multiplication and division first check for zero. Then add and subtract exponents.

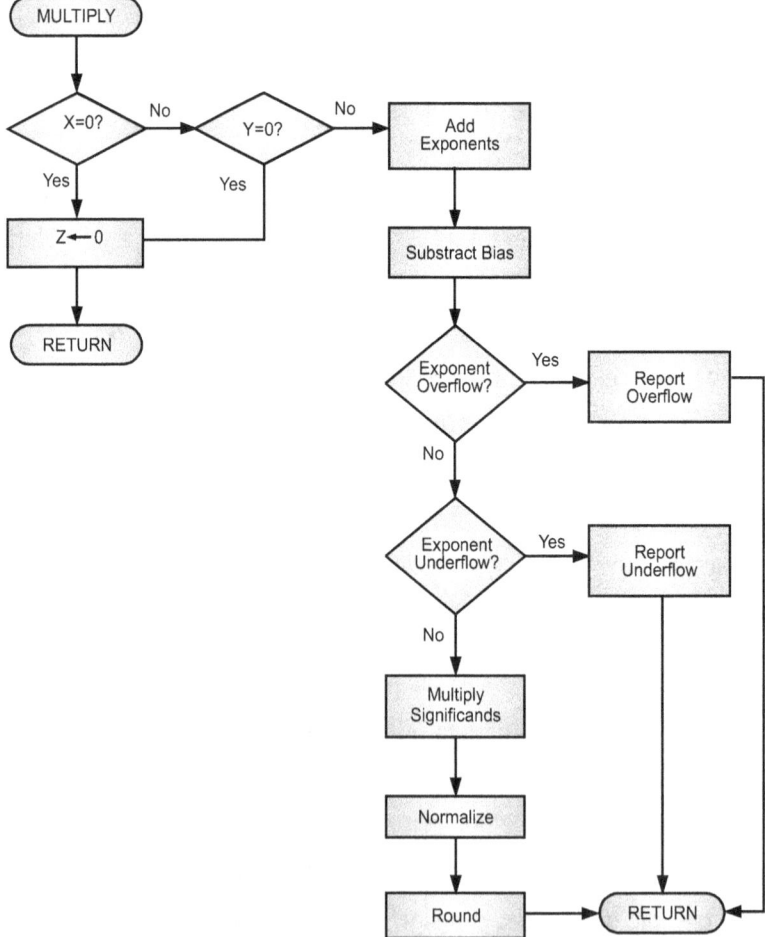

Fig. 3.7 : Floating point multiplication

Multiply or divide significant. Take care of sign of the bits. Then normalize the values. Round the values. All the intermediate results are in double length storage. Both the figures explain the steps involved in floating point multiplication and division.

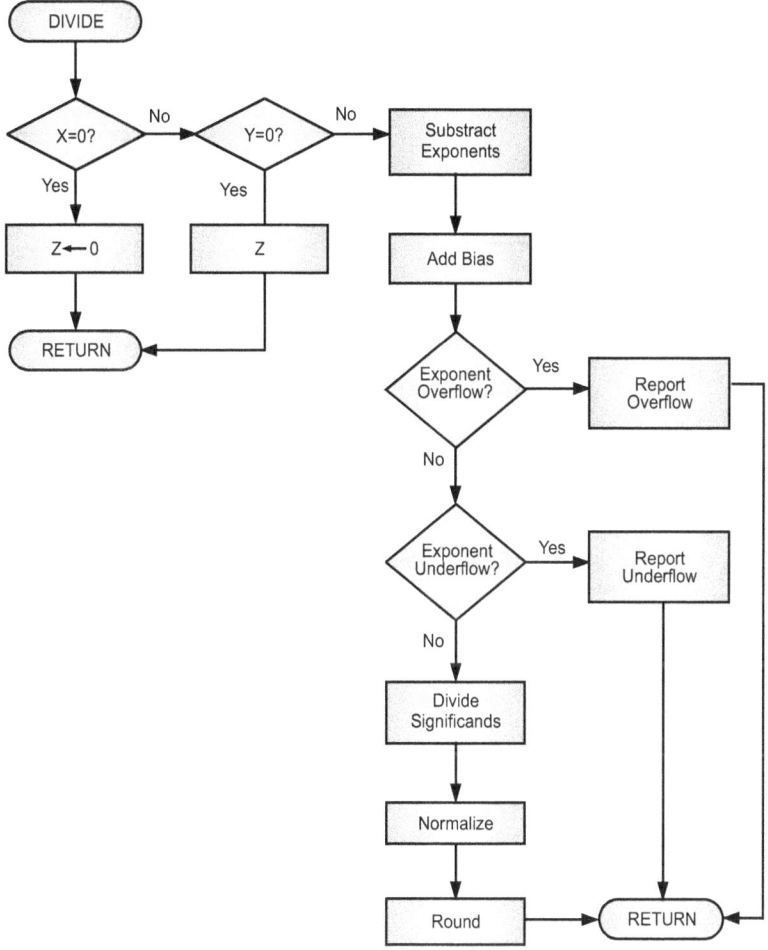

Fig. 3.8 : Floating point division

3.3   ARITHMETIC LOGIC UNIT

Various circuits used to execute data processing instructions are combined in a single circuit called an arithmetic logic unit (ALU). Simple ALUs that perform fixed point addition and subtraction as well as word-based logical operations are realized by combinational circuit.

3.3.1 Combinational ALUs

Simplest ALUs combine the functions of a two's complement adder-subtracter with those of a circuit that generates word based logic functions of the form f (x, y). For example, AND, XOR and NOT. Fig. 3.9 shown below outlines an ALU that has separate subunits for logical and arithmetic operations. A particular class of operation (logical or arithmetic) to be performed is determined by a "mode" control line m attached to a two way multiplexer that channels the required result to the output bus Z.

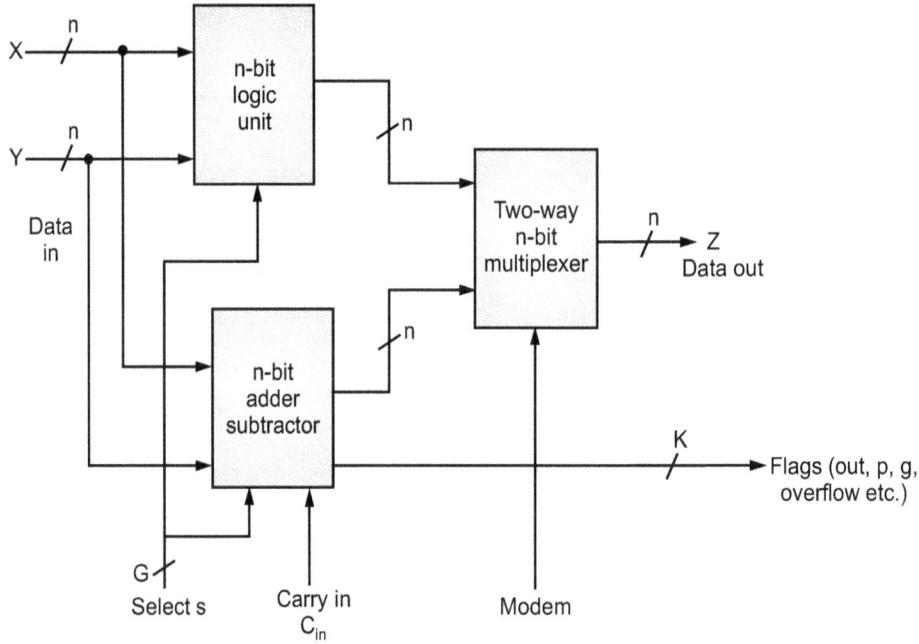

Fig. 3.9 : Basic n-bit ALU

Specific operation performed by the desired subunit is determined by a "select" control line S as shown. ALUs logical operations are performed by bitwise i.e. same operation f is applied to every paid of data lines $x_i y_i$. The maximum number of distinct logical operations of the form f (x_i, y_i) is 16, which is the number of distinct truth tables of two Boolean variables. Hence, the select bus needs to be of size 4 at most. S can be used to select up to 16 different arithmetic operations, such as X + Y, X − Y, Y − X, X + 1, X − 1.

The logical operations in previous Fig. 3.9 can be obtained by generating all four minterms of f (x_i, y_i) namely.

$$m_3 = x_i y_i, \quad m_2 = \overline{x_i}\, y_i, \quad m_1 = x_i\, \overline{y_i}, \quad m_0 = \overline{y_i}\, \overline{y_i}$$

For every pail $x_i y_i$ of data bits and by using control lines $s = s_3 s_2 s_1 s_0$ to select desired subsets at the minterms to be URed together. If we construct sum-of-product expression.

$$f(x_i, y_i) = x_3 S_3 + m_2 S_2 + m_1 S_1 + m_0 S_0$$

$$= x_i y_i S_3 + x \bar{y_i} S_2 + \bar{x_i} y_i S_1 + \bar{x_i} \bar{y_i} S_0 \qquad \ldots(1)$$

Here, we can find every combination of $S_3 S_2 S_1 S_0$ produces a different function. For example :

$S = 0110$ makes $f(x_i, y_i) = x_i \bar{y_i} + \bar{x_i} y_i$, which is EXCLUSIVE-OR. Because of the bitwise nature of the logic operations, we can replace x_i and y_i in equation (1) with n-bit words X and Y.

$$f(x, y) = XYS_3 + X\bar{Y}S_2 + \bar{X}YS_1 + \bar{X}\bar{Y}S_0 \qquad \ldots(2)$$

Apart from all simplicity, the ALU of Fig. 3.9 is more expensive and slower. For $n = 4$, the logic subunit employs about 25 gates and inverters. The multiplexer in Fig. 3.9 also requires additional gates. Thus, we can implement the logic unit directly using equation (2) using several n-bit word gates as shown in Fig. 3.10. Adder subtractor can be designed be any of the techniques presented earlier with appropriate addition connections to X, Y and S.

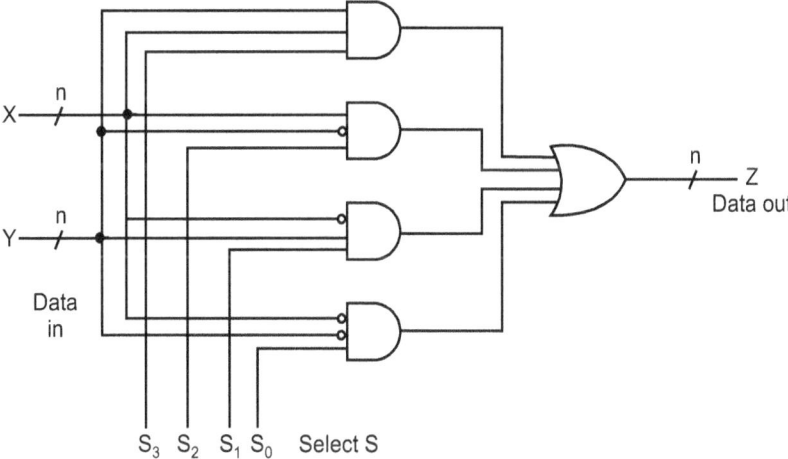

Fig. 3.10 : n-bit logic unit that realizes all 16 bits variable functions

3.3.2 Sequential ALUs

As we have seen, both multiplication and division can be implemented by combinational logic. But, it is impractical to merge these operation with addition and subtraction in single. Combinational multipliers and deviders are costly in terms of hardware. Also, they are slower in performance. n-bit combinational multiplier or divider is typically composed of n or more levels of add-subtract logic, making multiplication and division at least n-times slower than addition and subtraction. The number of gates in the multiply-divide logic is also greater by factor of about n. Hence, except when n is very small, complete ALUs are usually constructed from low-cost sequential circuits where add and subtract each take one clock-cycle while multiplication and division are multicycle operations.

3.3.2.1 Basic Design

Fig. 3.11 shows a widely used sequential ALU design that aims at minimizing hardware costs.

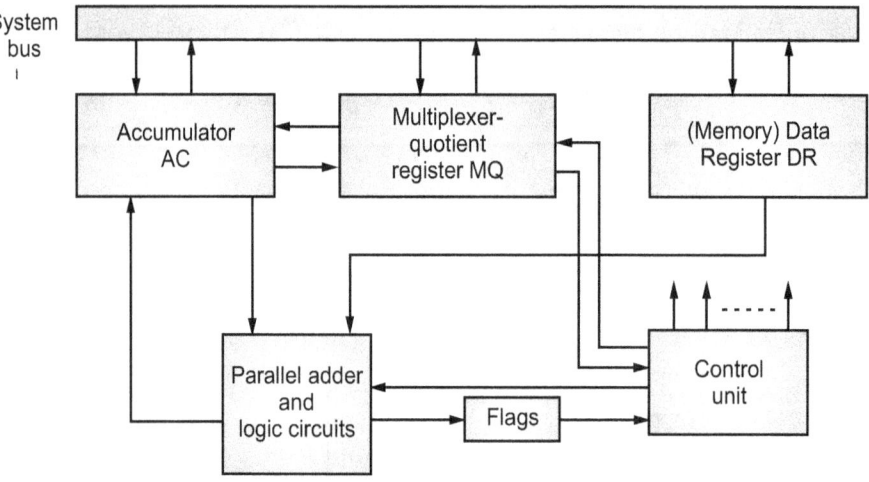

Fig. 3.11 : Structure of a basic sequential ALU

Here, it is intended to implement multiplication and division using one of the sequential digit-by-digit shift add/subtract algorithms discussed earlier. Three one-word registers are used for operand storage, the accumulator (AC), multiplier-register quotient (MQ) and data register (DR). AC and MQ are organized as a single register AC. MQ capable of left and right shifting. Additional data processing is provided by a combinational ALU capable of addition, subtraction, and logical operations. We will refer to this unit as the add-subtract unit. This unit derives its inputs from AC and DR and places its result in AC. The MQ register is so called because it stores the multiplier during multiplication and the quotient during division.

DR stores the multiplicand or devisor, while the result (product or quotient and remainder) is stored in the register pair AC. MQ. The role of these is as follows :

Addition	$AC = AC + DR$
Subtraction	$AC = AC - DR$
Multiplication	$AC \cdot MQ = DR \times MQ$
Division	$AC \cdot MQ = \dfrac{MQ}{DR}$

AND	AC = AC and DR
OR	AC = AC or DR
EXCLUSIVE-OR	AC = AC xor DR
NOT	AC = not (AC)

3.4   PIPELINE PROCESSING

Pipelining is a general technique for increasing processor throughout without requiring large amounts of extra hardware.

3.4.1   Introduction

A pipeline processor consists of a sequence of m-data processing circuits, called stages or segments, which collectively perform single operation on a stream of data operands through them. Every stage performs some processing but, final result is obtained at the end of entire pipeline. As shown in Fig. 3.12 a stage S_i contains a multiword input register or latch R_i and a datapth circuit C_i that is usually combinational. R_i's hold partially processed results as they move though the pipeline. They also serve as buffers that prevent neighboring stages from interfering with one another. a common clock signal causes the R_i's to change state synchronously. Each R_i receives a new set of input data D_{i-1} from the preceding stage S_{i-1} except for R_1 when data is supplied from an external source. D_{i-1} represents the results computed by C_{i-1} during the preceding clock period. Once D_i is loaded into R_i, C_i proceeds to use D_{i-1} to compute a new data set D_i. Thus, in each clock period, every stage transfers its previous results to the next stage and computer a new set of results.

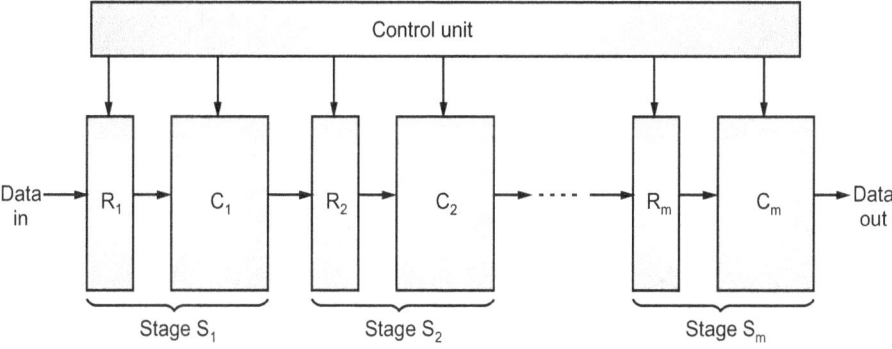

Fig. 3.12 : Structure of a pipeline processor

Advantage of pipeline is that m-stage pipeline can simultaneously process up to m independent sets of data operands. These data sets move through the pipeline stage by stage so that when pipeline is full, m separate operations are being executed concurrently, each in different stage. Consider, each stage of the m-stage pipe takes T seconds to perform its local suboperation and store its results. T is a clock period of pipeline. Delay or latency of the pipeline i.e. time to complete single operation is therefore mT. However, the throughout of the pipeline i.e. maximum number of operations completed per second is I/T.

Fig. 3.13 illustrates the behaviour of the adder pipeline when performing a sequence of N floating point additions of the form $x_i + y_i$ for the case N = 6. Add sequences of this type arise when adding two N complement real (floating point) vectors. At any time, any of the four stages can contain a pair of partially processed scalar operands denoted (x_i, y_i) in Fig. 3.13. The buffering of the stages ensures that S_i receiver as inputs the result computed by stage S_{i-1} during the preceding clock period only. If T is pipelines clock period, then it takes time 4T.

This valve is approximately the time required to do one floating point addition using a non-pipelined processor plus the delay due to the buffer register once all four stages of the pipeline have been filled with data, a new sum emerges from the lost stage S_4 every T seconds. Consequently, N consecutive addition can be done in time (N + 3) T, implying that the four- stage pipeline speedup is

$$S(4) = \frac{4\,(N)}{N + 3}$$

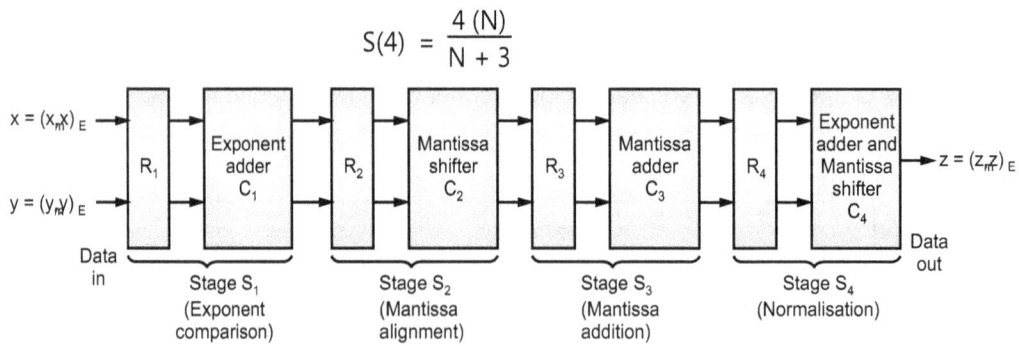

Fig. 3.13 : Four stage floating point adder pipeline

3.4.2 Pipeline Design

Fig. 3.14 shows the register level design of a floating point adder pipeline. The circuits that perform the mantissa addition in stage S_3 and the corresponding buffer are enlarged as shown by broken lines in Fig. 3.14 to accommodate full-size fixed point operands. To perform a fixed point addition, the input operands are routed through S_3 only, bypassing the other three stages. This Fig. is an example of a multi function pipeline that can be configured either as a four stage floating point adder or as a one-stage fixed point adder.

A floating point adder can have as few as two stages and as many as six e.g. a five stage adders have been built in which the normalization stage S_4 in Fig. 3.10 is split into two stages, one to count the number K of leading zeros (or ones) in an unnormalised mantissa and a second stage to perform the k shifts that normalize the mantissa.

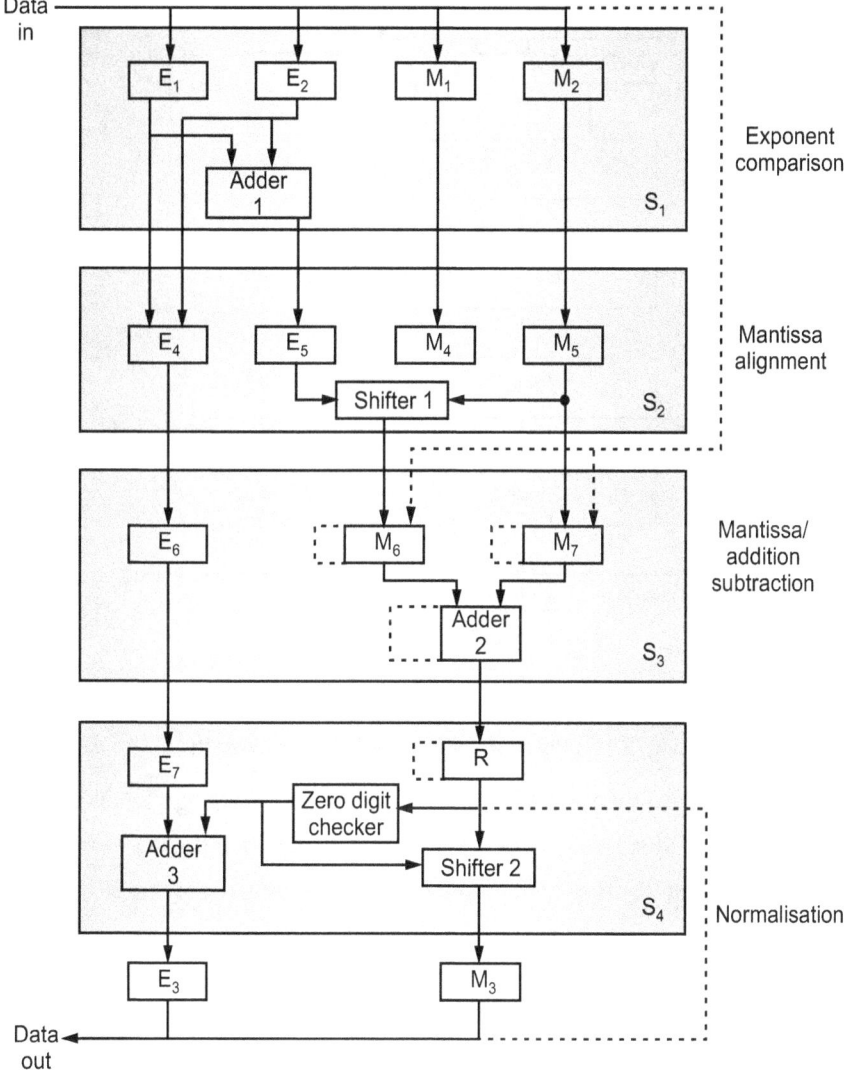

Fig. 3.14 : Pipelined version of the floating point adder

3.4.3 Feedback

The usefulness of a pipline processor can sometimes be enhanced by including feedback paths from the stage outputs to the primary inputs of the pipeline. Feedback enables the results computed by certain stages to be used in subsequent calculations by the pipeline. Fig. 3.15 explains the same.

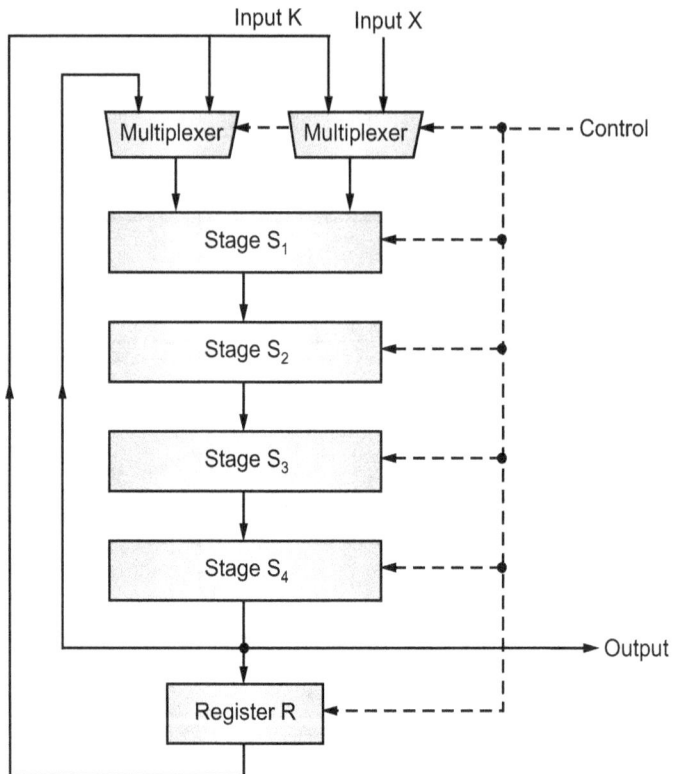

Fig. 3.15 : Pipelined adder with feedback paths

Here, a feedback path has been added to the output of the final stage S_4, allowing its results to be feedback to the first stage S_1. A register R has also been connected to the output of S_4, so that stages results can be stored indefinitely before being feed back to S_1.

The input operands of the modified pipeline are derived from four separate sources, a variable x that is typically obtained from a CPU register or memory location, a constant source K that can apply such operands as the all 0 and all 1 words. The output of stage S_4, representing the result computed by S_4 in the preceding clock-period and finally, an earlier result computed by the pipeline and stored in the output register R.

MULTIPLE CHOICE QUESTIONS (MCQ's)

1. For design of complex data path units such as multipliers and floating point adders ... pipeline is applied

    (a) software   (b) firemware   (c) hardware   (d) All

2. 1/T is maximum number of operations completed per second. This is also called......

    (a) latency   (b) delay   (d) Throughput   (d) frequency

3. Which statement is true about pipeline design ?

    (a) suboperations should have approximately same execution time.

    (b) to apply pipeline, operation should get subdivided into multi-stage sequential suboperations

    (c) fast buffers must be placed between stages

    (d) all above

4. DR register in sequential ALU is used for storing ......

    (a) multiplicand   (b) multiplier

    (c) divisor   (d) both (a) and (c)

5. In case of multiplication, in the sequential ALU ... stores product.

    (a) $AC \cdot MQ$ (b) $MQ \cdot AC$ (c) $DR \cdot MQ$ (d) $DR \cdot AC$

6. In case of division, in the sequential ALU ......stores remainder and ......stores quotient.

    (a) AC, MQ   (b) MQ, AC   (c) DR, MQ   (d) DR, AC

7. Select correct statement

    (a) Register file is also known as multiport high speed RAM

    (b) General purpose register is usually known as register file

    (c) Register file therefore needs several access ports

    (c) (b) and (c)

    (e) all above

8. In ... , k copies of the m-bit ALU are connected in the manner of a ripple carry adder to form a single, ALU capable of processing km-bit words directly.

    (a) spatial expansion   (b) temporal expansion

    (c) general expansion   (d) all of these

9. In ... one copy of the m-bit ALU in the manner of serial adder performs an operation of km-bits words in k consecutive steps.

    (a) spatial expansion   (b) temporal expansion

    (c) general expansion   (d) all of these

10.   Bit-sliced ALU uses ......

(a) Spatial expansion   (b) temporal expansion

(c) general expansion   (d) all of these

11.   ...... includes multi-precision processing.

(a) spatial expansion   (b) Temporal expansion

(b) General expansion   (b) all of these

12.   In signal division, the operands are preprocessed to transform them into ...... value.

(a) +ve   (b) – ve

(c) both (a) and (b)   (d) Neither (a) nor (b)

13.   In floating point arithmetic, in case of division if the dividend is zero then result is ......

(a) one   (b) zero   (c) ∞   (d) Any of these

14.   In division of binary number, first bits of dividend are checked from left to right until the set of bits examined represents a number ...... the divison.

(a) greater than or equal to   (b) equal to

(c) less than   (d) less than or equal to

15.   In restoring division algorithm, if the result of subtraction is ...... then it needs restoring of register A.

(a) + ve   (b) – ve

(c) both (a) and (b)   (d) None of these

16.   Non-restoring division algorithm needs restoring of remainder if remainder is

(a) + ve   (b) – ve

(c) both (a) and (b)   (d) neither (a) nor (b)

17.   Select false statement about combinational ALU ?

(a) simple in design   (b) less expensive

(c) slower   (d) none of these

18.   Which are subunits of combinational ALU ?

(a) logic unit   (b) add/ sub unit

(c) multiplexer   (d) all of these

19.   Which of the following are the subunits of sequential ALUs ?

(a) accumulator   (b) multiplier quotient register

(c) data register   (d) all of these

20. MQ register in the sequential ALU is used to store
     (a) quotient   (b) multiplier
     (c) remainder   (d) both (a) and (b)

21. The front end of Intel Nehalem pipeline organization can decade upto ...... instructions in one cycle.
     (a) 1   (b) 2   (c) 3   (d) 4

22. The front end of intel Nehalem pipeline organization supports ......hardware threads.
     (a) 1   (b) 2   (c) 3   (d) 4

23. Front end of intel Nehalem pipeline includes enhancement in
     (a) branch handling   (b) loop detection
     (c) MSROM   (d) all of these

24. In Intel Nehalem pipeline, the instruction fetch unit (IFU) can fetch upto ...... bytes of aligned instructions bytes each cycle from the instruction cacho.
     (a) 2   (b) 4   (c) 8   (d) 16

25. In Intel Nehalem pipeline, the scheduler can dispatch upto ...... micro-operations in one cycle.
     (a) 2   (b) 4   (c) 6   (d) 8

26. In Intel Nehalem pipeline, the instruction Queue (IQ) buffers the ILD processed instructions and can deliver upto ...... instructions in one cycle to the instruction decoder.
     (a) 2   (b) 4   (c) 6   (d) 8

27. In Intel Nehalem pipeline, the ...... is located inside the IDQ to improve power consumption.
     (a) loop stream decader   (b) power saver
     (c) idle register   (d) all of these

28. The instruction decoder supports micro fusion to
     (a) improve front end throughput
     (b) increase the effective size of queues in scheduler
     (c) Re-order buffer (ROB)
     (d) All above

29. ......merges two instructions into a single micro operation.

(a) micro-fusion   (b) macro-fusion

(c) mini-fusion   (d) none of these

30. The instruction queue supports ......to combine adjacent instructions into one micro-operations where possible.

(a) micro-fusion   (b) macro-fusion

(c) mini-fusion   (d) all of these

ANSWERS

1.	c	2.	c	3.	d	4.	d	5.	a
6.	a	7.	e	8.	a	9.	b	10.	a
11.	b	12.	a	13.	c	14.	a	15.	b
16.	b	17.	b	18.	d	19.	d	20.	d
21.	d	22.	b	23.	d	24.	d	25.	c
26.	b	27.	a	28.	d	29.	b	30.	b

QUESTIONS

1. Explain floating point arithmetic.   **[May 04, 05, 06, 09, 10, 12. Dec. 03, 06, 07, 10]**

2. Draw the flowchart for floating point addition and explain.

[May 04, 05 , 06, 10, 12, Dec. 03]

3. Draw and explain flowchart for floating point subtraction.   **[Dec. 06]**

4. Explain the design of ALU using combinational circuit.   **[May 11]**

5. Differentiate between combinational and sequential ALU.   **[Dec. 11, 12]**

6. Explain the design of ALU.   **[May 13]**

7. How instruction execution is done in 4-stage pipeline ?   **[Dec. 11, May 12]**

8. What are the advantages of pipeling.   **[Dec. 11, 12, May 12]**

CONTROL DESIGN ORGANIZATION

4.1 BASIC CONCEPTS

A digital system is divided into two parts a data path unit and control unit. The data path is a network of functional and storage unit capable of performing certain micro operations on data words. While, the purpose of control unit is to issue control signals to the data path. These control signals enters the data path at 'control points', where they select the functions to be performed at specific times and route the data through the appropriate ports of the data path unit. In short, control unit logically reconfigures the data path to implement some specified instructions or program.

CPU's data path contains circuits to perform arithmetic and logical operations on words such as fixed point or floating point numbers. The internal structure of the data path circuit DP of a small microprocessor is depicted in Fig. 4.1.

It contains a register file RF for temporary storage of operands, two functional units F_1 and F_2 responsible for data processing and multiplexers to allow the data to be steered through DP. Typical functional units are an ALU performing addition, subtraction and logical operations, a shifter or a multiplier. The control unit CU receives external

4.1.1. Implementation Methods

During Implementation two approaches to control unit design have evolved. One approach views the controller as a sequential logic circuit or finite state machine that generates specific sequences of control signals in response to externally supplied instructions. As shown in Fig. 4.2(a), it is designed with goals of minimizing the number of components used and maximizing the speed of operation. Here, once the unit is constructed, the only way to implement changes in control unit behaviour is by redesigning the entire unit. Such a circuit is called Hardwired. On the other hand micro programmed control unit has the structure built around a storage called control memory, where all the control signals are stored in a program like format. It is shown in Fig. 4.2(b) the control memory stores a set of microprograms designed to implement or emulate the behaviour of the given instruction set.

Each instruction causes the corresponding microprogram to be fetched and its control information extracted in a manner that resembles the fetching and execution of a program from main memory instructions or commands. Which it converts into sequence of control signals that the CU applies to DP to implement a sequence of register transfer operations.

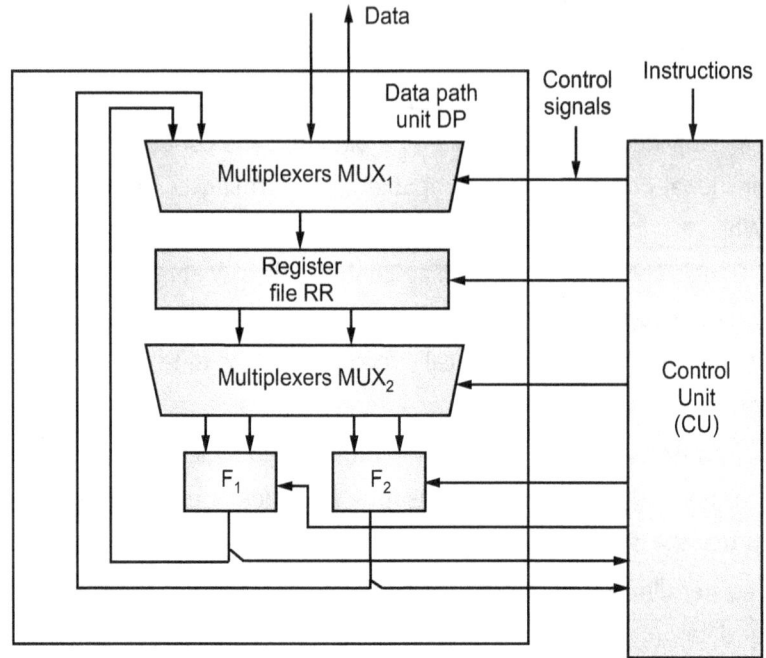

Fig. 4.1 : Processor composed of a datapath unit DP and a control unit CU

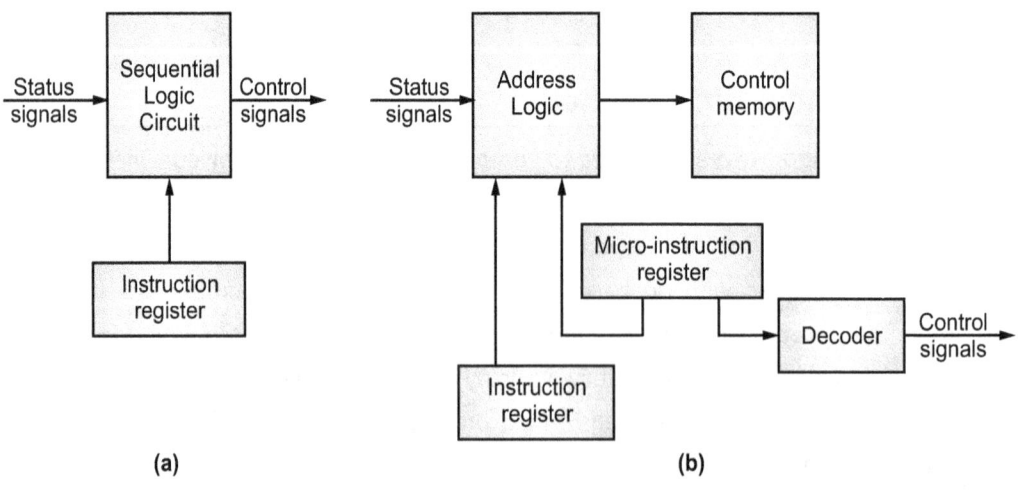

(a)   (b)

Fig. 4.2 : (a) Hardwired (b) Microprogrammed Control unit

4.2 HARDWARE CONTROL

In design method, two approaches are used. These method are representation of those used in practice, but they are suitable only for small control units such as might be encountered in simple RISE processors or application specific controllers.

Method 1 : The classical method of sequential circuit design. It attempts to minimize the amount of hardware, in particular, by using only $[\log_2 P]$ flip-flops to realize a p-state circuit.

Method 2 : An approach that uses one flip-flop per state and is known as the one hot method. While expensive in terms of flip-flops, this method simplifies CU design and debugging.

4.2.1 State Tables

The behaviour required of a control unit, like that of any finite state machine, can be represented by a state table of the general type shown in Table 4.1 (a). The rows of the state table correspond to the set of internal states {S}. These states are determined by the information stored in the machine at discrete points of time (clock cycles). Let X and Z the input and output variables.

Table 4.1 (a)

Inputs

State	I_1	I_2	I_m
S_1	$S_{1,1}, O_{1,1}$	$S_{1,2}, O_{1,2}....$	$S_{1,m}, O_{1,m}$
S_2	$S_{2,1}, O_{2,1}$	$S_{2,2}, O_{2,2}....$	$S_{2,m}, O_{2,m}$
S_n	$S_{n,1}, O_{n,1}$	$S_{n,2}, O_{n,2}....$	$S_{n,m}, O_{n,m}$

Table 4.1 (b)

Inputs

State	I_1	I_2	I_m	Output
S_1	$S_{1,1}$	$S_{1,2}$	$S_{1,m}$	O_1
S_2	$S_{2,1}$	$S_{2,2}$	$S_{2,m}$	O_2
S_n	$S_{n,1}$	$S_{n,2}$	$S_{n,m}$	O_n

The columns correspond to the combinations of the X signals that can be applied to the machine and are denoted by (I_j). The entry in row S_i and column I_j has the form $S_i, j \rightarrow S_{i,j}, O_{i,j}$ $S_{i,j}$ where $S_{i,j}$ is the next state of the machine that results from the application of input combination I_j, and O_{ij} denotes the output signals that appear on Z whenever the machine is in state S_i with input I_j applied control units have a feature that favours as slightly different state table. Their output signal valves often depend on the current state S_i only and so are independent of the input combination I_j. If all outputs are of this type, the circuit is called a micro machine. In case to represent the machines behaviour in the more compact format of table 4.1 (b). Where the output signals associated with each row are placed in separate column.

4.2.2 Design of Hardwired Control Unit   [May 06. 08, 09, June 07]

1. Sequence counter method : This is the most popular method conveniently employed for design of controller of moderate complexity. It uses counter for timing purposes.

2. Delay element method : This method depends on the use of clocked delay elements for generating the sequence of control signals.

3. State table method : This scheme employs the traditional algorithmic approach to sequential circuit design using classical state table method.

4. PLA method : It uses programmable logic array.

Under the control of a set of programmed instructions $I_1, I_2, ..., I_{i+1}, ...$ the CPU changes states (say) S_1, S_2, S_1, S_{i+1}. Fetching and executing any instruction. Then it is changes the state of CPU in a specified sequence say $S_{i1}, S_{i2}, ... S_{ij}, S_{i(j+1)}$. While the CPU is in state S_{ij}, a set of micro–operations are executed whereby CPU changes state to $S_{i(j+1)}$.

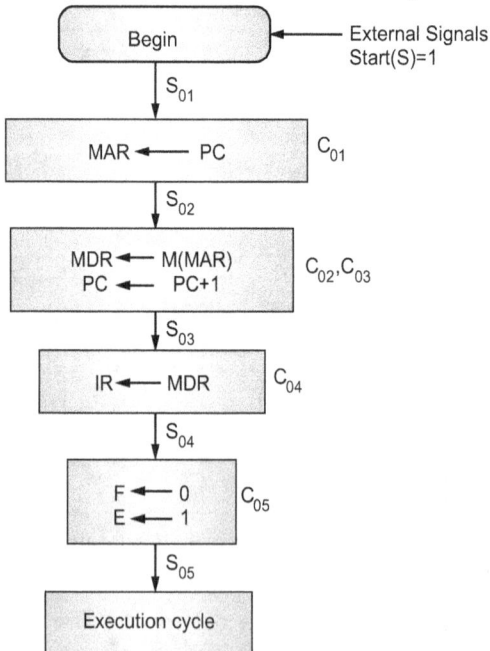

Fig. 4.3 : Controller Specification for fetch cycle

The controller generates the control signals associated with the set of micro–operations causing the state change of CPU.Hence, the flowchart specifying the sequence of micro–operations associated with fetch and execution cycles of an instruction provides directly the controller specification.

To generate the control signals C_{01}, (C_{02}, C_{03}), C_{04}, C_{05} in the specified order on accepting the external start signal $S = 1$.

Design of Hardwired control unit

1. Sequence Counter Method :

Step 1 : Identify the distinct phases in the flowchart.

Step 2 : Identify maximum number of sequential micro–operations (say k) in each of the phases.

Step 3 : Execute these k number of sequential operations with the help of Mod counter.

Step 4 : The counter output can be decoded and used to generate k control signals in a sequence to execute k micro–operations.

Step 5 : At the end, counter can be reset with E (execution) and F (fetch) being set to '1' and '0' respectively to start execution phase.

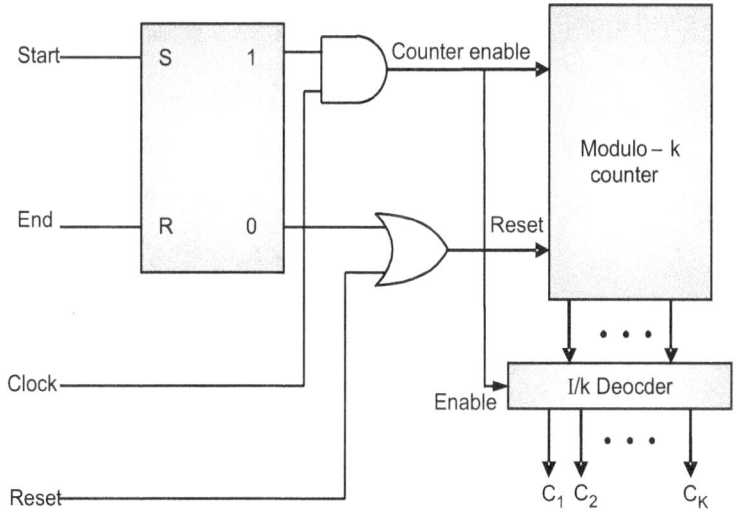

Fig. 4.4 : Modulo k sequence counter

2. Delay element method :   (May 2005, Dec. 2006)

It is simplified form the scheme is illustrated in Fig. 4.5 for designing a controller having the behaviour method noted in Fig. 4.3 for fetch cycle.

The ith block in the flowchart is replaced be delay element D_i having a delay of di unit. The control signals necessary to execute the micro–operations noted in the it" block are generate directly from line input to D_i. The time span t_i is the time elapsed from the beginning to the point while executions of the micro–operation(s) associate with the ith block of the flowchart get completed. Then

$$t_i - t_{i-1} = d_i$$

i.e. the delay block Di introduces a delay of di after which the control signals associated with the $(i+1)^{th}$ block may be generated.

The control signals or groups of control signals from the control unit are activated in a proper sequence. There is specific time delay between activation of two contiguous control signals. To ensure synchronous operation, the delay elements are implemented by D flip–flops and controlled by a common clock signal.

A control unit using delay elements can be constructed directly from flowchart that specifies required control signal sequences. There are some rules to drive control circuit from flowchart :

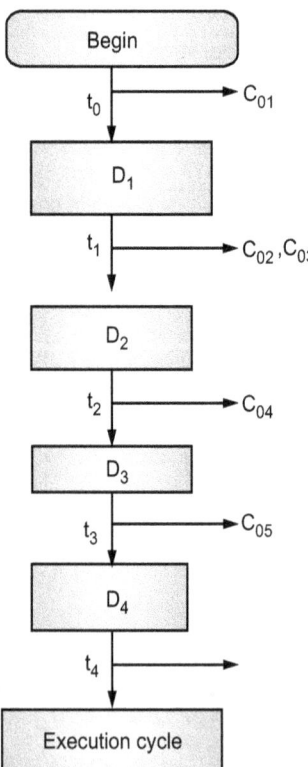

Fig. 4.5 : Control unit based on delay element method for fetch cycle

Rule 1 : Each sequence of two successive micro–operations requires a delay element. The signals that activate the control lines are taken directly from the input and output lines of the delay element as shown in Fig. 4.6 (a). The signals that are intended to activate same control line are logically ORed to get one common output signal as shown in Fig. 4.6 (b).

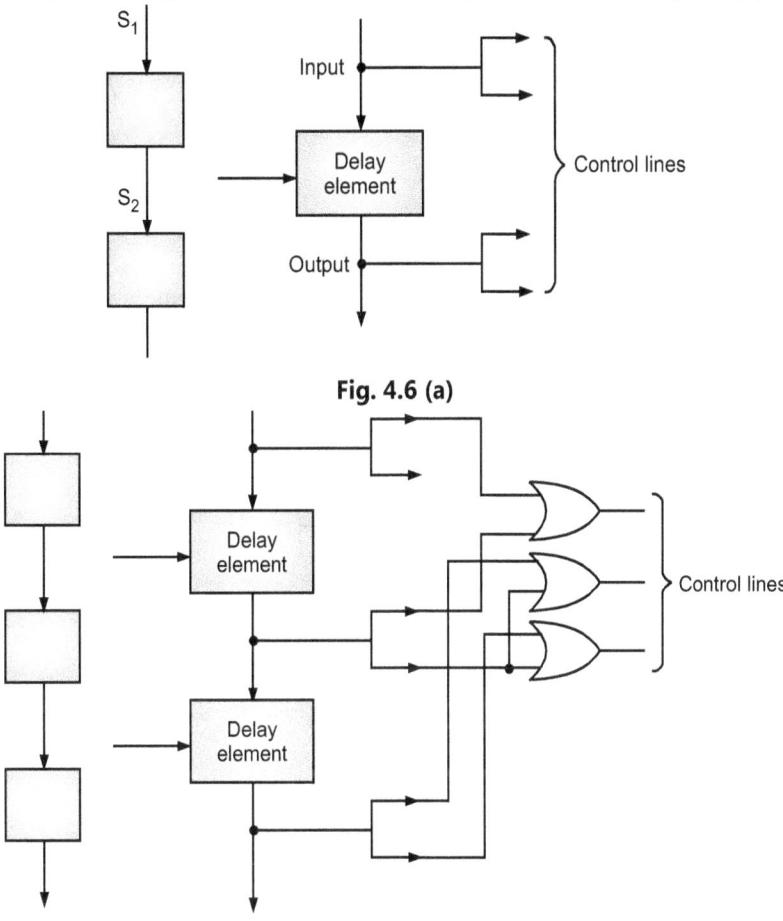

Fig. 4.6 (a)

Fig. 4.6 (b)

Rule 2 : In lines in the flowchart merge to a common Ilne are transformed into input OR gate, as shown in Fig. 4.7.

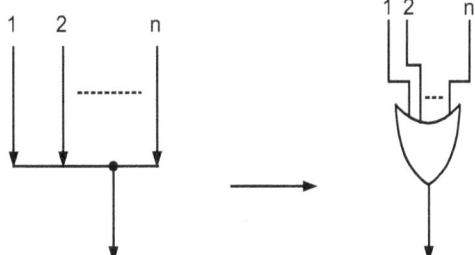

Fig. 4.7

Rule 3 : A decision box can be implemented by two AND gates, as shown in Fig. 4.8.

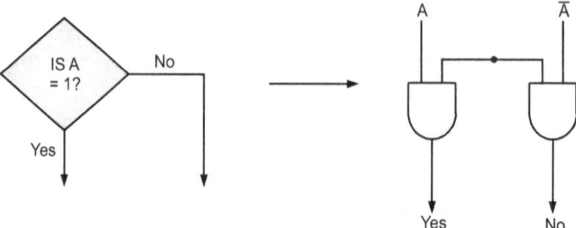

Fig. 4.8

Fig. 4.9 shows final circuit.

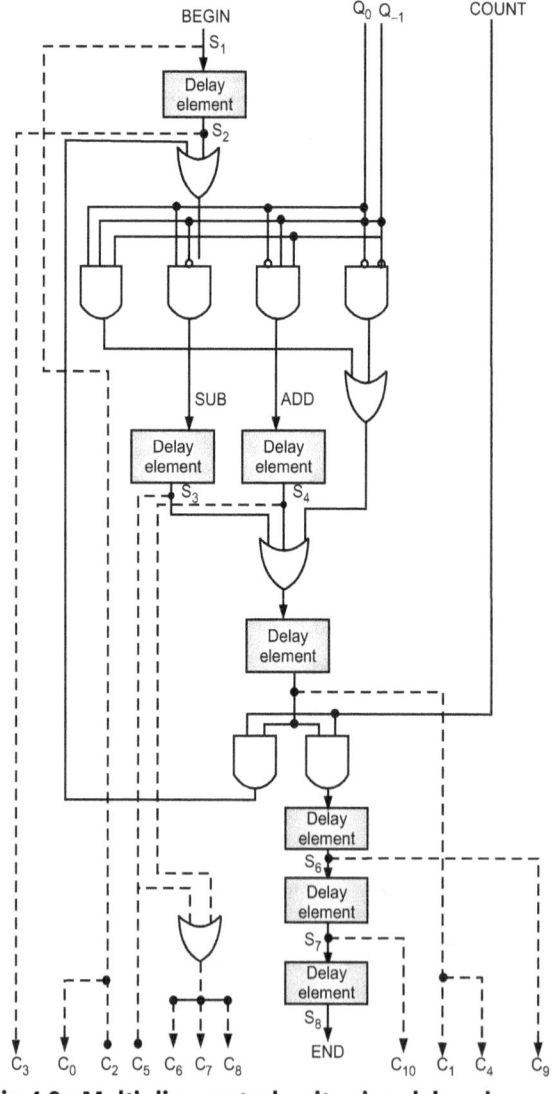

Fig 4.9 : Multiplier control unit using delay elements

Advantages of Delay element method

1. Simple design since there is no encoding and decoding of control unit states.

2. Less number of combinational logic elements.

3. Minimum design turnaround time, since there is direct correspondence of the controller structure.

Disadvantages of Delay element method

1. For an n state controller while the sequence counter method needs login flip–flops, the delay element method needs n number of delay elements each having one or more flip–flops.

2. Synchronization of widely distributed delay elements is often difficult to achieve.

3. **State Table Method :**

In the flowcharts shown in Fig. 4.3, state has been marked above each block of the flowchart. This can be viewed as the state of the controller which generates the control signals to control the microperations. A controller in state S_i on receiving the primary input signals I_j switched over to state S_i while generating the output signals C_i. The set of output signals executes the micro–instructions.

The control structure realizing the behaviour noted in the flowchart can be designed by executing following steps :

1. State Assignment : States are assigned as shown in the flowchart. Each such state specifics a particular state of the controller at the specific time.

2. State minimization : A set of states $(S_1, S_2,... S_n,)$ can be merged to a single state S' if that states are compatible.

3. State encoding : State variables are defined and states are encoded in terms of state variables.

Next flip–flops are selected to realize the state variables and the combinational circuit is designed to implement the state transition and the output signals as specified in the state transition table.

Example : Flowchart for 2's complement multiplication.

We can associate a state with every micro–instruction block, as shown in Fig. 4.10. Giving 9 states labelled S_0 through S_8. State represents idle or waiting state of the control unit. There are 4 primary input signals BEGIN, COUNT and Q_{-1}. So there are 16 possible input combinations.

Table shows a state table for the control unit which is directly derived from flowchart. Each entry indicates the next state followed by a list of control signals that are activated.

For example, for S_1, the next state is S_2 and is reached by activating control signals C_0 and C_2.

So state table entry is S_2, C_0, and C_2.

Certain state–and–input–signal combinations should not occur during normal operation, so the corresponding table entries are left blank.

For example, BEGIN signal should assume the 1 value only when the control unit is in the idle state So. Similarly, COUNT (which becomes 1 when counter count = 0) is never 1 in state S_2, since counter is loaded with count n in the preceding state S_1.

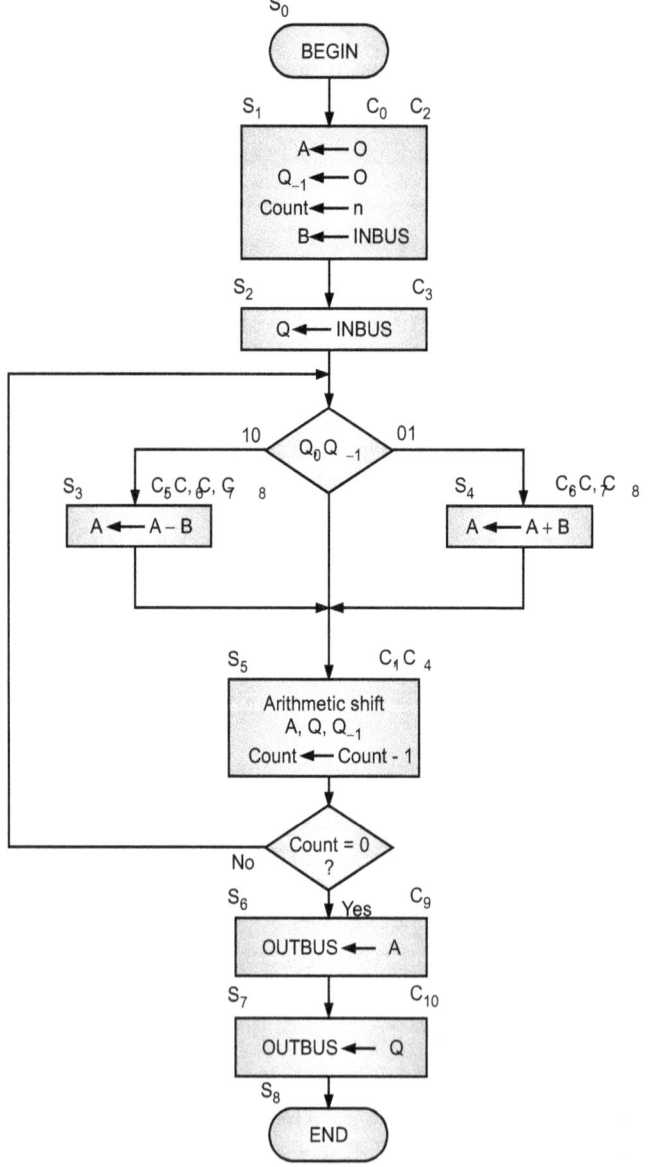

Fig. 4.10 : Flowchart for 2's complement multiplication

Table 4.2 : State Table

BEGIN	COUNT	Q_0	Q_{-1}	S_0	S_1	S_2	S_3	S_4	S_5	S_6	S_7	S_8
0	0	0	0	S_0	S_2, C_0, C_2	S_5, C_3			$S_5, C_1, C_4,$			
0	0	0	1	S_0	S_2, C_0, C_2	S_4, C_3		S_5, C_6, C_7, C_8	S_4, C_1, C_4			
0	0	1	0	S_0	S_2, C_0, C_2	S_3, C_3	S_5, C_5, C_6, C_7, C_6		S_3, C_1, C_4			
0	0	1	1	S_0	S_2, C_0, C_2	S_2, C_3			S_5, C_1, C_4			
0	1	0	0	S_0	S_2, C_0, C_2				S_6, C_1, C_4	S_7, C_9	S_8, C_{10}	$S_{10},$ END
0	1	0	1	S_0	S_2, C_0, C_2				S_6, C_1, C_4	S_7, C_9	S_8, C_{10}	$S_{10},$ END
0	1	1	0	S_0	S_2, C_0, C_2				S_6, C_1, C_4	S_7, C_9	S_8, C_{10}	$S_{10},$ END
0	1	1	1	S_0	S_2, C_0, C_2				S_6, C_1, C_4	S_7, C_9	S_8, C_{10}	$S_{10},$ END
1	0	0	0	S_1								
1	0	0	1	S_1								
1	0	1	0	S_1								
1	0	1	1	S_1								
1	1	0	0	S_1								
1	1	0	1	S_1								
1	1	1	1	S_1								
1	1	1	1	S_1								

Disadvantages of state table method :

1. The manual design process for the state table method based controller design becomes extremely difficult. Also, the computation time to automate the design process grows exponentially.

2. High design cost and time.

4. PLA Method.:

The control unit designed methods discussed so far are suitable only for small control units due to their size and complexity. In modern computer VLSI technology based circuitry is used for the design of control unit. One such structure PLA is discussed here.

AND and OR both arrays can be programmed to implement combinational logic functions. As shown in Fig. 4.11 (a) Xi, X2, X3 are input signals and fl, f2, f3 are combinations of input signals as outputs.

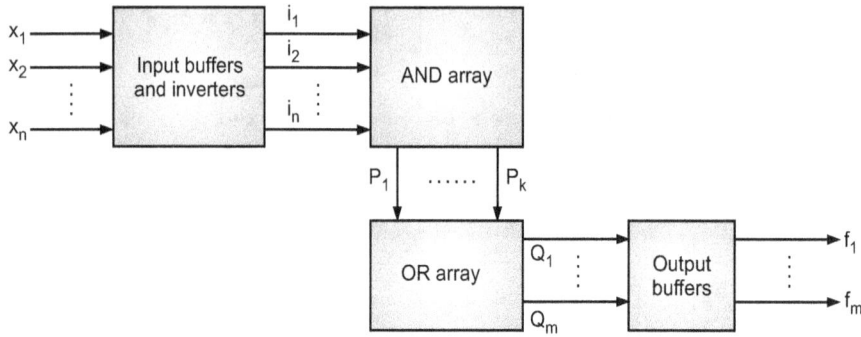

Fig. 4.11 (a) : Block diagram of PLA

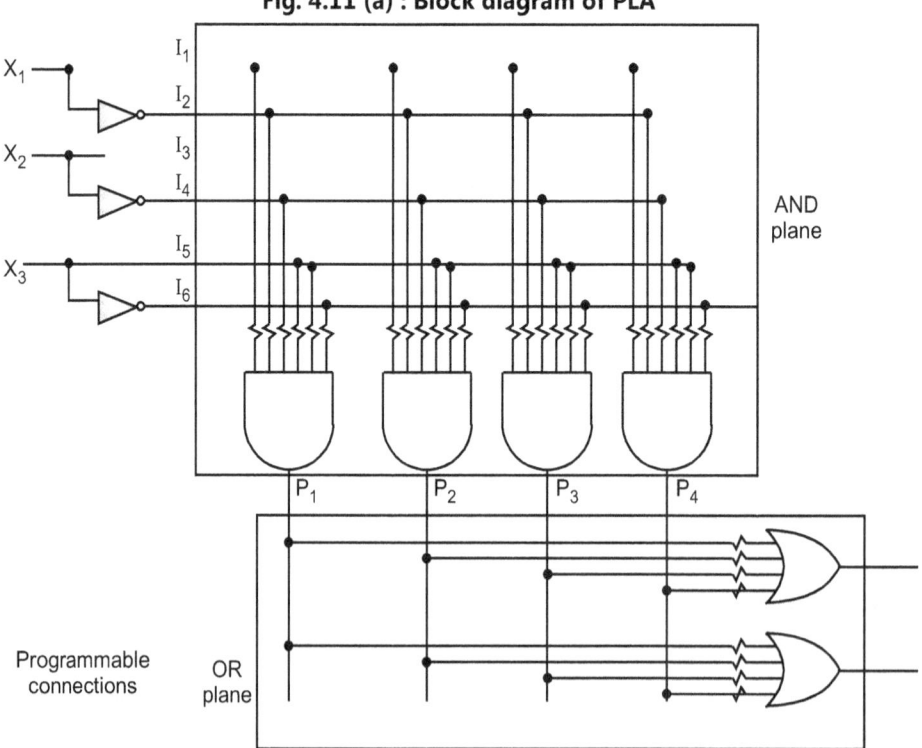

Fig. 4.11 (b) : Function Structure of PLA

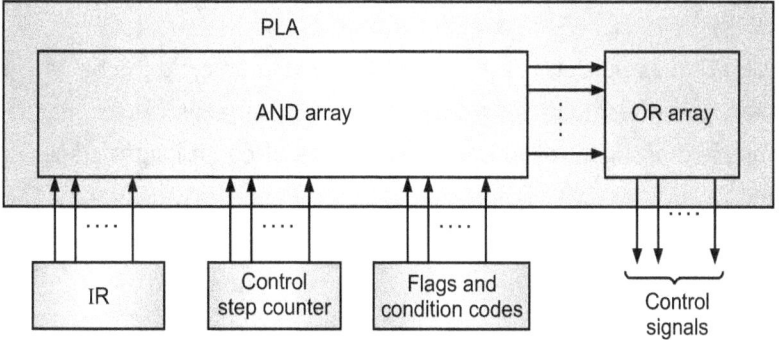

Fig. 4.12 : Control unit implementation using PLA

4.2.3 Advantages of Hardwired Design

- A higher speed operation.
- The smaller implementations.

4.2.4 Problems with Hard Wired Design

- Sequencing and micro–operation logic gets complex.
- Difficult to design, prototype, and test.
- Resultant design is inflexible, and difficult to build upon (Pipeline, multiple computation units etc.).
- Adding new instructions requires major design and adds complexity quickly.

4.3   MICROPROGRAMMED CONTROL

A microprogrammed control unit on the other hand makes use of a micro sequencer from which instruction bits are decoded to be implemented. It acts as the device supervisor that controls the rest of the subsystems including arithmetic and logic units, registers, instruction registers, off–chip input/output, and buses.

Microprogrammed control in which a dedicated microcontroller executes a microprogram to generate the signals.

4.3.1 Basic Concepts

- **Micro–operations :** We have already seen that the programs are executed as a sequence of instructions, each instruction consists of a series of steps that make up the instruction cycle fetch, decode etc. Each of these steps are, in turn, made up of a smaller series of steps called micro–operations.

- **Micro–operation execution :** Each step of the instruction cycle can be decomposed into micro–operation primitives that are performed in a precise time sequence. Each micro–operation is initiated and controlled based on the use of control signals/lines coming from the control unit.

- **Micro–instruction :** Each instruction of the processor is translated into a sequence of lower–level micro–instructions. The process of translation and execution are to as microprogramming.

- **Microprogramming :** A microprogram consists of a sequence of micro–instructions in a microprogramming.

- **Microprogrammed Control Unit :** It is a relatively logic circuit that is capable of sequencing through micro–instructions and generating control signal to execute each micro–instruction.

- **Control Unit :** The control Unit is an important portion of the processor.

The control unit issues control signals external to the processor to cause data exchange with memory and 1/0 unit. The control Unit issues also control signals internal to the processor to move data between registers, to perform the ALU and other internal operations in processor. In a hardwired control unit, the control signals are generated by a micro–instruction are used to controller register transfers and ALU operations. Control Unit design is then the collection and the implementation of all of the needed control signals for the micro–instruction executions.

4.3.2 Branch Address Modification using Bit–ORing and Wide– Branch Addressing   [Dec 2007]

In a microprogram to reduce complexity of branching, how to do branch address modification using bit – ORing and wide–branch addressing.

Bit–ORing : In this technique, the branch address is determined by ORing particular bit or bits with the current address of the micro–instruction.

For example, if the current address is 170, and branch address is 172, then the branch address can be generated by ORing 02 (bit 1), with the current address.

Wide–Branch Addressing : Generating branch addresses becomes more difficult as the number of branch addresses increases. In such situations programmable logic array (PLA) can be used to generate the required branch address. This simple and inexpensive way of generating branch addresses is known as wide–branch addressing.

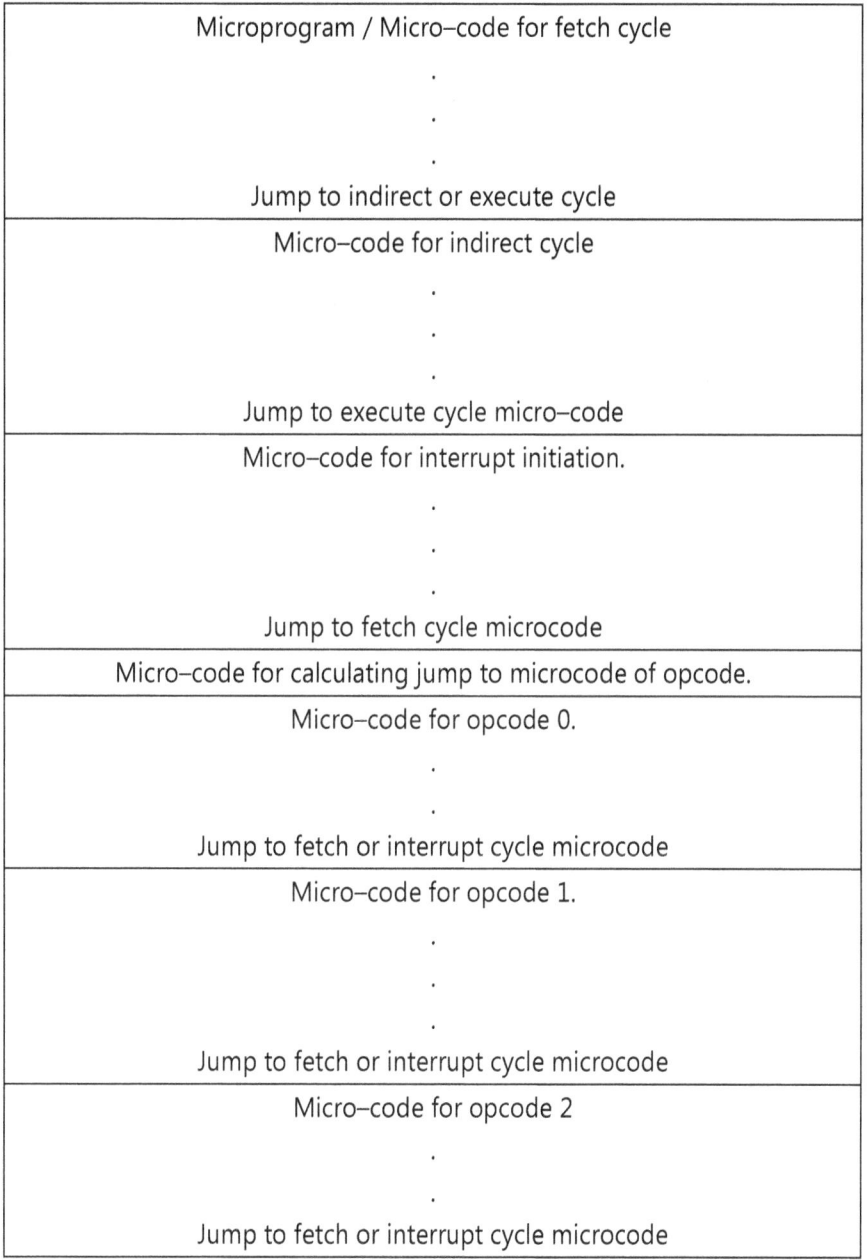

Microprogram / Micro–code for fetch cycle
.
.
.
Jump to indirect or execute cycle
Micro–code for indirect cycle
.
.
.
Jump to execute cycle micro–code
Micro–code for interrupt initiation.
.
.
.
Jump to fetch cycle microcode
Micro–code for calculating jump to microcode of opcode.
Micro–code for opcode 0.
.
.
Jump to fetch or interrupt cycle microcode
Micro–code for opcode 1.
.
.
Jump to fetch or interrupt cycle microcode
Micro–code for opcode 2
.
.
Jump to fetch or interrupt cycle microcode

Fig. 4.13 : Instruction execution steps

Here, the opcode of a machine instruction is translated into the starting address of the corresponding micro–routine. This is achieved by connecting the opcode bits of the instruction register as inputs to the PLA, which acts as a decoder. The output of PLA is the address of the desired micro routine.

4.3.3 Microprogramming Advantages   [May 06]

1. It is Simplifies the design of control unit.
2. It is cheaper and less error prone to implement.
3. Control functions are implemented in software rather than hardware.
4. The design process is orderly and systematic.
5. More flexible – adapt to changes in any organization, at any time.
6. Complex function can be realized efficiently.
7. Very powerful instruction sets.
8. Generality – Multiple instruction sets on same machine.
9. Compatibility.
   - Easy to be backward compatible in one family.
   - Many organizations, same instruction set.
10. Improvement in performance.
11. A high degree of parallelism in data paths e.g., multiple bit micro–instructions are performed in one cycle.

4.3.4 Microprogramming Disadvantages

1. Costly to implement.
2, Microprogrammed control slower than hardwired control unit because of following reasons :
   - Micro–instruction interpreted at execution time.
   - Interpretation is internal to CPU.
   - Interpret one instruction at a time.

4.4   MICRO-INSTRUCTION

4.4.1 Definition of Micro–instruction

An instruction that controls data flow and instruction–execution sequencing in a processor at a more fundamental level than machine instructions.

The control unit seems reasonably simple device. Nevertheless to implement a control unit as an interconnection of basic logic elements is no easy task. The design must include logic for sequencing through micro–operations, for executing micro–operations, for interpreting opcodes and for staking decisions based on ALU flags. It is difficult to design and test such a piece of hardware. Furthermore, the design is relatively inflexible. For example, it is difficult to change the design if one wishes to add a new machine instruction.

4.4.2 Classification of Micro–instructions

Micro–instructions can be classified as vertical and horizontal.

1. Horizontal Micro–instruction :

Individual bits of micro–instructions correspond to individual control lines. A horizontal micro–instruction has following attributes

1. Long format.
2. Horizontal micro–instructions are long and allow maximum parallelism since each bit controls a single control line.
3. No decoding is needed in horizontal micro–instructions

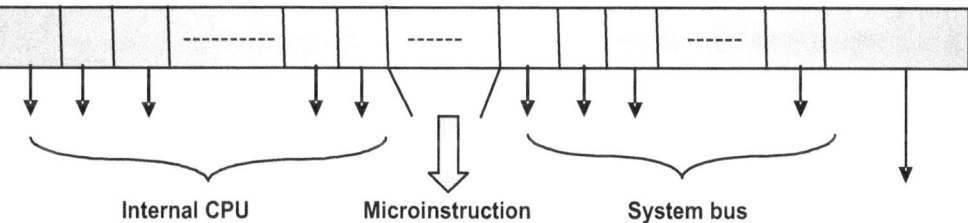

Fig. 4.14 : Horizontal Micro–instruction

Format of horizontal micro–instructions is as follows

1. There is one–bit for each internal control line.
2. There is one–bit for each system bus control line.
3. There is condition field for each condition for conditional branching.
4. Address field stores the address field of the micro–instructions to be executed next when a branch is taken.

Horizontal Micro–instructions Advantages

1. Can control a variety of components operating in parallel. So efficient hardware utilization.
2. Horizontal control unit is faster.

Horizontal Micro–instructions Disadvantages

1. Each bit directly controls each micro–operation
2. Control word bits are not fully utilized.
3. CS becomes large so, Costly.

2. Vertical Micro–instruction :

It allows encoding of control information

A vertical micro–instruction has following attributes

1. Short format. Because of the encoding vertical micro–instructions are much shorter than horizontal ones.
2. In vertical micro–instructions control lines are coded into specific fields within a micro–instruction.
3. Decoders are needed to map fields of k bits to possible 2k bits possible combinations of control lines.

   E.g. 3–bit fields in a micro–instruction could be used to specify any one of eight possible lines.
4. Control lines encoded in the same field cannot be activated simultaneously. Therefore vertical micro–instructions allow only limited parallelism.

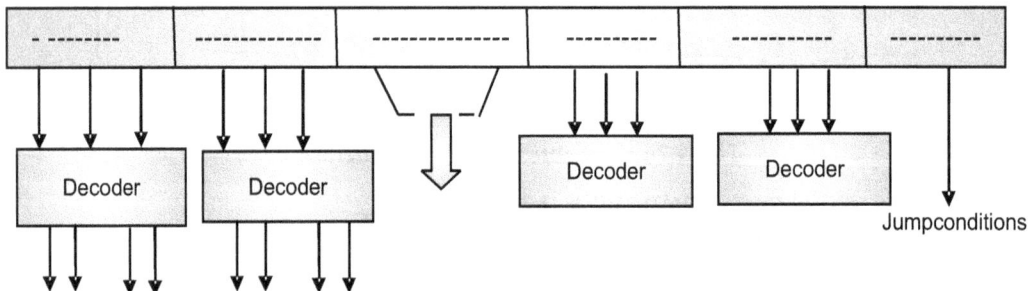

Fig. 4.15 : Vertical micro-instruction

As the CPU may need hundreds of control signals, the control word will be inevitably long. To reduce the length of the control word, groups of control signals that are mutually exclusive (only one of them need be asserted at a time) can be encoded to form shorter fields. This shorter form of control word is called vertical organization.

For example, if only 1 of a group of 8 signals is needed at any time, they can be encoded into a field of $\log_2 8 = 3$ bits, instead of 8 bits. The price to pay is the time delay needed for decoding the encoded field.

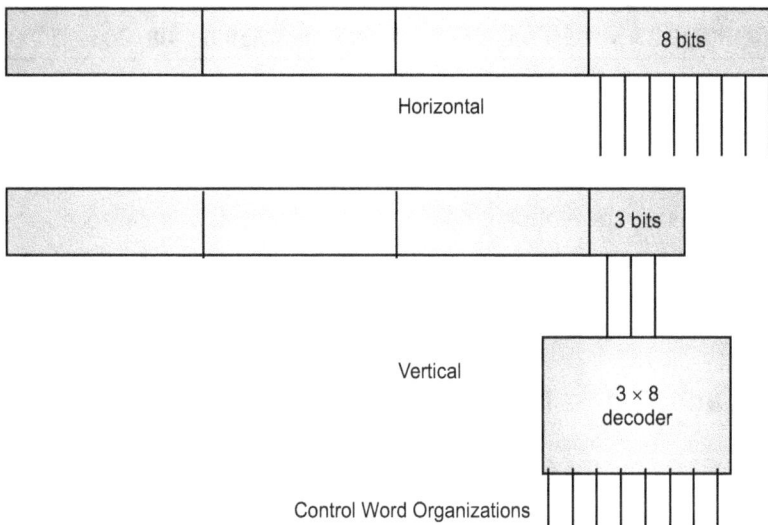

Fig. 4.16 : Control Word Organizations in horizontal and vertical micro–instruction

Vertical Micro–instructions Advantage

Vertical implies a short micro–instruction word.

Vertical Micro–instructions Disadvantages :

1. Decoders are required because of encoded micro–instruction fields.
2. It allows only limited parallelism.

4.4.3 Distinguish between Horizontal and Vertical Micro–instruction [Dec. 07, 08, 09, 10, May 2010, 11]

Table 4.3 : Difference between horizontal and vertical Micro–instruction

Sr. No.	Horizontal Micro–instruction	Vertical micro–instruction
1	In this each bit of units represents a control signal	It allows encoding of control information.
2	Decoders are not needed	Because of higher degree of encoding complex decoders are needed
3	Long format	Short format
4	High degree of parallelism	Allows limited parallelism
5	Limited encoding	Considerable encoding of the control information

4.5 MICROPROGRAMMED CONTROL UNIT ➤ [May 06, 08, 2010, 11 Dec. 08, 09]

Microprogramming is an orderly method of designing the control unit of a conventional computer (Wilkes 1951). The term microprogramming is based on the analogy between sequence of transfer required to execute a machine instruction and the sequence of individual instructions in conventional user program. Each step is called micro–instruction and complete set of steps required to process a machine instruction is called the microprogram.

4.5.1 Basic Layout of a Microprogrammed Control Unit

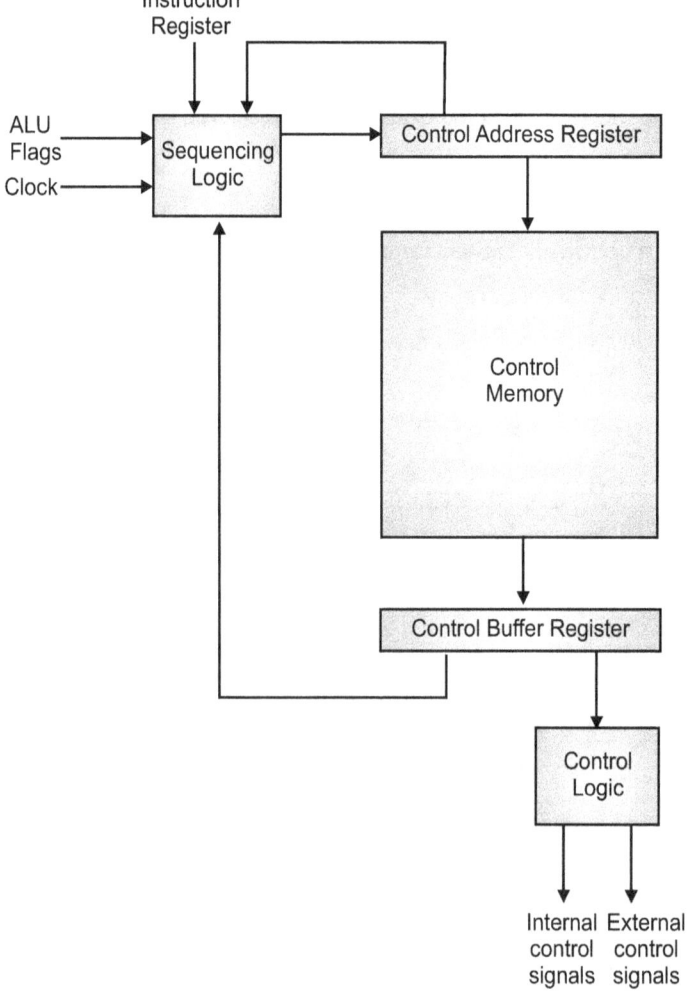

Fig. 4.17 : Functioning of Microprogrammed Control Unit

The control unit Functions as follows :

1. To execute an instruction the sequencing logic unit issues a READ command to the control memory.

2. The word whose address is specified in the control address register is read into control buffer register.

3. The content of the control buffer register generates the control signal and next address information for sequencing logic unit.

4. The sequencing logic unit loads a new address into the control address register based on the next address information from the control buffer register and the ALU flags. All this happens during one clock pulse.

The last step just listed needs elaboration. At the conclusion of each micro–instruction, the sequencing logic unit loads a new address into the control address register. Depending on the value of the ALU flags and the control buffer register, one of three decisions is made :

• **Get the next instruction :** Add 1 to control address register.

• **Jump to a new routine based on a Jump micro–instruction :** Load the address field of the control buffer register into the control address register.

• **Jump to a machine instruction routine :** Load the control address register based on the opcode in the IR.

4.5.2 Grouping of Control Signals in Microprogrammed Control

[Dec. 2005, May 2008]

A simple way to structure micro–instructions is to assign one–bit position to each control signal required in the CPU. However, this scheme has one drawback, i.e. assigning individual bits to each control signal results in long micro–instructions, because the number of required signals is usually large. Moreover, only a few bits are used in any given instruction.

The solution of this problem is to group the control signals.

Grouping of control signals : Grouping technique is used to reduce the number of bits in the micro–instruction.

Let us consider single bus CPU having different control signals, as shown in Fig. 4.25

Gating Signals : IN and OUT signals.

Control Signals : Read, Write, Clear A, set carry in, continue operation, end etc.

ALU Signals : Add, Sub etc.

There are total 39 signals and hence each micro–instruction will have 39 bits. It is not necessary to use all 39 bits for every micro–instruction because by using grouping of control signals we minimize number of bits for micro–instruction.

Ways to reduce number of bits in micro–instruction

1. Most signals not needed simultaneously.

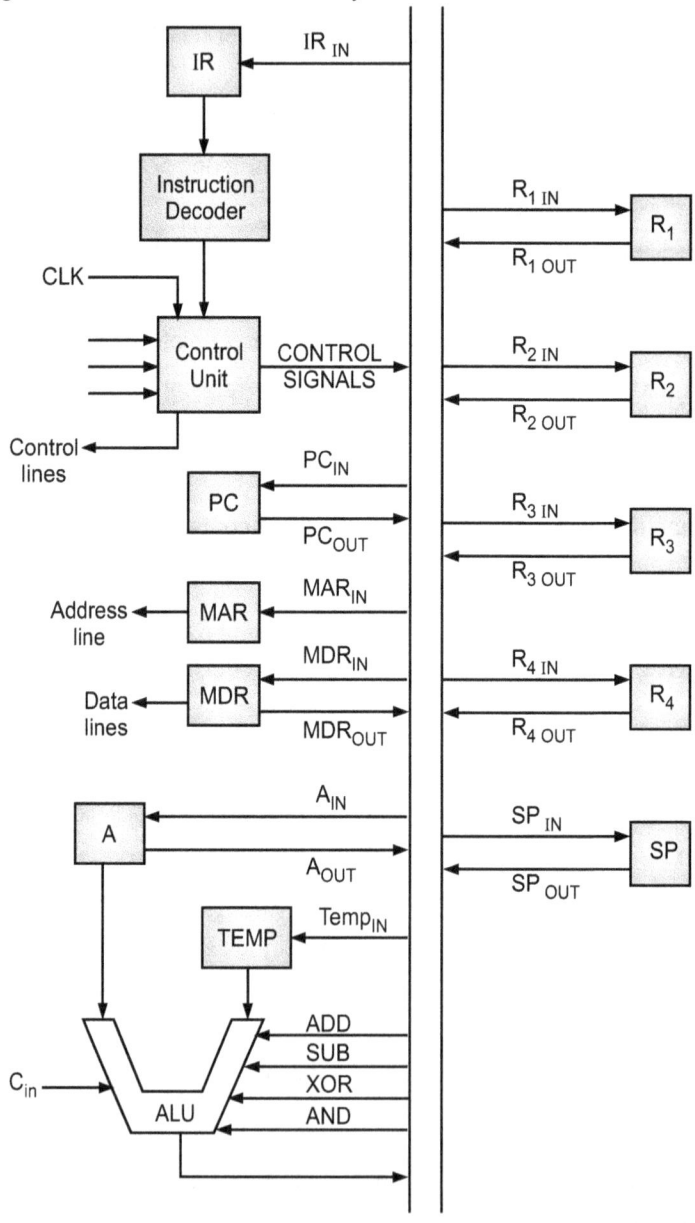

Fig. 4.18 : Single Bus CPU structure with control signals

2. Many signals are mutually exclusive e.g. only one function of ALU can be activated at a time.

3. A source for data transfers must be unique which means that it should not be possible to get the contents of two different registers on to the bus at the same time.

4. Read and write signals to the memory can't be activated simultaneously. So with these suggestions 39 control signals can be grouped in 8 different group.

Table 4.4 : Groups of Control Signals

G_1 (4–Bits) : IN grouping		$G2$ (4–Bits) OUT grouping	
0000	No Transfer	0000	No Transfer
0001	IR_{IN}	0001	PC_{OUT}
0010	PC_{IN}	0010	MDR_{out}
0011	MDR_{IN}	0011	$R_{1\ OUT}$
0100	MAR_{IN}	0100	R_{2OUT}
0101	A_{IN}	0101	R_{3OUT}
0110	$TEMP_{IN}$	0110	R_{4OUT}
0111	R_{1IN}	0111	SP_{OUT}
1001	R_{2IN}		
1010	R_{3IN}		
1011	SP_{IN}		
G_3 (4 – bits) : ALU Functions		**G_4 (2 – Bits) : RD/WR Control Signals**	
0000	ADD		
0001	SUB	00	No Action
..	⎱ 16 ALU	01	Read
..	⎰ Function	10	Write
1111	XOR		
G5 (1–Bit) : A Register		**G_6(1-Bit) : Carry**	
0	No Action	0	Carry in to ALU = 0
1	Clear A	1	Carry in to ALU = 1
G_7 (1 – Bit)		**G_8 (1 – Bit) : Operation**	
0	No Action	0	Continue operation
1	WMFC	1	End

The total numbers of grouping bits are 18. So, we minimized 39–bits micro–instruction to 18–bit micro–instruction. Grouping results in small increase in the required hardware as it becomes necessary to use decoding circuits to translate bit patterns of each group into actual control signals.

4.5.3 Hardwired Control versus Microprogrammed Control

[May 05, 2010, 11, June 07, Dec. 05, 06, 08, 09, 10]

Hardwired control is a control mechanism to generate control signals by using appropriate finite state machine (FSM). Microprogrammed control is a control mechanism to generate control signals by using a memory called control storage (CS), which contains the control signals. Although microprogrammed control seems to be advantageous to CISC machines, since CISC requires systematic development of sophisticated control signals, there is no intrinsic difference between these 2 control mechanisms.

The pair of "micro–instruction–register" and "control storage address register" call be regarded as a "state register" for the hardwired control. Note that the control storage can be regarded as a kind of combinational logic circuit. We can assign any 0, 1 values to each output corresponding to each address, which can be regarded as the input for a combinational logic circuit.

Difference between Hardwired and Microprogrammed control

Attribute	Hardwired control	Microprogrammed control
Speed	Fast	Slow
Control functions	Implemented in hardware.	Implemented in software.
Flexibility	Not flexible to accommodate new system specifications or new instructions.	More flexible to accommodate new system specifications or new, instructions.redesign
Ability to handle large/complex instruction sets	Some what difficulty	Easier
Ability to support operating systems and diagnostic features	Very difficult (unless anticipated during design).	Easy.

Design process	Somewhat complicated.	Orderly and systematic.
Applications	Mostly RISC microprocessors.	Mainframes, some micro–processors
Instruction set size	Usually under 100 instructions	Usually over under 100 instructions
ROM size	...	2k to 10K by 20–400 bit micro–instructions
Chip area efficiency	Uses least area	Uses more area.
Generation of signals	By using appropriate finite state machine (FSM).	By using a memory called control storage.

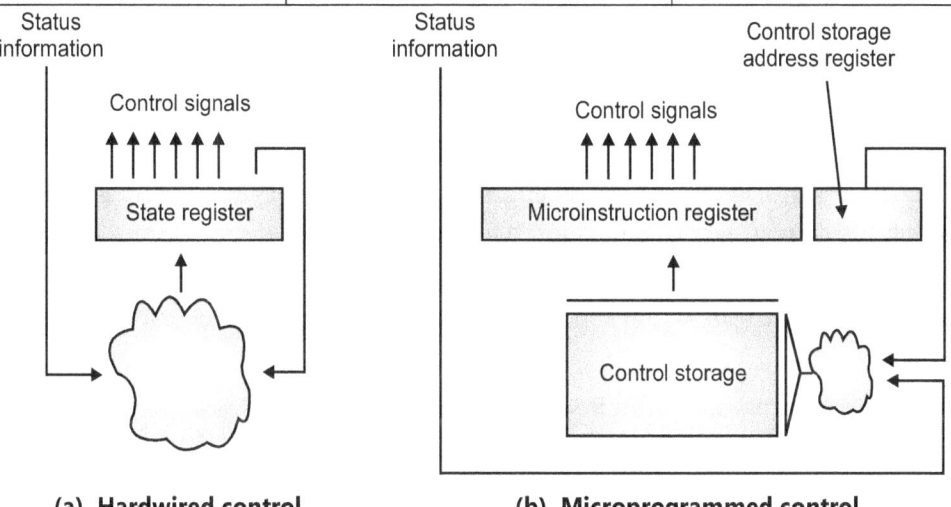

(a) **Hardwired control**   (b) **Microprogrammed control**

Fig. 4.19 : Difference between Hardwired control and microprogrammed control

4.6 MICRO-INSTRUCTION SEQUENCING   [Dec. 05,]

Two basic tasks performed by a mciroprogrammed control unit are as follows :

1. **Micro–instruction sequencing :** Get the next instruction from the control memory.

2. **Micro–instruction execution :** Generate the control signals needed for execution.

In designing a control unit, these tasks must be considered together, because both affect the format of the micro–instruction and the timing of the control unit.

Design considerations in micro–instruction sequencing :

Two concerns are involved in the design of micro–instruction sequencing technique :

1.   **The size of micro–instruction :** Minimizing size of control unit reduces the cost of component.

2.   **The address generation time :** To execute micro–instructions as fast as possible. In Executing a microprogram, the address of the next micro–instruction to be executed is in one of these categories.

- Determined by instruction register
- Next sequential address
- Branch

The first category occurs only once per instruction cycle, just after an instruction is fetched. The second category is the most common in most designs. However, the design cannot be optimized just for sequential access. Branches, both conditional and unconditional, are a necessary part of a microprogram.

4.6.1 Sequencing Techniques

Based on the current micro–instruction, condition flags, and the content of the instruction register, the Control memory address must be generated for the next microinstruction. A wide variety of techniques have been used. We can group there into three general categories.

Three general categories for a control memory address are as follows –

- Two address fields
- Single address field
- Variable format

1. Two Address Field :

In Fig. 4.20, the branch control logic with a two address field is illustrated.

This is the simplest approach. A multiplexer is provided that serves as it destination for both address fields plus the instruction register. Based on an address–selection input, the multiplexer transmits either the opcode or one of the two addresses to the control address register (CAR). The CAR is sub–sequently decoded to produce the next micro– instruction address. The address–selection signals are provided by a branch logic module whose input consists of control unit flags plus bits front the control portion of the micro–instruction.

Although the two–address approach is simple. It requires more bits in the micro–instruction than other approaches.

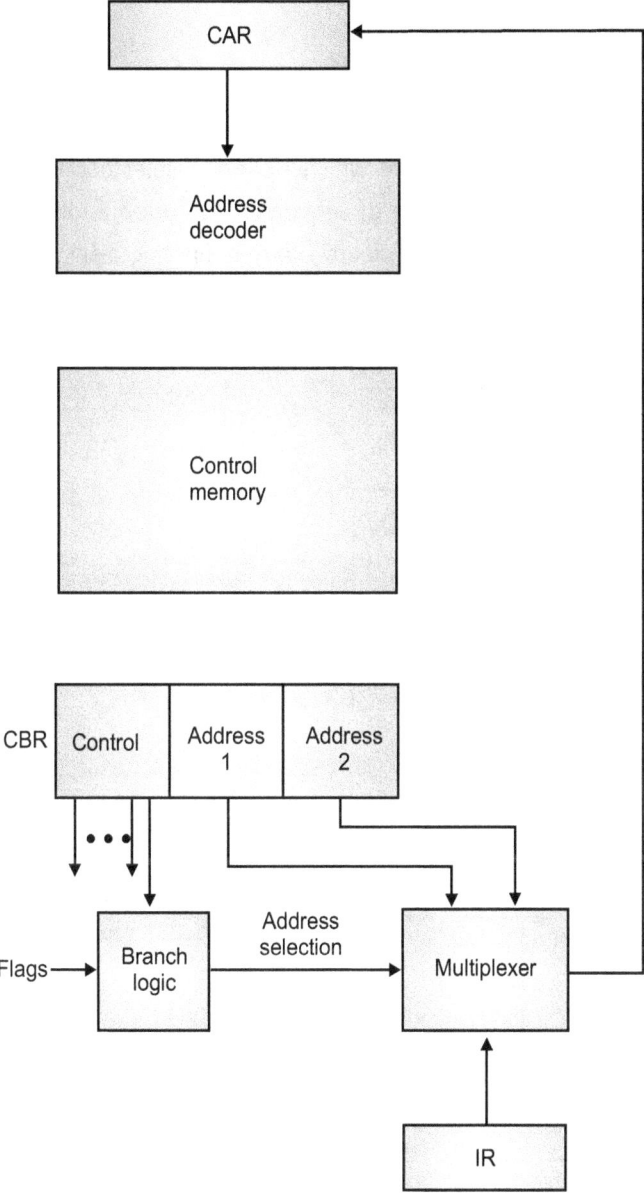

Fig. 4.20 : Branch Control Logic two address fields

2. Single Address Field :

A common approach is to have a single address field (Fig. 4.21). With this approach, the options for next address are as follows :

A single address field present in the micro–instruction with the following options for next address :

1.   Address field

2.   Based on OPcode I instruction register.

3.   Next sequential address.

The address selection signals determine which option is selected. This approach reduces number of address field to one. In case of sequential execution address field not used. So, micro–instruction encoding does not efficiently utilize entire micro–instruction.

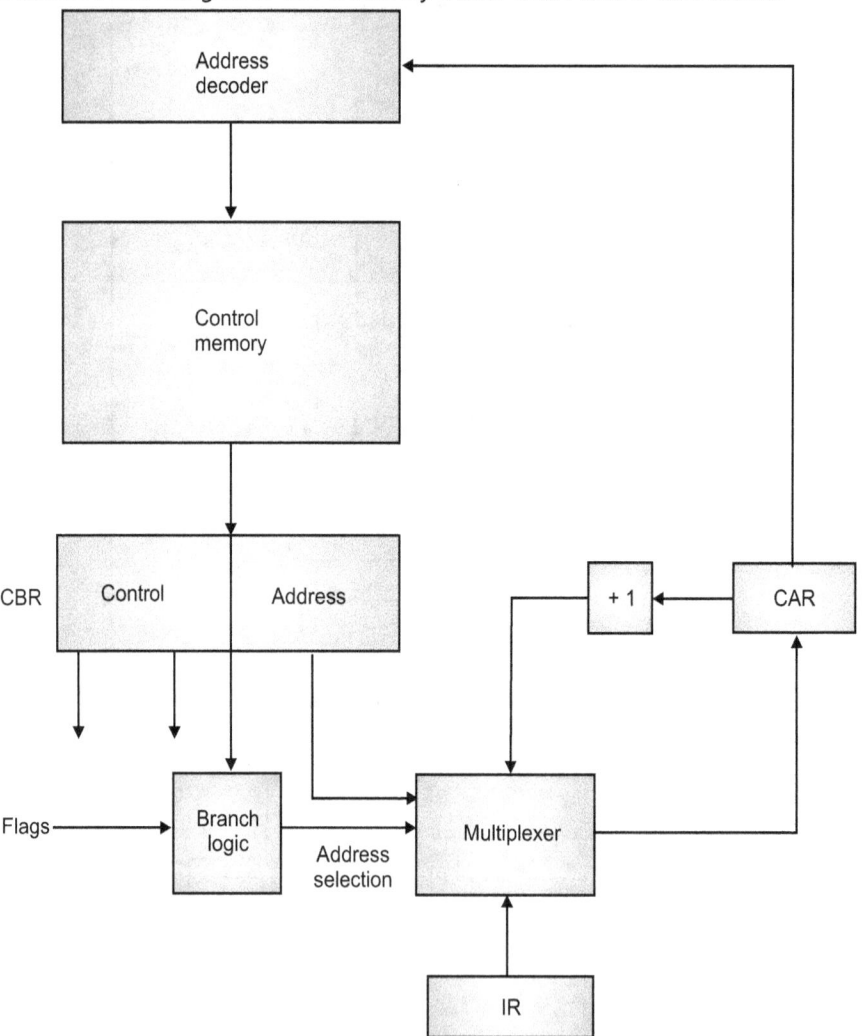

Fig. 4.21 : Branch Control Logic single address field

Advantages of single address field format

Reduces number of address field to one.

Disadvantages of single address field format

In case of sequential execution address field not used. So, micro–instruction encoding does not efficiently utilize entire micro–instruction

3. Variable Format Addressing :

In this approach, there are two entirely different micro–instruction formats. One–bit

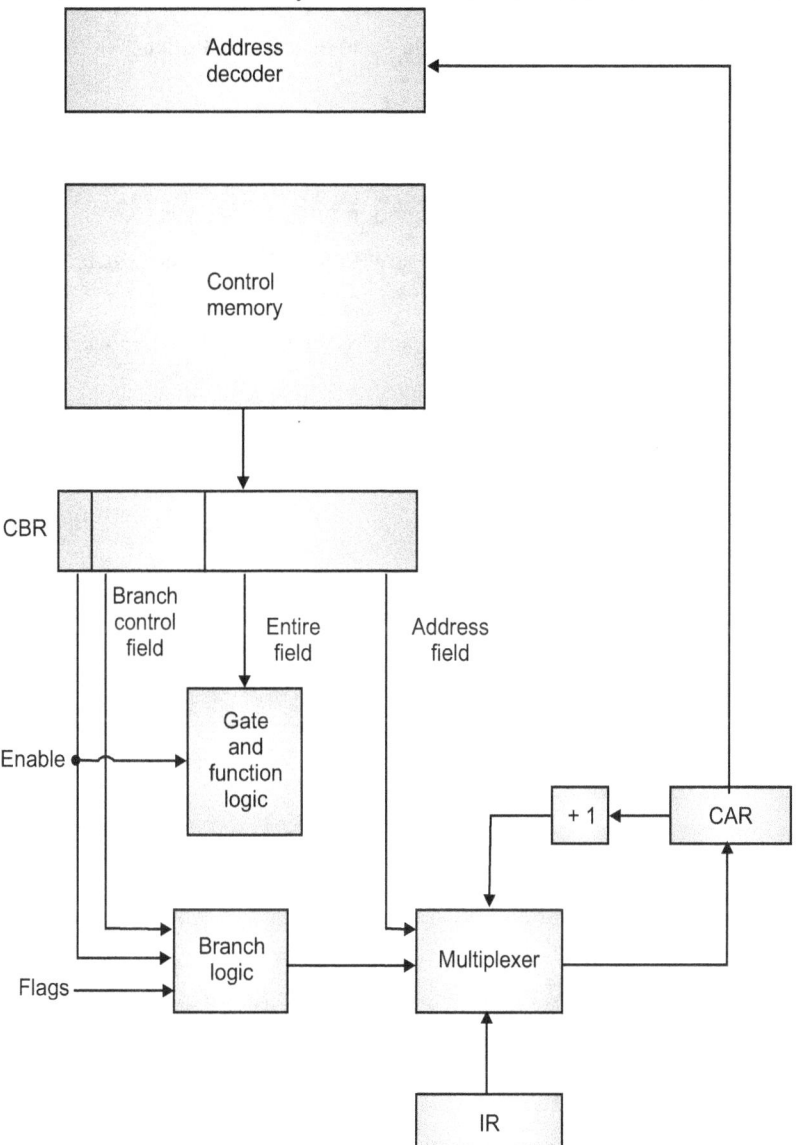

Fig. 4.22 : Branch Control Logic, Variable Format

designates which format is being used. In the first format, the remaining bits are used to activate control signals. In the second format, some bits drive the branch logic module, and the remaining bits provide the address. With the first format, the next address is either the next sequential address or an address derived from the instruction register. With the second format either a conditional or unconditional branch is specified.

Disadvantages of variable format :

One entire cycle is consumed with each branch micro–instruction. With other approaches, address generation occurs as part of the same cycle as control signal generation, minimizing control memory access.

These all approaches described are general. Specific implementation will often involve a combination of these techniques.

The next micro–instruction address is determined in one of five ways

1. Next sequential address : The control unit's control address register is incremented by 1.

2. OPcode mapping : At the beginning of each instruction cycle, the next micro–instruction address is determined by the opcode.

3. Subroutine facility : The address of subroutine is loaded in control address register and executes subroutine.

4. Interrupt testing : Certain micro–instructions specify a test for interrupts. If an interrupt has occurred, this determines the next micro–instruction address.

5. Branch : Conditional and Unconditional branch micro–instructions are used.

MULTIPLE CHOICE QUESTIONS

1. Which of the following registers in a single bus organisation of processor are inaccessible to the programmer
   - (a) Temp
   - (b) y
   - (c) z
   - (d) all of these

2. ...... coordinates the input and output devices of a computer system.
   - (a) Processor
   - (b) ALU
   - (c) Control Unit
   - (d) None of these

3. Which registers are used as temporary register
   - (a) Y
   - (b) z
   - (c) a and b
   - (d) none of these

4. The ...... bus is set of lines that carry information about where in memory data is to be transferred to or form

(a) data   (b) address

(c) control   (d) all of these

5. The ...... bus are the lines that actually carry data being transferred.

(a) address   (b) control

(c) data   (d) none of these

6. The ...... bus control how bus functions and allow users of bus to signal when data is available.

(a) control   (b) data

(c) address   (d) single

7. The control unit of a computer ......

(a) accepts input data

(b) generates control signals to execute an instruction

(c) stores data in the memory

(d) all of above

8. The programmer can not access following registers

(a) IR   (b) MAR and MDR

(c) Y, Z and Temp   (d) PC

9. Which of following are special purpose registers.

(a) stack pointer   (b) index registers

(c) pointers   (d) all of these

10. ALU, data registers and interconnecting bus combinely form ......

(a) data path   (b) address path

(c) control path   (d) all above

11. In a single bus organization ...... data ...... can be transferred over the bus in a clock cycle.

(a) single, word   (b) double, word

(c) signel, byte   (d) double, byte

12. Instructions written in a proper sequence to execute a particular task is called ......

(a) algorithm   (b) program

(c) function   (d) procedure

13. After branching...... is fetched for execution

(a) First instruction of program

(b) instruction following branch instruction in program

(c) last instruction of program

(d) instruction of target address

14. JB Next is ......
    - (a) condition branch
    - (b) unconditional branch
    - (c) loop
    - (d) none of above

15. CALL NEXT, is ......
    - (a) conditional branch
    - (b) unconditional branch
    - (c) loop
    - (d) none of above

16. After execution of instruction, PC = ...
    - (a) PC + 1
    - (b) PC + 2
    - (c) PC + size of (current instruction)
    - (d) PC + Size of (next instruction)

17. The ...... is used to select the two inputs.
    - (a) multiplexer
    - (b) demultiplexer
    - (c) Encoder
    - (d) decoder

18. Registers Ro through R (n –1) includes ......
    - (a) general purpose register
    - (b) special purpose register
    - (c) both (a) and (b)
    - (d) none of these

19. Job of programmer to select and write appropriate instructions one after the other in a proper sequence is called as ......
    - (a) programming
    - (b) instruction sequencing
    - (c) algorithm
    - (d) instruction routing

20. Once an instruction is executed, then next will be executed is described as ......
    - (a) straight line execution
    - (b) branching
    - (c) instruction decoding
    - (d) instruction fetching

21. ...... register is used to fetch address of next instruction to be executed
    - (a) MAR
    - (b) PC
    - (c) MDR
    - (d) IR

22. Depending upon the condition specifies transfer the control of program of specified routine is called ......
    - (a) instruction sequencing
    - (b) looping
    - (c) unconditional branches
    - (d) conditional branching

23. Without checking any condition, transfer program control to some another loop is called......
    - (a) conditional branching
    - (b) unconditional branching
    - (c) looping
    - (d) instruction sequencing

24. Each instruction cycle has following steps......
    - (a) execute, fetch, indirect, corrupt
    - (b) indirect, execute, interrupt fetch
    - (c) fetch, indirect, execute, interrupt
    - (d) none of these

25. ...... cycle occurs at beginning of each instruction cycle
    (a) execute   (b) fetch
    (c) interrupt   (d) indirect

26. ...... is connected to address lines of the system bus.
    (a) MAR   (b) MBR
    (c) PC   (d) IR

27. ...... is connected to data lines of the system bus.
    (a) MAR   (b) MBR
    (c) PC   (d) Ir

28. ...... holds the last instruction fetched.
    (a) PC   (b) IR
    (c) MAR   (d) MBR

29. In which of the following cases operand fetch is required.
    (a) If operand is present in CPU
    (b) If operand is an immediate data
    (c) If operand is present at some address
    (d) None of these

30. Which cycle does not involves a small, fixed sequence of micro-instructions and same micro operations are not repeated each time around.
    (a) fetch   (b) Indirect
    (c) Interrupt   (d) execute

31. Execution of an instruction requires following cycles
    (a) Fetch operand, decode instruction
    (b) Decode instruction, fetch operands, perform operation, store result
    (c) Perform operation , decode instruction
    (d) decode instruction, perform operation, store result

32. ...... microperations transfer binary information from one register to another.
    (a) Register transfer   (b) Arithmetic microperations
    (c) Logic microperation   (d) Shift microperations

33. In branch instructions new address is loaded into
    (a) stack register   (b) memory address register
    (c) memory data register   (d) program counter

34. ...... micro operations perform arithmetic operations on numbers stored in registers.
    (a) Register transfer   (b) Arithmetic
    (c) Logic   (d) Shift

35. ...... micro operations perform bit manipulation operations on non-numeric data stored in registers.
    (a) Register transfer   (b) Arithmetic
    (c) Logic   (d) Shift

36. ...... micro operations perform shift operations on contents of register.
    (a) Register transfer   (b) Arithmetic
    (c) Logic   (d) Shift

37. ...... micro operation doesn't change contents of registers.
    (a) Register transfer   (b) Arithmetic
    (c) Logic   (d) Shift

38. In ...... instruction bits directly generate the signals.
    (a) hardwired control   (b) microprogrammed control
    (c) micro-instruction sequencing   (d) None of these

39. In ...... a dedicated microcontroller executes a micro-program to generate signals.
    (a) hardwired control   (b) microprogrammed control
    (c) microinstruction sequencing   (d) all of above

40. There is specific time delay between activation of two contiguous control signals in ......method.
    (a) sequence counter   (b) state table
    (c) PLA   (d) delay element method

41. Each instruction consists of a series of steps that, in turn, made up of a smaller series of steps called as ......
    (a) micro-operations   (b) micro-controller
    (c) micro-processor   (d) instructions

42. A ...... consists of a sequence of micro instructions in a micro-programming.
    (a) program   (b) algorithm
    (c) microprogram   (d) micro-instruction

43. An instruction that controls data flow and instruction execution sequencing in a processor at more fundamental level than m/c instructions is called as ......
    (a) micro-program   (b) conditional instruction
    (c) micro-instruction   (d) none of these

44. PLA means ......
    (a) programmable logic analysis   (b) programmable logic array
    (c) programmable logical addressing (d) programmable logic algorithm
45. Horizontal micro-instruction has ...... format.
    (a) long   (b) short   (c) double
46. Vertical micro-instruction has ...... format.
    (a) long   (b) short   (c) double
47. No decoding is needed in ...... micro-instructions.
    (a) vertical   (b) horizontal
48. Decodes are required in ...... mico-instruction
    (a) horizontal   (b) vertical
49. Hardwired control is implemented in ......
    (a) software   (b) hardware
50. Microprogrammed control is implemented in ......
    (a) hardware   (b) software
51. Speed of hardwired control is ...... than microprogrammed control.
    (a) slow   (b) same as   (c) fast
52. The number of bits required in horizontal microinstruction are ...... compared to vertical microinstruction.
    (a) less   (b) same as
    (c) more   (d) none of these
53. Sequence counter, Delay-elements, state-table, PLA are the methods for design of ...... control unit.
    (a) microprogrammed   (b) hardwired
    (c) (a) and (b)   (d) (a) or (b)
54. If IR is an 8-bit register, then instruction decoder generates ...... signals one for each instruction.
    (a) 16   (b) 32   (c) 64   (d) 256
55. A microprogrammed control unit ......
    (a) implemented in hardware
    (b) contains instruction set size usually under 100 instructions
    (c) faster than hardware wired unit
    (d) facilitates easy of new instructions.

56. The microinstruction MAR ← PC is executed to ......

    (a) Fetch operand from memory

    (b) Fetch an instruction

    (c) stores result in memory

    (d) To fetch register value

57. MDR ← M (MAR) is executed to ......

    (a) Data from memory put to data bus

    (b) Data from memory is put on address bus

    (c) Data from memory is put on control bus

    (d) None of above

58. M (MAR) ← MDR operations is ......

    (a) memory read   (b) memory write

    (c) data read   (d) data write

59. To transfer contents of memory location z into register R2 use following instruction

    ......

    (a) Z ← R2   (b) R2 ← Z

    (c) R1 ← Z   (d) Z ← R1

60. To transfer contents of register R2 into register R1 use following instruction ......

    (a) R2 ↔ R1   (b) X ← R2

    (c) R2 ← R1   (d) R1 ← R2

61. To transfer contents of register R2 into memory location Y.

    (a) R2 ← R1   (b) X ← R2

    (c) Y ← R2   (d) R2 ← Y

62. ...... means contents of R1 plus R2 transferred to R3.

    (a) X ← R1 + R2   (b) R3 ← R1 + R2

    (c) R3 ← R1 + 1   (d) R3 ← R2 + 1

63. ...... means contents of R1 minus R2 transferred to R3.

    (a) X ← R1 – R2   (b) R1 – R2 ← X

    (c) R1 – R2 ← R3   (d) R3 ← R1 – R2

64. ...... means contents of register R1 and memory location X is added and result is stored in memory location Z.

    (a) R1 + X ← Z   (b) Z ← R1 + X

    (c) X ← R1 + Z   (d) Z ← R1 + 1

65. ......means contents of memory locations Z is subtracted from register R1 and result is stored in memory location Y.

    (a) Y ← R1 – Z   (b) Y ← Z – R1

    (c) Y ← R1 + Z   (d) Y ← R1 + R2

66. shl instruction is for a ......

    (a) logical shift left   (b) logical shift right

    (c) logical shift left and right   (d) logical shift right and then left

67. shr instruction is for ......

    (a) logical shift right   (b) logical shift left

    (c) logical shift right and then left   (d) logical shift left and then right

68. Negative flag will have value '1' when result is ......

    (a) greater than 0   (b) less than 0

    (c) 1   (d) borrow or carry is generated

69. Zero flag is set to '1' when result is ......

    (a) greater than 0   (b) less than 0

    (c) 0   (d) 1

70. Overflow flag will have value '1' when result ......

    (a) is one   (b) is negative

    (c) is zero   (d) has arithmetic overflow

71. Carry flag will have value '1' when result

    (a) is one   (b) is zero

    (c) borrow or carry is generate   (d) has arithmetic overflow

72. An instruction may contain ...... address(es).

    (a) 0 or 1   (b) 2

    (c) 3   (d) any of above

73. The instruction Add is ...... address instruction.

    (a) 0   (b) 1

    (c) 2   (d) 3

74. The instruction Add Y is ...... address instruction.

    (a) 0   (b) 1

    (c) 2   (d) 3

75. The instruction Add Y, Z is ...... address instruction.

    (a) 0   (b) 1

    (c) 2   (d) 3

76. The instruction Add X, Y, Z is ...... address instruction.

    (a) 0   (b) 1

    (c) 2   (d) 3

77. Memory transfer operations ...... register contains the address in address bus.

    (a) MAR   (b) MDR

    (c) IR   (d) All of above

78. In memory transfer operations ...... register contains the data in data bus.

    (a) MAR   (b) MDR

    (c) IR   (d) All of above

79. The control signals generated for operation MAR ← PC are ......

    (a) PCin, MARin   (b) PCin, MARout

    (c) PCout, MARin   (d) PCout, MARout

80. The control signals generated for operation MDR ← M (MAR) are ......

    (a) MARin, RAMout, MDRin system   (b) MARout, RAMout, MDRin system

    (c) MARout, RAMin, MDRin system   (d) MARout, RAMout, MDRout system

81. The control signals generated for operation PC ← PC + 1 are ......

    (a) PCout, MARin, Zin, PCin   (b) PCout, MARout, Zin, PCin

    (c) PCin, MARin, Zout, PCin   (d) PCout, MARin, Zout, PCin

82. The control signals generated for IR← MDR (opcode) are ......

    (a) MDRout, opcode, IRout   (b) MDRout, opcode, IRin

    (c) MDRin, opcode, IRin   (d) MDRin, opcode, IRout

83. The delay elements are implemented by ...... and controlled by a common clock signal.

    (a) T flip-flops   (b) D flip-flops

    (c) SR flip-flops   (d) JK flip-flops

84. In delay element method, the signal that activate same control signals are ...... to get one common output signal.

    (a) Anded   (b) ORed

    (c) XORed   (d) XNoRed

85. In delay element method, a decision box can be implemented by two ...... gates.

    (a) AND   (b) OR

    (c) XOR   (d) NOR

86. We can associated a state with every micro-instruction block in ......

    (a) Delay element method   (b) State table method

    (c) PLA method   (d) Sequence counter method

87. In ...... control memory is organized as a program logic array.

    (a) Sequence counter method   (b) Delay element method

    (c) Wilkes control method   (d) State table method

88. In ...... control unit, control memory is used

    (a) microprogrammed   (b) Hardwired

    (c) (a) and (b)   (d) None of above

89. In ...... control unit, control memory is absent,

    (a) microprogrammed   (b) Hardwired

    (c) (a) and (b)   (d) None of above

90. The hardwired control unit based system contains ...... instructions.

    (a) smaller   (b) larger

    (c) both (a) and (b)   (d) None of above

91. The microprogrammed control unit based system contains ...... instructions.

    (a) smaller   (b) larger

    (c) both (a) and (b)   (d) None of above

92. The hardwired control units find more applications in ...... processors.

    (a) CISC   (b) RISC

93. The microprogrammed control units find more applications in ...... processors.

    (a) CISC   (b) RISC

94. ...... control unit required less chip area.

    (a) Hardwired   (b) Microprogrammed

95. ...... control unit required more chip area.

    (a) Hardwired   (b) Microprogrammed

96. ...... control unit generates signals using appropriate finite state machine (FSM).

    (a) Hardwired   (b) Microprogrammed

97. The ...... is subsequently decoded to produce next micro-instruction address.

    (a) memory address register   (b) control address register

    (c) program counter   (d) memory data register

98. The ......encoding method identifies functions within the machine and designates fields by function type.

    (a) Functional Encoding   (b) Resource Encoding

    (c) Indirect encoding   (d) All of above

99. The ...... encoding views the machine as consisting of set of independent resources and devoted one file to each.

    (a) Functional Encoding   (b) Resource Encoding

    (c) Indirect encoding   (d) All of above

100. Microprogramming can be used for Data management system.

    (a) False   (b) True

101. Microprogramming can be used for real time data.

    (a) False   (b) True

102. Microprogramming can be used for emulation.

    (a) True   (b) False

103. Special processors can be designed through microprogramming.

    (a) True   (b) False

104. Microprogramming can be used for ......

    (a) software diagnostics   (b) Hardware diagnostics

    (c) Micro diagnostics   (d) All of above

105. Microprogramming allows instruction set of machine to be changed and be tailored to specific applications.

    (a) True   (b) False

106. Microprogramming can be used to improve effectiveness of higher order programming languages.

    (a) True   (b) False

107. Security can be provided against illegal access using microprogramming.

    (a) True   (b) False

108. Microprogramming can be used in airborne system

    (a) True   (b) False

109. Microprogramming can be used in input output processing.

    (a) True   (b) False

ANSWERS

1.	d	2.	c	3.	c	4.	b	5.	c
6.	a	7.	b	8.	c	9.	d	10.	a
11.	a	12.	b	13.	d	14.	a	15.	b
16.	c	17.	a	18.	c	19.	b	20.	a
21.	b	22.	d	23.	b	24.	c	25.	b
26.	a	27.	b	28.	b	29.	c	30.	d
31.	b	32.	a	33.	d	34.	b	35.	c
36.	d	37.	a	38.	a	39.	b	40.	d
41.	a	42.	c	43.	c	44.	b	45.	a
46.	b	47.	b	48.	b	49.	b	50.	b
51.	c	52.	c	53.	b	54.	d	55.	d

56.	b	57.	a	58.	b	59.	b	60.	d
61.	c	62.	b	63.	d	64.	b	65.	a
66.	a	67.	a	68.	b	69.	c	70.	d
71.	c	72.	d	73.	a	74.	b	75.	c
76.	d	77.	a	78.	b	79.	c	80.	b
81.	d	82.	b	83.	b	84.	b	85.	a
86.	b	87.	c	88.	a	89.	b	90.	a
91.	b	92.	b	93.	a	94.	a	95.	b
96.	a	97.	b	98.	a	99.	b	100.	b
101.	b	102.	a	103.	a	104.	d	105.	a
106.	a	107.	a	108.	a	109.	a		

QUESTIONS

1. Draw and explain single bus organization of the CPU.   **[May 10, 13, Jan 12]**

2. Draw the neat diagram of single bus organization of the CPU showing ALU, all types of register and the data paths among them.   **[May 11]**

3. Compare single bus organization with multiple bus organization of CPU.   **[Dec. 12]**

4. With the help of diagram explain internal structure of CPU.   **[Dec. 12]**

5. Explain the sequence of operations needed to perform processor functions.

    (i) fetching a word from memory

    (ii) performing on arithmetic or logical operation.   **[May 12]**

6. For a single bus organization of CPU, write micro-operations and control signals for unconditional branch instruction.   **[May 10, 13]**

7. Explain in detail state table design method for hardwired control.   **[May 13]**

8. What are different design methods for hardwired control units ? Explain any one.

                                                      [May 10, 12]

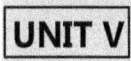

MEMORY AND I/O ORGANIZATION

5.1 INTRODUCTION

We realize that one of the most important aspects of a computer is its capability to store large amounts of information in what we normally call "memory." Specifically, it's random access memory (RAM), and it holds volatile information that can be accessed quickly and directly. And considering the ever growing system need for speed and efficiency, understanding double-data-rate (DDR) memory is important to system developers.

With improvements in processor speeds, RAM memory has evolved into high performance RAM chipsets called DDR synchronous dynamic RAM (SDRAM). It doubles the processing rate by making a data fetch on both the rising and falling-edge of a clock cycle. This is in contrast to the older single-data-rate (SDR) SDRAM that makes a data fetch on only one edge of the clock cycle.

In addition to well-known computer applications, DDR memories are widely used in other high-speed, memory demanding applications, such as graphic cards, which need to process a large amount of information in a very short time to achieve the best graphics processing efficiency. Blade servers using many blades, or single purpose boards, powered by a single, more efficient power supply also need fast memory access. This allows the blades to quickly transmit reliable information among each other and create greater opportunities to reduce power consumption. Memory devices are also required in networking and communications applications with tasks ranging from simple address lookups to traffic shaping/policing and buffer management.

5.2 DDR MEMORY CHARACTERISTICS

DDR memory's primary advantage is the ability to fetch data on both the rising and falling edge of a clock cycle, doubling the data rate for a given clock frequency. For example, in a DDR200 device the data transfer frequency is 200 MHz, but the bus speed is 100 MHz.

DDR1, DDR2 and DDR3 memories are powered up with 2.5, 1.8 and 1.5 V supply voltages respectively, thus producing less heat and providing more efficiency in power management than normal SDRAM chipsets, which use 3.3 V.

Temporization is another characteristic of DDR memories. Memory temporization is given through a series of numbers, such as 2-3-2-6-T1, 3-4-4-8 or 2-2-2-5 for DDR1. These numbers indicate the number of clock pulses that it takes the memory to perform a certain operation, the smaller the number, the faster the memory.

The operations that these numbers represent are the following: CL, tRCD, tRP, tRAS, CMD. To understand them, you have to keep in mind that the memory is internally organized as a matrix, where the data is stored at the intersection of the rows and columns.

- **CL:** Column address strobe (CAS) latency is the time it takes between the processor asking memory for data and memory returning it.

- **tRCD:** Row address strobe (RAS) to CAS delay is the time it takes between the activation of the row (RAS) and the column (CAS) where data is stored in the matrix.

- **tRP:** RAS precharge is the time between disabling the access to a row of data and the beginning of the access to another row of data.

- **tRAS:** Active to precharge delay is how long the memory has to wait until the next access to memory can be initiated.

- **CMD:** Command rate is the time between the memory chip activation and when the first command may be sent to the memory. Sometimes this value is not informed. It usually is T1 (1 clock speed) or T2 (2 clock speeds).

5.2.1 Types of DDR Memories

There are presently three generations of DDR memories:

1. DDR1 memory, with a maximum rated clock of 400 MHz and a 64-bit (8 bytes) data bus is now becoming obsolete and is not being produced in massive quantities. Technology is adopting new ways to achieve faster speeds/data rates for RAM memories.

2. DDR2 technology is replacing DDR with data rates from 400 MHz to 800 MHz and a data bus of 64 bits (8 bytes). Widely produced by RAM manufacturers, DDR2 memory is physically incompatible with the previous generation of DDR memories.

3. DDR3 technology picks up where DDR2 left off (800 Mbps bandwidth) and brings

the speed up to 1.6 Gbps. One of the chips already announced by ELPIDA contains up to 512 megabits of DDR3 SDRAM, with a column access time of 8.75 ns (CL7 latency) and data transfer rate of 1.6 Gbps at 1.6 GHz. The 1.5V DDR3 voltage level also saves some power compared to DDR2 memory. What is more interesting is that at an even lower 1.36 V, the DDR3 RAM runs fine at 1.333 GHz (DDR3-1333) with a CL6 latency (8.4 ns total CAS time), which matches the CAS time of the fastest current DDR2 memory.

5.2.2 DDR3 Memory Interface Controller Overview

Designing a DDR3 memory controller from scratch can be very difficult. Multiple tradeoffs and many interactions between features must be considered. Using a proven IP Core saves the significant development, test and debug time that would be spent developing an in-house design. A proven IP Core also reduces the support burden, since it is backed by the developer. Most importantly, the use of a proven IP Core allows the designer to focus effort on the unique features of the design that deliver higher value to the end customer. As an example, the LatticeECP3 DDR3 Memory Controller IP Core has been proven using a third party verification suite. It has also been implemented and thoroughly tested using the LatticeECP3 I/O Protocol Board.

A block diagram of a memory controller is shown in Fig. 5.1. The Configuration Interface at the top of the diagram is used to set the various options in the design. The DDR3 I/O modules are implemented using I/O primitives. The Command Decode block decodes user commands and generates a sequence of internal memory commands, depending on the status of each bank and row. The Command Application block translates each command sequence into memory commands that meet the functional and timing requirements of the target memory device. The Data Path block interfaces with the DDR3 I/O modules and is responsible for generating the read data and read data valid signals during read operations. The Read Data Deskew module aligns data from each 8-bit lane, adjusting for any potential clock skew. This creates a user side read data bus that is correctly timed to the system clock. The Write Leveling block adjusts the DQS to CK relationship for proper data capture. The ODT block improves the signal integrity of the memory channel by independently controlling the termination resistance for any or all DDR3 SDRAM devices.

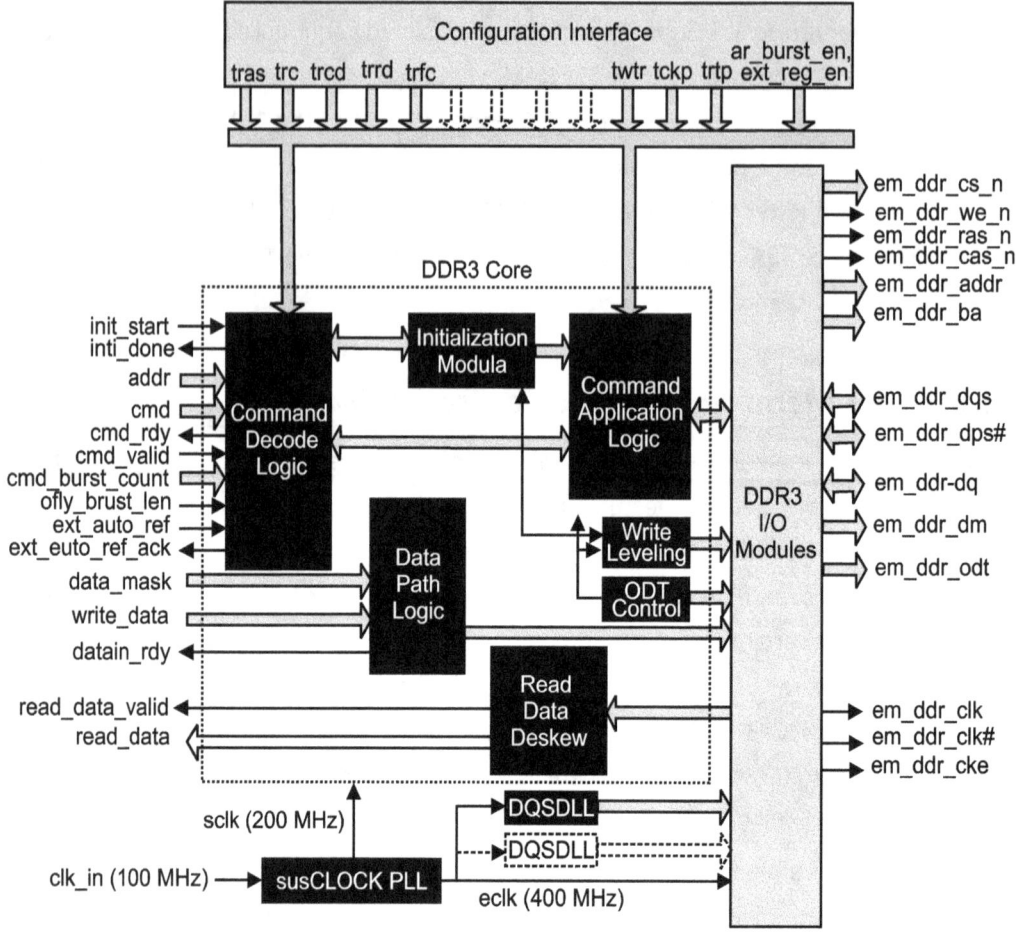

Fig. 5.1 : DDR 3 Memory Controller IP core Block Diagram

5.3 NON-UNIFORM MEMORY ACCESS

Non-uniform memory access (NUMA) is a computer memory design used in multiprocessing, where the memory access time depends on the memory location relative to a processor. Under NUMA, a processor can access its own local memory faster than non-local memory (memory local to another processor or memory shared between processors). The benefits of NUMA are limited to particular workloads, notably on servers where the data are often associated strongly with certain tasks or users.

Limiting the number of memory accesses provided the key to extracting high performance from a modern computer. For commodity processors, this meant installing an ever-increasing amount of high-speed cache memory and using increasingly sophisticated algorithms to avoid cache misses. But the dramatic increase in size of the operating systems and of the applications run on them has generally overwhelmed these cache-processing improvements. Multi-processor systems without NUMA make the problem considerably worse. Now a system can starve several processors at the same time, notably because only one processor can access the computer's memory at a time.

NUMA attempts to address this problem by providing separate memory for each processor, avoiding the performance hit when several processors attempt to address the same memory. For problems involving spread data (common for servers and similar applications), NUMA can improve the performance over a single shared memory by a factor of roughly the number of processors (or separate memory banks).

Ofcourse, not all data ends up confined to a single task, which means that more than one processor may require the same data. To handle these cases, NUMA systems include additional hardware or software to move data between memory banks. This operation slows the processors attached to those banks, so the overall speed increase due to NUMA depends heavily on the nature of the running tasks.

Fig. 5.2 below shows One possible architecture of a NUMA system. The processors connect to the bus or crossbar by connections of varying thickness/number. This shows that different CPUs have different access priorities to memory based on their relative location.

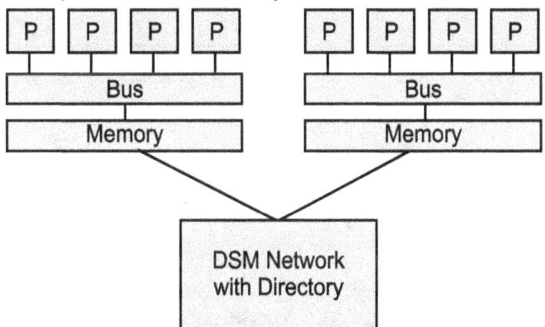

Fig. 5.2 : NUMA Architecture

5.4 UNIFORM MEMORY ACCESS (UMA)

Uniform memory access (UMA) is a shared memory architecture used in parallel computers. All the processors in the UMA model share the physical memory uniformly. In a UMA architecture, access time to a memory location is independent of which processor makes the request or which memory chip contains the transferred data. Uniform memory access computer architectures are often contrasted with non-uniform memory access (NUMA) architectures. In the UMA architecture, each processor may use a private cache. Peripherals are also shared in some fashion. The UMA model is suitable for general purpose and time sharing applications by multiple users. It can be used to speed up the execution of a single large program in time critical applications.

Types of UMA architectures :

1. UMA using bus-based symmetric multiprocessing (SMP) architectures
2. UMA using crossbar switches
3. UMA using multistage interconnection networks

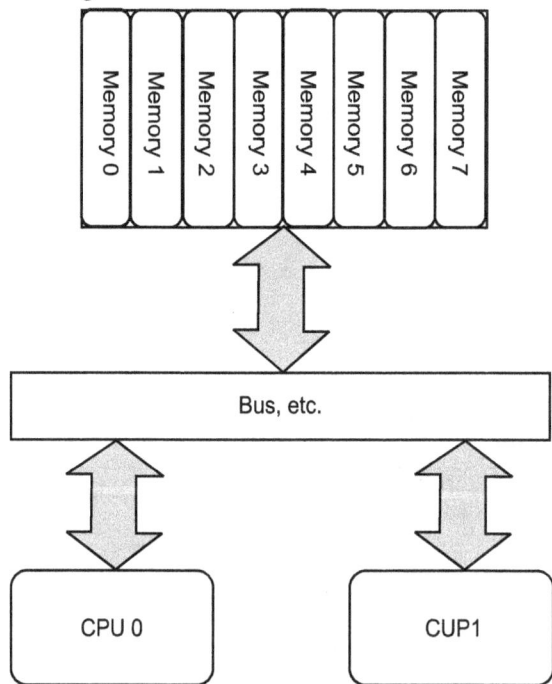

Fig. 5.3 : Generalised Architecture of UMA

5.5 I/O INTERFACING TECHNIQUE

Important components of any computer system are CPU, memory and I/O devices. The CPU fetches instructions (opcodes and operands/data) from memory, processes them and stores results in memory.

I/O devices can be interfaced to a computer system I/O in two ways which are called interfacing techniques.

1. Memory mapped I/O   2. I/O mapped I/O

5.5.1 Memory Mapped I/O

Here the total memory address space is partitioned and part of this pole is devoted to I/O addressing as in Fig. 5.4.

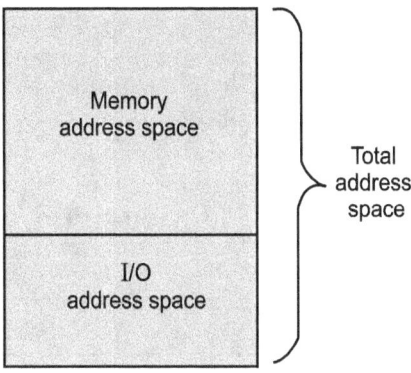

Fig. 5.4 : Address space

When this technique is used, a memory reference instruction that causes data to be fetched from or stored at address specified, automatically becomes an I/O instruction if that address is made the address on an I/O port.

Advantage :

Usual memory related instructions are used for I/O related operations the special I/O instructions are not required.

Disadvantages :

The memory address space is reduced.

5.5.2 I/O Mapped I/O

If we do not want to reduce the memory address space. We allot a different I/O address space, apart from total memory space which is called I/O mapped I/O techniques as shown in Fig. 5.5.

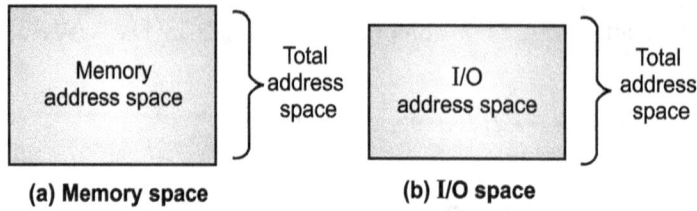

(a) Memory space

(b) I/O space

Fig. 5.5 : Address Space

Advantage :

Full memory address space is available.

Disadvantage :

Memory related instructions do not work. Therefore, processor can only use this mode if it has special instructions for I/O related operations such as I/O read, I/O write.

5.5.3 Comparison of Memory Mapped and I/O Mapped I/O

Memory Mapped I/O	I/O Mapped I/O
1. Memory and I/O share the entire address range of processor	Processor provides separate address range for memory and I/O devices.
2. generally, processor provides more address lines for accessing memory. Therefore, more decoding is required control signals.	Generally, processor provides less address lines for accessing I/O. Therefore, less decoding is required.
3. Memory control signals are used to control read and write I/O operations.	I/O control signals are used to control read and write I/O operations.
4. In this device, address is 16 bit. Thus A_0 to A_{15} lines are used to generate device address.	In this I/O devices address is 8-bit. Thus A_0 to A_7 or A_8 to A_{15} lines are used to generate device address.
5. $\overline{\text{MEMR}}$ and $\overline{\text{MEMW}}$ control signals are used to control read and write I/O operations.	$\overline{\text{IOR}}$ and $\overline{\text{IOW}}$ control signals are used to control read and write I/) Operations.
6. Data transfer is between any registor and I/O devices.	Data transfer is between accumulator and I/O devices.

5.6 DIRECT MEMORY ACCESS (DMA)

Definition :

A direct memory access (DMA) is an operation in which data is copied (transported) from one resource to another resource in a computer system without the involvement of the CPU. The task of a DMA-controller (DMAC) is to execute the copy operation of data from one resource location to another. The copy of data can be performed from:

1.   I/O device to memory

2.   Memory to I/O device

3.   Memory to memory

4.   I/O-device to I/O device

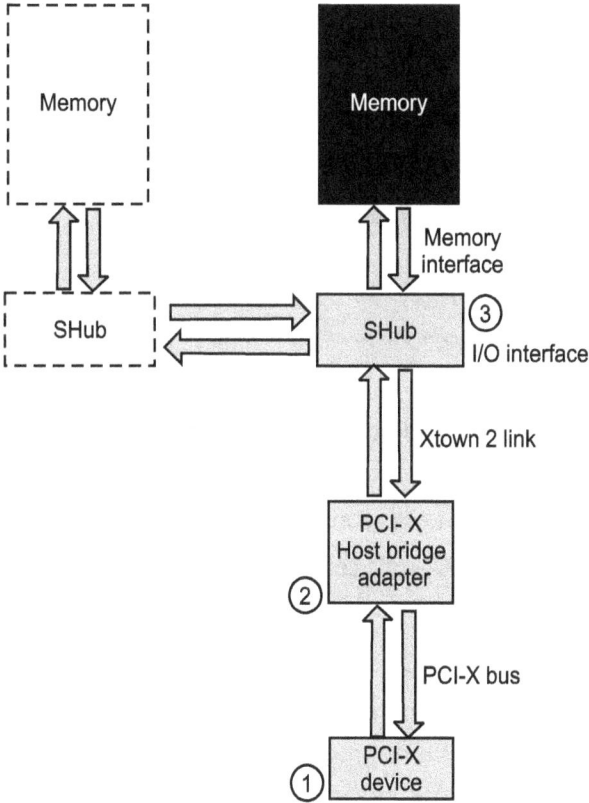

Fig. 5.6 : DMA

A DMAC is an independent (from CPU) resource of a computer system added for the concurrent execution of DMA-operations. The first two operation modes are 'read from' and write to' transfers of an I/O device to the main memory, which are the common operation of a DMA-controller. The other two operations are slightly more difficult to implement and most DMA controllers do not implement device to device transfers.

The flow depicted in Figure is as follows:

1. PCI-X device places the DMA request on the bus.
2. PCI-X host bridge adapter places the DMA request to the directly connected SHub's I/O interface.
3. Since this is a request to locally attached memory, the request is satisfied by the local SHub's memory.

5.6.1 DMA Operations

A lot of different operating modes exist for DMACs. The simplest one is the single block transfer copying a block of data from a device to memory. Here, only a short list of operating modes is given:

- single block transfer
- chained block transfers
- linked block transfers
- fly-by transfers

All these operations normally access the block of data in a linear sequence. Nevertheless, there are more usefull access functions possible, as there are: constant stride, constant stride with offset, incremental stride.

The DMA mechanism can be configured in different ways. The most common amongst them are:

(a) Single bus, detached DMA - I/O configuration.

(b) Single bus, Integrated DMA - I/O configuration.

(c) Using separate I/O bus.

(a) Single bus, detached DMA - I/O configuration

In this organization all modules share the same system bus.The DMA module here acts as a surrogate processor. This method uses programmed I/O to exchange data between memory and an I/O module through the DMA module.

• For each transfer it uses the bus twice. The first one is when transferring the data between I/O and DMA and the second one is when transferring the data between DMA and memory. Since the bus is used twice while transferring data, so the bus will be suspended twice. The transfer consumes two bus cycle.

The interconnection organization is shown in the Fig. 5.7.

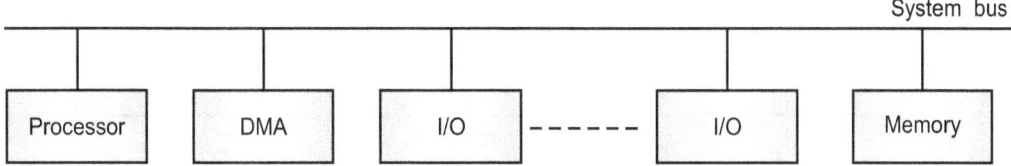

Fig. 5.7 : Single bus arrangement for DMA transfer

(b) Single bus, Integrated DMA - I/O configuration

By integrating the DMA and I/O function the number of required bus cycle can be reduced. In this configuration, the DMA module and one or more I/O modules are integrated together in such a way that the system bus is not involved.

- In this case DMA logic may actually be a part of an I/O module, or it may be a separate module that controls one or more I/O modules.

- The DMA module, processor and the memory module are connected through the system bus. In this configuration each transfer will use the system bus only once and so the processor is suspended only once.

- The system bus is not involved when transferring data between DMA and I/O device, so processor is not suspended. Processor is suspended when data is transferred between DMA and memory. The configuration is shown in the Fig. 5.8.

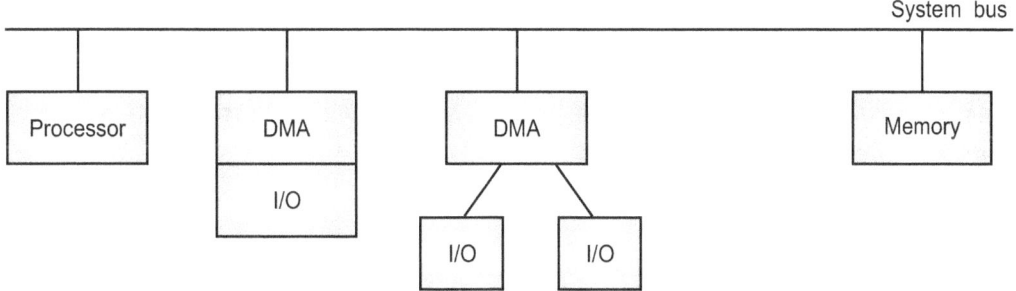

Fig. 5.8 : Single bus integrated DMA transfer

(c) Using separate I/O bus

In this configuration the I/O modules are connected to the DMA through another I/O bus. In this case the DMA module is reduced to one.

- Transfer of data between I/O module and DMA module is carried out through this I/O bus. In this transfer, system bus is not in use and so it is not needed to suspend the processor.

- There is another transfer phase between DMA module and memory. In this time system bus is needed for transfer and processor will be suspended for one bus cycle. The configuration is shown in the Fig. 5.9.

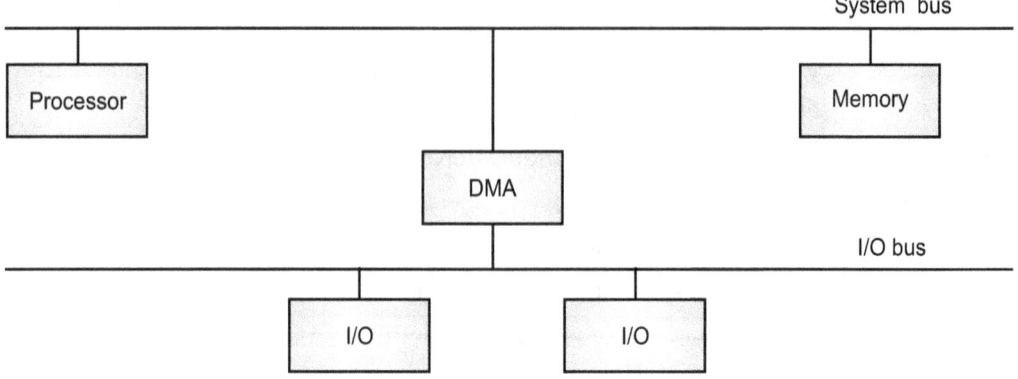

Fig. 5.9 : Seperate I/O bus for DMA transfer

5.7   PARALLEL AND SERIAL BUSES

A parallel bus is one where each bit has its own copper wire, e.g. for a 32-bit bus there may be 32 data lines and 32 address lines and control lines line R/W etc. There is usually a strobe line that says when the data bits are valid.

Examples of parallel bus : PCI, IDE, SCSI.

A serial bus is one where bits are sent in sequence on the same wire. There is usually some framing information to identify the start of a frame of data, such as a long gap. **Examples of serial bus:** SATA, USB, I2C.

5.7.1 Serial Buses

Serial Buses transfer data one bit at a time. These bits arrive at their destination in a timed sequence, called the "baud" rate, one after the other. To signal that a full byte crossed a serial bus, bytes of data, which represent eight bits, are preceded with "start" and "stop" bits. To check for errors in communication, the stop bits, along with the baud rate, are used to determine if all bits arrived properly.

5.7.2 Parallel Bus

The parallel bus, as opposed to the serial bus, does not send bits one at a time. A parallel port contains several connections laying parallel to one another, running between the same two pieces of hardware. Each connection can send one bit. An eight-bit parallel port can transmit one full byte of data.

Uses

Typically, parallel bus connections are used in computer devices and hardware connections, or for a printer connection. The internal workings of a computer require fast transfer speeds, and the parallel setup ensures that data gets where it needs to go quickly. Serial connections occur in certain peripherals that users can attach to a computer, such as a Universal Serial Bus (USB) device like an external hard drive or an MP3 player.

5.7.3 PCI Bus

The PCI bus was developed in the early 1990's by a group of companies with the goal to advance the interface allowing OEM's or users to upgrade the I/O (Input-Output) of personal computers. The PCI bus has proven a huge success and has been adopted in almost every PC and Server since. The latest advancement of the PCI bus is PCI-X. PCI-X is a 64-bit parallel interface that runs at 133 MHz enabling 1 GB/s (8 Gb/s) of bandwidth. Though other advancements are in the works, including DDR, for the PCI bus, they are perceived as falling short. They are too expensive (too many pins in the 64-bit versions) for the PC industry to implement in the mass volumes of PCs and that they don't offer sufficient bandwidth and advanced feature set required for the servers of the future.

• Essentially, a bus is a channel or path between the components in a computer. Bus connect components to the computer's processor which include hard disks, memory, sound systems, and video systems and so on.

PCI bus is known as the Peripheral Component Interconnect (PCI).

5.7.4 System Bus vs. PCI Bus

Few years ago, the processors were so slow, the bus ran at the same speed as the processor, and there was one bus in the machine. Today, the processors run so fast as most computers have two or more buses. Each bus specializes in a certain type of traffic. A typical desktop PC today has two main buses :

• The first one, known as the system bus or local bus, connects the microprocessor (central processing unit) and the system memory. This is the fastest bus in the system.

- The second one is a slower bus for communicating with things like hard disks and sound cards. One very common bus of this type is known as the PCI bus. These slower buses connect to the system bus through a bridge, which is a part of the computer's chipset and acts as a traffic cop, integrating the data from the other buses to the system bus.

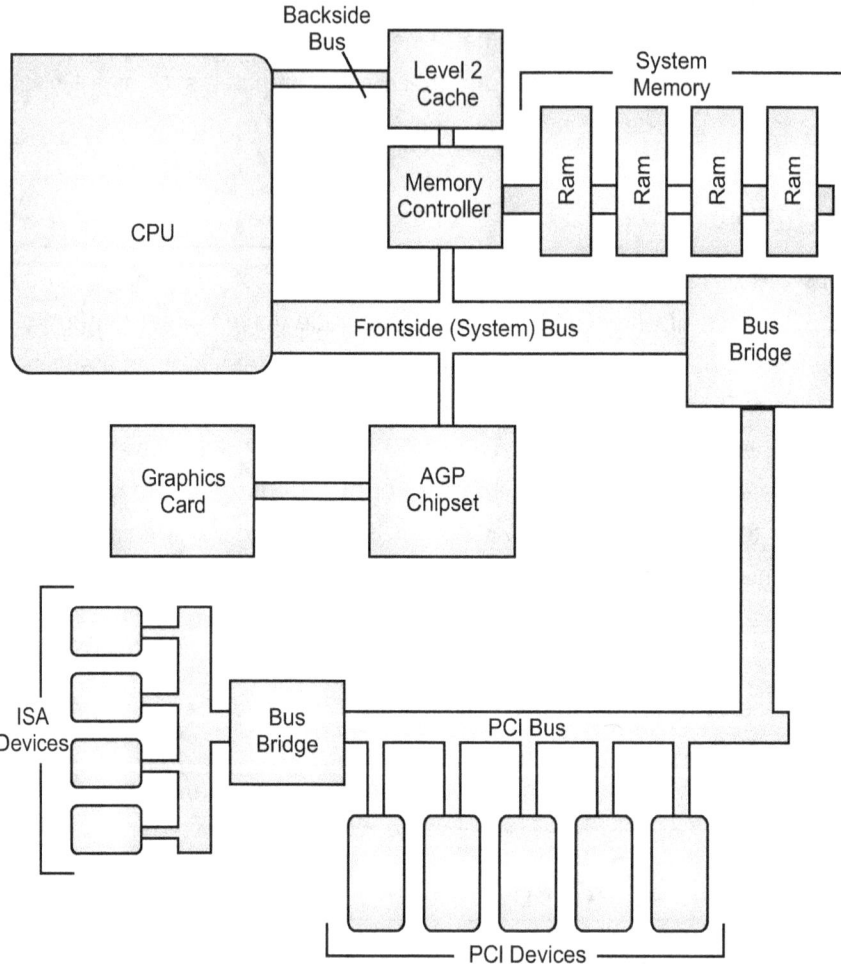

Fig. 5.10 : various buses connected to the CPU.

5.7.5 PCI History

During the early 1990s, Intel introduced a new bus standard for consideration, the Peripheral Component Interconnect (PCI) bus. It provides direct access to system memory for connected devices, but uses a bridge to connect to the front side bus and therefore to the CPU.

Basically, this means that it is capable of even higher performance than VL-Bus while eliminating the potential for interference with the CPU.

5.7.6 PCI cards use 47 pins

• PCI cards use 47 pins to connect (49 pins for a mastering card, which can control the PCI bus without CPU intervention). The PCI bus is able to work with so few pins because of hardware multiplexing, which means that the device sends more than one signal over a single pin. Also, PCI supports devices that use either 5 volts or 3.3 volts.

- PCI is synchronous bus architecture with all data transfers being performed relative to a system clock (CLK).
- In PCI terminology, data is transferred between an initiator which is the bus master, and a target which is the bus slave.

• A PCI bus transfer consists of one address phase and any number of data phases.

• PCI provides separate memory and I/O port address spaces for the x86 processor family, 64 and 32 bits, respectively. Addresses in these address spaces are assigned by software.

• A third address space, called the PCI Configuration Space, which uses a fixed addressing scheme.

• It allows software to determine the amount of memory and I/O address space needed by each device.

5.7.7 PCI command codes/Bus cycles

• There are 16 possible 4-bit command codes, and 12 of them are assigned. the least significant bit of the command code indicates whether the following data phases are a read (data sent from target to initiator) or a write (data sent from an initiator to target).

• PCI targets must examine the command code as well as the address and not respond to address phases which specify an unsupported command code.

C/BE	Command Type
0000	Interrupt Acknowledge
0001	Special Cycle
0010	I/O Read
0011	I/O Write
0100	Reserved

0101	Reserved
0110	Memory Read
0111	Memory Write
1000	Reserved
1001	Reserved
1010	Configuration Read
1011	Configuration Write
1100	Multiple Memory Read
1101	Dual Address Cycle
1110	Memory-Read Line
1111	Memory Write and Invalidate

➤ **0000: Interrupt Acknowledge**

This is a special form of read cycle implicitly addressed to the interrupt controller, which returns an interrupt vector. The 32-bit address field is ignored. Generates an interrupt acknowledge cycle on an ISA bus using a PCI/ISA bus bridge.

➤ **0001: Special Cycle**

The address field of a special cycle is ignored, but it is followed by a data phase containing a payload message. The currently defined messages announce that the processor is stopping for some reason (e.g. to save power). No device ever responds to this cycle; it is always terminated with a master abort after leaving the data on the bus for at least 4 cycles.

0 x 0000	**Processor Shutdown**
0×0000	Processor Shutdown
0×0001	Processor Halt
0×0002	x86 Specific Code
0×0003 to $0 \times$ FFFF	Reserved

➤ **0010: I/O Read**

This performs a read from I/O space. All 32 bits of the read address are provided; so that a device can (for compatibility reasons) implement less than 4 bytes worth of I/O registers. If the bytes enabled request data not within the address range supported by the PCI device, it must be terminated with a target abort. Multiple data cycles are permitted.

➤ **0011: I/O Write**

This performs a write to I/O space.

➤ **010x: Reserved**

A PCI device must not respond to an address cycle with these command codes.

➤ **0110: Memory Read**

This performs a read cycle from memory space. Because the smallest memory space a PCI device is permitted to implement is 16 bytes, the two least significant bits of the address are not needed; equivalent information will arrive in the form of byte select signals. They instead specify the order in which burst data must be returned. If a device does not support the requested order, it must provide the first word and then disconnect.

If a memory space is marked as "prefetchable", then the target device must ignore the byte select signals on a memory read and always return 32 valid bits.

➤ **0110: Memory Write**

This operates similarly to a memory read. The byte select signals are more important in a write, as unselected bytes must not be written to memory.

Generally, PCI writes are faster than PCI reads, because a device can buffer the incoming write data and release the bus faster. For a read, it must delay the data phase until the data has been fetched.

➤ **100x: Reserved**

A PCI device must not respond to an address cycle with these command codes.

➤ **1010: Configuration Read**

This is similar to an I/O read, but reads from PCI configuration space. A device must respond only if the low 11 bits of the address specify a function and register that it implements, and if the special IDSEL signal is asserted. It must ignore the high 21 bits. Burst reads are permitted in PCI configuration space.

Unlike I/O space, standard PCI configuration registers are defined so that reads never disturb the state of the device.

➤ **1011: Configuration Write**

This operates analogously to a configuration read.

➤ **1100: Memory Read Multiple**

This command is identical to a generic memory read, but includes the hint that a long read burst will continue beyond the end of the current cache line, and the target should internally prefetch a large amount of data. A target is always permitted to consider this a synonym for a generic memory read.

➢ **1101: Dual Address Cycle**

When accessing a memory address that requires more than 32 bits to represent, the address phase begins with this command and the high 32 bits of the address, followed by a second cycle with the actual command and the low 32 bits of the address.

➢ **1110: Memory Read Line**

This command is identical to a generic memory read, but includes the hint that the read will continue to the end of the cache line. A target is always permitted to consider this a synonym for a generic memory read.

➢ **1111: Memory Write and Invalidate**

This command is identical to a generic memory write, but comes with the guarantee that one or more whole cache line will be written, with all byte selects enabled. This is an optimization for write-back caches snooping the bus. If the write is performed using this command, the data to be written back is guaranteed to be irrelevant, and can simply be invalidated in the write-back cache.

5.7.8 PCI timing diagrams

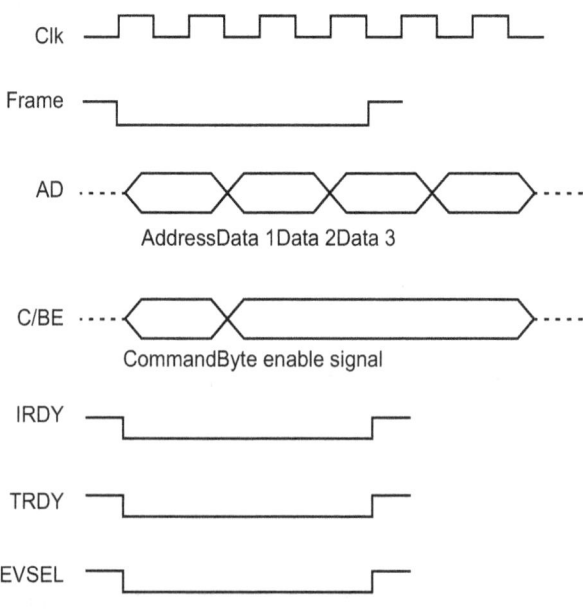

Fig. 5.11 : PCI timing diagrams

PCI transfer cycle, with wait states. Data is transferred on the rising edge of CLK at points labeled A, B, and C.

Signal timing

- All PCI bus signals are sampled on the rising edge of the clock. Signals nominally change on the falling edge of the clock, giving each PCI device approximately one half a clock cycles to decide how to respond to the signals it observed on the rising edge, and one half a clock cycle to transmit its response to the other device.

- The PCI bus requires that every time the device driving a PCI bus signal changes, one turnaround cycle must elapse between the time the one device stops driving the signal and the other device starts. The combination of this turnaround cycle and the requirement to drive a control line high for one cycle before ceasing to drive it means that each of the main control lines must be high for a minimum of 2 cycles when changing owners is it necessary to insert additional delay to meet this requirement.

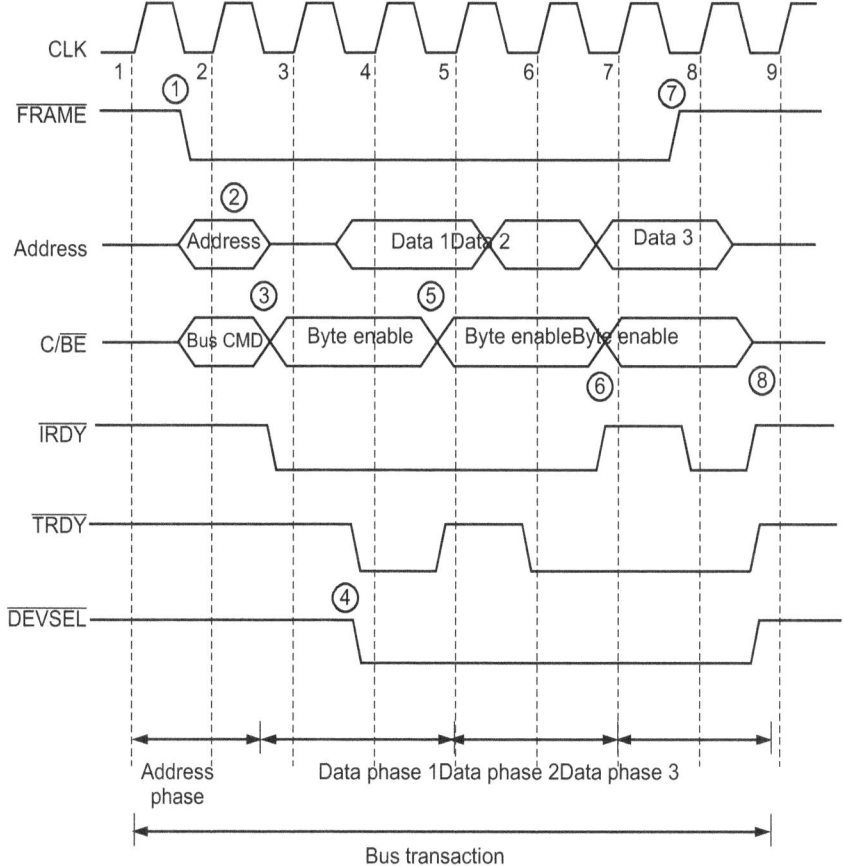

Fig. 5.12 : Address Phase and timing diagram

Arbitration

- Any device on a PCI bus that is capable of acting as a bus master may initiate a transaction with any other device. To ensure that only one transaction is initiated at a time, each master must first wait for a bus grant signal, GNT#, from an arbiter located on the motherboard. Each device has a separate request line REQ# that requests the bus, but the arbiter may "park" the bus grant signal at any device if there are no current requests.

- The arbiter may remove GNT# at any time. A device which loses GNT# may complete its current transaction, but may not start one (by asserting FRAME#) unless it observes GNT# asserted the cycle before it begins.

- The arbiter may also provide GNT# at any time, including during another master's transaction. During a transaction, either FRAME# or IRDY# or both are asserted; when both are disserted, the bus is idle. A device may initiate a transaction at any time that GNT# is asserted and the bus is idle.

5.8   SCSI CONTROLLER (SMALL COMPUTER SYSTEM INTERFACE CONTROLLER

A SCSI controller, also called a host bus adapter (HBA), is a card or chip that allows a Small Computer System Interface (SCSI) storage device to communicate with the operating system across a SCSI bus.

The actual implementation of a SCSI controller varies by manufacturer. SCSI controllers can reside in a hard drive's PCI slot or can be a chip built into the mother board. When an end user sends a request, the operating system sends the SCSI command to the controller, which then sends it to the storage device.

Like all components on a SCSI bus, a SCSI controller is given a unique identifier.

A computer is full of busses or highways that take information and power from one place to another.

- For example, when you plug an MP3 player or digital camera into your computer, you're probably using a universal serial bus (USB) port.

- Your USB port is good at carrying the data and electricity required for small electronic devices that do things like create and store pictures and music files. But that bus isn't big enough to support a whole computer, a server or lots of devices simultaneously.

For that we need SCSI.

- Small Computer System Interface, or the SCSI standards define commands, protocols, and electrical and optical interfaces. The Small Computer System Interface (SCSI) is a parallel I/O bus and protocol that permits the connection of a variety of peripherals including disk drives, tape drives, modems, printers, scanners, optical devices, test equipment, and medical devices to a host computer.

- It's a fast bus that can connect lots of devices to a computer at the same time, including hard drives, scanners, CD-ROM/RW drives, printers and tape drives The SCSI bus connects all parts of a computer system so that they can communicate with each other.

- SCSI is an intelligent interface: it hides the complexity of physical format. Every device attaches to the SCSI bus in a similar manner.

- SCSI is a peripheral interface: up to 8 or 16 devices can be attached to a single bus. There can be any number of hosts and peripheral devices but there should be at least one host.

- SCSI is a buffered interface: it uses hand shake signals between devices, SCSI-1, SCSI-2 have the option of parity error checking. Starting with SCSI-U160 (part of SCSI-3) all commands and data are error checked by a CRC32 checksum.

- SCSI is a peer to peer interface: the SCSI protocol defines communication from host to host, host to a peripheral device, and peripheral device to a peripheral device.

5.8.1 SCSI Types

SCSI has three basic specifications:

1. **SCSI-1:** The original specification developed in 1986, SCSI-1 is now obsolete. It featured a bus width of 8 bits and clock speed of 5 MHz.

2. **SCSI-2:** Adopted in 1994, this specification included the Common Command Set (CCS) 18 commands considered an absolute necessity for support of any SCSI device. It also had the option to double the clock speed to 10 MHz (Fast), double the bus width from to 16 bits and increase the number of devices to 15 (Wide), or do both (Fast/Wide). SCSI-2 also added command queuing, allowing devices to store and prioritize commands from the host computer.

3. **SCSI-3:** This specification debuted in 1995 and included a series of smaller standards within its overall scope. A set of standards involving the SCSI Parallel Interface (SPI), which is the way that SCSI devices communicate with each other, has continued to evolve within SCSI-3. Most SCSI-3 specifications begin with the term Ultra, such as

Ultra for SPI variations, Ultra2 for SPI-2 variations and Ultra3 for SPI-3 variations. The Fast and Wide designations work just like their SCSI-2 counterparts. SCSI-3 is the standard currently in use.

5.8.2 Controllers, Devices and Cables

• A SCSI controller coordinates between all of the other devices on the SCSI bus and the computer. Also called a host adapter, the controller can be a card that you plug into an available slot or it can be built into the motherboard. The SCSI BIOS is also on the controller. This is a small ROM or Flash memory chip that contains the software needed to access and control the devices on the bus.

• Each SCSI device must have a unique identifier (ID) in order for it to work properly.

• Internal devices connect to a SCSI controller with a ribbon cable. External SCSI devices attach to the controller in a daisy chain using a thick, round cable. (Serial Attached SCSI devices use SATA cables.)

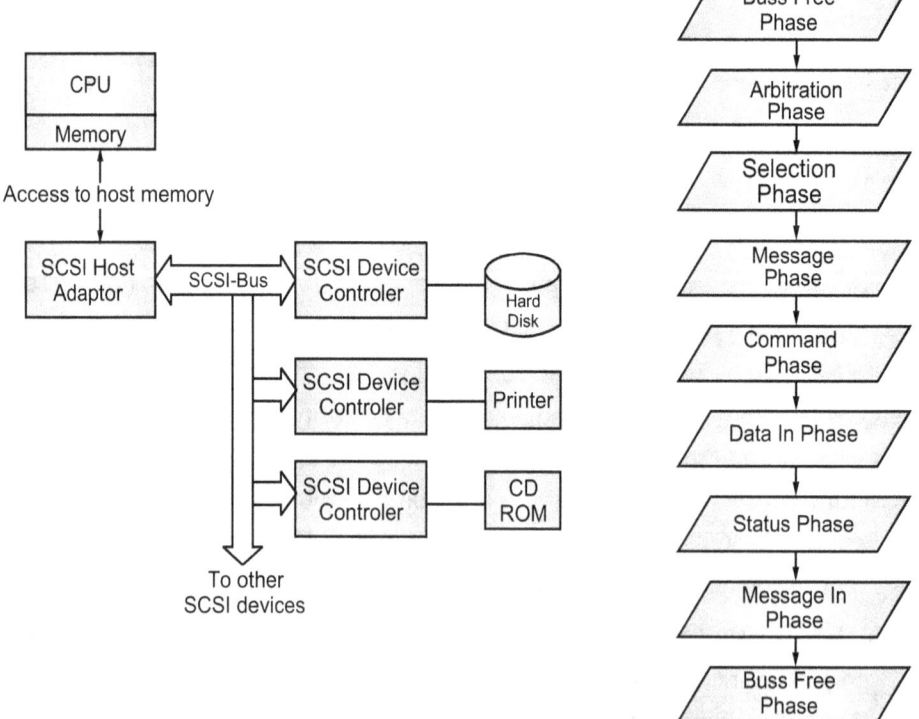

Fig. 5.13 : SCSI Configuration   **Fig. 5.14 : SCSI Bus Phases**

The cable itself typically consists of three layers:

> ➤ Inner layer: The most protected layer, this contains the actual data being sent.

> ➤ Media layer: Contains the wires that send control commands to the device.

> ➤ Outer layer: Includes wires that carry parity information, which ensures that the data is correct.

• When two devices communicate on the bus, one device initiates the communication to the target, and the target performs the task. SCSI devices usually have a fixed role as an initiator or a target, although some devices can perform both roles.

5.8.3 SCSI Bus signals

The SCSI bus uses eighteen signals. Nine are control signals used to develop logical bus phases, and nine are data signals, including parity, for messages, commands, status, and data.

The state of the SEL, BSY, and I/O signals and the sequence of the phases determine when the Bus Free, Arbitration, Selection, and Reselection phases are entered.

Table 1 describes the nine control signals.

• The Selection or Reselection phase can be entered onl form the Arbitration phase.

• The Arbitration phase can be entered only from the Bus Free phase.

• The Bus Free phase can be entered from any of the other phases (although some transitions are caused by errors).

I/O determine the current phase, you need to know information about the previous phase and the state of the signals. The initiator and target drive these signals to change from one phase to another phase.

Table 5.1 : SCSI Bus Signals

Signal	Description
BSY(BUSY)	An 'OR-tied signal which indicates that the bus is being used.
SEL(SELECT)	A signal used by an initiator to select a target or by a target to reselect an initiator.
C/D (CONTROL/DATA)	A signal driven by a target to indicate whether or not control or data information is on the data bus. True indicates control.

I/0 (INPUT/OUTPUT)	A signal driven by a target to control the direction of data movement on the data bus. True indicates input to the initiator. This signal is also used to distinguish between selection and reselection phases.
MSG (MESSAGE)	A signal driven by a target during the Message phase.
REQ (REQUEST)	A signal driven by a target to request a REQ/ACK data transfer handshake.
ACK (ACKNOWLEDGE)	A signal driven by an initiator to acknowledge a REQ/ACK data transfer.
ATN (ATTENTION)	A signal driven by an initiator to indicate the condition (initiator has a message for the target).
RST (RESET)	An 'OR-tied' signal and hard Reset condition.
DB (7-0,P) (DATA BUS)	Eight data-bit (DB) signals, plus a parity-bit signal that form a Data Bus. DB (7) is the most significant bit and has the highest during the Arbitration phase. Bit number, significance, and priority decreases downward to DB (0). A data bit is defined as one when the signal value is true, and defined as zero when the signal value is false. Data parity DB (P) shall be odd, but parity is undefined during the Arbitration phase.

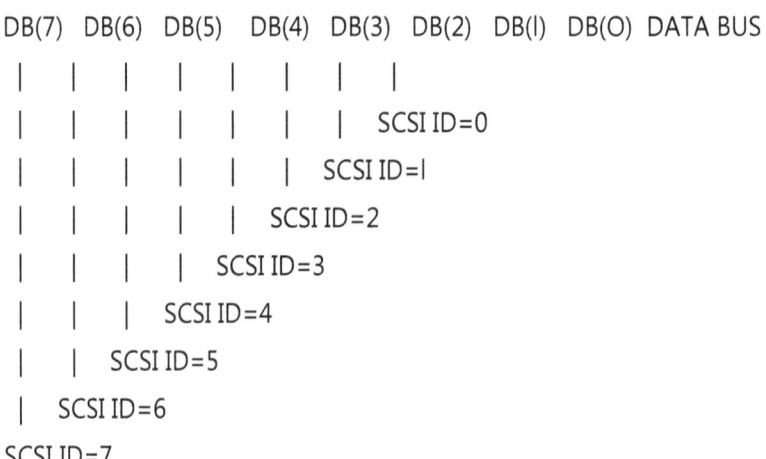

```
DB(7)  DB(6)  DB(5)   DB(4)  DB(3)  DB(2)  DB(I)  DB(O)  DATA BUS
  |      |      |       |      |      |      |      |
  |      |      |       |      |      |      |   SCSI ID=0
  |      |      |       |      |      |   SCSI ID=I
  |      |      |       |      |   SCSI ID=2
  |      |      |       |   SCSI ID=3
  |      |      |    SCSI ID=4
  |      |   SCSI ID=5
  |   SCSI ID=6
SCSI ID=7
```

Fig. 5.15 : SCSI ID Bits

A SCSI device usually has a fixed role as an initiator or target, but some devices are able to assume either role. In most cases, the host is the initiator and the device is the target.

An initiator may address up to eight peripheral devices that are connected to a target. These are called Logical Units Numbers (LUNs). Digital devices currently only support a single LUN per device.

5.8.4 SCSI Bus Phases

- The Small Computer System Interface bus can be time-shared, which results in greater usage of bus bandwidth. This is how it works: while one device is using the bus, other devices may be active and performing internal activities.
- System performance is significantly increased when devices disconnect and reconnect to the bus. During the bus phases devices must first contend for access to the bus.
- Then a physical path is established between the initiator and target. The SCSI bus cannot be in more than one phase at a same time.

The SCSI architecture includes eight distinct phases:

- Bus Free phase
- Arbitration phase
- Selection phase
- Reselection phase.
- Command phase
- Data phase
- Message phase
- Status phase

- The SCSI bus can never be in more than one phase at any given time. Unless otherwise noted in the following description, signals that are not mentioned shall not be asserted.

Bus Free Phase

- The Bus Free Phase is used to indicate that no SCSI device is actively using the SCSI bus and that it is available for subsequent users. SCSI devices shall detect the Bus Free Phase after SEL and BSY are both false for at least a bus settles delay. SCSI devices shall release all SCSI bus signals has a bus clear delay after BSY and SEI, become continuously false for a bus settle delay.

- If a SCSI device requires more than a bus settle delay to detect the Bus Free Phase then it releases all SCSI bus signals within a bus clear delay minus the excess time to detect the Bus Free Phase.

- The total time to clear the SCSI bus does not exceed a bus settle delay plus a bus clear delay. Initiators normally do not expect Bus Free Phase to begin because of the target's release of BSY except after one of the following occurrences:

  - After a Reset condition is detected.

  - After an Abort message is successfully received by a target.

  - After a Bus Device Reset message is successfully received by a target.

  - After a Disconnect message is successfully transmitted from a target.

  - After a Command Complete message is successfully transmitted from a target.

  - After- a Release Recovery message is successfully received by a target.

The Bus Free Phase may also be entered after an unsuccessful selection or reselection, of SEL rather than the release of BSY that first although in this case it is the established the Bus Free Phase.

- If an initiator detects the release of BSY by the target at other times, the target is indicating an error condition to the initiator. The target may perform this transition to the Bus Free Phase independent of the state of the ATN signal. The initiator manages this condition as an unsuccessful I/0 process termination.

- The target terminates the I/0 process by clearing all pending data and status information for the affected logical unit or process.

- The target may optionally prepare sense bytes that could be read by a Request Sense command.

- When an initiator detects an unexpected Bus Free condition it is normal that a Request Sense command is attempted to obtain any valid sense information that may be available. If the error that caused the Bus Free termination of the I/0 process is still present, the Request Sense command may not be successful.

Arbitration Phase

The Arbitration Phase allows one SCSI device to gain control of the SCSI bus so that it can assume the role of an initiator or target. The procedure for an SCSI device to obtain control of the SCSI bus is as follows:

1. The SCSI device shall first wait for the Bus Free Phase to occur. The Bus Free Phase is detected whenever both BSY and SEL are simultaneously and continuously false for a minimum of a bus settle delay

2. The SCSI device waits a minimum of a bus free delay alter detection of the Bus Free Phase (that is after BSY and SEL are both false for a bus settles delay) before driving any signal

3. Following the bus free delay in step (2), the SCSI device may arbitrate for the SCSI bus by asserting both BSY and its own SCST ID, however the SCSI device does not arbitrate (that is assert BSY and its SCSI ID) if more than a bus settle delay has passed since the Bus Free Phase was last observed

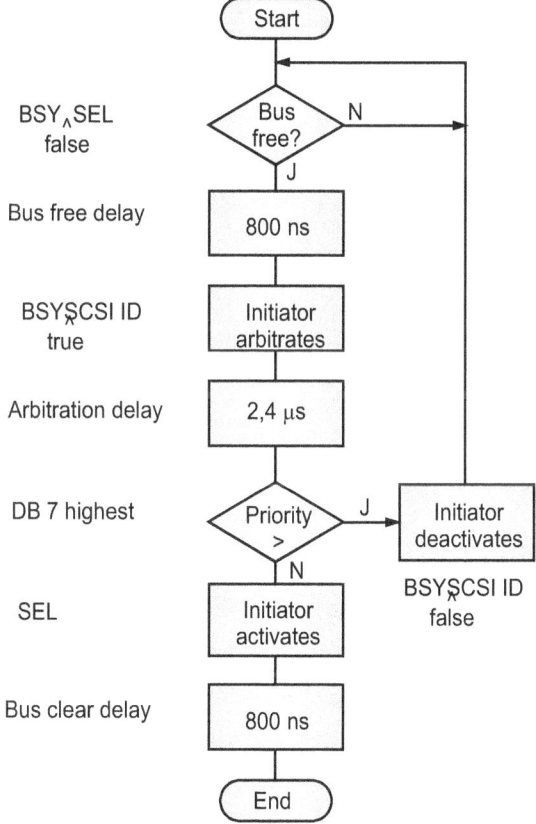

Fig. 5.15 : SCSI Arbitration

4. After waiting at least an arbitration delay (measured from its assertion of BSY) the SCSI device examines the Data Bus If a higher priority SCSI ID bit is true on the DATA BUS (DB(7) is the highest), then the SCSI device has lost the arbitration and the SCSI

device releases its' signals and returns to step (1)' If no higher priority SCSI ID bit is true on the Data Bus, then the SCSI device has won the arbitration and it asserts SEL. Any other SCSI device that is participating in the Arbitration Phase has lost the arbitration and releases BSY and its SCSI ID bit within a bus clear delay after SEL becomes true. A SCSI device that loses arbitration returns to step (1)

5. The SCSI device that wins arbitration shall wait at least a bus clear delay plus a bus settle delay after asserting SEL before changing any signals.

Selection Phase

The Selection Phase allows an initiator to select a target for the purpose of initiating some target function for example the Read or Write command.

During the Selection Phase the I/0 signal is negated so that this phase can be distinguished from the Reselection Phase.

• The SCSI device that won the arbitration has both BSY and SEL asserted and has delayed at least a bus clear delay plus a bus settle delay before ending the Arbitration Phase. The SCSI device that won the arbitration becomes an initiator by not asserting the I/0 signal. The initiator sets the Data Bus to a value which is the OR of its SCSI ID bit and the target's SCSI ID bit. The initiator then waits at least two deskew delays and releases BSY. The initiator then waits at least a bus settle delay before looking for a response from the target.

Selection Phase

DB(0)	DB(l)	DB(2)	DB(3)	DB(4)	DB(5)	DB(6)	DB(7)
1	0	0	0	0	0	1	0

• In this example, SCSI ID 6 (host) has asserted both its own SCSI ID (DB (6)) and that of a device (DB (0)). The target determines that it is selected when SEL and its SCSI ID bit are true and BSY and I/0 are false for at least a bus settle delay. The selected target examines the data Bus in order to determine the SCSI ID of the selecting initiator. The selected target is BSY within a selection; this is required for correct operation of the time-out procedure. The target shall not respond to a selection if bad parity is detected. Also, if more than two SCSI ID bits are on the Data Bus, the target does not respond to selection.

Reselection Phase

• Reselection is an optional phase that allows a target to reconnect to an initiator for the purpose of continuing some operation that was previously started by the initiator but was suspended by the target. For example, a host system may have requested a Read from a disk. The disk can disconnect and Reconnect if the Read involves a time consuming seek operation to be performed. This is one of the optimization features of SCSI.

- The initiator determines that it is reselected when SEL, I/O and its SCSI ID bit are true and BSY is false for at least a bus settle delay. The reselected initiator may examine the Data Bus in order to determine the SCSI ID of the reselecting target. The reselected initiator then asserts BSY within a selection abort time of its most recent detection of being reselected; this is required for correct operation of the time-out procedure. The initiator does not respond to a Reselection Phase if bad party is detected. Also, the initiator may not respond to a Reselection Phase if other than two SCSI ID bits are on the Data Bus.

- After the target detects BSY, it also asserts BSY and wait at least two deskew delays and then release SEL. The target may then change the I/O signal and the Data Bus. After the reselected initiator detects SEL false, it releases BSY. The target continues asserting BSY until it relinquishes the SCSI bus.

Information Transfer Phases

The Command, Data, Status, and Message Phases are all grouped together as the Information Tansfer Phases because they are all used to transfer data or control information via the Data Bus.

- The C/D, I/O, and MSG signals are used to distinguish between the different Information Tansfer Phases. The target drives these three signals and therefore controls all changes from one phase to another.

- The initiator can request a Message out Phase by asserting ATN, while the target can cause the Bus Free Phase by releasing MSG, C/D, I/O and BSY. The Information Tansfer Phases use one or more REQ/ACK handshakes to control the information transfer.

- Each REQ/ACK handshake allows the transfer of one byte of information. During the information transfer phases BSY remains true and SEL remains false.

- Additionally, during the Information Tansfer Phases, the target shall continuously envelope the REQ/ACK handshake(s) with C/D, I/O and MSG in such a manner that these control signals are valid for a bus settle delay before the assertion of REQ of the first handshake and remain valid until after the negation of ACK at the end of the handshake of the last transfer of the phase.

Information Transfer Phases

Signal

MSG	C/D	I/O	Phase Name	Direction of Transfer	Comment
0 0	0	Data out	Initiator to Target	Data	
0 0	1	Data in	Initiator from Target	Phase	
0 1	0	Command	Initiator to Target		
0 1	1	Status	Initiator from Target		
1 0	0	*			
1 0	1	*			
1 1	0	Message Out	Initiator To Target	Message	
1 1	1	Message In	Initiator From Target	Phase	

Key : 0 = False

1 = True

* = Reserved for future specification

Asynchronous Information Transfer

- The target controls the direction of information transfer by means of the I/0 signals. When I/0 are true, information is transferred from the target to the initiator. When I/0 is false, information is transferred from the initiator to the target.
- If I/O is true (transfer to the initiator),
- If I/O is false (transfer to the target)
- When ACK becomes true at the target, the target reads DB(7-0,P) then negates REQ. When REQ becomes false at the initiator, the initiator may change or release DB(7-0,P) and negates ACK. The target may continue the transfer by asserting REQ, as described above.

Synchronous Data Transfer

- Synchronous data transfer is only used in data phases. It is used in a data phase if a synchronous data transfer agreement has been established between the target and initiator.
- The REQ/ACK offset specifies the Maximum number of REQ pulses that can be sent by the, target in advance of the number of ACK pulses received from the initiator, establishing a pacing mechanism.

- If the number of REQ pulses exceeds the number of ACK pulses by the REQ/ACK offset, the target shall not assert REQ until alter the leading edge of the next ACK pulse is received. • The target asserts the REQ signal for a minimum of an assertion period. The target shall wait at least a transfer period from the last transition of REQ to false before asserting the REQ signal.

- The initiator sends one pulse on the ACK signal for each REQ pulse received. The ACK signal may be asserted as soon as the leading edge of the corresponding REQ pulse has been received.

- The initiator asserts the ACK signal for a minimum of an assertion period. The initiator waits at least the greater of a transfer period from the last transition of ACK to true or for a minimum of a negation period from the last transition of ACK to false before asserting the ACK signal.

- If I/O is true (transfer to the initiator), the target first drives DB(7-0,P) to their desired values, waits at least one deskskew delay plus one cable skew delay, then assert REQ. DB(70,P) shall be held valid for a minimum of one deskew delay plus one cable skew delay plus one hold time after the assertion of REQ. The target asserts REQ for a minimum of an assertion period.

- The target may then negate REQ and change or release DB(7-0,P). The initiator reads the value on DB(7-0,P) within one hold tirne of the transition of REQ to true. The initiator then responds with an ACK pulse.

Command Phase

The Command Phase allows the target to request command information from the initiator.The target shall assert the C/D signal and negate the I/0 and MSG during the REQ/ACK handshake(s) of this phase.

Data Phase

The Data Phase is a term that encompasses both the Data In Phase and the Data Out Phase.

(a) Data In Phase

The Data In Phase allows the target to request that data be sent to the initiator from the target. The target asserts the I/0 signal and negate the C/D and MSG signals during the REQ/ACK handshake(s) of this phase.

(b) Data Out Phase

The Data Out Phase allows the target to request that data be sent from the initiator to the target. The target negates the C/D, I/0, and MSG signals during the REQ/ACK handshake(s) of this phase.

(c) Status Phase

The Status Phase allows the target to request that status information be sent from the target to the initiator. The target asserts C/D and I/0 and negates the MSG signal during the REQ/ACK handshake of this phase.

(d) Message Phase

The Message Phase is a term that references either a Message In, or a Message Out Phase. Multiple messages may be sent during either phase. The first byte transferred in either of these phases is either a single-byte message or the first byte of a multiple-byte message. Multiple-byte messages are wholly contained within a single message phase.

(e) Message In Phase

The Message In Phase allows the target to request that message(s) be sent to the initiator from the target.

The target asserts C/D, 1/0, and MSG during the REQ/ACK handshake(s) of this phase.

(f) Message Out Phase

The Message Out Phase allows the target to request that message(s) be sent from the initiator to the target. The target invokes this phase in response to the Attention condition created by the initiator.

5.8.5 SCSI Bus Conditions

The SCSI bus has two asynchronous conditions; the Attention condition and the Reset condition. These conditions cause the SCSI device to perform certain actions and can alter the phase sequence.

1. **Attention Condition**

   - The Attention condition allows an initiator to inform a target that the initiator has a message ready. The target may get this message by performing a Message Out Phase.

   - The initiator creates the Attention condition by asserting ATN at any time except during the Arbitration or Bus Free Phases.

   - The initiator asserts the ATN signal before negating ACK for the last byte transferred in a bus phase.

   - The initiator negates ATN before asserting ACK when transferring the last byte of the messages.

- If the target detects that the initiator failed to meet this requirement, then the target goes to Bus Free Phase.

2. Reset Condition

- The Reset condition is used to immediately clear all SCSI devices from the bus.
- All SCSI devices release all SCSI bus signals (except RST) within a bus clear delay of the transition of RST to true. The Bus Free Phase always follows the Reset condition

5.8.6 SCSI Bus Phase Sequences

- The order in which phases are used on the SCSI bus follows a prescribed sequence. The Reset condition can abort any phase and is always followed by the Bus Free Phase.

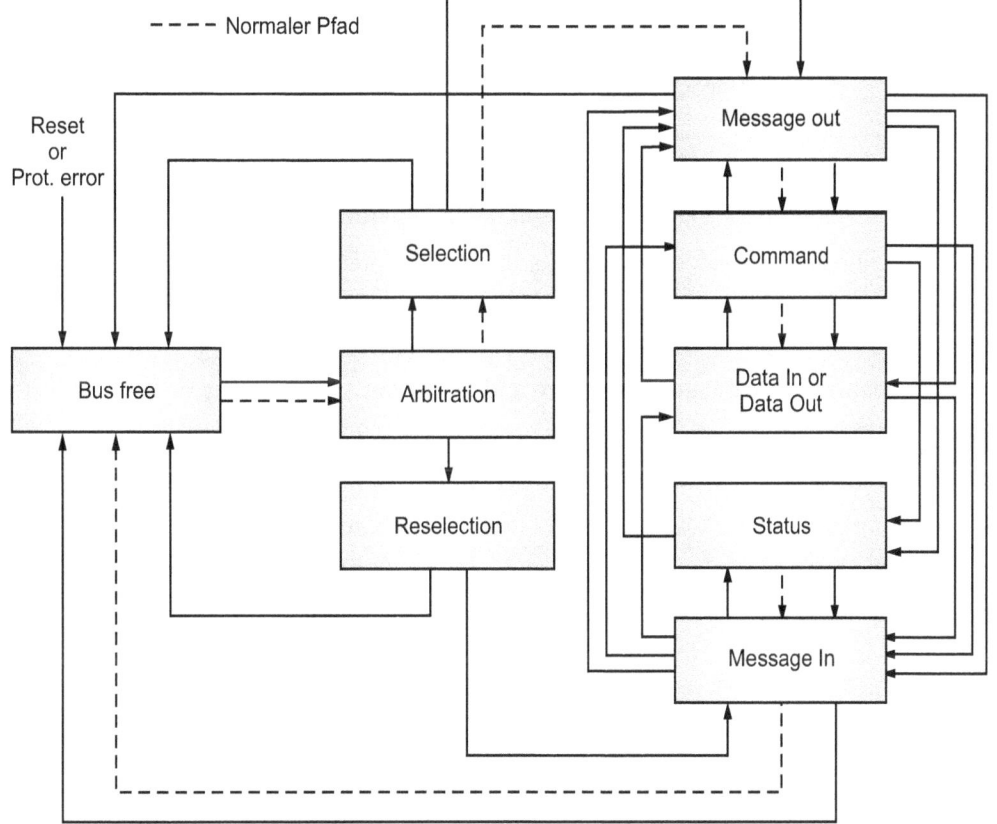

Fig. 5.16 : SCSI Phase Sequences

- Also any other phase can be followed by the Bus Free Phase but many such instances are error conditions.

- The normal Progression is from the Bus Free Phase to Arbitration, from Arbitration to Selection or Reselection, and from Selection or Reselection to one or more of the Information Transfer Phases (Command, Data, Status, or Message).

- Normally, the final Information Humanster Phase is Message In Phase where a Disconnect, Command Complete, or Linked Command Complete message is transferred, followed by Bus Free phase.

5.8.7 SCSI Pointers

Consider the system shown in Fig. 5.17 in which an initiator and target communicate on the SCSI bus in order to execute an I/0 operation.

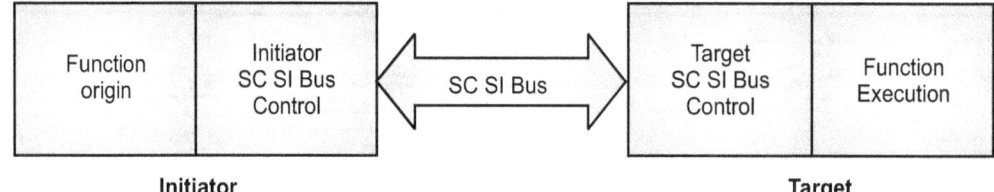

Fig. 5.17 : Simplified I/0 Operation

The SCSI architecture provides for two sets of three pointers within each initiator. The first sets of pointers are known as the current (or active) pointers. These pointers are used to represent the state of the interface and point to the next command, data, or status byte to be transferred between the initiator's memory and the target. There is only one set of current pointers in each initiator.

The second sets of pointers are known as the saved pointers.

The saved status pointer always points to the start of the status area for the current PO process. At the beginning of each I/0 processes, the saved data pointer points to the start of the data area. It remains at this value until the target sends a Save Data Pointer message to the initiator. In response to this message, the initiator stores the value of the current data pointer into the saved data pointer.

The Target may restore the current pointers to their saved values by sending a Restore Pointers message to the initiator.

The initiator then moves the saved value of each pointer into the corresponding current pointer. Whenever an SCSI device disconnects from the bus, only the saved pointer values are retained.

The current pointer values are restored from the saved values upon the next reconnection.

5.8.8 SCSI Messages

- **Abort**

This message is sent from the initiator to the target to clear the present I/0 process plus any queued I/O process for the I-T-x nexus.

- **Bus Device Reset**

This message is sent from an initiator to direct a target to clear all current I/0 processes on that SCSI device.

- **Command Complete**

This message is sent from a target to an initiator to indicate that the execution of a command has terminated and that valid status has been sent to the initiator. After successfully sending this message, the target enters the Bus Free Phase by releasing BSY. The target considers the message transmission to be successful when it detects the negation of ACK for the Command Complete message with the ATN signal false.

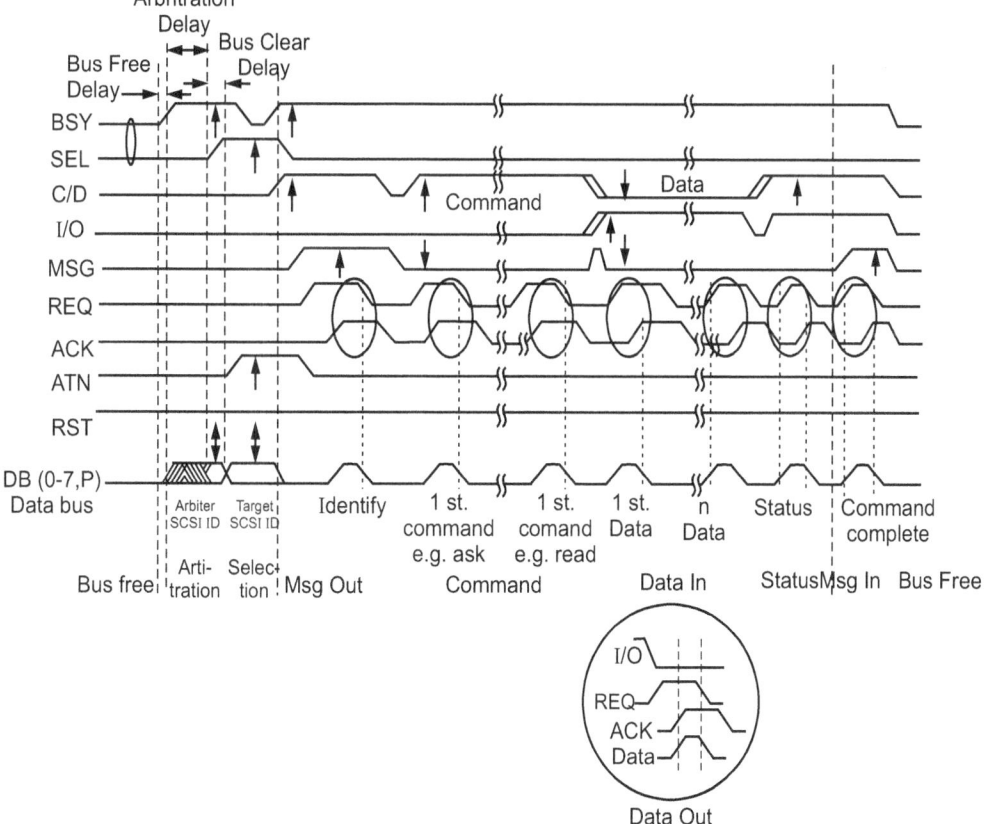

Fig. 5.18 : SCSI Timing Diagram

- **Disconnect**

This message is sent from a target to inform an initiator that the present connection is going to be broken (the target plans to disconnect by releasing BSY), but that a later reconnect will be required in order to complete the current I/O process.

This message may also be sent from an initiator to a target to instruct the target to disconnect from the SCSI bus.

- **Identify**

The Identify message is sent by either the initiator or the target to establish an I - T - L nexus or an I-T-R nexus. Fig5.43 shows an example of the SCSI signals, its sequence and the timing.

5.9 USB PORTS

USB is short form of Universal Serial Bus, an external bus standard that supports data transfer rates of 12 Mbps. A single USB port can be used to connect up to 127 peripheral devices, such as mice, modems, and keyboards. USB also supports Plug-and-Play installation and hot plugging. the USB system is so flexible and is able to support so many devices so easily. The Universal Serial Bus gives a single, standardized, easy-to-use way to connect up to 127 devices to a computer.

5.9.1 USB Cables and Connectors

Connecting a USB device to a computer is simple. You find the USB connector on the back of your machine and plug the USB connector into it.

If it is a new device, the operating system auto-detects it and asks for the driver disk. If the device has already been installed, the computer activates it and starts talking to it. USB devices can be connected and disconnected at any time.

Many USB devices come with their own built-in cable, and the cable has an "A" connection on it. If not, then the device has a socket on it that accepts a USB "B" connector.

The USB standard uses "A" and "B" connectors to avoid confusion:

- "A" connectors head "upstream" toward the computer.
- "B" connectors head "downstream" and connect to individual devices.

By using different connectors on the upstream and downstream end, it is impossible to ever get confused. If you connect any USB cable's "B" connector into a device, you know that it will work. Similarly, you can plug any "A" connector into any "A" socket and know that it will work.

5.9.2 USB Hubs

Most computers that you buy today come with one or two USB sockets. With so many USB devices on the market today, you easily run out of sockets very quickly. For example, on the computer that I am typing on right now, I have a USB printer, a USB scanner, a USB Webcam and a USB network connection. My computer has only one USB connector on it, so the obvious question is, "How do you hook up all the devices?"

The easy solution to the problem is to buy an inexpensive USB hub. The USB standard supports up to 127 devices, and USB hubs are a part of the standard.

A hub typically has four new ports, but may have many more. You plug the hub into your computer, and then plug your devices (or other hubs) into the hub. By chaining hubs together, you can build up dozens of available USB ports on a single computer.

Hubs can be powered or unpowered.The power (up to 500 milliamps at 5 volts) comes from the computer. If you have lots of self-powered devices (like printers and scanners), then your hub does not need to be powered or none of the devices connecting to the hub needs additional power, so the computer can handle it. If you have lots of unpowered devices like mice and cameras, you probably need a powered hub. The hub has its own transformer and it supplies power to the bus so that the devices do not overload the computer's supply.

5.9.3 The USB Process

When the host powers up, it queries all of the devices connected to the bus and assigns each one an address. This process is called enumeration devices are also enumerated when they connect to the bus. The host also finds out from each device what type of data transfer it wishes to perform:

- **Interrupt** - A device like a mouse or a keyboard, which will be sending very little data, would choose the interrupt mode.

- **Bulk -** A device like a printer, which receives data in one big packet, uses the bulk transfer mode. A block of data is sent to the printer (in 64-byte chunks) and verified to make sure it is correct.

- **Isochronous -** A streaming device (such as speakers) uses the isochronous mode. Data streams between the device and the host in real-time, and there is no error correction.

The host can also send commands or query parameters with control packets.

The Universal Serial Bus divides the available bandwidth into frames, and the host controls the frames. Frames contain 1,500 bytes, and a new frame starts every millisecond. During a frame, isochronous and interrupt devices get a slot so they are guaranteed the bandwidth they need. Bulk and control transfers use whatever space is left.

5.9.4 USB Features

The Universal Serial Bus has the following features:

1. The computer acts as the host.
2. Up to 127 devices can connect to the host, either directly or by way of USB hubs.
3. Individual USB cables can run as long as 5 meters; with hubs, devices can be up to 30 meters (six cables' worth) away from the host.
3. With USB 2.0,the bus has a maximum data rate of 480 megabits per second.
4. A USB cable has two wires for power (+5 volts and ground) and a twisted pair of wires to carry the data.
5. On the power wires, the computer can supply up to 500 milliamps of power at 5 volts.
6. Low-power devices (such as mice) can draw their power directly from the bus. High-power devices (such as printers) have their own power supplies and draw minimal power from the bus. Hubs can have their own power supplies to provide power to devices connected to the hub.

USB devices are hot-swappable, meaning you can plug them into the bus and unplug them any time.

Many USB devices can be put to sleep by the host computer when the computer enters a power-saving mode.

The devices connected to a USB port rely on the USB cable to carry power and data.

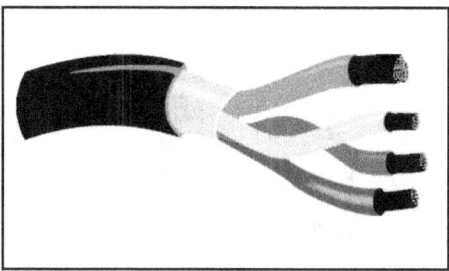

Fig. 5.19 : Inside a USB cable: There are two wires for power +5 volts (red) and ground (brown) and a twisted pair (yellow and blue) of wires to carry the data.

The cable is also shielded

5.10 CASE STUDY : INTEL NEHALEM MEMORY ORGANIZATION

Intel is now shipping microprocessors using their new architecture code named "Nehalem" as a successor to the Core architecture. This design uses multiple cores like its predecessor, but claims to improve the utilization and communication between the individual cores. This is primarily accomplished through better memory management and cache organization. Some benchmarking and research has been performed on the Nehalem architecture to analyze the cache and memory improvements.

OVERVIEW OF NEHALEM

A. Architectural Approach :

The approach to the Nehalem architecture is more modular than the Core architecture which makes it much more flexible and customizable to the application. The architecture really only consists of a few basic building blocks. The main blocks are a microprocessor core (with its own L2 cache), a shared L3 cache, a Quick Path Interconnect (QPI) bus controller, an integrated memory controller (IMC), and graphics core. With this flexible architecture, the blocks can be configured to meet what the market demands. For example, the Bloom-field model, which is intended for a performance desktop application, has four cores, an L3 cache, one memory controller, and one QPI bus controller. Server microprocessors like the Beckton model can have eight cores, and four QPI bus controllers. The architecture allows the cores to communicate very effectively in either case. The specifics of the memory organization are described in detail later.

Fig. 5.20 is an example of an eight-core Nehalem processor with two QPI bus controllers.

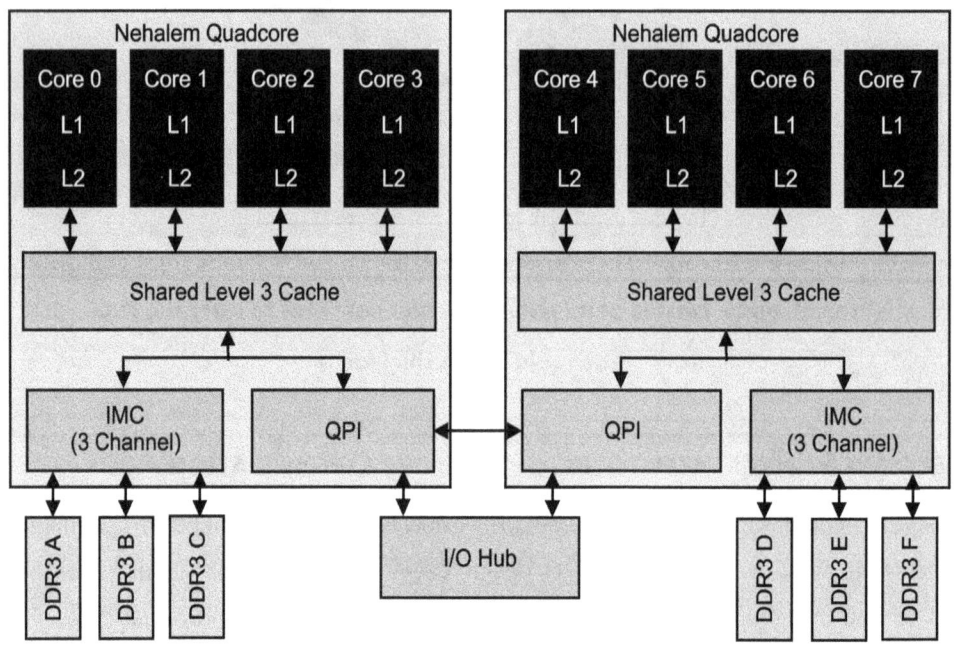

Fig. 5.20

B. Branch Prediction :

Another significant improvement in the Nehalem microarchitecture involves branch prediction. For the Core architecture, Intel designed what they call a "Loop Stream Detector," which detects loops in code execution and saves the instructions in a special buffer so they do not need to be continually fetched from cache. This increased branch prediction success for loops in the code and improved performance. Intel engineers took the concept even further with the Nehalem architecture by placing the Loop Stream Detector after the decode stage eliminating the instruction decode from a loop iteration and saving CPU cycles.

C. Out-of-order Execution :

Out-of-order execution also greatly increases the performance of the Nehalem architecture. This feature allows the processor to fill pipeline stalls with useful instructions so the pipeline efficiency is maximized. Out-of-order execution was present in the Core architecture, but in the Nehalem architecture the reorder buffer has been greatly increased to allow more instructions to be ready for immediate execution.

D. Instruction Set :

Intel also added seven new instructions to the instruction set. These are single-instruction, multiple-data (SIMD) instructions that take advantage of data-level parallelism for today's data intensive applications (like multimedia). Intel refers to the new instructions as Applications Targeted Accelerators (ATA) due to their specialized nature. For example, a few instructions are used explicitly for efficient text processing such as XML parsing. Another instruction is used just for calculating check sums.

E. Power Management :

For past architectures Intel has used a single power management circuit to adjust voltage and clock frequencies even on a die with multiple cores. With many cores, this strategy becomes wasteful because the load across cores is rarely uniform. Looking forward to a more scalable power management strategy, Intel engineers decided to put yet another processing unit on the die called the Power Control Unit (PCU). The PCU firmware is much more flexible and capable than the dedicated hardware circuit on previous architectures. Figure 2 shows how the PSU interacts with the cores. It uses sensors to read temperature, voltage, and current across all cores in the system and adjusts the clock frequency and supply voltage accordingly. This enables the cores to get exactly what they need, including putting a core to sleep if it is not being used at all.

QUESTIONS

1. Distinguish between SDR and DDR of main memory which one is more efficient? Why?
2. What are the types of DDR memories?
3. With neat block diagram explain DDR3 memory controller?
4. Explain Non-uniform and uniform memory access (NUMA and UMA)
5. What are I/O interfacing techniques? Illustrate.
6. Compare memory mapped and I/O mapped I/O.

7.   What is DMA? What are its advantages and disadvantages?

8.   Write a note an parallel and serial buses.

9.   What is PCI? Explain use of PCI in computer organization.

10. Briefly explain SCSI (Small Computer System Interface).

11. Explain intel Nehalem architecture in detail.

ADVANCED COMPUTER ORGANIZATIONS

6.1 THE AMD MULTICORE OPTERON

This includes addition, subtraction, multiplication and division through arithmetic of binary.

Multicore design uses two or more cores on single physical processor. We illustrate here Bulldozer design of AMD multicore opteron.

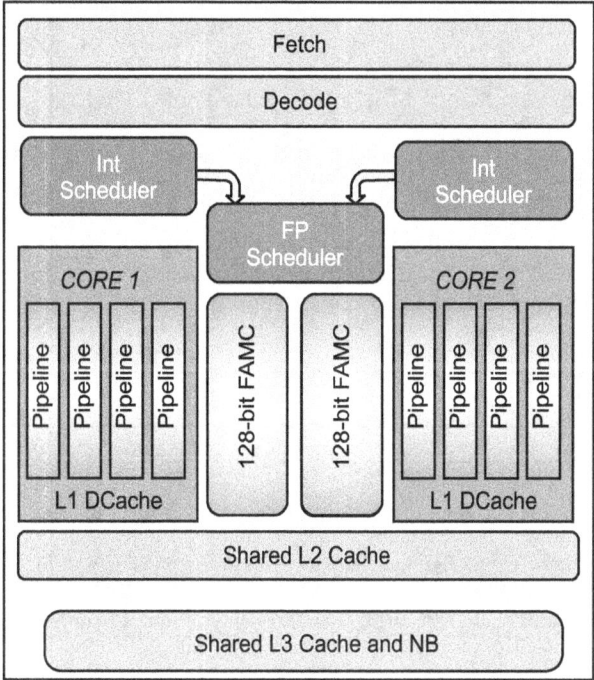

Fig. 6.1

AMD Bulldozer series opteron :

In the diagram above, the core is not really a core in the traditional sense that we have been using that word, since some elements of what we have been thinking of as a core are shared across multiple integer and floating point units in the Bulldozer design while others are doubled up as you might expect from past Opteron designs.

"By sharing some components, we can reduce both power consumption and costs, but also scale performance," says John Fruehe, director of server product marketing at AMD, who walked El Reg through the Bulldozer design.

The "core" in the Bulldozer design is a single-threaded, four-pipeline integer unit, which as you can see will have its own scheduler and its own L1 cache. This is essentially the same structure as the K8 Opteron integer unit, according to Fruehe, who says that 90 % of the workload an Opteron has to cope with runs through the integer unit. Rather than giving each core its own fetch and decode unit, the Bulldozer puts a slightly wider fetch and decode unit on the module, which allows them to share it.

As you can see in the diagram, the Bulldozer module has a shared floating point scheduler and two 128-bit floating point units, which debuted with the quad-core "Barcelona" Opteron 2200s and 8200s two years ago. (These FP units can do two 64-bit double-precision operations per clock or four 32-bit single precision operations). What is neat about the Bulldozer design is that either "core" in the module can grab the scheduler and if the other core is not doing floating point, then it can take all 256 bits and do four double precision or eight single precision ops in a clock.

6.2   THE SUN ULTRASPARC T1

The UltraSPARC® T1 multicore processor is the basis of the Sun Fire T2000 server. The UltraSPARC T1 processor is based on chip multithreading (CMT) technology that is optimized for highly threaded transactional processing. The UltraSPARC T1 processor improves throughput while using less power and dissipating less heat than conventional processor designs.

Depending on the model purchased, the processor has four, six, or eight UltraSPARC cores. Each core equates to a 64-bit execution pipeline capable of running four threads. The result is that the 8-core processor handles up to 32 active threads concurrently.

Additional processor components, such as L1 cache, L2 cache, memory access crossbar, DDR2 memory controllers, and a JBus I/O interface have been carefully tuned for optimal performance. See Fig. 6.2.

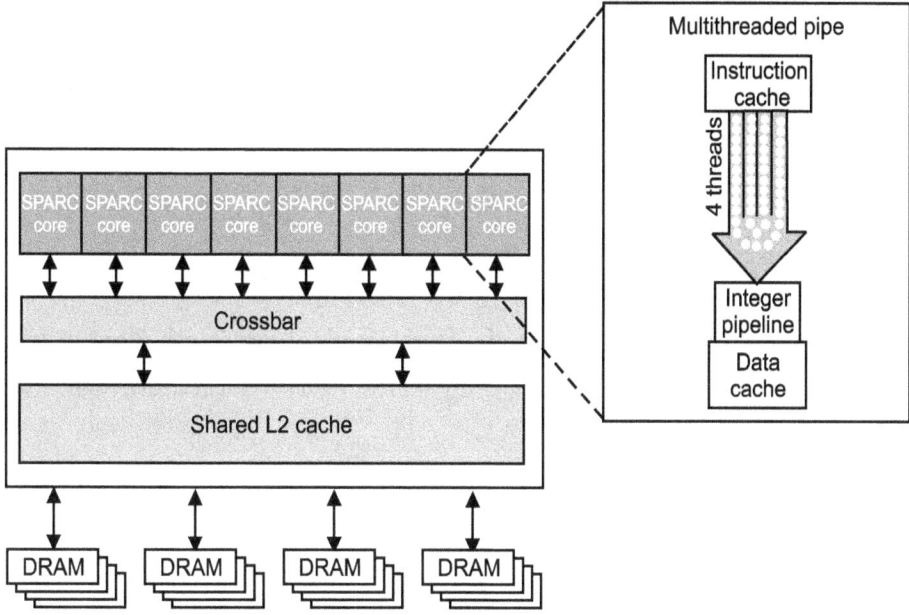

Fig. 6.2 : UltraSPARC T1 Multicore Processor Block Diagram

Power and cooling requirements are becoming primary concerns for many data center managers. Servers equipped with ever more power-hungry microprocessors are pushing power and cooling limits to meet increasing computational demand. In order to alleviate this trend, data centers need processors that use less power and generate less heat. Ideally, the processor maximizes the performance per power while minimizing the processor's power density.

While several vendors have attempted to mitigate the power issues using traditional methods, Sun's UltraSPARC T1 processor offers the most innovative and effective solution. Designed from the ground-up, the UltraSPARC T1 processor employs multiple architectural techniques to maximize performance per power while minimizing power density. This fundamentally new approach to processor design enables the UltraSPARC T1 processor to be more suitable for dense rack-mount implementations in the data center than other contemporary processors.

Another vital element in the UltraSPARC T1 processor's power architecture is the operating system. Enhancements to the Solaris Operating System (Solaris OS) such as the thread scheduling algorithm maximize performance and minimize power dissipation.

The UltraSPARC T1 processor has eight independent 64-bit execution pipelines (cores). Each core is capable of selecting from four active threads. The result is a processor that provides for up to 32 different threads or processes to be executing simultaneously on a single chip (As in Fig. 6.2). The aggregate throughput is approximately 5 to 15 times better than contemporary processors.

In addition, the power density for the UltraSPARC T1 processor is several times less than other contemporary processors, making the UltraSPARC T1 processor more suitable for dense rack-mount installations in the data center. The power density increasing over time with improved transistor density and increased processor complexity.

6.3 THE IBM CELL BROADBAND ENGINE (CBE)

The Cell Broadband Engine (Cell BE) processor is the first implementation of the Cell Broadband Engine Architecture (CBEA), developed jointly by Sony, Toshiba and IBM. In addition to Cell BE's use in the upcoming Sony PlayStation® 3 console, there is a great deal of interest in using it in Cell BE-based workstations, media-rich electronics devices, video and image processing systems, as well as several other emerging applications.

The Cell BE includes one POWER™ Processing Element (PPE) and eight Synergistic Processing Elements (SPEs). The Cell BE architecture is designed to be well-suited for a wide variety of programming models, and allows for partitioning of work between the PPE and the eight SPEs.

Introduction :

Until recently, improvements in the performance of general-purpose processor systems were primarily derived from higher processor clock frequencies, wider issue super-scalar or deeper super-pipeline designs. However, without a commensurate increase in the memory speed, these approaches only led to increased memory latencies and even more complex logic to hide them. Further, not being able to have a large number of concurrent accesses to memory, complex cores end up under-utilizing the execution pipelines and memory bandwidth. Invariably the end results can be poor utilization of the chip area and a disproportionate increase in power dissipation relative to overall performance.

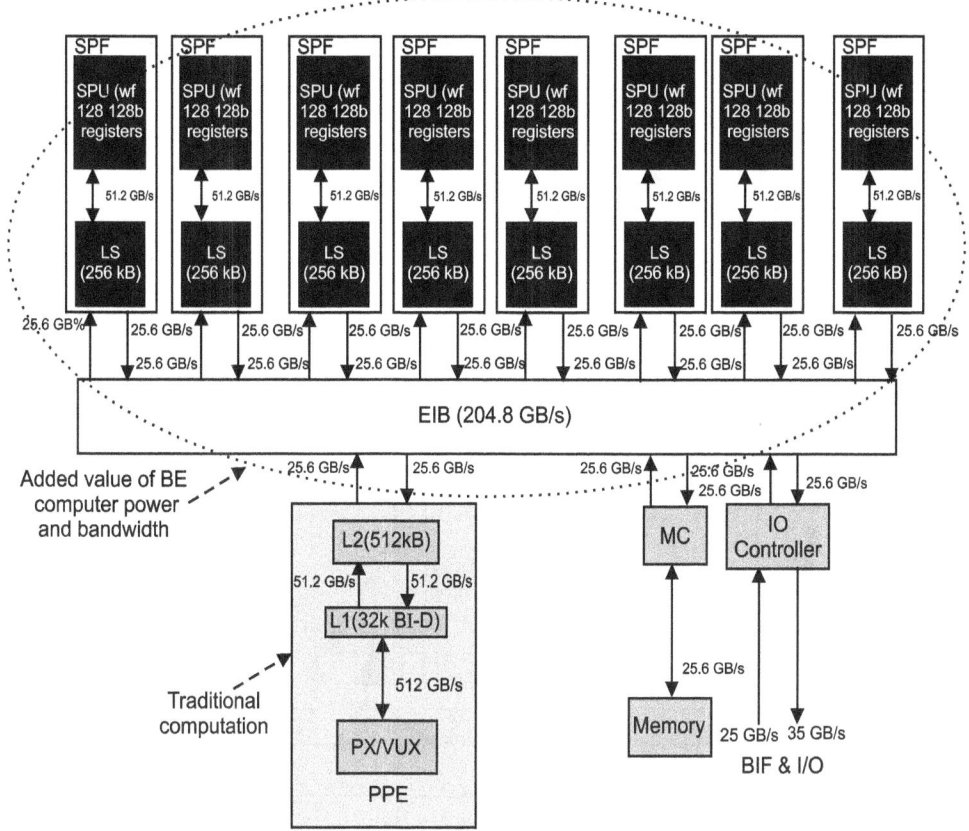

Fig. 6.3 : Cell BE Processor Block Diagram

Fig. 6.3 shows a high-level view of the first implementation of Cell BE. It includes a general-purpose 64-bit POWER Processing Element (PPE). In addition, the Cell BE incorporates eight Synergistic Processing Elements (SPEs) interconnected by a high-speed, memory-coherent Element Interconnect Bus (EIB). This initial implementation of Cell BE is targeted to run at 3.2 GHz.

The SIMD units on the eight SPEs provide the majority of the computational power of the Cell BE. When using single-precision floating-point fused multiply-add instructions, the eight SPEs in the first-generation Cell BE chip can perform a total of 64 floating-point operations per cycle.

The integrated memory controller (MIC) provides a peak bandwidth of 25.6 GB/s to an external XDR memory, while the integrated I/O controller provides peak bandwidths of 25 GB/s (for inbound) and 35 GB/s (for outbound). The EIB supports a peak bandwidth of 204.8 GB/s for intra-chip data transfers among the PPE, the SPEs, and the memory and the I/O interface controllers.

6.4 INTEL IA -64

With the Pentium 4, the microprocessor family that began with the 8086 and that has been the most successful computer product line ever appears to have come to an end. Intel has teamed up with Hewlett-Packard (HP) to develop a new 64-bit architecture, called IA-64. IA-64 is not a 64-bit extension of Intel's 32-bit x 86 architecture, nor is it an adaptation of Hewlett-Packard's 64-bit PA-RISC architecture. Instead, IA-64 is a new architecture that builds on years of research at the two companies and at universities. The architecture exploits the vast circuitry and high speeds available on the newest generations of microchips by a systematic use of parallelism. IA-64 architecture represents a significant departure from the trend to superscalar schemes that have dominated recent processor development.

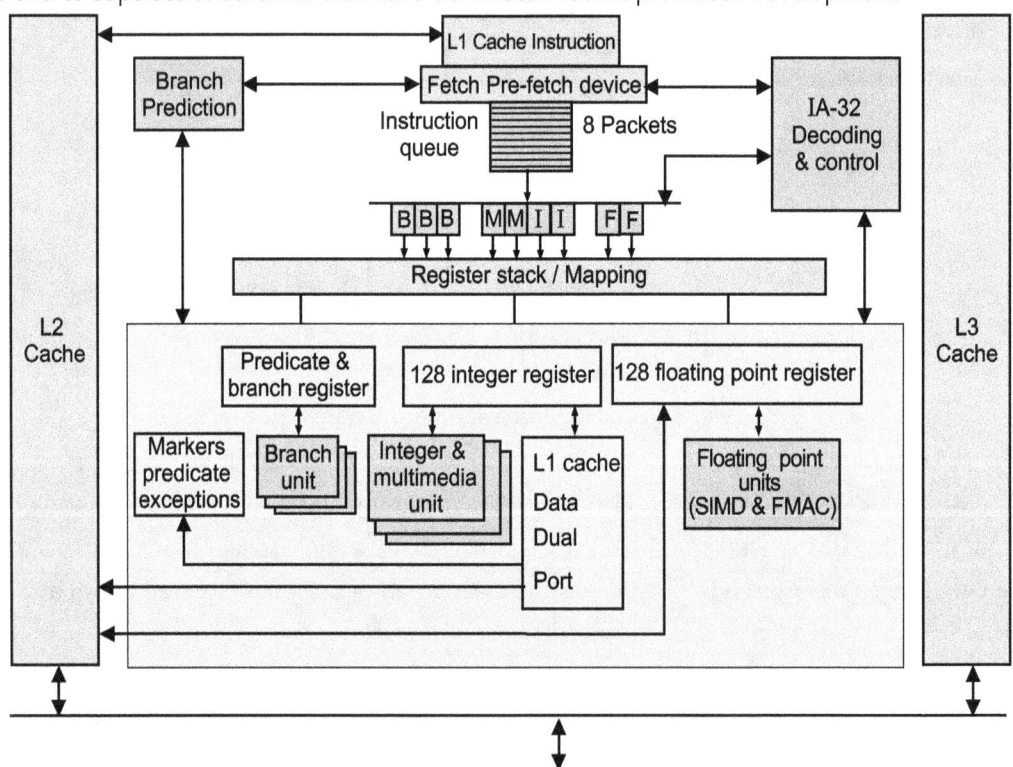

Fig. 6.4 : IA-64 block diagram

Fig. 6.4 explains block diagram of IA-64.

The basic concepts underlying IA-64 are:

- Instruction-level parallelism that is explicit in the machine instructions rather than being determined at run time by the processor.
- Long or very long instruction words (LIW/VLIW).

- Branch predication (not the same thing as branch prediction).

- Speculative loading.

Intel and HP refer to this combination of concepts as explicitly parallel instruction computing (EPIC). Intel and HP use the term EPIC to refer to the technology, or collection of techniques. IA-64 is an actual instruction set architecture that is intended for implementation using the EPIC technology. The first Intel product based on this architecture is referred to as Itanium. Other products will follow, based on the same IA-64 architecture.

6.4.1 General Organization

The key features are :

- **Large number of registers :** The IA-64 instruction format assumes the use of 256 registers: 128 64-bit registers for integer, logical, and general-purpose use, and 128 82-bit registers for floating-point and graphic use. There are also 64 1-bit predicate registers used for predicated execution, as explained subsequently.

- **Multiple execution units :** A typical commercial superscalar machine today may support four parallel pipelines, using four parallel execution units in both the integer and floating-point portions of the processor. It is expected that IA-64 will be implemented on systems with eight or more parallel units.

The register file is quite large compared with most RISC and superscalar machines. The reason for this is that a large number of registers is needed to support a high degree of parallelism. In a traditional superscalar machine, the machine language (and the assembly language) employs a small number of visible registers, and the processor maps these onto a larger number of registers using register renaming techniques and dependency analysis. Because we wish to make parallelism explicit and relieve the processor of the burden of register renaming and dependency analysis, we need a large number of explicit registers.

The number of execution units is a function of the number of transistors available in a particular implementation. The processor will exploit parallelism to the extent that it can. For example, if the machine language instruction stream indicates that eight integer instructions may be executed in parallel, a processor with four integer pipelines will execute these in two chunks. A processor with eight pipelines will execute all eight instructions simultaneously.

Four types of execution unit are defined in the IA-64 architecture :

- **I-unit :** For integer arithmetic, shift-and-add, logical, compare, and integer multimedia instructions

- **M-unit :** Load and store between register and memory plus some integer ALU operations

- **B-unit :** Branch instruction.

- **F-unit :** Floating-point instructions.

6.5 i5 / i7 ARCHITECTURES

The code-named "Lynnfield" Core i7 and Core i5 processors prove to be an interesting bunch. When the original LGA1366 Core i7 Bloomfield processors were released in late 2008, they offered undeniably excellent performance. Unfortunately, they also came at a high price point. Many consumers chose to stay with Intel's processors predating the company's new Nehalem microarchitecture. To combat this and move the market ahead, Intel launched a series of processors for mainstream consumption at a lower price point. Based on the Lynnfield core fabricated using a 45 nm process, and packaged into the new LGA1156 socket, Intel hopes to provide consumers with a price break in conjunction with the new P55 chipset.

The main difference between Bloomfield and Lynnfield besides the socket boils down to the replacement of Intel's high bandwidth 25.6 GB/s QuickPath Interconnect (QPI) link with the slower 2-4 GB/s DMI (Direct Media Interface) chip to chip link, as well as deletion of one of the memory controllers. The latter means that rather than having triple channel memory, Lynnfield processors will only support dual channel. Users familiar with Intel's previous designs should also be familiar with the company's DMI interface; however, it is now integrated onto the processor, rather than the Northbridge, to replace the legacy Front Side Bus. This reduces the physical size and number of pins required for the processor, but having different sockets for Nehalem microarchitecture processors may prove inconvenient with regards to the upgrade path in the future.

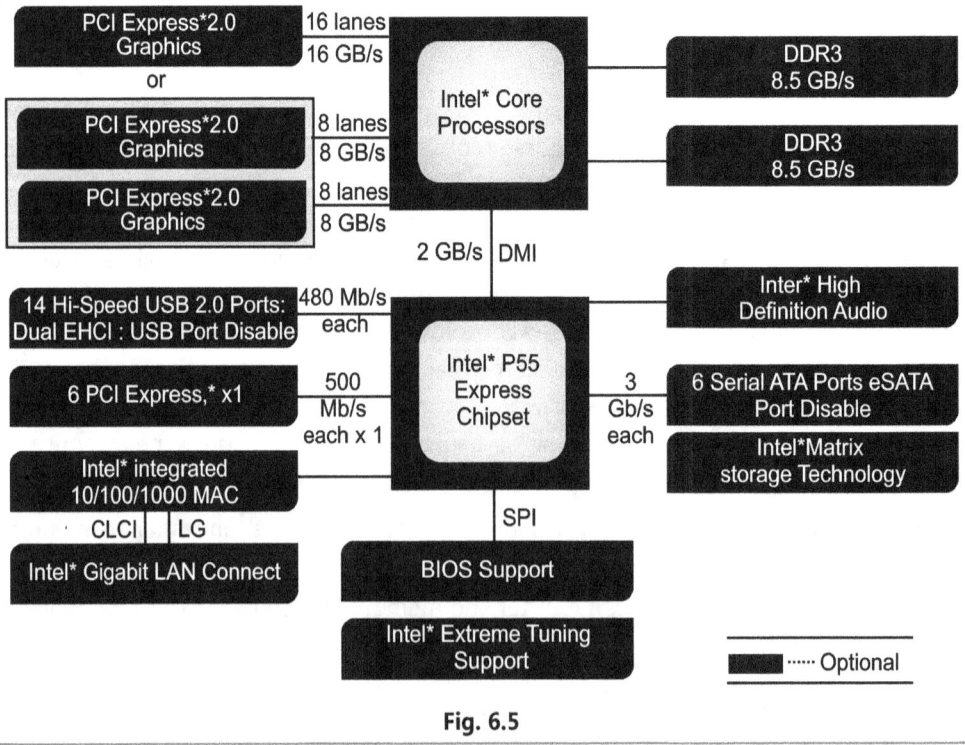

Fig. 6.5

In addition to the DDR3-1333 64-bit wide on-die memory controller, Intel also integrated 16 PCI Express 2.0 lanes into the processor to overcome the inherent bandwidth limitation of the DMI interface. There are only two chips on the LGA1156 platform, as seen in the block diagram above. What was previously known as the Southbridge takes care of the standard connection interfaces such as providing up to 14 USB ports and 6 SATA ports, as well as providing six additional PCI Express lanes for PCIe based devices such as Ethernet. As many Northbridge functions are now on the CPU itself as aforementioned, the P55 chipset doesn't do nearly as much as it did in the past – Intel resolved to call it the Platform Controller Hub, or PCH, instead.

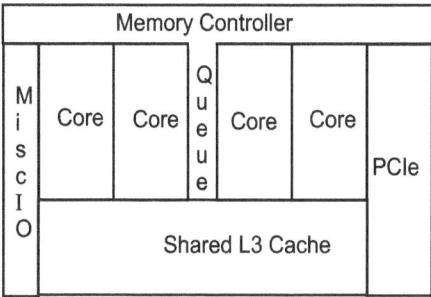

Fig. 6.6

Back onto the specifications and design of the processor itself, the 900-series Intel Core i7 processors have 731 million transistors whereas the Lynnfield CPUs (700 and 800 series for Core i5 and Core i7, respectively) have 774 million transistors jammed into a die size of 296 mm². Each core has 64 kB of L1 cache and 256 kB L2 cache. All four cores share a relatively large 8MB L3 cache for all Lynnfield processors which includes the Core i5-750 and all 800-series Core i7s thanks to its native quad core design. With all four cores finally joined together on a single die, it is a significantly more elegant engineering-wise than "gluing" two dual core processors into a single package, as Intel has previously done with the Core 2 Quad. Not only does this decrease the amount of heat generated, it also eliminates the FSB overhead when cores not on the same die needs to communicate with each other.

With the elimination of the front side bus design on the Core i5-750, the clock speed of the processor is now determined by the base clock times the multiplier. The default base clock on all Lynnfield CPUs is 133 MHz, setting the default multiplier at 20x to give its 2.66 GHz frequency. Meanwhile, the integrated memory controller and L3 cache can now operate on their own separate frequency called the Uncore Clock, which is determined by the base clock times the uncore multiplier.

One of the newest features to come with Intel's latest generation of CPUs is Turbo Mode, it dynamically overclocks the processor beyond specification to attain higher performance, limited either by current temperature or capped to its 24x multiplier. This means that the Intel Core i5-750 can boost up to 3.192 GHz, temperature permitting. Speaking of which, the TDP for this processor is rated at 95 W. Because of the variations in accuracy with regards to running Turbo Mode on in benchmarking, we disabled it when obtaining our test results. Generally speaking, our results were obtained with no Turbo Boost kicking in, yo. Just good old constant clock speed for maximum accuracy.

Other innovations new to the Nehalem microarchitecture are its innovative power management features. In conjunction with numerous integrated power sensors, the Power Control Unit (PCU) chip that actively monitors and manages the performance of the processor. This allow features such as the aforementioned Turbo Mode, as the PCU is capable of dynamically adjusting the voltage and frequency of its CPU cores to provide both performance boost where needed, and reduced power consumption during idle conditions. Thanks to the Power Gate Transistor, idling cores can also be completed shut down, and put into C6 sleep mode, to further save electricity.

6.6 NVIDIA GPU ARCHITECTURE

GPU accelerated computing is the use of a graphics processing unit (GPU) together with a CPU to accelerate scientific, engineering, and enterprise applications. Pioneered in 2007 by NVIDIA, GPUs now power energy-efficient data centers in government labs, universities, enterprises, and small-and-medium businesses around the world.

How Applications Accelerate with GPUs ?

GPU accelerated computing offers unprecedented application performance by offloading compute-intensive portions of the application to the GPU, while the remainder of the code still runs on the CPU. From a user's perspective, applications simply run significantly faster.

CPU VERSUS GPU :

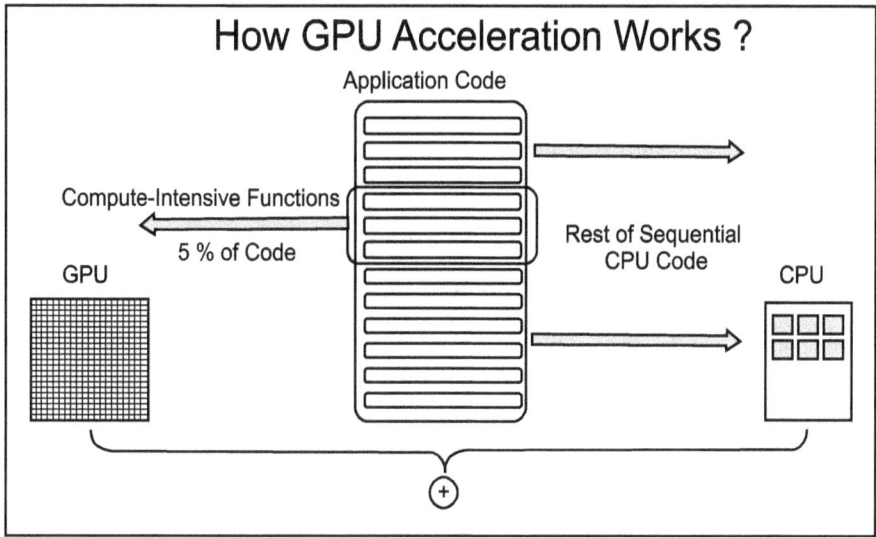

Fig. 6.7

A simple way to understand the difference between a CPU and GPU is to compare how they process tasks. A CPU consists of a few cores optimized for sequential serial processing while a GPU consists of thousands of smaller, more efficient cores designed for handling multiple tasks simultaneously.

GPUs have thousands of cores to process parallel workloads efficiently :

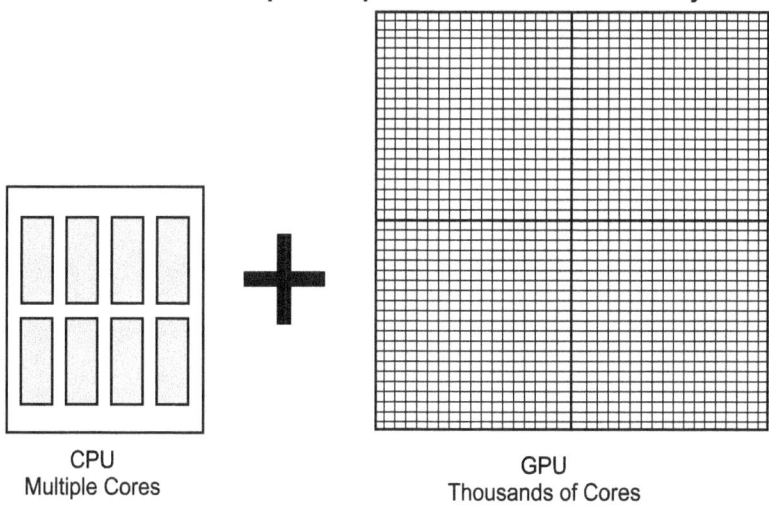

Fig. 6.8

6.6.1 What Is Gpu Computing ?

GPU computing is the use of a GPU (graphics processing unit) together with a CPU to accelerate general-purpose scientific and engineering applications. Pioneered five years ago by NVIDIA, GPU computing has quickly become an industry standard, enjoyed by millions of users worldwide and adopted by virtually all computing vendors.

GPU computing offers unprecedented application performance by offloading compute-intensive portions of the application to the GPU, while the remainder of the code still runs on the CPU. From a user's perspective, applications simply run significantly faster.

CPU + GPU is a powerful combination because CPUs consist of a few cores optimized for serial processing, while GPUs consist of thousands of smaller, more efficient cores designed for parallel performance. Serial portions of the code run on the CPU while parallel portions run on the GPU.

All NVIDIA GPUs-GeForce®, Quadro®, and Tesla®- support GPU computing and the CUDA® parallel programming model. Developers have access to NVIDIA GPUs in virtually any platform of their choice, including the latest Apple MacBook Pro.

QUESTIONS

1. State and explain functions of AMD multicore optron ?
2. What is multicore processor ? Illustrate AMD multicore.
3. With neat block diagram explain sunultraspare T processore.
4. Distinguish between AMD and sunultraspare Architecture.
5. Write a note on IBM (CBF).
6. Why $6C_1$-bit processor is faster than 32-bit processor ? Explain with Intel IA-64.
7. Distinguish between i3, i5 and i7 series of intel.
8. What is GPU ? How it is different from CPU ?
9. Explain NVIDIA GPU architecture.

www.ingramcontent.com/pod-product-compliance
Lightning Source LLC
Chambersburg PA
CBHW081143020726
47504CB00009B/1976